FORBIDDEN SEDUCTION

Andreia Solomon Burke

L.A Press Release

2014

ISBN:0956194613

ISBN-13:978-0-9561946-1-9

10 9 8 7 6 5 4 3 2

FORBIDDEN SEDUCTION

To Jackie
You mean the world to
me and I love you
for what you mean to
me / us!
love
Andrea

Dedication

I dedicate this novel to my guardian angels:
my mother, Carolyn L. Solomon and my sister
Beverly Renee Solomon. I miss you both every second,
every minute, every hour,
of every day.

Special Acknowledgements

To my Editor, Natasha Dailey, I can't express how grateful I am to you for editing my novel; the peace you've given me is invaluable. I looked in the UK and US for someone to take it on, when all I had to do was pick up the phone and call my niece.
Love you to pieces.

FORBIDDEN SEDUCTION

Lane

On the morning that my mother was to be laid to rest, the sun beamed down on us as brightly as she had done all of her life. I was happy, yet surprised to see that my dad handled the morning as well as he had. However, I knew it would be only a matter of time before the realization hit him and he'd be faced with the harsh fact that his Lynn wouldn't be home by suppertime. I found myself unnervingly baffled by how calm I'd been from the night I received that dreadful call from Char to this point. I ascribed my behavior to the fact that I had stuffed my pain down so deeply, because it allowed me to function for my dad.

By eight o'clock, I had already been in overload as my dad and Clay stood guard over me since the moment I awoke. Every time I thought I'd have a small quiet minute to myself, they appeared from out of nowhere. As our family and friends started to arrive at my parents' house, I sneaked away from my dad and a watchful Clay. I wanted only a few precious minutes to myself to reminisce on some of the last times I had shared with my mother.

I escaped to my parents' room, sat down in my mother's rocking-chair, and stared out of the bay window where I used to sit as a child while my mother read to me. I just needed some calm while we waited for the cars to pick us up from our Brooklyn Brownstone to take us to the church. Charmine had called earlier and explained that she and Anthony would have to meet us at the church as their morning flight from Atlanta had been delayed.

Char's presence in my life meant the world to me, and I was so grateful to have her in my life. She's been such a good friend, who has been there for me at whatever stage I was at in my life. I also had to credit Clay—that man hadn't left my side from that night. The way he took charge certainly helped me get to this point reasonably sane.

I sat unusually serene and listened as our doorbell rang continuously with the flow of people who wanted to pay their last respects to my mother. I heard my aunt Bernice as she directed people to either the living room or the kitchen, depending upon if they had brought any food with them. My mother complained for years about how she felt Aunt Bernice would just come over to our house and take charge of it. And although they didn't have the best relationship, my mother would have been very appreciative of how well my aunt had taken care of me and my dad during this time. I was jarred from my thoughts as my cousin, Beverly, called my name through the closed door before she knocked. I told her to come in. "Hey Lane, how you doin'?" she asked, but before I responded she went on. "I want you to know how sorry I am about Aunt Lynn; she was always my favorite aunt."

"I know, Bev. Thank you."

Beverly placed her cold hands on my shoulders and paused. "And one more thing...this probably ain't the right time for you to hear this. You probably won't even care, but I bumped into Dre at the DMV yesterday. And I told him about Aunt Lynn's funeral." I stopped rocking in my chair and braced myself for what she'd say next. "Lane, he asked me for the address to the church because he's coming to the funeral." Beverly was right, the timing was inappropriate but I was glad that she told me. I didn't want any chaos today between Dre and Clay—especially not today.

I watched the back of the door as Beverly closed it, and I found myself in a peculiar mode. I was almost contented that I'd get to see Dre, even with Clay being present. My aunt Bernice yelled out from the kitchen for my cousin, Rasheed, to answer the door as someone knocked quite loudly. "Ma, it's the funeral limo driver," Rasheed yelled back to her. "He said he'll be downstairs." When I heard what Rasheed said, I felt nauseated all over again—it was the moment that I had dreaded. I had become light-headed as I attempted to stand and lost my footing. I plummeted backward just as Clay entered the room, and he caught me seconds before I landed on the floor.

"C'mon Baby, I got you. Are you okay?" he asked and held me upright.

"I thought I was," I said and smoothed out my black dress.

"Hold onto me." Clay wrapped his arm around my waist. As we left my parents' room, my dad had also come to check on me. He grabbed a tight hold of my free arm and escorted me downstairs to the car. When we approached the car, my aunt Bernice was already seated and my dad ushered me in beside her. He waited until Clay ducked his tall physique in the seat across from us, and then he climbed in next to me. As I sat cushioned between my aunt and father, my head throbbed from the gloominess which had left me completely drained. I wished at that moment I could have been going anywhere but where we were headed.

My teary eyes scanned the contents of the limo which lacked all of the amenities of a good night out. It looked a lot different from the party limos I had become accustomed to since meeting Clay. Instead of the flashing lights, loud music, and a mini bar stocked with alcohol—this limo was stocked with: tissues, smelling salts, and Mahalia Jackson which was being played softly through the speakers.

My dad wept quietly as he held my hand in his the entire way to the church. Clay sat across from me, and each time I looked in his direction, his eyes were locked on mine. My aunt's intermittent cries sounded like wounded cats which only added to my unendurable headache. I noticed the limo had slowed down, and when I looked out of the window to my left, there stood a crowd of people. They all looked on grievously as the driver pulled in the space marked: Reserved For the Family. Charmine emerged through the crowd of people and pushed her way through to the doors of the limo—I could tell she'd been crying as her tears hadn't fully dried.

Before the driver could get out of the limo, Char yanked the door open, reached past Aunt Bernice, and pulled me out. The driver waited until I exited the car before he proceeded to help my aunt and dad from the car. Clay had gotten out of the car and stood behind me as I cried uncontrollably on Charmine's shoulder. Anthony walked over to Charmine and dried her tears with a handkerchief he pulled from his suit pocket. He held onto her as my dad and Clay walked me into the church.

Everything from that point became fragmented images that blinked off and on in my head. I remember when we entered the church and seeing my mother; she looked like a sleeping, graceful angel. I remember that my dad collapsed as the pallbearers placed my mother on their shoulders. I remember a man with dark shades on as he leaned against a shade tree at the Eternal Gardens cemetery. And lastly, I remember the minister's last words were: ashes to ashes and dust to dust. . .

Back at my parents' house, the mood lightened when stories of how my parents met filled the room. Each story was a remembrance to her loving, caring spirit. I listened as our family and friends shared their stories to what a wonderful wife, mother, and friend she had been to all who knew her. Everyone who spoke had such a heartwarming story, but when I felt it had all become too much for me to hear, I excused myself to my old room and Char followed. We laid on my bed amid all my stuffed animals and sorority pillows my mother made for me when I first pledged. "It was a beautiful service, Lane," Char said. I nodded slightly as that was all I had strength enough to do. Char had even started to share her own encounters with my mother. "Do you remember that night we were at the club and she called? You lied and said we were at church revival."

That story brought an easy smile to my face "I do. She asked me why I was at church so late, and why was it so noisy. I thought for sure I was going to hell when I told her that the choir had people falling out from the Holy Ghost." I knew the memories of my mother such as those would always keep a smile on my face. We talked a bit more before my cousin, Beverly, knocked on my door again. "Come in," I said. Beverly entered my room. Her normal, boisterous demeanor seemed tamed even for today. "What's the matter with you Bev?"

Beverly announced something that wiped the fleeting smile completely from my face. "I hate to interrupt y'all, but you have a visitor," she said.

"Who is it?"

"It's Dre." Char and I looked at each other as if we were in a horror film, the scene right before we knew one of us was about to be killed off. I leaped to my feet and walked closer to Beverly.
"Where is he now?" I whispered.

"He's at the door," she said, with her face all screwed-up. "I'm not stupid—you know I wouldn't let him in the house with Clay here. Now do you see why I wanted you to know this earlier?"

"Where is Clay?" I asked.

"He's in the living room with everybody else," she said.

"Let me go! I have something I want to tell him," Charmine said, and she hopped off my bed.

"No, Char, I'll go. I know what you want to tell him, and it's nothing nice. Anyway, he's only here to pay his respects, and there's nothing wrong with that." I immediately left my room before Clay could have spotted us. When I walked out of my room to see Dre, my insides felt about as nervous as Beverly's face looked. Beverly had completely shut the front door and when I opened it, I knew instantly who the man behind the dark shades at the cemetery was. Dre.

"How you doin', Lane?" Dre took off his shades, lowered his eyes, and shook his head. "Aww, I don't even know what to say to you. When I saw your cuz down at the DMV and she told me, I couldn't believe it." He cringed as he spoke, and he appeared to be genuinely hurt.

"I know. I couldn't believe it either. I still can't. I was just here less than a month ago. No, she wasn't doing great, but I never expected this."

"How's Mr. King holding up?"

"He's doing as well as can be expected—they've been together over forty-years." Just as I said that out loud it pained me to think how my dad would recover or if he would ever recover.

"Can I see him? I wanna show my respect. "

"I don't think this is the time, Dre. We have a lot of people here, and at the moment, they seem to have taken his mind off of everything," I said. I just hoped he bought it—I couldn't dare risk Clay bumping into him.

"I got you. Just let him know I asked about him. How long you staying in Brooklyn?"

"I can't answer that right now. I have to play it by ear. I have my dad to think about."

"Well, take my number and call me if you need some company while you here." Immediately my shoulders rose, and I backed up to the door. "Not like that, Lane. If you just want someone to 'talk' to," he corrected. I apologized to him for being on edge, and I watched him subtly as he wrote down his number on the back of a barber's card. Dre had always been a very good-looking man, and nothing changed about that. He had smooth caramel skin, lustful eyes, and a body that was drool worthy. He always kept a low haircut to show off his wavy texture, and he smelled good enough to eat. When he handed me his card, I began to feel guilty about the thoughts that entered my mind about him. Not only should my thoughts be only with my mother but with Clay who's just a room away.

"Thank you for dropping by, Dre. We didn't leave on such a good note the last time we saw each other, so this means a lot to me," I said and took the card from his hand.

"You know I'm gon' always care about you. I mean it, call me if you want someone to kick it with, and don't forget to tell your dad I stopped through."

"Thanks, Dre. I'll tell him." Dre reached out and gave me a hug. After a minute long embrace, I realized it was more than just a condolence hug as Dre's hands caressed the small of my back. Dre and I were still in an embrace when I felt a strong presence behind me.

"Lane, you want to introduce me to your friend?" Clay asked. Dre finally released me as if we were caught in a lewd act.

"Oh, Clay. You scared me," I said and stepped back from Dre's hug.

"I know I did," he said.

"You remember me, we've met before. I'm Dre," he said and extended his hand for Clay to shake. Clay looked at me as if he wanted to say, not you again. Clay's eyes never left mine as he addressed Dre.

"Dre? Aight, listen. We appreciate you coming by, but I got it from here."

"No Dawg, it ain't even like that. I just came through to pay my respect to Lane and the family. I wanted to make sure Lane was alright that's all," Dre said.

"Lane is fine. And like I said 'Dawg,' I got it from here." Clay ended any further conversation between them and closed the door in his face. I didn't know how I should have reacted, so I obeyed Clay's silent command and followed him back into the house. Clay walked ahead of me to go back into the room he had been in with my dad. I reached for his arm because I wanted to explain what he had just seen, but when Clay pulled away from me. I rejoined Char in my bedroom.

"What took you so long? Did Dre give you any trouble?" Char asked.

"No, he didn't, but Clay did. Clay came to the door while Dre and I were hugging," I said in an exhausted state.

"Clay came to the door? What'd he say?"

"He didn't want to talk about it now, so I left him alone."

"Wow, this is too much." Charmine was right. It was too much that I just buried my mother. It was too much that the man I love witnessed me being held by my ex, and it was too much that I didn't want Dre to let me go. But I couldn't dare voice that out loud, not even to Char. "Listen Char, let me go check on my dad and at least speak to Anthony properly. He was kind enough to travel all this way, and I haven't said two words to him." We walked in the den where my dad, Anthony, and Clay held camp for most of the afternoon.

My dad appeared to be fine, and by this time, he had changed his stories to sports. I would have found this to be odd, but Char had assured me his behavior was normal. Charmine referenced this to her first year in college when she studied psychology before she decided she wanted to become an attorney. However, she warned me that when he did break, he would need me there to help him through it. When I approached Anthony, he rose from his seat. I gave him a big hug and thanked him for coming. He told me not to mention it. He said he just wished it could have been under happier circumstances, and I agreed.

Clay suggested I put something in my stomach—he said he noticed that I hadn't eaten anything all day. When I declined, he went to the kitchen, and in spite of what I said, he returned with a small plate of food. "Try to eat a little bit you'll feel better. That's probably why you can't get rid of your headache," he said.

"I can't get rid of my headache because I just buried my mother!" I yelled.

My dad shot me a look of disapproval, and shouted at me. "LANE! There's no cause for you to talk to Clay that way. He's only being concerned about you and was trying to help."

After my dad chastised me, I felt ashamed. "Clay, I'm sorry. I didn't mea---."

"No need to say sorry, Bae. I can't imagine what you're going through right now." Charmine, Anthony, and my dad excused themselves to the front room with the other guests. I hung my head in shame after I realized that they had left the room because my outburst had embarrassed Clay. "Lane, I know this isn't going to be easy for you, but I want you know I'm here for you, so don't push me away"

"I know that, Clay. I shouldn't have spoken to you like that. Please accept my apology."

"I told you there's no need for one, but of course I do."

After Clay had forgiven me, I felt even more ashamed of myself. I played with my food like a scolded child and pushed the potato salad from one side of my plate to the other.

As the afternoon went into the evening, my family and friends began to dwindle like the sunlight. One by one they expressed their condolences and said goodnight. My aunt Bernice and my cousins cleared the kitchen of all the mess and packed some food to take home with them as well. Aunt Bernice made sure my dad and I had at least a week worth of food stored in Tupperware in the fridge. After Aunt Bernice and her clan left, it was just us.

The five of us sat in the living room and talked about the day, and as we spoke, I was aware my mother's physical being wasn't there, but her presence filled the room. Char and Anthony had a late flight back to Atlanta, but stayed with us a bit longer before they went back to her parents' house so they could take them to the airport. My dad looked exhausted, so he finally conceded. After he told us all goodnight, he went to his bedroom. Char and I had a brief moment while Clay and Anthony got to know each other. "Lane, you know if I could stay another day I would, but my case goes to trial in the morning."

"You don't have to tell me that. I know if you could, you'd stay as long as I needed you to. I genuinely appreciate you and Anthony coming."

"I know, Sweetheart, but we better get going. I hate the thought of my parents driving on the expressway at night, but they insisted they wanted to take us to the airport...well, my mother insisted. You know my father still hasn't clicked with Anthony yet.

"He will. You see how well Anthony and Clay are getting along, and Clay doesn't like anyone.

"I see. Clay is one of the good ones, and I'm so happy you two worked that nonsense out."

"I am too.

"Well, this is it." I love you, Chica, and I'll call you when we get back."

"I love you too." Clay and I walked them downstairs to see them off, and when Clay came back upstairs, he flipped through a few channels and found a college football game on TV. I laid down with my head in his lap, and he massaged my temples while he watched the game. "That feels so good, Clay. I don't want you to stop," I said.

"Then I won't."

A week after my mother's funeral, my dad started to get back into his former daily routine. I got up early to prepare my dad's breakfast, but I found a note on the fridge—it read he had gone to the social club to have breakfast with his buddies. My dad had gone there for years after his good friend, Kernel, introduced him to the club. He always talked about what a good, hearty breakfast they served for under five dollars. I was really glad that he had a solid friendship with Kernel. Kernel had loss his wife just a year earlier to breast cancer, and I knew he could relate to what my dad was going through.

I decided since I was already up, I'd fix Clay some breakfast. I called out to him a few times, but he didn't answer. I walked up to the guest room where he slept, and the door was shut. I realized he hadn't heard me call him because he was engrossed in a heated discussion over the phone. I raised my knuckles to knock on the door, but decided against it. I walked back to the kitchen, put the coffee machine on, and poured us both a mug of coffee. When Clay had finished his phone conversation, he entered the kitchen and greeted me with a kiss on my forehead.

It was apparent he had been up for some time because he was fully dressed, and his locs were neatly pulled back from his handsome face. I offered to fix him a hot breakfast, but he opted to have a bagel with some cream cheese instead. As we sat at the table and ate our light breakfast, Clay hadn't mentioned what had transpired in his phone call from Shon. I didn't know how to just come out and ask, so I asked him several questions that I hoped would lead into what I had overheard.

"I bet Shon misses not having you at the studio. He can't handle business and womanize at the same time like he usually does."

"That's not gonna stop him."

"What about your new artists, are they alright?"

"Yeah, Bae, everything is good. What's up with all the questions about Shon and the studio?"

"Okay, Clay, I'm not going to hide this any longer. I overheard you on the phone with Shon, and you sounded quite upset. Are you sure everything is good back in Atlanta?" When he realized I had overheard his conversation he hesitated for a second, he scratched his eyebrow and leaned back in his seat.

"Nah, it's not all good. Some bullshit has happened that could potentially fuck up my company." And that's all he offered. When I nagged him to talk about it, he told me not to worry about it and that he'd handle it.

Throughout the morning, Clay still hadn't expressed any desire to return to Atlanta, even though his most trusted and capable partner kept calling. From what I gathered, Shon tried to convey to Clay how detrimental the situation was and how it required Clay's immediate attention. It seemed that Clay had dismissed the seriousness of the issue altogether and asked me what I wanted to do for the day. But when Shon called Clay for the fifth time and he went back into the guest room and shut the door, I followed him. I strained my ears to listen, and when I heard Clay ask if he could handle it by phone, I knew then I had no choice but to step in and urge him to go back to Atlanta to handle his business.

When Clay finished his conversation with Shon, I darted into my bedroom like I had been there the whole time. As Clay walked down the hall, I asked if I could to speak to him.

"Clay, I really appreciate you being here for me and my dad, but it's time you go back to Atlanta. You can't afford putting your company at risk. You could lose everything you've worked so hard for while you're here babysitting me."

"I'm not babysitting you. I just want to make sure you're good before I go back."

"But who knows when that'll be. It isn't like I have the sniffles, I've loss my mother. I may never fully recover from this, and as much as I would love for you to stay here with me, you can't. Don't worry, Clay, I have a lot of family and friends here to help me if I need them."

"Who? Like Dre?" he asked. The harshness of his tone had put me off and made me question his true motive for staying in Brooklyn.

"Dre? What does he have to do with this? Wait. Is he the real reason why you don't want to go back to handle your business?" Clay looked caught, and his facial expression told me the truth even if he wanted to lie.

"Are you serious, Clay? Here it is I'm thinking you couldn't bear to pull yourself away from me, because you were so concerned about me. But the truth is you don't trust me." I was hurt by his comment, and I turned to walk away, but Clay closed my bedroom door and slid his arm around my waist. I tried to remove his firm hold from away my waist, but he refused to let go.

"Lane, look at me," he asked. This time I refused to obey Clay's demand as easily, and kept my back towards him. "I'm sorry. I guess I am concerned about leaving you here with Dre. He basically lives up the street, but it has nothing to do with me not trusting you. When I saw you two all hugged up at the door last week, feelings arose in me that I thought I had gotten rid of when I was in high school. So yea, I'll man-up and admit I'm a bit nervous to leave you here, but believe me when I say I trust you with everything I have." He released me, and swept my hair from my back to expose my neck where he kissed me lightly. I was still angry at him, but I had begun to soften at his touch.

Clay's kisses weakened me, but I didn't want to submit to him fully. I couldn't believe that he would even suggest that something would happen between me and Dre if he went back to Atlanta. I turned to face him as I wanted to clear the air. "I apologized to you for having walked up on us. I know that must have put you in an unpleasant situation, especially knowing that we used to be in a relationship, but you also said you'd gotten over it. Listen Clay, you don't have to worry about... I love you."

Clay pulled me closer to him, and kissed me forcefully as if he had been starved for my affection, and by the way my body reacted I craved his touch just as much. I returned his starved kiss and in one motion, Clay pushed the laced pillows off my bed and gently laid me down on it. I felt the fire as it swelled in my body, and I welcomed his actions. I wanted him just as badly because we hadn't made love in more than a few weeks. As he touched me his hands felt like much needed therapy, and I allowed him to take over. Clay lifted my skirt above my waist and snatched off my floral panties. He placed his tongue in my moist treasure, and I gasped from pure bliss as he indulged me.

My mind swirled with delight as Clay's tongue found my sensitive spot, and I shuddered when Clay nibbled lightly on my clitoris until my legs had become rubbery. He then inched his tongue up my perspired body until his tongue met mine. I was so wet that Clay penetrated me easily with his iron manhood, and as he buried all of his thickness inside of me, I started to feel whole again. Our bodies moved harmoniously from the frantic rotation of my hips. Clay's breathing and pleasurable thrusts became frenzied as his eruption filled my insides. He swept the damp hair from my face as he continued to lie on top of me. "I love you, Lane," he said, and he lifted his head to look into my eyes.

"And I love you too, Clay."

"I just want you to remember that when I'm back in Atlanta," he said.

"So, you are going back to Atlanta?"

"Yeah, you convinced me. I never wanted you to think that I didn't trust you. It's Dre who I don't trust—I saw how he was looking at you when y'all were at the door," he said, and rolled over on his back. "That muthfucka still want you, and don't think for one minute because he knows we're together he won't try you."

"Clay, stop. Now, you're exaggerating. Dre is a good friend, and plus I wouldn't let that happen." Clay jumped up off my bed.

"'Good friend, since when? If he was so good, Lane, why aren't you still with him?" he snapped as he put his pants back on. I refused to go there and especially after the moment we had just shared.

"Okay Clay, I can see what you're saying, but you know what I meant." I dressed quickly and darted to the bathroom to escape this dead conversation. No sooner than I shut the bathroom door, I heard the front door shut and my dad's voice as he yelled out for us.

"Lane? Clay? Where are you two at?

"We're in the back Mr. King," Clay answered. I stayed in the bathroom and freshened up before I went out there to greet my dad.

"I'm in the bathroom, Dad. I'll be out shortly." My dad went to the living room and turned on the early afternoon news. I hurried myself as I wanted to talk to my dad and hear how his morning with his friend, Kernel had been.

I joined them in the living room as Clay explained to my dad that he needed to head back to Atlanta due to a crisis with his business. My dad grew very concerned about Clay's dilemma. "Are you taking my baby girl back with you?" I plopped down on the sofa next to my dad and planted a quick peck on his cheek.

"No dad, I'm not going back to Atlanta with Clay. Who'll take care of you if I'm gone?"

My dad responded to me as if he felt I was treating him like a child.

"Err, let me take a stab at this one, Lane. Me. Lane, there ain't no reason why you're not going back to your home and your life with Clay. I can take care of myself, young lady. Do I miss your mother? Of course I do. And I will until the good Lord sees fit to bring us back together again. So in other words, I'll be just fine," he said. My dad tapped the top of my hand a few times for assurance.

Clay's face had gotten as bright as stadium lights at a night game as he listened to my dad battle it out for me to go back to Atlanta with him. Clay studied my face for a reaction, but I refused to finch a facial muscle, because I knew he would have immediately booked a flight for me to go back to Atlanta with him. And even though I knew how badly Clay wanted me to return with him, he remained respectfully mute in the presence of my dad. Clay and my dad talked about the usual guy stuff while I searched for my phone as it rang, and when I finally found it, it had stopped. I looked at the screen, and it displayed I had a missed call, but I didn't recognize the Atlanta number. I thought it may have been Shon who tried to get in touch with Clay on my phone, but it rang again before I had a chance to find out from Clay. "Hello."

"Hi sweetie, it's Faizon." The southern belle squeaked out on the other end. "Before you say anything, I didn't know what to say to you, that's why I'm just now calling."

"Oh, Faizon, don't apologize. I understand," I said. And I really did. Her baby would have turned one-year old on the same day of my mother's funeral if it had survived. And to add salt to her gaping open wound, she had also been harassed by Darnell via mail and phone calls. She had to have him served with a restraining order in prison. "You don't have to explain. Char told me that every time you two talked, you asked about me."

"I'm so glad you understand. I really do miss you. When are you coming back home?"

"I am home," I chuckled.

"All right smart-ass, you know I meant Atlanta!"

"I know, and you sound just like Clay asking me those questions. I honestly can't answer that now. It's all depending on my dad." I glanced down at my wrist watch and noticed that my time with Clay was almost over. He had an evening flight booked for later. "Faizon, I hate to cut our call short, but Clay will be leaving soon. Can I call you back?"

"Oh, Clay is flying back today?

"Yeah, he's packing right now as a matter of fact."

"Sure you can, but I have a favor to ask you before we hang up.

Actually, it's a favor I'd like to ask Clay, but since we haven't officially met I was hoping that you'll ask him for me."

"I'm sure he will if he can. What is it?"

"Ask him if he'll help me launch my clothing line?"

"You must have heard about his new entertainment and event planning division?"

"Yeah, Girl. You know how quickly things spread in Atlanta. I've heard about a few events he's done for some people here, and the word around ATL is Clay Roberts is the man."

"Sure, I'll ask him. Girl, I know you must be excited and nervous at the same time, but you'll tell me all about it when I call you back later tonight. Thanks for calling, Faizon."

"Thanks, Lane, and kiss your dad for me. I hope Clay has a safe flight, and hopefully I'll talk to him when he gets back to Atlanta. Bye sweetie."

By the time I walked back in the guestroom, Clay had all of his things packed. Although I had coerced him to leave, I felt funny knowing that I would be here for an indeterminate time without him. Since the day Clay and I had gotten back together we hadn't spent a day apart, and now in a matter of hours I would officially be in a long distance relationship. Clay grabbed his wallet from out of his back pocket and sifted through a slew of his credit cards and pulled out one of his Amex cards. He casually took my hand and placed the limitless card in it.

"Take this just in case there's an emergency or anything you might want, but I'm hoping that you'll use it to get a plane ticket," he said.

"Clay, please. Let's not start that conversation again, not now. We have less than an hour together before you have to leave, and I've already made up my mind." I tried to force the card back in his hands, but he was adamant and refused to take it back.

"I don't understand what the problem is now? Your dad has just given you his blessings to come back with me." I explained to Clay exactly what I felt and what I thought he needed to hear. I told him I couldn't dare leave my dad so soon after my mother passed, and as soon as I felt my dad was doing well enough for me to leave, I would. What had me scared to let Clay go back to Atlanta without me was—I hadn't been able to get Dre out of my mind since I saw him. I fought hard not to think about him, but I couldn't help the way that I felt for him. I had thought about Dre everyday since he stood at the front door of my parents' home finer than ever. And when he hugged me, he ignited feelings within me I didn't know I still had for him.

My dad was sad to see Clay leave. They bonded so nicely during the time Clay had been in Brooklyn, and it was obvious that Clay felt the same way. My dad offered to go with us to the airport, but promptly changed his mind. He said he wanted us to have our last moments of privacy. While I called for a cab, my dad and Clay said their goodbyes. I watched them as they hugged each other, and I listened as my dad offered Clay some advice. You would have thought that my dad was sending his only son off to war the way they carried on.

"Don't worry about us too much, Clay. I'll send her back home to you sooner than you think, and if she keeps up with this long face she might even beat you home," he said.

They both seemed to have found that funny. I was just so happy to see my dad laugh again—truly laugh.

"But in all seriousness, Clay, I want to thank you from the bottom of my heart for all you've done for us; if Lynn would have lived, she would have loved you too. Have a safe trip home, Son." They hugged it out once more before the cabbie blew his car horn.

"Thank you, Mr. King, and please don't hesitate to call me if you want anything, and I mean anything."

"Thanks, Son, but I don't think we'll be needing anything."

"I didn't say 'need' Mr. King." My dad wasn't familiar with Clay's hang-up with that word, but I told my clueless dad that I'd explain it to him when I got back home. I kissed my dad on the cheek and told him I'd be back shortly. Before Clay and I made it down the stairs, the impatient cab driver honked for us again, but when he saw us in his view he jumped out of the cab and opened the trunk for Clay's luggage. As I slid into the back seat of the cab, I shivered from the unusually cold March weather. I heard a loud thud from the sound of the trunk being closed, and when they entered the cab, Clay told the cabbie that we wanted to go to JFK airport.

Clay interlocked his fingers with mine and gave me a sweet peck below my earlobe. We hadn't spoken a word to each other until we approached the Nassau expressway. Clay finally broke the silence when he asked me if I was I feeling all right.

"I'm fine, Clay. But if I'm totally honest, a part of me wishes I were going back with you today. I just can't find it in me to leave my dad so soon."

"At the risk of me sounding like a selfish man, I guess I have to say I understand that. But the selfish man in me wishes that you were coming back with me."

I felt like such a hypocrite when I pledged to Clay that my decision to

14

stay in Brooklyn was purely for my dad's sake. While in the back of my head, I had hoped to have the opportunity to take Dre up on his offer to call him if I ever needed someone to talk to. However, I wasn't totally lying when I told Clay that part of me wanted to be back in Atlanta, because I knew I would miss him terribly. I peered out the window to hide my guilt from Clay, and before I realized it, we had merged onto the JFK expressway. With only minutes away from the airport, and all the thoughts that swarmed in my head, I had almost forgotten about my phone conversation with Faizon.

"Clay, I almost forgot. My friend, Faizon, wants you to call her when you get back to Atlanta."

"About what?" he asked.

"She didn't go into much detail, but she wants you to help her with her clothing line launch.

"I'll have to direct her to Shon or Nikole—they handle the event planning side of the business.

"I know, but if you do this for me I'll really appreciate it. She's gonna need someone with your expertise to help her."

"Lane, I don't know if I can do it personally. Don't forget the reason I'm leaving is because I have a lot to contend with when I get back home."

"Please, Clay. This will be my chance to show you off, let her know I'm seeing a BOSS!"

Clay chuckled loudly, "Aight, I hope you know I'm only doing this because you asked and I love you."

"Thanks, Clay. I love you too. I'll give you her number; just give her a call when you get settled."

The cab driver asked us again what airline we wanted, and when Clay reminded him that we wanted Delta, he parked in the drop-off lane and asked if I wanted him to wait on me. I was prepared to tell him he could leave because I wanted to wait with Clay until his flight left, but Clay insisted that he wait for me. The cabbie got out of his car, opened the trunk for Clay, and pulled out his luggage as I stood on the curb. Clay paid the cabbie for a round-trip, and after he pocketed his fare, the stout man hopped back in his car causing it to bounce. Clay looked at me with those chestnut eyes of his and had me regret my decision to not be on that plane with him. He kissed me several times on my lips as I clung to him afraid to let him loose, and my eyes welled up with tears.

"Don't cry, Bae. I don't want to leave you like this. All you have to do is say the word and you could be on that plane with me."

"I know I could, Clay. I'll be fine."

"Well, it's about that time," he said, as he glanced at his watch. "I love you Lane. With my soul, I love you. I'll call you as soon as I get in, be good," he said. Clay walked through the automatic doors, and I stood at the back door of the cab with my arms wrapped around my body. I watched as Clay maneuvered through the crowded airport until he was completely lost from my sight.

"Are you ready, Miss?" the cabbie yelled through the opened back window.

"I guess I am."

I got back into the poorly kept cab with the ripped leather backseat. I opened my bag and pulled out my small compact mirror to assess the damage I had caused to my face from crying. The cabbie turned his radio volume on low, but I could still hear Mint Condition's, "Pretty Brown Eyes" and I lost it again. The cabbie peeked at me through his rearview mirror and asked if I wanted him to turn the radio off. I told him that it wasn't necessary and that I would be fine. I was almost home when Char called; she wanted to know if Clay made it off safely. I told her how confused I was over my decision, and wondered if I should have gone back to Atlanta with Clay. Again, she assured me my feelings of uncertainty were absolutely normal and that I'd experience a lot more indefiniteness before this was all over.

I didn't want to have this conversation with her in the cab, so I told her I would call her later. "Char, I'm almost home from the airport, so I'll call you later on tonight."

"Okay, Lane. Call me before nine o'clock because my baby is taking me out."

"Where y'all going?"

"Girl, there's no telling. Anthony just told me to be ready, and I'm gon' be ready!" We both laughed. "Oh yeah, Faizon told me she finally caught up with you."

"Yeah, she did. It was so good hearing her voice. She told me about all the craziness happening with Darnell too. I can't believe the nerve of that bastard."

"Can you believe that? Anyway, it's all good now...we hope. I'm about to head into a hearing so don't forget to call me. And before nine!" she insisted.

"I will, stop trippin'." Seconds after I placed my phone back into my bag, I received another call. I thought it may have been my dad to check up on me, but I looked at the number it wasn't from home. "Hello." I said.

"What's up, Lane. It's Dre."

I was stupefied when I heard Dre's voice. What a coincidence that he would call me as Clay probably hadn't left the runway yet. "Hi, Dre." I made certain my tone remained calm, reserved, not too excited. "How are you?"

"I'm good. I was just thinking about you and I thought I'd ring you. What are you and dude up to today?"

"Well, me and 'dude' aren't doing anything today—Clay just left for Atlanta. Why do you wanna know?"

"I was gonna shoot by your crib, but I didn't want another confrontation between me and ole boy. I thought I'd give this being respectful shit a try, you know, call before I just showed up at your door." The more Dre spoke to me, the more I squirmed to the sound of his voice. I had become so involved in my conversation with Dre, I hadn't realized that the cab had stopped. The cabbie knocked on his Plexiglas partition, and pointed to my house.

"Thank you," I told the driver and exited the cab.

"Thanks for what?"

"Not you Dre, the taxi driver. Look, Dre. I literally just dropped Clay off at the airport. I'm about to walk into the house, call me later. Bye Dre." I pressed the end button without giving Dre a chance to breathe another word. I walked in the house and went inside the living room where I heard the TV. My dad had a few of his fishing buddies over, and I almost hated to interrupt them. They all sat on the edge of their seats—their eyes glossed over—glued to the TV screen. You would have thought they were watching a Cinemax After Dark flick, but instead it was just a fishing program. I popped my head in the doorway and greeted the room full of retirees. They all looked up from the screen long enough to say hello and back to the screen they went. My dad excused himself and followed me as I walked towards my room.

"So did Clay make it off all right?" he asked.

"Yeah, he did."

"Are you okay?"

"I'm fine, Dad. I think I'm going to take a short nap."

"Lane, I really hoped that Clay would have gotten you to change your mind about staying here."

"No, da---"

"No, Lane, wait. Let me finish," my dad interrupted. "You've known me all your life, and there's one thing I hope you'd be able to say and that is I've never stripped you of your happiness and neither has your mother for that matter. Clay makes you happy. Hell! It'd be obvious to Stevie

Wonder that he's crazy about you, so why in the world would I stop you two from starting a life together?" My dad rested his elbow on my dresser and waited for me to reply.

"I know you've never stood in the way of my happiness, and me staying here with you isn't the end of my life. It's just something I need to do, something I want to do."

"Not for me, Lane...for you." He left me in my room and rejoined his buddies back in the living room. I sat down on my bed and pulled off my black Camilla Skovgaard boots, slipped into my comfy sweats, and my Bugs Bunny furry slippers. After I got comfortable, I went into the kitchen, put in a load of laundry, and cleaned up the kitchen. When I finished my mini clean up, I fixed a glass of orange juice and grabbed a piece of cold chicken that my aunt Bernice had stored in Tupperware for our dinner. I looked up at the duck shaped clock on the wall before I went back to my room and noted that in less than an hour Clay should be landing in Atlanta. I guzzled the glass of ice cold orange juice and went back in my room. I slid my mentally tired body onto my bed until my back was rested against the wall and thought about what my dad just told me.

I looked in the side drawer of my nightstand and pulled out my journal. I had started to write an entry when Clay called and said he had just landed and was headed to the studio where he planned to meet Shon about what's happened since he'd been gone. Before we hung up, he said he wanted me to know how badly he missed me already. I told him I felt the same.

"I didn't expect this at this time in my life," he said.

"What's that?" I asked.

"You. I didn't expect you. I didn't expect to love anyone the way I love you. That's why I wanted you to come back with me."

"Clay, I need you to trust me, and know that I need to do this."

"I do trust you. I even respect what you're doing, but if you want me to keep it real, I can't help but to think that Dre will think he still has a chance with you."

"Well, he doesn't, and you shouldn't let that worry you."

"But it does. I'm a man and I know how another man thinks. The second he finds out that I'm back in Atlanta he'll try to get at you. You're already vulnerable and he's going to use that to his advantage."

"Give me more credit than that, Clay. In order for someone to take advantage of me would mean I'd have to allow it, and that's not going to happen." I told Clay to put all of his doubts about Dre and me out of his mind. I assured him that he had fabricated this love reunion with Dre in his own head. As Clay and I talked, I heard my dad's guests tell him they would see him tomorrow at the club. After Clay and I hung up, I continued to write in my journal—I wrote how Clay's concerns weren't completely outlandish and how rattled I'd been after Dre unexpectedly called me shortly after Clay boarded the plane.

After I jotted down all the day's events in my journal, I laid down across my bed and started to read a book. I heard my dad on the phone; he had called in an order at the Rib Shack down the street from us. When I peeked my head in the door of his room, he had just put the phone down. "You're up? I thought you were still asleep. I just got off the phone with the Rib Shack for our dinner. I hope you're in the mood for some ribs?"

"I wasn't sleeping, I was reading a book. And I sure am in the mood for some ribs. Did you get some of their macaroni and cheese too?"

"You know I did, I even got us some cobbler"

I smiled at his delight. "That sounds so good, Daddy. What time is it by the way?"

"It's nearly eight-thirty. Why?"

"Nothing really, I just told Char I'd call her before nine o'clock." As we waited for our food, I went to the kitchen, pulled out two plates from the cabinet, and made a fresh pitcher of lemonade. When the food arrived my dad brought the food into the kitchen, and I fixed our plates while my dad set up the trays in his bedroom. We watched an episode of American Idol and rooted for our favorite contestants as we ate. I heard what my dad said about going back to Atlanta with Clay, but I looked at how happy he had been and I knew that I had made the right decision to stay.

Charmine

My day had gone to shit! I had ripped my twenty-five dollar stockings before I even entered the courtroom and lost both of the cases I tried. Now, the caterer for my wedding has pulled out because she's become a Muslim. She claimed she can't be around pork or alcohol any more. So with just two months before my wedding, I have to scramble to find another caterer. I was blessed that Faizon had offered to make my wedding dress as a gift. She's already showed me a few of her sketches, and I loved them all.

My day had turned out so horribly that I nearly canceled my date with Anthony because of it, but I knew that he looked forward to our evening together. I asked Lane to call me before Anthony and I went out, but when I looked at my watch it was nearly nine o'clock, and I wondered if Lane was going to call at all. I went inside my bag and pulled out my phone to call her. Just as I was about to press her number, my phone vibrated, and Lane's face popped up. "What's up, Chica? I was just about to call you," I said.

"Nothing, Dad and I just got done eating. I rushed through my cobbler and ice cream so I could talk to you before your hot date. How was your day?"

"Girl, we're not even gonna go there—everything went haywire today. Tell me why 'Angela the caterer' has now become 'Aamira the Muslim?' So as of today I don't have a caterer."

"Stop playing!"

"I wish I was. When are you coming back 'cause I'm going to need all the help in the world with this wedding? Do you realize I have just a little over two months?"

"Yeah, I do realize that, but I honestly don't know when I'm coming back to Atlanta. I have to stick around a little longer for my dad's sake."

"What is your dad saying about all of this?"

"He's telling me he'll be fine without me if I go back to Atlanta, but he doesn't know what he wants at the moment."

"No, Lane, it sounds like you don't know what you want."

"What do you mean by that? This is the second time you've said that to me, and now my dad is saying the same thing. Now please, will you tell me what you're talking about?" I was slightly hesitant to give Lane my opinion on why she felt the overwhelming need to stay with her dad, but I knew our relationship was cemented and we could talk about anything.

"I believe you're feeling guilty for not being there for your mom during her illness and then her ultimately death." Lane sighed heavily, but that was her only rebuttal. I nearly thought she had considered to hang up on me. "Lane? You still there?" I asked.

"Yeah, I'm still here. But I totally disagree with what you've just said. I love how you think your one semester of psychology has you thinking you can analyze me, but you're all wrong."

"I hope so, but you did ask." I tried to change the subject because it was one of two things: either Lane was in deep denial, or I was wrong, but I didn't think I was wrong in this case.

"I did, but it's not true. Although I was living in Atlanta, I was always there for my mother."

"So, why don't you think you can do the same for your dad now?"

"I can, but I choose not to." Lane and I could have gone back and forth on this subject all night, but I didn't have the energy for it. So, I lied and told her Anthony was walking in the office, and I would call

22

her sometime tomorrow. My day had been horrible enough without having a blown-out argument with Lane over something she wasn't ready to admit.

When Anthony arrived ten minutes later, he looked so handsome. He had a bouquet of flowers in one hand and a bottle of champagne in the other. I didn't give him the chance to shut my office door before I had leaped on him causing him to nearly drop the contents in both his hands. "What's with the champagne?" I asked.

"It's for later," he said nonchalantly. "If I'd known that flowers and champagne would make you this happy you would have gotten them everyday," he said.

"They do, but I'm happier to see you right now." I gave him a long passionate kiss. Anthony tossed the champagne and the flowers on the Italian leather chair beside us and backed me up against the door. He slowly unbuttoned my blouse, but when he reached my third button I stopped him; I stripped down to my baby blue bra and panties. Anthony watched in fascination as I unhooked my bra and it fell to the floor. He jiggled the door handle to check if it had been locked as I stood there partially naked and waited for him to have me. "Where do you want me?" I asked.

Anthony's eyes scanned my office and pointed to my desk. I walked over, pushed the phone, desk lamp, and the stack of files to one side. I slid onto its surface, and it was there that Anthony made love to me tenderly and generously. Anthony's body shuddered one last time before he buried his face in my heaving cleavage. "Ahh that was good, Charmine. Love you," he said.

"I love you back." Anthony slipped out of me and grabbed for his pants. I couldn't move. My body felt weak from our quick, yet ravenous escapade. Anthony had the body of a sexy fitness trainer, and I admired it while he got dressed. I apologized to him for the sexual distraction, which I thought had caused us to miss our reservation. Anthony looked at me strangely and asked me what reservation had I caused us to miss. When I reminded him that he asked me to be ready at nine o'clock, he grinned.

"We don't have dinner reservations. I wanted to take you to your early wedding gift."

"Anthony, our wedding isn't for two months."

"I know Darling, that's why I said *early*. I want to give it to you tonight." I got dressed quickly as the mention of an early wedding gift peaked my curiosity. Anthony put the flowers and the bottle of bubbly in my leather bag, I straightened my desk and hid any remnants of an episode of steamy crazed sex. You see, I had an extremely nosy administrative assistant. I caught her one day going through one of the partner's desk drawers. I cautioned her that if I ever caught her going through my things like that, she'd be fired instantly. It was only because the said partner was a certified asshole that I even turned a blind eye and my back.

I turned off the lights in my office, and Anthony guided me safely out of the darkened room. Once we were outside, Anthony opened the passenger's side door to our Land Rover and helped me in. The nightlife in Atlanta started on Thursday nights as evidenced by the loud music and laughter that filled the streets of Buckhead as we drove to my wedding gift. We were in the car for less than fifteen minutes before Anthony stopped the vehicle in front of an unoccupied office in midtown Atlanta. "Why did we stop here?" I asked.

"That is your wedding gift," he said, and pointed to the large windowed office. "That, Darling, is the new home of: Martin & Martin."

I nearly jumped out of my damn skin when I realized Anthony had just secured our future with the purchase of our very own law office.

"OH-MY-GOD!" I screamed and jumped out of the car. "You are the best thing that's ever happened to me." I peered through the window to get a glimpse of the inside. Anthony was at the door of our new office and suspended a large set of keys from his hand.

"Why are you peeking through the window when you can you go inside?" he asked. When he opened the door, I could smell the newness of the office. It was packed with huge boxes and other office furniture items still securely wrapped in plastic.

"I can't believe this...when did you do all this?" I asked.

"I have my ways. Are you happy?"

"Absolutely!" I rubbed his face and told him how much I appreciated him. The moment felt magical, and I never wanted it to end. We sat on the packed boxes in the office and sipped on the champagne. We talked for hours about what the future held for us and now for the future of Martin & Martin.

We both had an early morning the next day and decided we'd better call it a night. We lived in Gwinnett County, which was a trek to our current office in Atlanta, so when Anthony agreed to relocate, it made me very happy. It was soon after Anthony asked me to marry him that he put his house on the market because we needed more space. We've had a few prospective buyers, but no one had come close to our asking price. As Anthony drove us home, I looked out the window, red-eyed and quiet. Anthony thought I had fallen asleep because I was so quiet, but when he realized I wasn't he struck up a conversation. "Are you all right, Babe? Are you having reservations about the new office," he asked.

"No! Not at all. I was sitting here thinking about Lane, wishing she could have just a pinch of my happiness right now. She's going through so much, and I don't know how to help her." Anthony took his right hand off of the steering wheel and caressed my thigh.

"I know, Darling. It must be a lot on her and you as her good friend." I tried not to think about Lane because I felt like I wanted to cry, but I was too exhausted to find any tears. When Anthony and I finally arrived home, I was so done I went straight to my bed where thankfully I stayed until the next morning.

Every time my alarm clock beeped, I slapped the snooze button like I was a contestant on Family Feud, and I hugged my pillow even tighter. Anthony just couldn't take it any longer, he stormed into the bedroom, turned off my alarm, and insisted I get out of bed. He advised me to get up and get to my day started unless I wanted a repeat of the previous day. That was all I needed to hear. I wouldn't have wished my yesterday on my worst enemy. I sprung from my bed and walked into the shower. I left my car in the parking lot of our office building in Buckhead, so Anthony had to drive us both to work. And because of the twelve times I had pushed the snooze button, I tried my best to hurry before Anthony lost his head. He was a fanatic for being everywhere on time, and because of that, I skipped a hot breakfast and grabbed only a cereal bar.

When Anthony and I stepped outside I welcomed the bright sun and hoped the morning's warm weather was an indicator that we could look forward to an early spring. Anthony rushed me so badly that I nearly forgot to grab the few swatches of material I picked out for Jayla's junior bridesmaid dress. Jayla, Anthony's niece, decided at the last minute she wanted to have a role in our wedding. I didn't mind as I thought it was a great gesture to unite our families.

Faizon and I had planned to meet for drinks after court to finalize any changes I may have wanted to my dress and the date of the last fitting. I had so much on my plate in the upcoming months: a wedding, a house move, and now our law firm—I just hoped I hadn't bitten off more than I could chew. I had also hoped that Lane would have made a decision about when she'd return to Atlanta, but each time I asked her about it she evaded my inquiries. If I hadn't learned anything else from Lane's experience, I learned to appreciate my time with my mother and to call her more frequently. My mother and I weren't nearly as close as Lane and her mother had been, but I couldn't bear the thought of something happening to her, and now I made more of an effort to talk to her.

Anthony drove like a maniac down I-85, but I dared say a word as I knew I was the cause of his erratic need for speed. Anthony told me that after work he was going by his parents for dinner and asked me if I wanted to join him. I told him that I would've loved to have gone with him if I weren't meeting Faizon concerning Jayla's dress. He gave me one of those snide side-looks. "You do know my parents think you're avoiding them, don't you?"

"Now why in the heck would they think that? Look at what they've given me." I winked at him, and ran my fingers through his silky, light brown hair. "Please send my apologies, but I'm sure if you tell them I'm meeting with Faizon after work about the dresses for the wedding, they'll understand that."

"I'll tell them, but this is the third time that you've been a no-show. It may now appear to them as avoidance."

I knew I had canceled on them before, but I hadn't realized it had been three times and that they've kept count. "Ah, Baby. I do see where they might think that, but you know differently. How about I prepare a nice meal for them next week? You know, a goodwill gesture."

"I don't want you to go through all that trouble. I just wanted you to be aware of what they're saying to me."

"It's no trouble at all. I'll call your mother on Sunday and make all the arrangements."

"Thanks, Babe," he said, and tooted his lips sideways for me to kiss so he wouldn't have to take his eyes off of the bumper-to-bumper traffic.

When it came to the wedding issues it seemed like everyday I had more and more to do. I needed another pair of hands and those hands were back in Brooklyn attached to Lane's body. I had to make it my mission to get her back in Atlanta. It was a miracle that with all that went wrong Anthony and I made it to the office on time. We kissed discretely in the hall before we departed and went our separate ways. I headed straight to my office because I had a hearing first thing, but first I needed to grab some files before I went down to the Fulton County courthouse. Bella, my nosy assistant, greeted me at the door of my office.

"Good morning, Ms Grant. How are you this morning?"

"I'm well, Bella, how are you?" I asked, but remained focused while I searched for my files.

"I'm good, thanks." I could tell she was in a talkative mood this morning, and I immediately put her to work.

"That's good, Bella. Bella, please find the Rubin case for me and put it on my desk."

"Sure thing Ms Grant." She walked over to the file cabinet and looked for the case I requested.

"Someone must have had a sweet time here last night." I didn't acknowledge her statement immediately, because I didn't want to give her allegation any credence. But, in my head I wondered what had Anthony or I left behind to make her come to that conclusion. I still hadn't looked up from my desk, but I wanted to know what she was on about.

"What do you mean, Bella?" I asked coolly.

"When I came in this morning there were rose petals in the crevice of the chair, and under your desk." Whew, that's all? I didn't know what this chick was going to say she found. I knew I had ripped my stockings off and forgotten to put them in the trash, but they had been ripped from that morning and not due to our lovemaking. Annoyed with Bella's amateur detective skills, I encouraged her to stay on task and look for the file as I requested. Bella noted I was being short with her and took the hint. She placed the file on my desk and exited my office without uttering another word. I looked in my bag to ensure I had my throat lozenges and a spare pair of pantyhose. Once I saw I had everything in place, I left the office.

En route to the courthouse, Faizon called to make sure that we were still on for later. I warned her that my morning case may be longer than I expected, but we were definitely still on. Faizon told me that she was fine if my time in court had been extended, because she had made a slight change to our plans herself. Faizon explained that she needed to meet with Clay about the launch of her new clothing collection and how she'd heard that Clay was the man to see in Atlanta to make things happen.

Faizon asked me had I remembered to bring the fabric samples for Jayla's dress, and I told her they were already in my bag. Before we said our goodbyes, she asked me to call her as soon as I stepped out of court. I approached the courthouse and darted my car in an empty parking space. I rushed through the courthouse building because the Honorable Miller was presiding over this case, and he had a reputation for being a bastard if you were late. No sooner than I stepped in the courtroom and greeted my client, the bailiff cleared his throat and said, "All rise for the Honorable Clark Miller."

Faizon

The Georgia weather is just one of the reasons I'm glad that I was born in the south. It was the month of March, and if you wanted to, you could get away with just wearing a pair of shorts and a t-shirt. But from the moment I became serious about designing my own clothes, I've been my own walking billboard. Every time I stepped out of my front door, I wore my own creations and today was no different. I'd never met Clay before and I wanted my attire to make an impression, so I chose to wear one of my signature designs, a sophisticated black jumpsuit; it was made for the perfect woman with perfect curves like me.

After I finished dressing, I looked at myself in the mirror, and I rubbed my hands over my flat stomach and tried to imagine myself being pregnant again. I wanted to know what it felt like to be a mother so badly, but I had been robbed of that precious gift, and I guess now I'll never know. It still haunts me today when I think about what Darnell's wife said during the trial—that losing my baby was karma for me sleeping with 'her' husband. I've had more than just a few questionable relationships over the past few years, but I never expected my affair with Darnell to end in such a heinous way for which my baby paid with its life—and nearly

29

cost me mine.

I guess being an only child and getting everything I've always wanted, even if it belonged to someone else contributed to me being very unpopular with other women. And to be honest, I still don't place high on the list for attracting true friends. Charmine and Lane are exceptions, both of them are supportive, caring, independent, and secure within themselves and some of those traits I simply do not possess. It's because of Lane's caring nature that she had arranged for Clay to handle the launch of my clothing collection at a fraction of what he would normally charge.

When Clay and I spoke over the phone, I was very appreciative that he agreed to meet me so soon after he returned from New York. He seemed enthusiastic about bringing my vision to life and had me all pumped up just speaking about it. Clay named a long list of Atlanta's most prominent heavy-hitters, and he promised he would have them at my launch and I hoped he could deliver. We agreed to meet at a newly opened cafe on 11th and Peachtree that bragged of its seventy plus pastries on display daily and European coffees. One of my poor habits is that I'm chronically late for everything, but I wanted to be respectful of Clay's time, so I arrived at the cafe fifteen minutes early and took a window table.

My server asked if I wanted to wait for my guest before I ordered, I told her I would, but I wanted to have a glass of mint water with lime while I waited. I stared out of the window and people-watched as they took advantage of the beautiful weather. I was convinced that my clothing line was much needed as I was disgusted with the hoodrat fashions these women pranced around in: short-shorts and cheap skimpy dresses up to their cesarean incisions. I scanned the parking lot of the cafe for Clay and hoped I would have recognized him when he arrived. I didn't have the pleasure of meeting Clay like Charmine had because just as Clay and Lane had started to date, I was recuperating from my ordeal with Darnell which kept me out of the loop. I remembered seeing him from a distance the one time that he picked Lane up from my house, but he never left his car and it was only for a brief minute in the night.

Just as my server had returned with my water I noticed a black BMW X1 entered the parking lot and parked. I didn't suspect that it was Clay as the driver hadn't gotten out of the car immediately. I picked up my glass and sipped on the refreshing taste of mint, when this tall delectable man stepped out of the BMW. I closed my eyes and said a quick prayer. Dear Lawd, please don't let him be my friend's man, because he-is-oh-so fuckable. But I was afraid it was him. From my recollection, Clay had locs and so does this man. I licked my lips and adjusted my boobs before I called out to him and prompted him to come over. "Clay, I'm over here," I said. He spotted me and proceeded to walk over. I was unsure of how I should have greeted him. Do I hug him? Do I kiss him? But he extended his hand and introduced himself to me, so I settled for that.

"Hello Faizon, I'm Clay," he said, and gestured for me to take my seat. I had a huge lump in throat and had to take another sip of my water before I responded.

"Hi Clay, thanks for coming."

"No problem, glad I can help. Can I get you something before we get started?" he asked.

"Ah... yeah, I'll have something." He raised two fingers in the air for our server and she came right over to us with an electronic device that she used to tap in the orders. I ordered something light, because I knew I would have dinner with Charmine after Clay and I finished here. "I'll have an Eiskaffe and an almond croissant." After I placed my order I watched as his eyes scanned my body up and down. I wanted to know what he was thinking so I asked him had I ordered too much. He asked me did I have ice cream in my coffee every morning and how I stayed in such good shape. In my traditional style of flirtation I told him that I'm a very physical being which I think made him uneasy. He quickly looked to our server and ordered a latte.

"Aight, Faizon. How do you want Platinum Plus Entertainment to help you?" How I wanted him to help me was way too inappropriate for a first meeting, especially since he's Lane's man. So, I started with how I wanted his company to help me with my clothing launch. Clay told me that he had just signed a young lady whose sound was similar to Elle Varner, and he felt she would appeal to the vibe of the night's event. He could've told me Barney Rubble was going to perform and it would not have mattered. I just wanted to have our meeting prolonged, because I could have stared and listened to him all day. I had almost

31

forgotten this man even had a girlfriend. That was until he mentioned how badly he wished Lane had come back to Atlanta with him. I should have been ashamed of how I sat across from Lane's man and lusted over him the way I had, but I wasn't.

I expected Charmine to call me at any minute to let me know she was out of court. Meanwhile, I thoroughly enjoyed being in Clay's company and tried to milk our time together. To my right, I noticed there was a table of women who tapped one another under the table and giggled every time Clay smiled. Unbeknownst to them I knew exactly what those sly undercover taps were for. Lane, Charmine, and I had those very same moments when we would see a good-looking man in a club and then boast about what we'd do to him in bed.

We talked a bit more about how I started in the fashion industry and my introduction to the fashion world. Clay's phone vibrated and he answered the call. "Speak of the angel, it's Lane," he said. "Hello Bae, Faizon and I were just talking about you." I watched him as he spoke to Lane and wished I were her. "Yeah, I miss you too. (silence) No, you're not disturbing anything. We're about finish here anyway. I'll buzz you when I head back to the office." I hadn't realized my time had been up, but apparently it was by Clay's account. He ended their conversation with an 'I love you too.' and he tapped a button to end the call. "Lane sends her love," he said.

He searched out our sever to bring the check over. Clay insisted he pay our tab, and he gave his card to the server. While we waited for his payment to go through, I told Clay how pleased I was with what he had outlined for my launch so far. He assured me that after I was formally introduced to the Atlanta fashion scene, I would be a household name. As we walked out of the cafe, the table of dreamy-eyed women who were seated across from us watched our every move until we were outside. Clay walked me to my car and told me he would call me first thing Monday morning for some more information. He extended his hand for me to shake again, but this time I leaned in for a hug. I pressed my breasts deep into his chest and wrapped my tiny arms tightly around his gorgeous masculine frame.

My forwardness proved to be unwanted as Clay stepped back quickly, and freed himself from my hold. It had now become an awkward moment for the both of us. Clay's voice had gone a pitch higher as he reiterated he'd call me Monday, and then he nervously high-stepped it to his car. I waited in my car until I heard Clay's vehicle screech past mine, when I saw he was out of my eye's view, I threw my arms over the steering wheel and plunked my face onto my forearm. What had I just done? I couldn't believe what an ass I had made of myself with such an overt advance towards Lane's man. When Charmine called me, I was so tense that I jumped, and it caused me to inadvertently honk my own horn. "Hi Charmine, you finished with court? I asked.

"Yeah, Girl, and I got my mojo back! I won my case," she said.

"That's great. You should feel real good about that."

"Yes, I do. Are you still meeting with Clay or are y'all finished?"

"No... I mean yeah," I answered, quite flustered. "We're done for today."

"What's the matter with you? You all right?"

"Of course I am. I just didn't expect..."

"What, for Clay to be so damn nice looking? Girl, I know. That brotha is fiinnee," she said. "That's right, this is your first time seeing him up close. You were still recovering when they started dating, and then they had that brief breakup."

I had to play it off, I couldn't confess to Charmine that I could have allowed Clay to sex me right there on the cafe table. "Charmine, it's really not that serious, he looks alright. What I'm more concerned with is hoping I haven't over extended myself. I have a lot I need to get accomplished in the matter of two months. And my main concern is my launch, and not how good Lane's man looks."

"Pardon me! I'm glad we're on the phone and I can't smell you, 'cause your attitude stinks," she joked. I'm glad she did, because I needed something to lighten my mood and deflect how I had crossed the line with Clay. Charmine told me that she was headed my way and should be at our meeting location in thirty-minutes or less. After our call, I put the key in the ignition and drove to the restaurant. Clay's alluring face flashed several times in my mind which disturbed me. I didn't want to go there—not with him.

When I arrived at the restaurant, Charmine was already there sitting in her car. I tooted my horn as I passed her car. She got out of her car, walked to the entrance of the restaurant, and waited for me to park. I reached in the backseat and grabbed my sweater as it had become a bit chilly. "Damn, girl. You look better and better every time I see you," she said.

"And so do you. Anthony must be doing something right."

"He is. He got me to marry his ass." We laughed about that as we entered the restaurant. We stood at the reception area and waited to be seated. We may have been there two minutes before a very pleasant male server with female attributes and mannerisms came over and seated us.

"Hello, I'm Trent, and I'll be your server this evening. What can I start you ladies with today?" he asked. Charmine ordered a glass of red wine, and I asked for a 5 O'clock in the Morning. "Oohh Chile, I hope you ain't driving," he teased and made a clawing motion towards my face with his long blue fingernails.

"I'll be fine, thanks," I answered. After he collected our drink order and left, Charmine added her nine cents.

"He's right, you know. Are you driving, or do you plan to spend the night here?"

"It's been one of those days, plus I've had one before. They aren't as strong as people make them out to be."

"By whose account, Ned the wino? Let me stop, order what the hell you want and I'm paying." Trent returned with our drinks and asked if we were ready to place our food order. Charmine ordered the Premium Wagyu Beef, and I ordered the Pan Fried Calamari. Trent studied my outfit closely while he took our order.

"Good choices ladies," Trent said, his eyes fixated on me. "I see you make plenty of good choices. Gurl, I love how you working that jumpsuit."

"Thank you, I made this myself," I flaunted.

"That is HOT! I'd wear that," he said and walked away. Charmine looked like she wanted to add her commentary to our little chit-chat, but allowed me the opportunity to show off.

"So tell me what happened today with you and Clay?" Charmine asked as she took a long sip of her wine.

"What do you mean what happened today with me and Clay? Nothing happened. We met. We talked. We planned. And that's it!" Had I looked as if I'd done something? What made her ask me that?

"All right, calm down. Why are you being so defensive? I just wanted to know how your meeting went with Clay. I know this is a big deal for you to finally get your brand started, and I want you to know that it's important to me too."

"I apologize, Charmine. I've just been so tired," I said, and offered her another bogus excuse. "I haven't been sleeping well ever since Darnell started sending me letters from jail."

"Aw, forgive me, Hun. I've been so wrapped up with my wedding, and I haven't been a good friend to you. Of course, that would stress anyone out. What action has the jail taken, or do I need to pay them a visit?" If she only knew that it is I, who wasn't being a good friend to her with all my lies.

"No, Charmine, don't trouble yourself it's all been sorted now." When Charmine asked if making all of the dresses for her wedding contributed to my stress, I reinforced that making her wedding dress had done nothing but bring me joy. I eventually came down from my high horse and shared with Charmine what my meeting with Clay entailed. I told her and how impressed I was with his plans for my launch.

Trent brought our meals to the table, and he asked Charmine if she wanted a top-up on her wine. She told him 'no' unless he planned to drive us both home. "Bon appetite," he said and went to serve another table. After we devoured our incredibly tasty five-star meal, Charmine pulled out the new fabric for her junior bridesmaid dress. Immediately, I envisioned the perfect little dress.

"Now that's what I'm talking about—nice fabric, Girl."

"I'm glad, you like?"

"I do! When do you plan to bring Jayla to my house so I can fit her? Don't forget, we barely have two full months; May will be here before we know it."

"I know, I know, don't remind me. I'm having them over for dinner on Sunday, so I'll get with Emily, Jayla's mom, and set it all up, and then I'll get with you. Is that all right?"

"It'll have to be, but please don't wait until the last minute. I don't want to be sewing dresses the day of your wedding. It's bad enough Lane is M.I.A, and I still don't have her measurements. Is she still planning to be in the wedding?"

35

"Of course she is. She's been dealing with so much lately. But as for now, just work on the bridesmaids' dresses that are here in Atlanta."

Spiked with venom I lashed out. "Aren't we all. She's not the only one dealing with shit lately."

Charmine's face said it all. "I never want to make a comparison to what you and Lane have been through in the last year, because honestly I don't know if I could have survived any of it. But be reasonable, Faizon, Lane has just buried her mother. And at this very moment she's struggling with choices which will undoubtedly affect her personal happiness. Lane wants to be here in Atlanta with Clay, but she doesn't want to leave her dad so soon after he's just lost his wife. Surely, you can sympathize with that."

"I'm sorry, Charmine. I shouldn't have said that—I know it can't be easy for her. I'll call her and find out if she can email me her measurements." I had taken my frustrations out on an absent Lane, because I wanted to taste Clay as soon as I saw him step out of his car. Charmine stayed true to her word, she picked up the check and Trent expressed his gratitude to Charmine for the very generous tip she left him. He asked us again if we wanted a taxi to take us home, but we assured him we'd be fine and thanked him for his great service.

Charmine walked over to her car, put her bag in the backseat, and walked back over to me. "Thank you, for all that you're doing for me, and like I said earlier if you feel it has all become too much for you, just tell me." I tried to calm the apprehension that I created by telling Charmine not to worry about anything, that everything would be fine. She blew a kiss at me and ran back to her car. As I drove home, I could have kicked myself over what I said about Lane, and I thought about how difficult it must be for her. I imagined her having to come to such painstaking decisions so soon after her mother's death. Maybe it would be best if she stayed in Brooklyn with her dad. I'm quite sure she'd get over Clay in time. The least I could do is help her make the right decision—I mean... what are friends for?

Clay

I had only been gone for two weeks—and when I returned —all my shit was fucked up! My studio was burglarized and new artists making demands on some ole diva type shit like they're veterans. Then I do a favor for my woman's friend, and she tried to seduce me in broad daylight in a parking lot. And the worst of it is, I had to leave Lane in Brooklyn with that snake Dre. Lane might fall for that 'I only want to pay my respects 'cause I'm so sad' bullshit, but I ain't buying none of it.

I'd spoken to Lane everyday since I been back, and since the meeting with Faizon, she's asked me how the meeting went. I tried to avoid the topic of Faizon altogether, 'cause I don't know if I should tell her about how she pushed her tits all up in my chest. I really didn't want to put any more strain on Lane at the moment, and that's the last thing she'd want to hear about her so-called 'friend.' I hoped that I was wrong about this, but I didn't think I was. I'm not conceited nor am I arrogant, but I'm aware that women find me pleasing to the eye and coupled with the fact I'm in the music and entertainment industry, I'm used to women coming on to me all the time. I had a lot to deal with myself since being back, so I called on my man, Shon. The first time I called him his phone went straight to voice mail, but I kept calling until he picked up."What's up man?" Shon asked.

"What's up is, I need you to get down to the studio."

"Aw c'mon Clay, it's the weekend and my head ain't right. Me and Pam went out last night and we just crawled in the bed," he pleaded.

"Now, crawl back out and get down to the studio. I have a project for you.

"Alright, man, give me an hour," he said, and let out a sigh to let me know he was agitated.

"Cool. I'm leaving home now, and I'll meet you there." I snatched up some papers and left for the studio. Lane had become such a huge part of my life, and the project I had for Shon would eliminate any problems which might occur for me down the road. I wasn't going to allow anyone to fuck up what Lane and I had built. Not even her beautiful friend. When I pulled up in front of the studio, Shon was already there. I had no choice but to close the studio until we got the windows repaired from the break-in.

"Do you ever sleep?" Shon asked.

"No and neither should you until we get this shit back up and running," I said. Before we entered the building I turned to the street, and surveyed the area taking note of the constant flow of foot and car traffic. "I still don't know how these muthfuckas made it out the studio on this busy ass strip with computers, a mixing console, multi-track recorder, and a digital recorder without anyone seeing them."

"I know, man. Somebody banged us up real bad, but that's the nature of the business," he said indifferently.

"Nah, that's the nature of *my* business." I unlocked the boarded up door, and we stepped into the studio. Shon may have been too hung-over to detect the sarcasm in my tone, or he maybe he just couldn't be bothered. One thing was evident; he didn't want to be at the studio. I opened my office door and plugged in my laptop I brought from home, because everything else I owned was either in somebody's house or the pawnshop by now.

"So what's this top priority project you have for me?" he asked, and dropped his drunken body into the chair in front of my desk. "Do we have a new client? Singer, rapper?"

"Neither. She's a fashion designer... and she's a friend of Lane's. I want her put out there to all the key playas, from music, to sports, and all the wannabe celebrities here in Atlanta. We'll also introduce Amani that night, and let her do three tracks from her upcoming album. I want this event to have an upscale appeal, and I don't want any screw-ups which is why I want you to handle it. And bring Nikole in to help you," I directed.

"Does this friend have a name?"

"Faizon Hill."

"Faizon. Faizon Hill?" Shon asked, and pulled his expensive sunglasses from his face. "Faizon Hill is Lane's friend? Damn, baby is fine! I just read an article about her in the Atlanta Metro Observer a couple of weeks ago. They said she's the one to look out for in the 'A.' Why you letting me take the lead on this one, especially since she's Lane's friend? I would think you'd want to handle this one solo to get you some STP." Shon is well-known around the office for his womanizing, and coming up with his own crazy terminology, but I'd never heard him use that particular term before and I had to know.

"What the hell is STP, Shon?"

"Special Treatment Pussy," he laughed.

"That's what I'm trying to avoid."

"What you mean by that?" he quizzed.

"I think Faizon wants to give me some of her 'STP.' We met for the first time the other day at a cafe to discuss her launch and everything was cool. When we were in the parking lot about to leave, I went to shake her hand, and she gives me this long-ass lingering hug. Bruh, I nearly had to push her off me." I understood Shon's initial skepticism, because over the years Shon has heard me talk about all the pussy that gets thrown at me from all types of woman, so as I told him about Faizon, he gave me this bugged-out grimace.

"You want me to believe that Lane's friend came on to you in the parking lot after a business meeting?" he asked and put his sunglasses back on. He reeled back in his chair with laughter. "Clay, I know you think ALL the women in Atlanta want you, but I think you got this one wrong. I've seen her—it was just a sisterly hug."

"That wasn't no sisterly hug, Man. Sisters don't hug you until you can feel their nipples get hard against your chest. My dick responded to that shit and the whole nine, I had to make a dash for my car."

By this time Shon is hollin', telling me he wished he had my problems. "I don't know about that, Bruh. I've seen Faizon in the paper. I would have tapped that and suffered the consequences later."

"That's not me. I love Lane, and I don't get down like that. When I'm with a woman, I with her." I printed off the information Shon needed concerning my meeting with Faizon and what seemed to excite her about what we had discussed. I told him she expected to be called on Monday morning to give us some more information, and I reminded him to include Nikole, our entertainment manager. Nikole would definitely add the flair Faizon would expect on that night.

Due to the burglary, the studio was considered a crime scene and we couldn't touch much of anything. While Shon and I were still in my office I received a call from a Det. O' Hare from Fulton County. He told me that I could have my window repaired since they were able to lift some prints. After Shon and I talked about the logistics of Faizon's launch, there was no need to keep him any longer. So I told him I'd wait for the glass specialist to come out to replace the window, and he could go back home to spend the rest of the day with Pam. The technician from the glass shop called and stated he was on his way, so while I waited for him, I applied that time to go over Faizon's bio and head-shots to be used for her press release. I stared at her photo and agreed with Shon; Faizon is a strikingly beautiful ambitious woman. I found myself staring at her photo longer than I had liked, and I felt a sensation in my dick when I thought about her full sensuous breasts against my body.

When the glass technician buzzed the buzzer to the entrance, I welcomed the distraction from this gorgeous creature. Sid, the glass technician, assessed the damage to the window that was kicked in during the burglary, and promised me the job would be finished by late afternoon. As soon as he quoted me the price, I returned to my office and called Lane. I really needed to hear her voice. "Hi Baby, I was just about to call you," Lane said.

"What's up, Bae. So, you was thinking about me?" I asked.

"Always. Where are you?"

"I'm at the studio waiting for the window to be fixed. What's going on with you?"

"Nothing right now. I'm taking my dad out to eat dinner later on. I just hate you have to deal with all that foolishness. Has anyone come forth yet to offer any information about the break-in?"

"Nah, and I don't expect anybody to. You know ain't nobody

snitching; it's the law of the streets."

"Yeah, I know, and that's a damn shame. You've worked too hard to have some crackhead come and do that to your property."

"Don't let that worry you, Bae. Plus that isn't why I called you. I want you to know I love, and I miss you."

"Aahh I know you do, Clay. You know I love and miss you too."

"If that's true when are you coming home? I really want to see you."

"Clay, we've been through this already. Right now my dad needs me."

"I need you too!" I shouted. "I'm sorry Bae, I didn't mean to come at you like that. It's just that I'm missing you real bad right now."

"Clay, I know you do, but before you left you said that you understood that I needed to do this."

I know what I told her. That was when I was in Brooklyn, but now that I'm here I regret it. "I can't argue with you, because I did tell you that. Okay, Lane, I'm not gonna stress you about it any more. When you're ready, you're ready."

"Thanks, for understanding. By the way, you never told me how the meeting went with Faizon. Every time I ask you, you jump to another topic. Why is that?"

"How well do you know this broad?" I asked.

"CLAY! Don't call her that. I've known her about two years, and before you say anything, I know I should have told you that she can be a bit full of herself."

"A 'bit,'" I mimicked. "She's more than just a bit."

"All right, she's more than a bit, but that's just how she is. And don't forget you'll be doing me huge favor, and when I get back to Atlanta, I'll show you how much I truly appreciate it." I had to laugh as I thought about what Shon had just told me about the STP. "What's so funny?" she asked.

"Nothing, I just remembered something Shon said to me earlier. Aight, Bae, I'll do this just for you. And no matter how long you stay in Brooklyn, I won't let you forget that you owe me," I said.

"You won't have to remind me, because I always pay my debts," she laughed. "Call you tonight, love you."

"I love you too. Bye Bae." I changed my mind about saying

anything to Lane about what transpired with Faizon. She seems to think her friendship with Faizon is cool, and maybe Shon was right. It could've been a sisterly hug and I misinterpreted it. This is one time I prayed I was wrong.

Lane

Every time I spoke to Clay he tried hard to persuade me to return to Atlanta, and although there wasn't anything I'd love to do more, I didn't see that happening in the near future. Maybe there was some truth in Char's unsolicited psychoanalysis. I may have harbored some guilt about my mother which kept me here in Brooklyn, but whatever it was I wasn't going to make the same mistake twice.

My cousin, Beverly, called and invited me to a party out in Queens that her boyfriend was having for his sister. I tried my best to get out of it, but she persisted until I gave in. I asked my dad if he would he be okay if I went; he told me that he'd be fine, because he had made plans to participate in a chess tournament at the Brooklyn Armory with his buddies.

Since I was unsure about the length of time I'd be home for my mother's funeral, Charmine had only packed two weeks worth of clothing for me, which meant I had to go shopping for a few items. After a good breakfast, I got dressed and then called Clay before I left for the day. I picked up my phone and scrolled down to his name. "Good morning, Baby," I said.

"Good morning, to you," he yawned. "What you doing up so early?"

"I have a busy day. I'm surprised you're still asleep."

"I had a busy night."

"Why? What happened?"

"After the guy fixed the window at the studio this kid,

Countree, from Memphis came through. He said he heard about the studio and wanted to lay down some tracks. His joints were bangin' and we ended up kicking it at the studio 'til a little after four this morning."

"Whaat? He must have been hot. Anyway, I didn't want anything so I'll let you get back to sleep. I'll call you back tonight when I get in."

"No, wait, I'm up now. Where are you going that you won't be home until tonight?"

"Well, Char didn't pack a whole lot for me, so first I'm going to Manhattan to get some clothes, and later on tonight I'm going to a party that Beverly invited me to."

"Aight then, hit me up later when you get in. I wanna hear your voice to make sure you got in safely—no matter how late."

"You know I will. Talk to you tonight."

"Bye, Bae."

I phoned Charmine after I talked to Clay, but I wasn't surprised when she hadn't answered. I knew her weekend schedule like the back of my hand. She was either at the spa, or if she's had a busy week, she slept-in. And with her planning a wedding she hadn't only been busy, but I imagined stressed as well. Before I put my phone back in my bag, I scrolled down to call Faizon to hear from her and what she thought about Clay. But I changed my mind, and hit the end button when I remembered most stores closed earlier than normal on Sundays, and so I left for Manhattan. The spring weather had arrived, and although it was a bright sunny day, it was a bit chilly. As I walked to the train station, I bumped into a few of my old neighborhood acquaintances, and I stopped to talk a bit before I continued my journey.

I boarded the A train to Manhattan, and I wished I were back in Atlanta to enjoy the luxury of being driven around by Clay. There were times if he couldn't drive me personally he'd get me a driver for the day. I hadn't been on a train in over two years. I had almost forgotten about the horrid smells and unique personalities of the people who would showcase one or all of them at the same time. The train hadn't completely stopped at the station when I squeezed through the crowd of people who stood in front of the doors to the train. I wanted to be the first person who made a beeline to exit from the putrid steel transporter. I sprinted up the stairs which led me directly to 34th street, and I marveled at the wonderful aromas of freshly baked pretzels, pizzas, and sautéed onions from the famous New York hot dogs.

I browsed through a few shops before I entered Saks Fifth Ave, one of my favorite stores when I lived in New York. Since Beverly had never mentioned the dress code for the party, I riffled aimlessly through racks and racks of clothes unclear of what to buy for the party.

After I walked what seemed like the length of a football field around the store, I settled on two pair of pants, a few blouses, and one unbelievably sexy black dress. Before I left Saks, I made one last stop to the shoe department. I found the cutest pair of red peep-toe pumps that caught my eye to wear to the party. After I bought the shoes, I knew it was time for me to leave Saks, or I'd have to find a job in New York. I really couldn't afford to shop the way I had, but I refused to use the credit card Clay had left with me. I made my way back to the subway station. I had resisted the savory smells of hot dogs when I first got off the train, but on my way back home I gave in and decided to treat myself to the famous hot dog with all the fixings.

As I got closer to the subway, the thought of the smelly fumes and silly scams turned my stomach, so I finished my hot dog and hailed a taxi. In the time I lived in the Georgia I must have picked up a southern accent, and the taxi driver picked up on it. He attempted to swindle me as he explained his meter had been broken during an accident and told me the fare to Brooklyn was seventy-five dollars. But when I told him where he can shove his 'broken meter' and 'seventy-five dollars' he soon learned that I was a native New Yorker. The driver mumbled a few select words under his breath then tried to justify his actions. "Oh," he said. "I thought you were a tourist."

"You thought very wrong. And what difference does that make to the price?" I snapped.

"Brooklyn isn't my normal route; I sometimes get confused on the fare." I started to hail another taxi, because it was clear that this man was dishonest but I was tired, and time was of the essence. When we arrived in front of my house, I paid the $45.60 fare. I slammed his door hard when I stepped out of his taxi in protest of all the unsuspecting tourists who sat in his cab. When I got upstairs to my bedroom, I laid all my new outfits on my bed. I still hadn't decided what I wanted to wear, but I felt the need to be dressed causal comfortable, rather than sexy.

My dad still wasn't home when I arrived, so I called to check on him and he said he was fine. He was having dinner with a few of his buddies. I decided on the outfit that I would wear to the party and hung the other new purchases in the closet. I hopped in the shower, and soon after I stepped out, Beverly called to make sure I was still going with her. She said she was afraid that I would have backed out on her like I had done to so many times before. Once I assured her that I was going she said she'd pick me up at 7:30. While I had her on the phone I told her what I planned to wear to the party, and she offered her opinion. "Please, come up out that black. You wear that shit all the time—you ain't goin' to no funeral," she blurted, then realized she had put her foot in her mouth. "Lane...I didn't mean to say that. What I meant–"

"I know what you meant, Bev. I'm not offended, but you know I've always worn black."

"I'm sorry. Wear what you want to wear, just don't be too over-dressed, it ain't that type of party." I looked at the time and told her that we should get off the phone so I could finish getting dressed. She agreed, and once more she repeated the time they would pick me up. I took into account what Beverly had said about not being over-dressed and I chose the black pants and a low-cut black top that revealed two of my best assets. After I applied my make-up and stepped into my fire red pumps, I glanced at myself in the mirror. This was my first time getting dressed-up since the funeral, and I was quite pleased with how good I looked.

Beverly was at my house on time and she knocked quick and hard on my door as if she needed to pee really badly, so I rushed to let her in. "C'mon Girl, you ready?" she asked in a panicked voice. "Trigger is already in a fucked up mood."

"What do you mean he's already in a fucked up mood? And do I even need to be going to this party if it's starting off like this?" I asked. I stood by the front door fully dressed and too cute not to be going anywhere, but now I had some apprehensions about going.

"You know how he is, he'll be fine before the night is out," she insisted.

"Actually, I don't know how he is. I've never met him." I knew very little about him. Beverly had mentioned to me that he was in jail at the same time as Dre when he was wrongly incarcerated for murder, but that was all I knew of him.

"Girl, I thought you did. Anyway, just hurry up 'cause he's double parked and he can't afford no tickets; then he'll be looking for me or you to pay it." She turned her back and walked out the door. Beverly's paranoid behavior should have been a sign for me to get undressed and climb into my bed with some Ben & Jerry's Cookie Dough ice cream, but instead I locked the door and joined them in the car. When I entered the car, I caught a contact from the strong smell of weed. I reached my hand over the seat for a handshake and introduced myself to Trigger, but he sped off in a huff and grunted 'What's up'? From what I could see of his side profile he wasn't too bad looking, but I couldn't get with his permed ponytails.

Apparently, Trigger wasn't high enough, and he lit up another blunt that he and Beverly passed back and forth. His first kind gesture towards me was when he offered me a pull of his blunt which I respectfully declined. He looked at me through the rearview mirror like I had two heads and asked me was I a church girl. I told him that if I was, it had nothing to do with anything—I just didn't want to smoke any of his weed. Beverly was concerned about a measly parking ticket, and I prayed that we didn't get pulled over from all the smoke that escaped through the window. As we approached his sister's street, I could hear the loud music as we pulled up. I watched as the party invitees piled into the small brick detached house in Queens. Trigger told Beverly he had to make a run before he went inside, but told us to 'get out of the car.'

As we walked into the house to greet the birthday girl, the most marvelous smell of barbecued steaks flowed throughout the house. We made our way to the backyard where most of the people congregated. A few guys asked Beverly who I was as if I couldn't speak for myself, and by the looks of some of them I was happy that she chose to ignore them. We walked up on a small group of women talking in a back bedroom. One of the ladies turned around and noticed Beverly. "Bev! You finally got yo' black ass here," she squeaked and spilled most of her drink as she tottered through the other women. "Who this with you?" she asked pointing in my direction.

"This is my cousin, Lane," she replied and, then Beverly turned her face towards me. "Lane, this is Patrice, Trigger's sister."

"Happy birthday, Patrice. Nice to meet you."

"Thanks, Love," she responded and turned her attention back to Beverly.

"Where my crazy-ass brother at?" she asked. Beverly told her that Trigger had to make a stop and would be back shortly. They continued to talk as I looked around and took a tally of the men to women ratio. The men clearly outnumbered the women, and the number of men continued to grow throughout the night. My stomach growled nosily as the smell of the grilled barbecue reminded me that the last thing I had put in my mouth was a hot dog. I told Beverly that I'd be back, and I found my way to the backyard where the chef was doing his thang. He was a heavyset man, who had adorned himself in a chef's hat and an apron that read: Kiss Me Or You Won't Eat! There was a long line of guys with paper plates in their hands who looked like they were prepared to kiss him if he challenged them.

I stood patiently in the line where most of the men had already eaten two plates of the chef's grilled splendor and was back in line for their third helping. The chef took one look at me and yelled to the guys that even if they weren't, to at least try to act like gentlemen and let me pass. I surely appreciated his comment and made my way to the head of the line. As I passed I caught the glimpses of a few men as they stared at my breasts and made the usual lame sexual comments.

The chef took it upon himself to become my personal protector; he told the brash guys that if he heard them make another comment about my breasts, he would shut down the grill for the rest of the night. "Thank you," I said.

"You welcome, now what is it that you want on your plate?" he asked, as he twirled his spatula in the air like a professional foodie.

"I've been dying to try some of that steak since I arrived. I'll also take a burger and some of those grilled peppers on top of the steak."

"Damn, ma, you gon' be able to eat all that?"

"Watch me." We laughed as he obliged my request. I took one bite of the superbly marinated steak that disappeared like butter on my tongue, and it explained the line of grown men waiting for more. I hadn't had steak that delighted my palate like that since my Uncle Snuck took charge of the grill at our last family reunion. While I ate, the chef and I started a conversation, I learned that his name was Beef; he was the stepbrother of Trigger and Patrice. He told me that they didn't call him for many of their social gatherings unless they wanted him to do the grilling because of his skills. I felt bad for him that he knew he was being used, but he didn't seem to mind. And when I asked him about it, he said he was happy to do it because he could eat as much as he wanted and get as high as he wanted.

As I continued to talk to Beef, the line of testy, hungry, paper plate holders grew impatient as they waited for him to serve them. I used that as my cue to leave before it got ugly back there, so I rejoined Beverly and the birthday girl back inside the house. I squeezed through the crowd of women and men who were either too rude to allow me to pass freely or those who tried to cop a sneaky feel as I passed them. I soon realized that this wasn't the crowd I normally liked to party with, and I regretted I didn't have an alternative exit strategy.

It was confirmed that I should have never attended the party, when I walked into the back bedroom where Patrice and Beverly were engaged in a heated debate over which of the two could smoke the most weed. Trigger, who had returned from his 'run', threw several clear small plastic bags on the bed and told them to 'show and prove.' I refused to stay in the room to witness two grown women have a weed contest, but no matter which room I went into something crazier than the next was being performed. It felt as though I was in an episode of the Twilight Zone.

Everywhere I turned someone either hurled lewd comments at me or shot me eye daggers. So, I decided my safest bet was to go back out to the backyard where Beef was at and stay there. Once again, I squeezed by a group of men who refused to budge, and one guy, who appeared to be the spokesperson for the entire group, just couldn't contain himself and had an outburst. "Is that all you, baby? I like milk," he sniggered and looked around for cosigners. That's it! I've had it! I was about to read this idiot his rights until I heard a baritone voice in the crowd come to my rescue.

"Yo, dog, that's all me. Now what's up?" I turned around and stood face to face with Dre. My stomach flipped as Dre walked up to the vulgar mouthed guy and stood close enough to touch his nose. "I asked is there a problem?" Dre repeated.

"No, Man. We good," he said and walked away. Dre walked over to me, slid his arm around my waist, and pulled me into him. He kissed me on my neck to solidify his claim. I was extremely shocked to see Dre, but I was just as thrilled.

"What are you doing here?" I asked.

"I know the dude who's throwing the party."

"That's right, Beverly did mention you knew him, but I didn't know you knew each other well enough to hang out together."

"We got cool when we was in Riker's Island." Dre pulled me through the same crowd of people who just minutes earlier refused to budge and have now parted a path wider than the red sea. Dre continued to tell me that he and Trigger had lived in the same dorm on Riker's Island, and they stayed in contact when Dre got out. It had become clear to me that my invitation to this party wasn't by chance, but had been arranged by my cousin. I was so happy to see Dre at the party that I couldn't even be mad at Beverly. Anyway, it wouldn't have made any sense to be upset with her, she was probably so high by now she wouldn't have comprehended why I was angry. Dre and I found a quieter place in the back for us to talk. I asked Dre if he have any prior knowledge of me being at the party, surprisingly he was honest and told me he did.

I had a headache from the over powering smell of all the marijuana that circulated throughout the house, and I was beyond ready to leave. I left Dre in the back bedroom and went back to Patrice's room to inform Beverly that I was ready to leave. But just as I feared, she and Trigger were both asleep sprawled out across Patrice's bed. I shook Beverly as hard as I could several times to wake her. I wanted to tell her that I'd enough, and I was leaving. She barely opened her eyes, and when she did, she didn't even bother to ask how I would get home.

I stormed out of the room, went back to the room where I'd left Dre to tell him what happened, and that I was about to leave the party. Dre and I walked through the house to find Patrice because I wanted to say goodbye and tell her to inform my cousin that I had gone. I located

Patrice in the kitchen where she was cornered by some guy stuck in the eighties—he still had a Jheri Curl—wore a Le Tigre shirt and matching jacket. "Excuse me, Patrice," I interrupted. "I'm about to leave, and I want to thank you for having me. Could you please tell my cousin that I went home?"

"Okay, Jane. I will, and thanks for coming," she said. I was so damn glad to finally be rid of those folks; it didn't even bother me that she called me 'Jane.' I walked out of the door into the front yard and inhaled the fresh air, something I hadn't done in nearly three hours. My feet started to hurt badly, and the pain must have registered on my face, so Dre took my hand and guided me down the three steps. I asked him if he knew where the nearest cash machine was.

"Why do you need a cash machine?" he asked.

"How else do you expect me to get home? My ride home is high out of his mind and incapable of driving heavy machinery."

"I'm leaving too. Come home with me."

"Dre, you just got here. I'm not trying to kill your night, stay and enjoy the party." I realized a trap was being set, and I didn't want to be snared by Dre.

"I didn't come here to party. I thought this was my chance to see you, and now that I see you, I want you to come home with me," he said. He moved in closer to me, and I thought he was about to kiss me. As good as he looked tonight I would not have objected, but nervously I took one step backwards.

"I don't think that's a good idea, Dre." I couldn't explain it, but with all that's gone on between us he still had this unexplainable hold on me. And more importantly, I was afraid of what might happen if I went home with him.

"You might as well. We're out here in no man's land, and I don't have any idea of where a cash machine is. Or, you can wait here until Trigger and Beverly come down from their high. It's up to you." That definitely wasn't an option, so I chose to go home with Dre. He went back inside of Patrice's house and got a number to a cab service, and when he returned, he said the cab should be here in ten minutes. While we waited for the cab his cell phone went off. He pulled his phone out from his pants pocket, looked at the screen, and ignored the call. I asked him why he didn't answer. He said he knew who it was, and they weren't important. His response took me back to the many nights that I would call him when we were together—when he would send me straight to his voice mail—I wondered if that was what he told his conquest for the evening about me.

The ten minute wait for the cab took more like fifteen, and I shivered from the nippy night chill. When the cab arrived, I jumped in, kicked my shoes off, and ran my hands up and down the sleeves of my jacket to warm myself. After Dre gave the driver his address, he asked him to turn up the heat because I was cold. I rested my head on the back of the seat and closed my eyes. I was nearly asleep when I felt Dre's hand rest on my thigh. I opened my eyes, but I never turned to look at him. I simply took his hand off my thigh and placed it back in his own lap. "No, Dre. Don't," I said.

"I missed you, Lane." Just as he was about to make his power move on me, his phone went off again and just as before he looked at the number, but this time he turned it off completely. I joked with him that Renee, his girlfriend, wasn't going to be too happy with him for ignoring her calls all night, and he swore to me that they weren't together any more. I slightly raised my head from the seat and pursed my lips sideways to let him know that I didn't believe him. But when he admitted his affair with Renee was one of his biggest mistakes, he looked sincere, and I believed him. I was surprised to hear him say that, and I flashed back to the day I caught them in our bed when we were still a couple. The pain I felt seeing them together—the way he held and kissed her—I stayed in bed for weeks after that.

Dre and I were already in Brooklyn when I received a call from Beverly. "Hey, where you at?"

"Are you serious, Bev? I'm on my way home, where else would I be?"

"How and with who? Patrice told me you left with some fine brotha who looked like Idris Elba."

"Stop playing stupid, Bev. You knew she was talking about Dre, he already told me everything about how y'all set this whole thing up."

"Okay, okay. Please, don't be mad at me, they forced me to do it. Are you still with him?" she asked.

"I don't want to have this conversation with you right now, Bev. I'll call you tomorrow. And by the way your girl, Patrice, she won the smoke contest. She was still partying when I left, while that stuff had you and your boyfriend laid out on some real CSI shit."

"I'm not mad, but are you with Dr–." I didn't want her to know that I was still with Dre, so I hung up quickly.

I was upset when the truth unfolded, because she knows that I'm involved in a serious relationship, and as my cousin I never expected that from her. Frustrated, I turned off my phone, and stuffed it down into my bag. I wanted to be mad at Dre as well for his participation in it, but when I looked over at him, the night glow on his face made him look just that much more attractive and all was forgiven. It was then I knew I'd made a huge mistake—I even voiced my fear to Dre, but he persuaded me to continue the journey to his place.

As we approached Dre's neighborhood he instructed the cab driver to make a left turn, and stop in front of a 24 hour store. Dre told me to sit tight because he needed to grab a few things. Dre was out of the store as quickly as he went in, and came out with a brown paper bag in his hand. Once Dre re-entered the car, the cab driver made a U-turn; he drove through two more traffic lights and stopped in front of a run-down building.

While Dre waited on the cab driver to give him his change from the fare, I looked up at the drab dank building which consisted of six floors. The landscape of empty beer bottles, cigarette butts, and burned crack pipes of Dre's tenement was a far cry from Clay's well manicured greenery, where he and I would sometimes picnic. As we entered the building I was immediately accosted by the strong smell of urine and stale beer. I held my breath as Dre led us up the two flights of filthy stairs, and we stopped at door number seven. It was badly chipped and concealed by a poor paint job. Dre reached in his pocket and pulled out his keys. I was afraid that if Dre had moved any slower I would have passed out from the lack of oxygen to my brain as I hadn't breathed from the moment we entered the stairwell. So when he finally opened his door, I assisted him inside his apartment with a light nudge to his back

The second we entered the house I released the air from my lungs, and panted to get my breathing rhythm back on track. Dre turned to me with a crooked smirk on his face. "I see you haven't changed much," he said and shook his head from right to left. "You still dramatic."

I grinned at his comment. "I beg your pardon. Me? Dramatic?"

"Yes, you," he answered and tossed his keys on a small glass table in the kitchen.

"When did you move over here?" I asked.

"Me and Ren—," he backtracked. "I moved over here about six months ago."

"Anyway, Dre." He tried to look stumped about what I meant by that, and I wanted to let him know I heard what he was about to say. "You were about to say Renee. It's all right, you can mention her name. I don't know why you feel the need to keep lying to me." He bowed his head, and tried to look pathetic, but I ignored his dismal tactic. When he realized I hadn't fallen for his weak performance, he poured himself half a glass of rum from the bottle he had just purchased and added just a tinge of coke for some color. He offered me a glass of the rum and I accepted. Dre disappeared into the kitchen, and when he returned, he had one of those glasses you get when you buy a value meal from McDonald's. He filled half my glass with rum, one cube of ice, and no coke. I asked him to add some coke to mine, because it appeared as if he was trying to get me drunk so that he could take advantage of me. He laughed and said he hadn't thought about that, but since I had brought it up it wouldn't be such a bad idea.

As we sat shoulder to shoulder on his cramped loveseat and drank the convenient store rum, Dre asked me when I had known it started to go all wrong in our relationship. I told him that it was his lack of motivation to find a job, his inability to remain faithful, and putting his 'boys' before me, but the deal breaker was when he slept with Renee. But, when Dre switched gears and alluded to our previous incredible sex life, my body started to get warm all over. My first two glasses of rum, I was fine, but after that I lost count of my alcohol intake and hadn't conceived the amount of trouble I had gotten myself into. Between the rum I had consumed and the heat from the radiator that filled Dre's tiny apartment I had started to sweat. I removed my shoes and unbuttoned the first few buttons on my blouse, Dre placed my aching feet in his lap and massaged them. I reclined back on his loveseat and started to enjoy the warmth of his apartment, the massage, and my light buzz.

With my head rested comfortably on the loveseat's tattered throw pillows and my feet being pampered by Dre—the combination had lulled me into a light sleep. When Dre stopped the foot massage I instantly opened my eyes. "Please don't stop, Dre. It feels so good," I urged.

"You must be thinking about those nights when you use to come home late from work, and I'd give you the 'Dre special,'" he joked, as he continued to be attentive to my feet.

As he reminded me of those nights of the 'Dre special' I also remembered all the other specialties he had performed for me when we were together; impetuously, I lunged forward and kissed Dre tenderly on his mouth. Although my own actions shocked me, it didn't stop me. Dre appeared surprised and pulled away from me ever so slowly. "Are you sure about this, Lane?" he asked.

I slid my tight pants over my ass and threw them onto the floor. "Yes, Dre. I'm sure." Dre kicked off his Timberland boots and stepped his bowlegs out of his jeans quickly. I unbuttoned the rest of the buttons on my blouse, laid back onto the cramped loveseat, and waited in anticipation of my body being draped with Dre's. He touched my body with such a fiery familiarity, wanting me to beg for more. He knew I wanted him badly and inched his thick hard manhood inside my throbbing, wet sweetness. I clawed Dre's back as he pushed deep between my thighs, and my body quivered as his thickness pleased me. It felt insanely good to be in Dre's arms once again, and for a brief instant, I was almost able to forget about everything and everyone, even Clay. OH MY GOD! CLAY! How could I? Dre continued to pump his slippery dick in me, and he paid no attention to the rush of tears streaming down my cheeks until he climaxed.

"What are the tears for? Did I hurt you?" he asked. I couldn't speak. I pushed Dre off of me, grabbed my clothing, and ran to his bathroom in shame. I heard Dre rumbling around in his living room, and then it got quiet. I turned on the tap to the sink, cupped my hands and buried my face in the cold flowing water. Dre was on the move again as I heard him bump his way to the bathroom. "What's the matter with you?" he persisted.

I turned the water off and leaned against the back of the door and wailed. I had to get out of there. Not that it would have changed my inexcusable act of infidelity, but I felt I would have suffocated if I had remained any longer. Dre had given up on trying to find out what the source of my mini breakdown was. And when I finally left the confines of his bathroom, Dre sat bare chested on the loveseat and smoked a cigarette as if nothing had gone on. I refused to make eye contact with Dre as we communicated. "Have you seen my shoes?" I asked.

"Yeah, I put them on the side of the chair next to your bag. Are you planning to tell me why you bust out crying like that?"

"Why does it matter? You and Bev had this whole evening planned from the beginning! I'm in a relationship with Clay or did you forget that?"

"No, Lane, did you forget about it? Don't run that damsel in distress shit on me now; I know better. You knew what it was when you came here." There it was, a bit of blunt truth to the face. I walked over to the side of the chair and picked up my things. I refused to sit down and wobbled from side to side as I hurried to put my shoes on. Once I had them on, I headed straight for the door. Dre pulled me back by my arm and restrained me from leaving his house. "Are you crazy!? Where you running to at this time of night in this neighborhood? Sit yo' ass down and let me call you a cab." Angry, disappointed, and still slightly drunk I followed Dre's orders. I sat down on the same loveseat we had just finished making love, and I waited until he called a cab for me.

Dre walked into his kitchen, grabbed his phone from the table, and called a cab. Dre's phone hadn't been turned on but a minute before I heard the multiple alerts as they chimed from the incoming activity he'd missed during the time we spent together. I heard Dre clearly as he gave the dispatcher the details to send a cab to Franklin Avenue. He added that the person would already be downstairs waiting, and told them not to blow the horn. Before he joined me back in the living room, his phone rang, but this time I couldn't make out what he was saying, or who he spoke to as his tone had gotten very low and muffled.

He stayed in the kitchen and talked for about five minutes creating background noises so he could drown out his conversation. But not even the distracting sounds of running water prevented me from hearing him end his conversation with a whispered 'I love you too.' I hung my barely sober head in disgust as I had just played myself. Dre rushed back into the room, pulled his sweater over his head, slipped back into his Timbs, and threw on his jacket. "C'mon, let's boogey. The cab will be here in a few," he said.

"So that's it?" I asked.

"Is that it, what?" I shouldn't have been surprised by his nonchalant demeanor, but I guess I had expected more than him treating me like one of his cheap booty-calls.

"Never mind Dre, just forget about it...everything."

"If you're worried that your boyfriend will find out, you good. But tonight just proved one thing, I don't care who you're with, you and I will always have a connection."

"Tonight doesn't prove anything except I shouldn't drink."

"Lane, do yourself a favor and don't be one of those chicks that blames sleeping with men on the L.I.Q. You said it with your own mouth. You wanted it—that's why we fucked tonight—because you wanted to," he arrogantly drilled. He peeped at his watch, then dashed in the kitchen, and grabbed his keys from the table. I brushed past him as he locked the door to his apartment, I got downstairs first and waited for the cab to arrive. Dre was only seconds behind me and stood in the middle of the deserted street. He looked in both directions of the block to see the cab when it arrived. He watched me silently as I shifted from one foot to the other to stay warm, and a few minutes later I noticed some bright headlights headed in our direction. The cab slowed down each time it passed a building on the block as the driver searched for the address. Dre whistled loudly and waved to the cab to come down a little further. The cab driver heard Dre's whistle and sped up until he stopped in front of us. Dre watched me as I opened the door and slid in. "I'll call you tomorrow," he said.

"Don't bother. Tonight should've never happened and there will never be another," I snapped. Dre snorted his usual cocky chuckle, which I've always hated terribly. He used to do it all the time when we lived together which mockingly translated into 'we'll see.' Dre had always gotten a real pleasure out of having a person eat their words.

"So you say," he said and smiled smugly. Dre put his hands inside his pants pockets and stepped backward onto the curb. I watched Dre from my peripheral until he became a tiny blur on the sidewalk as the cab turned the corner of his block. I feared being seen by anyone who could have associated me with Dre, so I slouched down in the backseat of the cab. If I had wanted to humiliate myself any further I would have curled up on the backseat of the cab and bawled like a baby, but I was determined to keep it together until I got in my own house. The sky had transitioned from night to morning, and I wanted to know the time. I reached inside my bag, turned my phone back on, and checked the time. It was after four in the morning, and I hoped my dad wasn't too worried about me.

Just as it had occurred with Dre, my phone buzzed at an incessant rate within minutes of it being turned on. I looked through my call log for the missed calls. I had missed a call from Charmine, my dad, and three missed calls from Clay. The last call Clay made to me was clocked less than an hour earlier, and my stomach felt queasy to think what I had been engaged in at the time he called.

I didn't live too far from Dre, so I reached home fairly quickly. When I stepped out of the cab into the brisk early morning air, I knew I had created a world of deceit and lies from my thoughtless action. Although I knew my dad was a hard sleeper, I eased into my house and tip-toed into my room. Clay made me promise that I would call him as soon as I got in, so I knew he would not sleep until he heard from me. I pondered several different scenarios in my mind before I even dialed his number. I had to compose a story so airtight that it wouldn't leave any room for doubt. Once I put my nightgown on, I peeked in on my dad and his snores bellowed throughout his toasty room. I closed his door and went to the bathroom and brushed my teeth.

Snuggled under my goose-down comforter, I hit the speed dial button for Clay's number. After the third ring he answered the phone groggily. "You finally made it in, huh? I must have called you like three or four times," he said.

"I know, my phone died," I said.

"It's gotta be after five o'clock or close to it. That must have been some party, how did you get home?" he asked.

"It was okay. You know how those house parties come be."

"I do, but you didn't answer me. How'd you get home?"

"Beverly and her boyfriend," I lied easily. "That's partly why I'm just now getting in. Bev and her boyfriend got so high that he couldn't drive."

"I'm just glad you're home safe, Bae, that's the main thing. But if you would have called ten minutes later I would have been dead asleep."

"I'm sorry I woke you, Clay. You get some sleep and we'll talk in the morning."

"Aight, love you Bae. Buzz me tomorrow."

"I will. Love you too, Clay. Sleep well." I held the phone to my ear until he hung up. After I had lied through my teeth for most of our conversation, I couldn't explain why I'd risk my loving relationship with Clay for one reckless night with Dre. I vowed that Clay mustn't ever find out what had taken place in Dre's seedy apartment. I laid awake in my bed and tried hard to block Dre's touch and his kisses out of my mind. But each time I closed my eyes I felt the electrified sensation of Dre's hands caress my body as if he were right next to me. And what pained me most was the unimaginable truth Dre hurled at me tonight. It wasn't my intoxication that caused me to sleep with him —I wanted him.

FORBIDDEN SEDUCTION

Dre

A few days had passed since the party, and I still hadn't heard from Lane. No doubt she wanted to prove something to herself, 'cause she ain't have me fooled. I prided myself on knowing two things and that was money and women. From my teenage years I considered myself somewhat of a womenologist—that's how well I knew 'em, and Lane in particular. Lane hoped that I would have been crazy enough to believe that the only reason why she let me hit that was because she was drunk. She can talk that silly shit to her fake-ass Berry Gordy boyfriend, but I know her. I really know her.

I didn't always play with Lane's head; I cared a lot for her when we first got together. It was just an unfortunate situation when she caught me in bed with Renee. I felt like I had lost Lane, and she left me no choice, so I started doin' my own thing. One thing I wasn't gonna allow to happen to me was getting caught out there with no place to lay my head and no cleavage to lay it in. My moms had taught me better than that. She told me at an early age that I had a special gift with women, and the more she schooled me the better I got at the game. And from that day forward I ain't never tripped off these hoes. Although growing up I barely got to see my moms, when I did, she gave me the only jewels she could and that was to teach me how to get over on people.

Looking back on it now, I don't think she always made the best choices for us, but I know she did the best she could. I wasn't raised by my moms 'cause she had gotten strung out on crack when I was around twelve or thirteen-years-old. She was so addicted to the drugs and to the streets that she left my younger brother and me to fend for ourselves by any means necessary. And by the time we hit puberty, we had gained such a bad reputation in our neighborhood for robbing anything that wasn't nailed down that the parents in the neighborhood didn't want their kids to hang out with us fearing we'd get them involved. The social services had been called on my moms so many times that they threatened if they received one more call we'd be taken away from her. And that's when my grandmother, Big Mama, stepped in and raised me and my brother. When we went to go live with Big Mama, she told my moms that she didn't want her visiting us under any circumstances, or she'd call the cops herself.

That didn't stop my moms though. She would be high as hell and still sneak visits with us while Big Mama was at work. There were plenty of times that after she rummaged through all of Big Mama's stuff, she would come in my room for a talk. She would sit on my bed and ask me if Big Mama had given us any pocket change, and when I'd tell her she didn't, she'd say to me 'boy as fine as you are, you could have women eating out of your hands, and all you have to do is make 'em feel good.' And the older I got I realized there was a lot of truth in what she had told me. Most of the time all I had to do was shoot a little game in some of these chicks' ears, and they basically gave me the key to the city. Some of them would be so afraid that I'd cheat on them that they'd buy me a cell phone and paid the bill just to keep tabs on me. Forget about them wanting me to work, especially if they thought there were some fine females on the job, so they would willingly take care of me.

When I first met Lane she acted real bourgeois, and I thought she'd be a challenge for me, but I just had to work a lot harder for her than I did those other chicks. I felt that Lane was worth it though 'cause I considered her a triple 'G': good job, good looking, and good pussy. And once I got her to get rid of that knucklehead dude she was fucking with at the time, it was all good. When Lane and I first moved in together, it was tight. We enjoyed the fruits of her labor, and she didn't seem to mind that I wasn't working—at first. Then all of a sudden her best friend, Charmine, whispered some ole nonsense in her ear. She told her this, that, and the third and that's when our shit got all sloppy.

At first, Lane's bitch sessions would come about once a week, then that shit got outta hand. I had gotten real tired of Lane nagging me about not working and doing more shit around the house, so I started staying away from home more. One night when me and my man, Herc, was coming out of the strip club, I looked across the street and couldn't help but notice this chick. She was thick and had a real cute face. I walked over and started to kick it to her and she told me her name was Renee. We kicked it for a few more minutes before she gave me her number. I knew off top she wasn't the same caliber of woman as Lane, but after we met a couple more times, I found out that she had that, make a nigga wanna stay type pussy. And that was eventually the slow demise of me and Lane's relationship. I never expected or wanted Lane to pack up and move to Atlanta after she caught me slipping with Renee. But after she left for good, it fucked with me, and whenever I saw her cousin, Beverly, in the neighborhood I would ask about her. There was this one time I ran into Beverly while out shopping on 42nd street, and she told me Lane was kicking it with some dude who owned his own record label in Atlanta.

At first it didn't bother me too much that Lane had hooked up with this dude, but the more I thought of another man getting what was once mine every night, it started to mess with my head. I even thought about making a move down there to Atlanta, but that was short-lived because I'm Brooklyn 'til I die. Then, there was Renee to think of. When I caught that murder case, she stood stronger than a tree by my side until I was vindicated, and I couldn't just jet on her after that. And although I knew Lane loved me, she would have never stood with me like that.

So with Lane being back in Brooklyn, of course I wanted to test the waters. I wanted see how far she'd let me take it, and after the other night, I knew I was still in there. I had been thinking a lot about the other night, and I wanted to find out if Lane was in as much love as she claimed to be with this cat. I knew we could never do the commitment shit again, but I would like to be able to get with her when I wanted to. But if she realized I had lied to her about me and Renee not being together—I don't know how she'd react to that. I came pretty damn close to getting found out when Renee kept calling my cell while Lane was still at my crib. I had to shut it off and later tell Renee that my battery had died. It just worked out for me that Renee was in Harlem spending the night with one of her sisters. I think she may have believed me, but I'll never know that for sure. I checked my watch and it was almost six o'clock, and I still hadn't heard from Renee. Usually she'd be home from work or would have at least called by now. I was wondering where she was. I took out my cell and pressed her number. She answered her phone with her usual greeting. "What's up Boo?"

"What's up? Where you at, I'm starving."

"You must haven't checked your texts. I text you earlier that I'm getting my hair braided at Darlene's house tonight."

"How long is that gonna take, and what am I supposed to eat?" I asked.

"You really got to start checking your texts, Dre. I told you in the text that I won't be coming home at all. I haven't even got my hair yet, and it's gonna take Darlene all night because she be doin' a billion other things while she be braiding people's hair. So, I know I'll be spending the night."

"Spending the night? I thought you had to work tomorrow morning."

"I did, but I switched with Trish. Listen Boo, I'm about to enter the subway and my phone isn't gonna have good reception. I'll call you when I get to Darlene's. Kiss-Kiss."

"Alright, talk to you later." After hanging up, I started to wish I had checked my phone earlier. I had been thinking about Lane and I would have called her to see if she wanted to come through, especially now that I would be alone again tonight. But, the way she ran out of my apartment the other night she probably would have hung up on me. I figured I had nothing to lose and would give her a call after I got something to eat.

I walked down Franklin Ave. and wondered to myself what ever made me move back into an area that caused me so many bad memories; every other corner had a story. It was on the very same block I moved back to that I almost murdered a man when I walked up on him telling my moms to suck his dick. He was about to pull his shit out in broad daylight for her to do it for a rock, so I stomped a mud-hole in his ass while he held onto his dick. True, she was a crackhead and did the unmentionable to keep dope in her hands, but she was still my moms.

And the memories didn't stop there. As I walked further up the block and turned the corner by the liquor store that was the incident that caused me to move from the area. I remembered how just six years ago I passed that exact liquor store and saw a huge crowd gathered by the entrance of the door. As I got closer to the crowd I heard someone say as they walked off 'another crackhead bites the dust' and those words have never left me. I pushed my way through the crowd and looked down to see my mom's tiny lifeless abused body sprawled out on the street from a drug overdose. To think that at one time she looked exactly like Billie Holiday, and when the drugs took over, I couldn't even recognize her.

By the time I had approached the Rib Shack, I shook all those fucked up memories off and concentrated on the menu. Since I didn't have a reason to rush back home, I sat in one of the empty booths enjoyed my dinner and the game that was on the big screen. I had been tempted to call Lane since I found out Renee wasn't coming home and decided I would hit her up now. I didn't expect her to answer but she did. "Hi, Dre."

"Hello Lane, what's up?"

"Nothing much," she said.

"Why you talking like that? You alright?"

"Yeah, I'm fine. I guess I want to know why you're calling me."

"Why? I can't call you now, after what we experienced the other night."

"Dre, the other night was a mistake and we both know it."

"I don't. And I want to see you again, so why don't you shoot through later tonight, and we can have a repeat of the other night."

"I...I can't."

"Of course you can."

"No, Dre, really I can't. I'm with Clay."

"Lane, your body told me something different the other night. You love the way I make you feel, the way I touch you, and I just want to make you feel like that again. Spend the night with me." Lane went

65

silent which led me to believe she was considering my offer. "So what's up? You coming through or what?"

"Dre, don't put me on the spot like this."

"What time you coming?"

"I didn't say I was coming for sure."

"See, I can change all that, and have you coming all night." When I heard her laugh I knew I had her.

"I'll see, Dre, but I'm not promising you anything."

"I hear you. If you do decide to come, call me when you're on your way."

"Okay Dre, I will...IF I decide to come."

"Got you."

"Bye, Dre," she said and hung up. I finished off the last few bites of my rib dinner and left the spot. I called Renee back, but this time I called Darlene's house to make sure she was there and that her plans remained the same. Renee answered Darlene's house phone and confirmed she'd be spending the night at her sister's house and would see me tomorrow after work. On my way home I stopped by the store and got some condoms. The other night I allowed the heat of the moment to take over and I wasn't wrapped up, but tonight I would be prepared.

Charmine

Over the past week, Lane and Faizon had been acting quite strangely and extremely secretive. When I called Faizon to set up a day for Jayla to be fitted for her dress, I also asked her how things progressed with Clay handling her launch. When I mentioned his name, she hit the roof. I wouldn't have paid too much attention to her tantrum, but it had been the second time that Faizon reacted this way when I asked her about Clay. And Lane's disconnected deportment towards me was no better. On the few occasions that I had the pleasure to speak to Lane and ask her where she disappeared to at night, she dismissed the question altogether. Humph, I had less than two months before I'd be walked down the aisle for the second time in my marriage career. I thought I reserved the right to be distracted, but I guess not.

When Lane and I had talked, I strongly conveyed to her that I needed her measurements to be sent to Faizon, but Faizon called me daily to moan about Lane's lack of interest in my wedding, and I knew then my pleas had gone unanswered. I understood why Faizon was annoyed with Lane as she was a perfectionist, and she refused to be rushed at the last hour to make Lane's dress. But as of lately and unprovoked, Faizon had found fault in everything that Lane had done, and I didn't know where it had all stemmed from. While I tried to figure out what had gone wrong with those two, I still hadn't fully recovered from my Sunday dinner with Anthony's parents. His parents were from the old

South, and they still made some very inappropriate comments towards African Americans and didn't see anything wrong with it. But to keep the peace with my soon-to-be in-laws, I turned a deaf ear, bit my bottom lip, and two days after that meal I still had a migraine.

I sat in my office at the makeshift desk and pulled out my to-do list for the week ahead. I was pleased that I had just about crossed off most of the things on my list, except for Lane's measurements and the gifts for my bridesmaids. Anthony peeked his head in the office and asked me to make myself available, because we had to meet with the new contractors. So, I stashed my list in my bag and joined him out front in the empty office. After we finished our meeting with the contractors, Anthony was satisfied with their bid and their ability to do the job, so he hired them on the spot. I left Anthony at the office with the contractors and I went to do the fun part. I had been given the pleasurable task of picking out the furniture and décor for the office.

I had just pulled into the parking lot to one of Atlanta's largest office furniture suppliers and parked when my phone rang. "Hello, this is Charmine."

"Hi Char, it's me," said the caller.

"Me, who?"

"Lane. Who do you think it is?"

"Lane? Lane who?"

"Oh, shut up Char! You knew good and damn well it was me all along." Lane laughed. I wanted to continue with my salty act, but I was so glad that I had finally heard from her that I let my guard down.

"Hi, Chica. Where the hell have you been? I woulda had a better chance having lunch with President Obama. It's been almost impossible trying to catch up with you lately."

"You stoopid. How are you?"

"I'm great. Just missing my best friend, how are you?"

"I'm good, missing you just as much. But other than that, nothing much is going on here."

"Really? So why haven't I heard from you? I had to call your dad's house phone since you haven't been answering your cell phone, and one time he said you were out partying with Beverly."

"Yeah Girl, and that party was a mess."

"What happened?"

"Bev and her boyfriend, Killer... Trigger or whatever his name is got so high that I was damn near stranded out there in Queens. I had to get home the best way I could."

"Stop playing. I don't even know what would make you party with her like that anyway; you know how she gets down. Was it at a club?"

"No, it was at Bev's boyfriend's sister's house."

"See. A house party? You should've known better. So, how did you eventually get home?" Lane changed the subject altogether, which left me quite suspicious, so I asked her again. "Lane, how did you get home?"

"It was actually a blessing he came to the party. I probably wouldn't have made it home at all if I had waited on Bev and her junkie boyfriend."

"Well, just tell me and let me be the judge if *he* was a blessing or not."

"Girl...you're not even going to believe this, but it was Dre. And before you get bent all outta shape, we didn't plan this he just so happened to show up at the party."

"You've got to be shitting me. Dre? Lane, please tell me that nothing happened and that you went straight home."

"Charmine..." Now normally when Lane called me by my full name a confession was soon to follow, so when she had, I already knew what the deal was. Lane proceeded to tell me all the details of her and Dre's night of steamy lovemaking on his decrepit loveseat.

"Oh my God, Lane, why? Why would you do that?"

"I don't know why. The only logical explanation is that I was so drunk and missing Clay so badly."

"You had to have been more than just drunk to end up back in bed with that problem child. What about Clay? Did you ever stop to think about him?"

"Of course I did, and it has killed me every time I think about it. Especially when I talk to him."

"You know what? ...Never mind, I better not." I was exasperated and had been for a very long time with the "Dre Chronicles," and I felt I would have said something that would have offended Lane to her core. She knew it was coming, but she chose to go there anyway.

"You better not what? Say it, Char. I don't get why you are so upset?"

"There's so many reasons why I'm upset, starting with he's no good for you. Or have you forgotten why you left him and Brooklyn in the first place? Then there's Clay; the best thing that's ever happened to you. And you're going to throw it all away for DRE? But, here's the real kick in my teeth, I've been worried sick about you only to find out you've been out enjoying yourself at night with that crab. Actually, I'm glad you called, because I was going to call you tonight anyway to remind you that my wedding is in less than two months, and I still haven't received your measurements. So now I have to tell you this...if I don't have your measurements by Saturday morning, you won't be in my wedding."

"Charmine. Charmine!" Lane frantically called my name, and that was the last thing I heard as I pressed the end button to disconnect our call. I hated it when Lane and I had our blow-ups, especially when they had gotten so heated that it caused one of us to hang up on the other, but I just couldn't get over this one. It was I who sat with her when she couldn't lift a finger to do anything for herself when Dre cheated on her, and now she's willingly going to his bed. Lane called me over and over, but I didn't have the energy for a round two with her, so I ignored all of her calls. I sat in my car for nearly ten minutes and tried to rationalize Lane's irrational decisions. I concluded that Lane was a grown woman, and I just hoped that she knew what she was doing. She was so different from the strong confident women I met when we were in college.

When Lane and I first met, she was so different from me that I didn't like her at all. One day, we were in a student hall meeting, and she kept interrupting the student president with ideas she wanted to implement, because she felt her way was the 'best way to handle it.' I remembered I even told one of my dorm mates that I thought Lane was an obnoxious hothead with rebel tendencies. But, it would be those same characteristics I once hated about her, that made me love her as if she were my own sister.

Our first year in college I had a part-time job at a floral shop, and on this particular day, I returned to my dorm early from work and discovered my emergency money, laptop, and a few pieces of my jewelry had been stolen. Ironically, it was Lane who helped me retrieve all my belongings through one of the same programs she implemented for the students, and from that day, we've been the best of friends. I was angry with Lane at the moment but it wouldn't last, we've been there for each other through all of our highs and lows. It was evident that Lane was in one of her lows, and as her friend, I needed to be there for her and not judge her, so I called her back and just listened.

FORBIDDEN SEDUCTION

Faizon

Between my launch and Charmine's wedding I'd been positively busy every second for the last few weeks. I barely ate or slept at night, because I worked hard to make Charmine's wedding dress my entrance into the fashion industry as it would markedly showcase my talents as a serious designer. The beauty of it was that my launch was just a couple of weeks after Charmine's wedding, so my name would still be fresh on people's minds. I'd called Clay several times after our initial meeting to set up another one to finalize the venue and entertainment, but my calls had been routed to his business partner, Shon. Clay hadn't said anything to me directly, but it was apparent he instructed Shon to be in charge now.

When Shon and I first spoke over the phone he was so enamored with me; he sounded almost stalkerish, and I was a bit leery to meet him alone, so I chose a populated location for us to meet. The last thing I needed was another Darnell situation on my hands. It angered me that Clay avoided me, and I wasn't having it. He promised me that he would personally handle my launch, and I was going to hold him to that. I called his office, and luckily one of the reception staff put me straight through to him. "Hello, this is Clay Roberts"

"Hi, stranger. You promised to call me, but I haven't heard from you. What's the matter Clay, do I make you nervous?"

"Nah, that's crazy. Why would you think you make me nervous, 'cause you're beautiful? I'm around beautiful women all

73

day long."

"Oh, so you think I'm beautiful? Thank you."

It was clear I had caught him off guard as he tried to recover from his admission. "Err...you know what I'm sayin.' I work with beautiful half naked models all the time, so there's no need for me to be nervous around you," he said.

"So why won't you work with me like you promised?"

"Honestly, I thought you were supposed to be one of Lane's good friends, and I felt you was tryna push up on me."

"Push up on you? Why, because I gave you a hug? No, Love, you got that one all wrong. I admit I'm a little flirtatious, but that hug was harmless... unless you wanted it to mean more."

"No, of course not, and if I offended you I apologize."

"Apology accepted. And since we got this misunderstanding cleared up, it's no reason why we can't work together; we're adults. And don't forget, you did promise Lane that you'd be the one to handle it, plus that Shon guy is creepy. I get the impression he be jerking off while we're on the phone."

"Nah, I doubt that. Aight, then, I'll take you at your word if you're saying I got it all wrong, and it was harmless. And to show you that I am a man of my word, I'll finish what I started."

"Thank you, Clay. I feel so much better knowing that you're back on-board once again." Before we got off the phone we confirmed our next meeting date. After our conversation, there wasn't a shadow of doubt that Clay was definitely in love with Lane. Most guys would have seen how far they could have gone with me, girlfriend or not, especially if they thought I was the one who pushed up on them. But not Clay, he was put off by my forwardness—he acted as if I had stripped him of any chance to earn his Boy Scout loyalty badge. My friendship with Lane was important to me, but growing up I was taught not to put anyone's needs before mine. And if Clay was as committed to Lane as he claimed to be, then a little harmless flirting wouldn't shake their foundation, but it'll be fun trying.

Charmine called me just as I was about to go shop for the pearls I wanted to use for Jayla's junior bridesmaid dress. Charmine and I made arrangements for Jayla to be brought to my house on Friday afternoon after she finished with her ballet class. I told her if Lane didn't hurry up and get her shit together, she'd be wearing a dress from off the rack, because I refused to be rushed into making her a dress. After all, it was my name and reputation at risk, and I wasn't going to compromise that for anyone, not even Lane. I jotted down the date and time of Jayla's fitting in my planner and left for my trip to the fabric shop.

The days seemed to have evaporated as things had started to sneak up on me. I hoped that Charmine and Emily, Jayla's mom, appreciated my vision for her dress. I wanted her to have a classic look without making her look beyond her youthful preteen years. I chilled a bottle of Charmine's favorite wine and laid all my sketches out on my desk just in case I went too classic. I wanted Charmine and Emily to be able have some input, however, I wanted them to respect that I was the designer and would have the final say. I wanted to make sure everything was perfect before they arrived, so I gave everything on my list a once over. No sooner than I checked my clock for the time did I hear a knock at my door. I peeked through my peep-hole and saw it was my guests. "Hello all, come in, come in," I said as I invited them inside my house.

"Hi Faizon," Charmine said, as she entered and made the introductions. "This is Emily and Miss Jayla herself." We all greeted one another, and I led them to my living area to have a seat. Jayla appeared shy. She was still dressed in her pale pink tutu and white leotard. She was much taller than I had expected for a twelve-year-old, but I knew immediately I had chosen the perfect style dress for her ballerina frame. I poured the three of us adults a glass of wine and blended a fruit berry smoothie for Jayla. Charmine was charged to see the sketch, so I pointed to the sketch of Jayla's dress, and they all ranted about how beautiful it was and how much they adored the dress.

After the business part had been taken care of, we ladies sat around the table and talked while Jayla went upstairs and played dress-up in my sewing room. Charmine and I had another glass of wine, but Emily declined as she was the driver and needed to be sober. Charmine asked me if it would be an imposition if I took her home, because she wanted to hang out a bit longer. The minute I told her I would take her home, she kicked off her heels and curled up on my sofa with her glass of wine. Emily asked me if I was involved with anyone, and when I told her I wasn't, she seemed shocked. She said she couldn't believe that because I was 'so pretty.' However, I told her that I had someone in mind, but it was too early to tell what would come of it. "I didn't know you were seeing someone," Charmine said.

"Didn't you just hear me tell Emily it's too soon to talk about? If and when it becomes something then I'll tell you all about it."

Jayla came downstairs and told her mother she was getting sleepy, and was ready to go home. As Emily gathered their belongings to leave, she told me how very impressed she was with my talent. She mentioned she had a co-worker who was getting married and would definitely tell her about me. I stayed in the house while Charmine walked her future sister-in-law and niece to their car. When she re-entered the house, she grabbed the bottle of wine from the table and held it to the light to see how much of it was left. "Girl, please say you have some more of this?" I knew how much Charmine loves her Prosecco, but I've never known her to finish off an entire bottle and still want more in one night.

"I do, but you'll have to wait until I put in the fridge for a few minutes so it'll have a slight chill." I took another bottle from the wine rack and placed it in the fridge for it to get cold. "You must have had some week, what's going on?" I asked. Charmine walked over to the food cabinet, and turned her attention to a bag of sour cream and onion potato chips she found. She then went back over to the fridge, pulled out the bottle of lukewarm wine, and opened it.

"I'm beginning to think I've gone mad. What in the hell would possess me to take on all of this at the same time? Wedding, new home, our own firm...I'm scared Faizon," she said, as she fell backwards on the sofa with the glass of wine still clutched between her hands. I sat beside her, reached my arm around her, and leaned in.

"Charmine, don't worry. I promise you—it'll all turn out fine, you'll see. The dresses will be ready before this month is gone, the venue will be beautiful, and as soon as Lane sends me the stuff I require from her, I'll get started on her dress right away." Charmine slapped her left temple lightly and ran for her purse.

"I forgot to tell you, Lane emailed me her measurements this morning. I know it was a lot like pulling teeth but at least I finally got it," she said and handed me the email that Lane had sent to her.

"Well, it's about damn time, and I hope she doesn't think she's done us any favors having just sent it."

"It's all right Faizon, I'm so over her and Dre right now, it's ridiculous. But I knew the moment I threatened to yank her out of my wedding she'd move heaven and hell to get it to me." I slid up to the edge of my sofa and rested my elbows on my knees.

"Dre? You mean, Clay?" Charmine's head spun around so quickly, she stumbled horribly over her words as she tried to recover when she realized her mistake. Had Charmine begun to tell me something had gone wrong in Clay and Lane's relationship? I became intent on getting to the bottom of it all.

"Nothing. I shouldn't have said anything," she said.

"You did mean to say Dre, didn't you? What does Dre have to do with this?"

"I said forget about it, Faizon."

"No, Charmine, I won't forget about it. Something is wrong and it looks like it's really bothering you, so you might as well come clean. Has Lane been seeing Dre since she's been home?"

"I don't want to talk about it. I promised Lane."

"You can tell me the truth, or, you can let me come to my own conclusion. And anyway, I have the right to know; she's my friend too." Charmine thought about it for awhile before she decided to let me in on Lane's secret. And after each detail she revealed of Lane's night with Dre, she took a sip of wine. By the time she had fully disclosed how Lane had kept herself busy, she had downed her entire glass of wine. Charmine went on to tell me how Lane claimed she was under the influence when she slept with Dre and how it'd kill her if Clay ever found out, blah, blah, blah.

"You have to promise me, that you'll never tell Lane that I told you."

"Has she told Clay?"

"Don't be stupid, of course not. And that's exactly how you need to play when you meet with him again."

"Sure I will. What would I have to gain by telling Clay, Lane is sleeping with Dre?"

"Whoa Faizon! I never said they're 'sleeping' together, it was only the one time."

77

"Sure, if that's what makes you feel better." I wondered how Clay would have felt if he knew about Lane, would he run into my open arms? As a child, I was never good at keeping secrets, so I just hoped it wouldn't slip out at my next meeting with Clay, accidentally or otherwise.

Lane

I was glad that Charmine and I were back on speaking terms. I couldn't remember the last time we fell out like that. The situation had gotten real when she threatened to ban me from her wedding, and I knew then I had to pull my act together. As her best friend, I should have been there to give her support and not been a hindrance to her or her wedding. Charmine had invested a lot more than just money into this wedding. She had to learn how to love and trust someone again after her first attempt down the aisle was a farce. I didn't know if she'd ever fully be rid of the shame and humiliation it caused, but nonetheless on the surface she seemed to have recovered from it very well.

I hated that I told her about my sexual encounter with Dre; I knew she didn't get it, and I didn't expect her to. There were days I struggled with my poor decision-making, especially where Dre was involved. Char had asked me several times why I allowed Dre to walk all over me, and I never had a sound answer for her. I guess I described it best when I told her that when I'm with Dre, it felt like he had me under a spell. He was just that intoxicating. It was the way he touched me and made me want him even more. And I had been put to the test again when he called and invited me over to his house for the second time.

My mind fought hard to be able to tell him no, but my body craved for his touch, and my body won. The first time I slept with him I blamed it on the alcohol, but I couldn't hide behind that excuse for a second time. I went there purposely with the intentions of making love to him.

And after we made love the other night, I didn't dare make the same mistake in telling him that it would be the last time, but I hoped it would be. It had gotten extremely difficult for me to speak to Clay on the phone knowing what I had done to him... twice. I hated to think he could feel the way I felt when I discovered I had been cheated on by Dre, and now I've put him in the same boat. My blessing was that the only person who knew about Dre and me was Charmine, and I knew she'd never say anything to anyone.

It had been over a month since Mommy had passed, and my dad had done very well. He went out more with his other retired buddies, and when asked, he still tinkered around with the neighbors old cars that needed to be repaired. I tried to spend as much time with my dad as possible, and I had made plans for us to have dinner at this new Asian fusion restaurant in Brooklyn. He worked on his neighbor's car for most of the day, and I was starved, but I waited patiently as he washed the motor oil gunk from his hands and got dressed so we could leave. When he came out of the bathroom, he still had on the same stained shirt with motor oil on it and announced he was ready. "Err...dad, I know I'm only your daughter, but you could at least try to make a little effort to look nice going out?" I laughed. He looked down at his shirt and pulled it forward from his skin to get a better look.

"Aw, Baby Girl, I'm sorry."

"Don't be. Let me find you something," I said. I walked into his room and looked through his closet. I pulled out a nice tan cardigan and some black pants. "This is nice, put this on." I laid his clothes out on his bed, and he let out a hearty laugh. "What's so funny?" I asked.

"You reminded me of your mother just then, getting my clothes out for church."

"Yeah, and I bet you never tried to leave the house with her with old 10W-30 stains on your shirt either," I joked.

"You right," he said and took his newly selected outfit back into the bathroom and got changed. I went back into my room and waited some more while he got dressed and combed his hair again. My phone rang and it was Clay, I started not to answer but we hadn't spoken all day.

"Hello, Clay."

"What's up, Bae, how are you?"

"Good, but I'm about to leave out with my dad."

"Where are you two going?"

"Out to grab something to eat, so can I call you back?"

"The same way you called me back the other morning and last night?"

"Clay, I told you I fell asleep."

"You've been telling me a lot of bullshit these days, Lane. What's really going on? You give me the impression that I'm bothering you when I call, and I'm not good with that."

"No, you're not bothering me. I'm sorry I've made you feel like that, I really am, but I promise you that isn't the case. We'll talk tonight, I promise."

"Aight. Talk to you later," he said. He disconnected the call before I said goodbye. I didn't like who I had become. I had lied to Clay for weeks and I felt horrible. When my dad was finally dressed and presentable enough for the outside world, we left for dinner. It was a quiet evening at the restaurant, and we were both pleased with that. My dad had never been keen on trying new things and had to be coaxed into trying the restaurant's specialty, Hash Jafrezi. As we waited for our food, my dad brought up the subject of my relationship with Clay. He wanted to know where I saw my relationship with Clay headed.

"You know, Baby Girl, I really like Clay. I think he's a good man, and he is good for you."

"Thanks, dad, I agree with you. Clay's a great guy, and I'm blessed to have him, but what made you bring that up?"

"Nothing in particular. I just want you to know that I'll be fine here by myself, and there's no need for you to worry about me no more."

"I don't know where all of this is coming from, but okaayy. It sounds like you're kicking me out of my house, or can I still call it my house?"

"Of course it's your house. But if you need someone to give you a little kick back to Atlanta, I'm the man."

"Wow. How long have you been thinking about this? I assumed everything was fine with us."

81

"Everything is fine between us, and will always be. But ..."

"But what?"

"I'm afraid you're going to get yourself into trouble here, and lose Clay for good." Just as my dad started to go into details the waiter brought our food over. I grew impatient as I waited for the waiter to place our food in front of us and leave. I wanted to resume where my dad left off.

Our waiter had barely left the table before I asked my dad what he meant. "Afraid of what? And how would I lose Clay for good?" I asked.

My dad stared down in his plate of Hash Jalfrezi and took a small forkful of his food before he spoke. "I think you already know what I'm talking about, Lane."

"No dad, I really don't."

"I hope it's just a rumor, but your aunt Bernice seems to think you've hooked back up with that good for nothing Dre. She claims she heard it from Beverly and swears that's who you're with when you haven't been home at night." That bitch! But I bet she failed to tell Aunt Bernice how much weed she smokes, and that she's still dating that murderous thug, Trigger, while she was on her snitching spree. If it hadn't been for her being sucked into Dre's and Trigger's plot, I wouldn't have even been in this dilemma in the first place. I wished I could have disappeared from the table but I couldn't, and I hated that I continued with this lie but not to disappoint my dad, I had to.

"No, dad, that's not exactly true. Yes, Beverly and I did attend a party and Dre was there, but as far as me spending the night with him...no, that's a lie"

My dad's droopy face cheered up, and he slapped his hands together loudly. "I told your aunt Bernie I didn't care what Bev had told her, she had her information all wrong. One thing I know for sure, me and your mama ain't raise no fool. I knew you would never go back to him after how poorly he treated you. And the main reason I told her she was wrong was because I know you wouldn't do that to Clay." I felt sick. It felt like the few bites of food that I had enjoyed was about to be involuntarily expelled from my stomach and onto the table before us. I assured my dad that it had all been a huge misunderstanding and excused myself to the ladies room.

I rushed passed a group of ladies who stood in front of the mirrors reapplying their makeup, and found an empty stall. When I closed the door, I cried silently as not to be heard by the other ladies whom occupied the stalls on both sides of me. I had been here before with Dre's the lies and sneakiness, and now, I was the one doing the cheating. I cried until the veins inside my neck stiffened. I dried my tears and splashed some cold water on my face. I hurried back to our table, because I knew my dad would wonder why I had been gone so long. I sat down and hoped my dad wouldn't have noticed the redness in my eyes. "You okay, Baby Girl?" he asked.

"I'm fine, Dad. I see why you've always played it safe when it comes to your food, something didn't agree with me."

"Now, you see why I stick to my burgers and fries," he said. I glanced up from my plate periodically and looked my dad's way, only to respond to the few comments he made about his dish. When he noticed I had barely touched anything since my lengthy absence to the bathroom, he suggested we leave. I flagged down our waiter and he brought our check to the table. I was glad that my dad had made the decision to leave. I hadn't felt that awkward around my dad since my mother first told him I started my period. My dad made it crystal clear to me during dinner that he loved me, but I wouldn't be missed if I went back to Atlanta. He spoke candidly of his fear which was the slightest possibility of me getting back together with Dre, even if it was only for a cup of coffee.

When we got back home, my dad drank a glass of water and watched the night news before he went to bed. Dre called me twice since we had returned home from the restaurant, but I refused to take his calls. I may not have been strong enough to tell him personally, but he would soon realize I wasn't going to be doing any more late nights at his house. I looked at the time on my watch and wished I hadn't promised Clay I'd call him when I got home. I had already been put on the spot once by my dad, and Clay would be even more intrusive about my whereabouts in the night. I knew this conversation couldn't be avoided much longer. "Hi, Clay. Are you busy?"

"No, actually I was waiting on you to call. How was dinner?"

"My dad didn't seem to enjoy it; he's a beef and potatoes kinda guy. ...I miss you Clay."

"You miss me? You have a funny way of showing it. I've been calling, texting, and leaving you messages on your dad's house phone; it's like you playing me to the left or something."

"You know I would never do that. But honestly Clay, I do miss you."

"It's only a click and you can be here tomorrow morning."

"I can't leave that soon."

"Then stop tellin' me you miss me. Lane, do you ever plan to come back to Atlanta?"

"Of course I do, just not now. I have so many things to tie up here before I come back."

"I'm just gonna come out and ask you...is Dre one of those things?" The way he asked the question was like he already knew what had transpired between Dre and me. The silence was so loud I was sure that I popped a blood vessel in my head. I was pressed to make a paramount decision whether to tell the truth which would cost me my relationship with Clay or lie as I had been and pray he never found out.

"...Clay I have something I want to tell you," Clay discharged a breath from his gut so forcefully that I removed the phone from my ear. "I have seen Dre, BUT nothing happened. I promise you."

"Where? At your house? In the street? Where, Lane?"

"He was at that party I went to with my cousin. I didn't know he was gonna be there I swear to you!"

"The same god damn party you went to and didn't get home 'til four in the morning? Who the hell are you talking to, Lane?!"

"Clay, listen to me. I knew you'd be upset and that's why I didn't want to tell you, but I swear to you nothing happened between us at that party."

"Lane, are you tryna play me? I told you from the word go I don't have time for games. I want this shit to work, but you're gonna have to make an effort to make it work along with me." This new revelation had made Clay very angry, and he had every right to be. I've made the people I love very much quite angry with me this week. And just as Char had done a few days ago, Clay also issued me a serious ultimatum, and there was no funny punch line which followed. "If you haven't made up your mind about us by next month, I'm moving on, and I suggest you do the same."

84

FORBIDDEN SEDUCTION

After Clay stated his position on our relationship, he hung up on me. I laid in my bed repulsed by my untruthful and adulterous behavior. And in my selfishness I never fully considered how powerless Clay must have felt knowing that Dre had access to me at any time given our history. I had a lot at stake and needed to make a resolution that would make everyone happy, myself included.

FORBIDDEN SEDUCTION

Clay

I love Lane, and I wanted her in my life, but if she thought I was the type of man to be involved in a love triangle, she had the game twisted. I'd rather we went our separate ways than for us to end up hurting, hating, and disrespecting each other. I was raised in a house with three strong women: my mother, my grandmother, and baby sister. I was brought up to always treat women with respect. But, in the environment I grew up, the men disrespected the women as if it was a part of life. We lived in the worst housing project in Chicago, and every day was a challenge to make it from home to school safely. I had one good friend, Tony, who always had my back no matter what, and I had his. We escaped the madness of the projects through our love of music.

Growing up, I hated our Chicago apartment, it would get so cold that my mother had to put space heaters in all of the rooms—she'd turn them on the highest temperature and hung thick blankets over the door to keep the heat in. My grandmother watched me and my sister while my mother worked, because my mother worked two jobs. In the day she worked in a clothing factory, and at night, she did laundry for the Cook County Hospital. Regardless of how little money she made on these menial jobs, she always made sure my sister and I had everything we needed so we wouldn't feel deprived. And she constantly reminded us not to allow our current living situation to dictate our future.

The weekends were the best time for our family. My mother

would be off from both of her jobs, and we would take advantage of the little time we had together. My grandmother was a great cook, so she'd be in charge of the cooking; she could cook grass and make it taste like a gourmet meal. After all our weekend chores were done, my mother would pour herself a tall glass of Budweiser beer, then she'd pull out all of her old records and dance while my sister, Michelle, would sing and I would rap to them. It's because of those weekends as a teenager that I dreamed of one day owning my own record label. My semi-absent father paid us a visit every two weeks. His visits were on the same rotation as my mother's paydays, and when her money ran out, so did he.

The last time we saw my father, it was a frigid cold and rainy night, and I nearly beat him unconscious. It was the same night that Tony and I had walked home from this bomb-ass party and bragged about all the girls we had pulled. As we had gotten closer to our projects, Tony stopped dead in his tracks and pointed when he spotted my sister standing in front of our building. I ran towards the building at top speed, and as I approached the doorway, there stood my sister wearing only a flimsy t-shirt, pajama bottoms, and summer flip-flops on her feet. Even through the heavy raindrops I noticed she'd been crying, and her body trembled from the cold. As I wrapped my coat around her shivering body, I asked her what was the matter—she struggled to catch her breath, and then she said our father was upstairs; that was all she needed to say.

I told Tony to stay with her, and I bolted up the five flights of stairs; my strong legs taking two at a time. When I reached my floor, I forcibly pushed opened the door and there was my father with his large fists in the air. He was demanding that my mother give him some money and said he wouldn't hit her again if she did. My mother pleaded with him to stop, because she didn't have any more to give him. In his own rage and my mother's begging screams he hadn't noticed I entered the room, and it seemed to go in slow motion from there. When he lowered his fist to my mother's already bloody face, I grabbed it and started to beat him unmercifully. My mother's cries and pleas for me to stop seemed to fuel my anger, and I plummeted my fist in his face a few more times and promised that the next time I saw him, I'd kill him. And that was the last we saw of him, payday or not.

FORBIDDEN SEDUCTION

I swore to myself on that night if no one would treat the women in my life like queens, I would. And that's how I wanted to treat Lane if she'd only let me. But, I was not about to let her take advantage of my good nature and have me look like a fool while she decided if it was me she wanted. My assistant, Zoey, had brought in my mail and in it was an invitation to Charmine and Anthony's wedding. At least I knew even if Lane didn't come back to Atlanta for me, she'd positively be here for Charmine's wedding. I asked Zoey to RSVP back that I would attend, and before she left, she reminded me that I had a three o'clock appointment with Faizon in the office. Shon entered my office at that moment and overheard that Faizon was scheduled to come in. He asked me if I made a smart move when I pulled him off Faizon's event to handle it myself. I told him that I had gotten my wires crossed when I assumed she had made a pass at me, but we had talked about it and it was all cleared up. "I hope for your sake it was a misunderstanding, but it's all good," he said.

"I'm a big boy, Shon. I can handle Faizon."

"I was hoping you would let me handle her, she's a real tiger."

"You're punching above your weight, man. And don't you have something to do?" I found Shon's infatuation with Faizon comical, and I was done having this conversation with him.

Atlanta's celebrity population had grown so much over the years because of the music and buoyancy of the city itself. And a great deal of the success of the business I owed to Nikole, my entertainment manager. She had the foresight to see what direction I needed to take the business. It was she who encouraged me to build the entertainment division to partner with my record label, and within the first year we were hired to do mostly high profile events and made a name for ourselves in the industry. I'd finished a call with one of the more popular Housewives of Atlanta who booked us to do her birthday party when Zoey buzzed to tell me Faizon had arrived.

I asked Zoey to send Faizon in, and when she entered my office, she looked and smelled amazing. I was tongue-tied for a second or so, but I managed to be able to tell her to take a seat in the chair across from me. Faizon wore a white blouse which revealed the right amount of cleavage and a black skirt that embosomed her curvaceous lower body. Her lipstick complemented her molasses complexion, and her

89

straight hair was swept to one side. As we planned a theme for her launch, my attention diverted to her round protruding nipples seen through her white blouse. In all my professional years I'd never been overcome with such a strong urge to make love to a client and especially not a client with ties with my woman. Faizon and I had concluded our business meeting, and I hurried to get her out of my office before I said or did anything which could have been misconstrued. "That should be all for now, Faizon. I hope you're satisfied with what we've planned," I said.

"I sure it will exceed my expectations. I know you won't let me down."

"The success of your event is not an option for us. We're committed to make it happen for you. Now, if we're done I'll walk you out," I said, but Faizon remained seated. She crossed her long, shapely legs for me to admire in her black stockings and high-heeled shoes.

"That's fine on the business front, but now on a personal note how's Lane doing? I haven't spoken to her much, she always seems to be so busy nowadays," she said.

"She's fine," was all I offered, as Lane had been too busy for me as well.

"That's good to hear. I couldn't imagine being in her shoes; away from my good friends and my man for so long. Oh, but that's right, she does still have some friends there—that should make her nights a lot more pleasant. And doesn't she have an ex-boyfriend that still lives in Brooklyn? Well, anyway, I know you don't have nothing to worry about. I can only imagine when y'all talk Lane is dying to get back here to you."

Lane was trying to do something, but getting back here to me wasn't one of them. Faizon and I shook hands and I escorted her out of my office into the lobby. When I turned to walk back in my office, Shon along with a few other of the male staff who worked in the studio stood in the hall and watched her exit.

"She's got it goin' on," Shon blurted out and returned to his office. I told the others to go find something to do as well, and as they dispersed, I heard them as they talked trash about what they'd do to Faizon, given the chance. When I got back into my office, I sat at my computer and attempted to do some work. But as Faizon's scent drifted in the air and thoughts of her tempting breasts and legs filled my head, I realized I had made a big mistake when I took her event back from Shon.

I went home that evening, and I couldn't seem to think about anything except her. I poured myself a glass of Hennessy and put the basketball game on TV hoping that it would have distracted me, but even that didn't yield the fact that I desired Faizon. I tried to make sense of it. I accepted that I missed Lane badly and that I hadn't touched a woman since I left Brooklyn. I prayed I had convinced Lane to listen to reason and come back to me, or pretty soon I wouldn't be able to contain my sexual urges much longer. The more I tried to escape from my thoughts, the stronger they got. I fought it as hard as I could... but secretly Faizon had become my forbidden desire.

FORBIDDEN SEDUCTION

Faizon

One month to go before my life would be changed forever. I had finished with Charmine's wedding dress and even made her a little something special for her wedding night, and by the end of the week, I'd be finished with all the dresses. Charmine swore to me that Lane would be in Atlanta in enough time before the wedding, just in case I needed to make any alterations to her dress. Charmine seemed to be a lot surer than Clay was when I asked him about Lane's return; he became borderline aggressive at the question. I wanted to lower the boom and tell him that his saintly Lane wasn't in any hurry to come back to the warmness of the South, as Dre had kept her as warm as a thermal blanket on those cold New York nights. But, I had planted the seed which I knew had grown since Clay and I had last seen each other.

Most women detest what I stand for, but I could care less. I'm here to satisfy one person, and that's me. Should I put someone else's happiness before mine for the sake of a friendship? ...I don't think so. Lane and I had basically just met. I have shoes in my closet that I've had a lot longer than I've known Lane, and I'm supposed to deny my feelings because of a 'friendship.' As far as I was concerned, Clay's a free man to do what he what's to do, and to whom he wants to do it to.

I knew something was wrong when I asked him about Lane in our meeting; his face lacked that spark that was there when we first met, and he gushed at the mention of her name. Maybe he already knew about Lane and Dre. But, I had one more ruse for

Clay, and if he passed this, I'd know for sure his heart belonged to Lane, and I'd surrender. But, I was positive that wouldn't be the case this time around.

Charmine had treated me so wonderfully while I recovered at my parents' home from the severe beating I suffered by Darnell's hands that my parents offered to secure her wedding reception venue to show their gratitude. My mother, Charmine, and I were scheduled to look at some of the venues, so I picked up my mother first and then Charmine. We weren't at all impressed with the first two venues, however, when we arrived at the St. Regis Hotel, we immediately fell in love with the class and sophistication of their ballroom. Charmine said she could visualize herself being spun around on the ballroom floor in Anthony's arms. Charmine wrapped her arms tightly around my mother's neck and thanked her profusely for such an extravagant gift. It was quite obvious that Charmine wanted to have her wedding reception at the St. Regis, and while she took a few pictures on her cell phone for her parents to have a look, my mother disappeared with the Wedding Specialist to book the date.

After all the formalities had been finalized, Charmine and I dropped my mother back off at her home and we continued on to the Cosmopolitan Lounge. We wanted to celebrate how well everything had gone at the St. Regis with a few cocktails. Over the sounds of Adele's sultry tune being played, I told Charmine her dress was finished—she hardly believed me until I took out my phone and showed her the evidence with the photos I had taken of her dress. She reached down in her Marc Jacobs bag and pulled out a tissue as she teared up. I sat silently and allowed her, her moment. I expected that once she had seen her dress she'd be overcome with emotions, but it appeared she had a lot more on her mind. "Don't cry Charmine, everything is going to be beautiful, just as I told you it would."

"I know. I can't thank you or your parents enough, but I really hoped Lane would have been here to share in the happiest time of my life."

"I thought she would have been here too, but I've come to the conclusion that Lane is very selfish."

Charmine dabbed her eyes and looked at me strangely. "No, I wouldn't go that far. She's just gone through a trying time herself, and it's taking her longer than expected to get back on course."

"Wait, but didn't you have a lot going on? You still managed to drop everything to be at her beck and call in New York when she needed you. Look at what you had to go through just to get her measurements from her, and don't even get me started on how she's dogged out poor Clay."

"Listen, Faizon, I've been meaning to talk to you about that...I really shouldn't have told you about her and Dre. She told me what happened in the strictest of confidence, and regardless of what she's done, she's still our friend."

"You can call her friend, and I'll stick with calling her selfish." Charmine must have wanted to kill herself knowing that she had divulged too much of Lane's affairs to me. Charmine came up with several extraneous excuses for Lane's recent uncharacteristic behavior. Charmine ended our celebratory evening earlier than anticipated, and I assumed it was due to my lack of empathy for Lane's situation. I drove Charmine back to her house—the ride there was a bit ill at ease as we barely had spoken a word during our journey except for a few pleasantries, which were constrained. I never fooled myself by thinking Charmine's loyalties to Lane would dissolve just because she'd be draped in one of my creations on the most important day of her life, but I wanted to prove to Charmine that Lane wasn't as loyal.

I parked my car in the driveway of Charmine's house and waited for her to exit. She thanked me again for the eventful day and turned to walk in her house. I was just about to drive away when she yelled for me to stop and motioned for me to roll down my window. "I have to be honest with you," she said, while she glared at me sternly. "I'll be forever indebted to you and your parents for everything you've done, but I gotta tell you, I don't feel good about what you've said about Lane. I don't know what she's done to you, but she doesn't deserve it."

I listened to Charmine for about another minute as she told me her stance on friendships and how sacred they are to her before I stopped her and said. "I'm thrilled you had a good day, but I could give a shit what you think about how I feel about Lane. And if you're not too angry with me after this, I'll talk to you tomorrow. Goodnight." I drove off as Charmine stood in her driveway shocked by my confession. That night I slept better than I'd slept in a while as I couldn't wait to perform my next move on Clay.

I called Clay the next day and told him I had looked over the structure of the floor plans; however, I still had some trouble with the layout of the venue. He offered to send me a step-by-step email to explain the plans better, but I persisted I needed him to come over to talk me through it or else they'd be foreign to me. He said he couldn't make it until after eight due to a prior engagement, and I told him that would work, and I'd see him later on that evening.

With Charmine's dresses out of the way, I had just two more pieces I needed to finish for my collection, and one very special piece for a private showing coming up. Charmine called and she seemed to be in a much better frame of mind, she asked when she could pick up the dresses for her and Jayla. I told her to let them stay with me until the week of the wedding in case there were any last minute alterations to be made, she wasn't happy about it but she agreed and hung up. I had busied myself most of the day that I hadn't noticed the lateness of the hour.

I placed my finished garments in a bag and hung them on the clothing rail in my sewing room. I skimmed through my closet and matched a cute outfit together before I jumped in the shower as time had slipped away from me. I dabbed some of my favorite perfume behind my ears and knees before I walked downstairs to wait until Clay arrived. I waited so long that the scented candles I had lit had nearly burned themselves out, and I was very disappointed that Clay hadn't showed up at eight o'clock as he promised me. The time was well past eleven o'clock and it became apparent that Clay had forgotten about me, so I blew out what remained of the scented candles and turned off my living room lights. I had started to walk upstairs when there was a knock on my door. I hopped down from the two steps and ran to the door. Excitedly, I opened the door for Clay. God he was so handsome, and as always, he was well-dressed in a black shirt, black suit jacket, and some jeans.

I invited him inside and closed the door behind him. Clay followed me into my living room and waited for me to offer him a seat. His chestnut brown eyes were slightly glossed—his movements were a bit nervous and unbalanced, most likely from his intake of spirits from his earlier social engagement. And although his words weren't slurred, it was obvious he wasn't completely sober either. After he was seated comfortably, I offered him something to drink. "Thanks, I'll take of glass of Hennessy if you have it. Is that Elle Varner you're playing? She's hot right now," he commented and as I walked over to my wet bar to fix his drink, I appreciated that his eyes followed my every step.

"She is. I love her CD." As I poured his drink, he confirmed my presumption. He told me he attended a party for the launch of a new brand of Vodka, which had freely served its product throughout the evening.

"I brought the layout you wanted to see," he said and held out some papers for me to take.

I handed him his drink and took the document from his hand. I stood over him and pretended to care a little about the rolled up document he handed me. I removed the rubber band and opened it.

"Oh, I see. So, here is where the reception will be held?" I leaned down over him and pointed to an area on the paper. When he looked up at me to answer my question, his eyes met mine, and they stayed there until I repeated the question. "Clay. Is this the area?"

"Yeah, yeah," he said and swigged the remainder of his drink.

"That's it, and now that you understand I better be headed out. Thanks for the drink, Faizon." He placed the empty glass on the table and stood to leave.

"No, Clay, wait. I have one more important matter to resolve, and I need your advice." He looked down at his Switzerland made watch that adorned his wrist and sat back down in his chair.

"Okay, but I really should be leaving soon." Clay picked up a magazine from the table and started to read it as I left him to go upstairs. I knew if my plot proved successful there would be no turning back, and I've lost my friendship with Lane forever. And possibly Charmine's as well. But from the moment he stepped in my house I was sexually drawn to him and wanted to seduce him. Perfectly aware of the consequences, I continued to dress into my newest piece that I desperately wanted his opinion and his hands on it. I walked back downstairs and stopped in the doorway of the living room.

I stopped in the doorway of the living room as I wanted to make a grand entrance to command Clay's full attention. I placed my hands on my hips and crossed one leg over like I've seen the models do. "Ahem" I cleared my throat as I announced my return. When I had his undivided attention, I walked slowly over to him and watched as his eyes filled with lust as I modeled a chocolate colored lingerie one-piece which tastefully accented my full breasts and hardly covered my ass. Clay tossed the magazine back onto the table and rubbed his neat goatee with his fingers. I stopped in hands reach of him and twirled slowly to show him the back of my creation, I smiled as he nodded his head in adoration. "So, what do you think?" I asked.

"I think...I think I like it very much," he said, then smiled broadly. I pulled his tall masculine physique up from his chair and placed his warm hands around my tiny waist.

"And, I think I like you very much." I leaned in and gave him a soft sweet peck on the corner of his mouth. I felt his body stiffen as he tried to combat the temptation. He pulled away from my partially naked body, but I refused to relent. I placed my mouth back on his— and this time he returned my kiss with such a searing hunger that I felt the presence of his dick as it pressed against my thigh. I pushed him gently onto my sofa and wildly unbuckled the belt to his pants as I desperately wanted to taste him.

He watched me in astonishment as I frantically unzipped his pants and released his thick erect dick. I brushed my hair behind my ear and lowered my head to take him in my mouth, but Clay's sudden movement startled me as he grabbed my hands that were wrapped around his hardness. "No, Faizon. Get up!" he said. "We can't! I can't do this to Lane." He pushed me off of him and pulled up his pants. Clay slumped backwards onto the sofa and zipped his pants back up.

"She doesn't have to know."

"But I will, and I'm not doing that to her," he said affirmatively.

"While you're here trying to be man of the year, to her, do you have any idea how she spends her nights, and with who?"

"I know how she spends her nights," he said, as he buckled his belt. Clay's face looked disturbed at my accusation.

"Are you sure about that?"

"Faizon, you'll never make me cast doubt on my relationship with Lane. Am I really gonna believe you after the way you orchestrated this entire night? He snatched his suit jacket from the back of the chair and left. I grew incensed with how the night had turned out and swiped the venue's lay-out off my coffee table to the floor. Why didn't I just tell Clay about Lane when I first heard about it? He'll never believe me now, and I know I've lost any chance of us ever getting together. My next biggest move would be how to ingratiate myself with Clay again before he pulled himself and his company off my launch, and this time for good.

FORBIDDEN SEDUCTION

Charmine

Anthony and I were swamped with work, and with the opening of our own law firm in Atlantic Station, I had become quite stressed. However, the last week at our present firm marked a sad ending to a new and exciting beginning. As we prepared to leave, the partners, attorneys, office staff, and even clients of the firm wished Anthony and I all the best. I made an appointment to get my hair and nails done as I hadn't made time for myself with all that had gone on lately. As I passed through Fazion's neighborhood to get to my appointment, I realized that Faizon and I hadn't spoken to each other in the last few days. I needed to call her and get to the root of what had caused her to turn so nasty towards Lane.

I had met Faizon through Lane when we all went out to a jazz and blues bar one night. The moment I looked at Faizon, I knew instantly she had an unhealthy competitive and jealous streak in her. She hated to be outdone in anything—if you've been to Paris once—she's been there twice. Faizon always tooted her own horn. And there was nothing wrong with that, but she took confidence to another level. So, I expected nothing less from her. Where we differed was I've always been a confident woman, whereas Faizon needed a designer label, car, or a man to define her. And over the years of our friendship, I had to learn that Faizon is Faizon, and she wasn't going to change.

Anthony called me as I approached the hair salon and asked me if I would stop by the market to pick up some truffle oil for a dish he wanted to make. I flew off the handle at his request and screamed. "Why would you wait until now to tell me about the truffle oil? You've been home most of the afternoon, why didn't you just pick some up earlier?"

"Don't bother. I thought since we've both been too busy to have a proper meal, it would have been nice to prepare a special dish for you tonight. And in case you've forgotten, my car was taken in for maintenance this afternoon," he said.

Damnmit! I had forgotten about that. I felt horrible that I had spoken to Anthony like that. "Oh Sweetheart, I'm so sorry. That's such a sweet gesture, and I forgot about your car."

"Charmine, talk to me. What's been eating you lately?" he asked, concerned about my mood swings over the last few days.

"Aw...it's nothing. It's probably the stress of the move, and wedding getting the better of me—it's nothing to worry about. I'll pick up the truffle oil after I leave the salon, love you."

"I love you too, and you can talk to me. I'm here for you." I wished it were only the stress of the move and wedding, I could handle that. I was worried about how I would tell Lane that I had inadvertently told Faizon that she had slept with Dre. And once I found a way to break it to her I'd call her, but for right now I needed to be pampered. My hair stylist wanted to do something different to my hair, so I courageously let her. I figured I needed a new look anyway, and maybe a new-do would have lifted my spirits a bit. I flipped through a few hair magazines for a style I thought would be nice for my face structure, and I decided to go with the Kerry Washington look. After I had been shampooed and rolled, I was put under the dreaded hair dryer as the nail technician gave me a manicure.

After I stepped out of the hair salon, I felt like my old self with a new hairdo. I stopped at the market and picked up the oil Anthony asked for then headed home. When I got in the house, the magnificent aromas met me at the front door. Anthony took the bag with the truffle oil from my hands. "Thanks, Dear, this is the last ingredient I needed for this dish and then we can eat."

"Hey, hey, watch my nails," I scowled. "And where's my kiss?" Anthony looked over his shoulder and kissed me on my forehead.

"Would you mind fixing us a salad?" he asked. I held up my hands and wiggled my fingers to show him my freshly painted red nails. "Okay, scratch that. Can you manage pouring us some wine?" I pulled two wine glasses from the cabinet and poured us both a glass of red wine. "Oh yeah, Lane called the house. She said she tried calling your cell but it kept going straight to your voice mail." I reached inside my bag, pulled out my phone, and attempted to turn it on, but it was dead. I asked Anthony how she sounded and if she mentioned what she wanted. He said she sounded fine, and the only message was that I should call her when I got in. I was about to go into my bedroom and get the inevitable over with, but when Anthony placed a plate of grilled shrimp with a truffle oil vinaigrette and asparagus in front of me, I sat in the dining area and ate my specially prepared dish first.

As we ate our dinner, Anthony told me his mother wanted to talk to me about something that pertained to our wedding, and she'd like for me to give her a call. Although things had gotten much better between Anthony's parents and me, I still wasn't too thrilled to hear what she wanted to talk to me about. After we finished our delectable dinner, I told Anthony I would take care of the cleanup, because he cooked; he happily left the table to watch the game. I grabbed the cordless phone and dialed Lane's number. "It's about time you called me back! Now I can ask you, where the hell you've been all day?" Lane snapped playfully.

"Why hello to you too, Lane. What's going on?"

"Nothing, I missed you a lot today and wanted to talk to you. That's all."

"How sweet, I miss you too. Anthony told me you called, but I had to put something in my system. It's been one of those days."

"I'm sorry to hear that."

"It's fine. What did you want to talk to me about?"

"I've been thinking.... I've been thinking it's about time for me to come back to Atlanta."

"Are you serious?! Girl, when? Does Clay know?"

"Yes. I don't know. No. But, my dad and I have been talking about it over the past week. He seems to think it's time, and I think he may be right."

"That's the best freakin' news I've heard all day. And I know Clay is going to be over-the-moon when he hears it!" We giggled as loudly as two crazy teenagers. A displeased Anthony looked up from his game and turned up the volume to the TV.

"I know right. I've been trying to get him all day as well, but he hasn't returned my call yet. I hope he's not trying to get rid of me after all this."

"I doubt that, he's probably just been busy. Your man does run two businesses, you know."

"I know, and I had the weirdest dream the other night that he told me he didn't want me any more and that he found someone else."

"Well, if you keep fucking around with Dre it won't be a dream, it'll be a reality. And while we're on the subject of Dre I have something to tell you." I grabbed for my last bit of wine and chucked it down my throat.

"What is it?"

"I know you're gonna freak out, but please know it was an absolute mistake. I kinda let it slip out to Faizon that you and Dre slept together."

"YOU WHAT?!"

"I said, I told – – "

"I heard you. How in the hell did you "kinda" let that slip? And to Faizon of all fuckin' people. You know how that bitch is."

"I know Lane, and I'm so sorry. I've been beating myself up over it since the night I told her. But I don't think you have anything to worry about—she isn't gong to say anything to anyone. She made a good point, why would she?"

"You don't even put anything past her. That's why you still haven't told her the whole story about you and Kamel. You know that chick is triflin'. Damn, Charmine, do you even understand how hard it was for me to tell you, and we share everything. And for you to just blurt it out to *her* like that...I don't know."

"Lane, I wish I could take it back, but I can't. I just think you're really over reacting about this unnecessarily. Trust me, Clay will never find out." Lane tried to coolly continue our conversation, but I could tell that she was rattled to know that Faizon knew about it.

Before Lane and I got off the phone, I made her swear she wasn't still angry at me and that she'd stay away from Dre, but when she only swore that she'd stay away from Dre, I didn't push the issue. Anthony entered the kitchen as I had started to put the dishes in the dishwasher and told me he was ready for bed. He insisted I join him, so I finished up quickly and followed him. I laid in bed in complete darkness and silence as Anthony had fallen asleep as soon as his head hit his pillow, so I started to piece this fuzzy puzzle all together. Hmmm... Faizon's recent negative and insensitive comments directed at Lane. Clay's sudden trepidation to work with Faizon. Faizon's defensiveness when I asked about her and Clay's meetings. The pieces of the puzzle started to fit, and I had begun to smell a fashion conscious rat, but before I dozed off I prayed I was dead wrong.

I woke up to a day of dread, knowing I had to call my future mother-in-law and Faizon. I wanted nothing more than for Faizon to tell me I had never been so wrong as to suspect something may have went on between her and Clay. If I found out it had—I basically gave Faizon the ammunition she needed and wanted on a silver platter.

The partners and staff at Holland Thompson & Harrington had surprised me and Anthony with a farewell party on our last day at the firm. I had to be excused to the ladies room to have a moment by myself as I hadn't expected to be so moved by all the lovely words and gifts. By the time all the speeches and festivities were finished, Anthony's mechanic, Bruce, called and said he had parked Anthony's car in the lot. Anthony and I said our final goodbyes and walked hand-in-hand out of the office for the last time. When we got to Anthony's car, he packed all of our gifts in the vehicle. I hopped in my vehicle and followed him to our new office less than five miles away. The project manager for the extension was still on-site when we arrived. He said everything was on schedule, and we'd be able to open on our projected date. Things had progressed just as I had hoped. I just hoped our wedding and the move into our new house went just as smoothly.

While Anthony finished up with the project manager, I decided I'd call Mrs. Martin to find out what she wanted. "Hello, Mrs. Martin, this is Charmine."

"Hello Charmine, dear, how are you?"

"I'm well, thanks. Anthony mentioned that you wanted me to call you."

"Yes Dear, that's right. I wanted to know if was there anything Mr. Martin and I can do to contribute towards the wedding?"

"Oh, Mrs. Martin, that is really kind of you, but my family and I have it all covered."

"Mr. Martin and I can appreciate how proud you colored folks are, but please don't be too proud to ask us for any financial help if your family can't afford to bear the cost on your own. After all, this is our son's wedding, and we have family traveling from out of state. We would hate for Anthony's wedding to be some low budget embarrassment. We want it to be spectacular." I was all kinds of shocked when I heard this women reference African Americans as 'colored' in this day and age, and I completely overlooked the fact she insinuated my parents and I couldn't afford my wedding on our own. I was utterly dumbfounded by her ignorance and saw an opportunity for a teachable moment. I attempted to educate her on her outdated and offensive views, but the more I tried the angrier I had become.

"Mrs. Martin, I think it would be helpful for you to know that 'we' don't use the term 'colored' any more."

"Well, pardon me Dear, but I don't know how you can possibly be offended when you people change the names of your nationality as often as we hold presidential elections." After Mrs. Martin made that statement is when I realized a debate with Mrs. Martin would be futile and wasted energy on my behalf. I planned to spend the rest of my life with her son, and I would have plenty of time to enlighten her on her ignorance. I had never been so happy to end a phone call as I had with Mrs. Martin—not that the call I made to Faizon was any less stressful.

"What's going on, Girl?" Faizon asked.

"Nothing. I just off the phone with my crazy-ass future mother-in-law. Girl, tell me why she still calling us 'coloreds.'"

"Stop playing! Girrl, you surely have your work cut out for you. I can imagine all y'all now—sitting around the table for family dinners."

"Shut up, Faizon. Listen, what are you doing later on?"

"Nothing really, why? You wanna go out?"

"I was hoping that we could meet up at that coffee house near my house."

"This sounds serious," she said.

"I hope not, can you meet me?"

"Yeah, give me about an hour." We disconnected, and as I got dressed, I was a bit nervous about what I may have found out. I arrived at the coffee house first and sat at a table in the rear where it seemed less noisy. When Faizon entered, all heads turned to watch the southern belle's swag as she walked over to greet me. I knew that after her clothing line had gotten off the ground, it would only be a matter of time before I would have to make an appointment just to speak to her majesty. The barista came over and took our order. When I ordered the Cafe Bombon, Faizon shot me an unpleasant look.

"What's that look for?" I asked Faizon after the barista left our table.

"You should have ordered a skinny latte instead of that Cafe Bombon—it looks like you've already gained a few pounds; I don't wanna have to let your dress out on the morning of your wedding." Faizon took off her shades and placed them in her bag.

"Oh, no, you didn't. That's rude," I said, as I looked down and noticed a slight pooch around my mid-section.

"That isn't rude, that's the truth." Faizon scanned the coffee house of on-lookers who quickly looked off once they had been caught staring at her.

"Well, I'm glad that you're in the mood for telling the truth, because there's something I want to ask you."

"What is it?" she asked as she assisted the barista and took her macchiato off the tray.

"What's up with you and Lane, and why have you been so hard on her lately?"

"Oh here we go. The almighty lawyer wants to defend her poor and helpless friend. There's nothing up with us. I haven't even seen Lane in close to two months, so what could possibly be up?"

"That's what I've been wondering, but something is wrong. So, if there isn't anything wrong with you and Lane, has something happened between you and Clay?" With that question I hit the jackpot, and my lawyer skills had kicked in. I detected there was a hint of guilt from Faizon's abrupt and flustered shift. Just the mention of his name seemed to make her become unraveled. She put her shades back on her face and nervously tapped her   fingernails on the table. And in that instant I knew something questionable had gone on. Faizon tried to downplay any involvement with Clay other than he was hired to arrange her launch, but when I told her I knew that he had pulled himself off the project she looked bewildered and wanted to know how I knew about that.

"Have you been talking to Clay? What has he told you about us?"

"Us? So now there's an 'us'?"

"Charmine! Will you just tell me what he said?" she demanded very angrily.

"Relax. He hasn't said anything to me personally, but he did tell Lane he had to assign someone else to your event which seemed suspect."

"I don't know what he's told her, and honestly I'm not bothered. But I do know this, if she's so concerned about what's going on here in Atlanta, she'd stop sleeping with Dre and get her ass back here. Because if she doesn't want Clay, I know someone who does," she said and stood up proudly from her chair. She pulled a twenty-dollar bill from her wallet and tossed it on the table before she walked out. I knew then the bitch had gone mad. The way she strutted out of the coffee house was like she felt that Lane had come in between her and Clay.

I watched Faizon as she walked out, and I was a bit scared because I knew the war that was to come from all of this. Talk about timing, Lane couldn't have chosen a better time to return to Atlanta and claim what is hers. And if Faizon had stayed just a bit longer for me to tell her that Lane was coming back to Atlanta, she'd know it wasn't going to be as easy as she thought to claim Clay as hers.

Clay

Ever since that night at Faizon's I have replayed that scene over, and over a thousand times in my head, and I still can't believe I allowed myself to be played like that. I nearly went to bed with my woman's friend. What tripped me out the most was what Faizon had implied: am I to believe that on the nights I haven't been able to contact Lane she's been with Dr--- sheesh. I couldn't even say it. But even if that was what she meant, why should I have taken Faizon's word for anything after what she pulled?

It's true that Lane hasn't been herself for a while now, but then she's also suffered a tremendous loss. I was aight with her getting out and doing things with her friends. I hadn't been concerned with her partying until I found out that she lied to me about seeing Dre at the party. But after she explained she lied because she didn't want me to flip-out I gave her the benefit of the doubt. There were even some nights I laid in my bed worried that I had lost her for good. So, when Lane called to tell me she was coming home because she missed me badly, I deaded all that other shit that Faizon buzzed in my ear.

There was no way I could have ignored what almost happened between Faizon and I, and it had to be addressed before Lane touched down in Atlanta. I called Faizon several times because we needed to discuss that night, but she never picked up her phone. Later that evening after work, I called Lane so she could tell me the details of her arrival. "Hi, Clay."

"What's up Bae? What's going on?"

"I'm good. I was sitting here with my dad getting some stuff sorted."

"Do you want me to call you back?"

"No, I could use a break right now. What ya been up to today?"

"I've been looking at taking PPE to the next level. We've been getting booked for a lot of celebrity events lately which is why I'm focusing a lot more on the entertainment division.

"That's great news. By the way, speaking of celebrities how is Atlanta's biggest diva's launch going?"

"It's going. . . it's going. Lane, I know I asked you this before, but how well do you really know Faizon?"

"Yeah you have, and I'm starting to get concerned about it. Like I told you the last time you asked, I met her when I first moved to Atlanta and we've been friends since then. Now will you tell me why you keep asking me that? Has she done something?" Nothing much besides getting me to her house under false pretenses with the intentions of having me fuck her. Oh yeah, and I was so sexually attracted to her I was on the verge of letting it happen.

"Nah, it's just that I'm not too sure about her, and I think it's best you don't fuck with her when you get back."

"Whoa...that doesn't sound right. She hasn't done anything, but you don't think I should continue my friendship with her when I get back. I'm not sure I understand that. Just last week you went into this whole big spiel about honesty and how relationships thrive on it, so I need for you to be honest with me the same way. What has she done?"

I looked around my room as if the answers were plastered on my wall. I wanted to be truthful with Lane, but I wanted our relationship even more. I told Lane that Faizon was infatuated with me, and I added that it wasn't uncommon for this to happen to men in my industry. Lane wanted to know if she had made any disrespectful advances towards me, and I only admitted to the flirtatious hug in the parking lot. I couldn't bring myself to tell Lane about the other night; I would have certainly lost her for sure. Lane asked if that hug had been the reason I put Shon in charge of Faizon's event. When I confirmed that was the reason, Lane stated she knew how Faizon got down and couldn't wait to confront Faizon. I couldn't have let that happen without the full truth being exposed, so I stayed on the phone until I coaxed Lane into letting me handle Faizon my way.

I tried to keep Lane off the subject of Faizon, so I asked her to tell me a little more about her timeline back to Atlanta. She told me that she'd be in Atlanta in two weeks just in time for Charmine's wedding and that she had also talked to her old boss at the bank and had her old job back. Now that Lane had given me the date of her return, I had to ascertain that Faizon's story collaborated with mine just in case Lane had confronted her. I called Faizon again and just like it had done earlier; it went straight to her voice mail. I left a message for her to get in touch with me. I told her it was urgent. I failed to include it concerned Lane's homecoming, because something told me she wouldn't have deemed it urgent if she had that piece of information.

About ten minutes after the third time I tried to reach Faizon, my phone rang and I hoped it was her, but it was Shon instead. He called to say he had an extra floor seat ticket to the Hawks vs. Lakers game at the Phillips Arena, and the ticket was mine if I wanted it. I told him of course I wanted it, and I would meet him at the front gate of the arena. We met up as planned and stopped by the concession stand for some beers. As Shon and I stood there, my mind wandered back to the night that Lane and I had met at that same spot as she stood in line for her refreshments. Shon interrupted my thoughts and asked me where I had gone because I had zoned out on him. So I told him the whole story of how Lane and I met. "Man, we were right here in this same spot when I noticed her. What's so crazy, if I recall correctly, Faizon and Charmine were with her that night."

"Yo, no disrespect but I gotta ask... Lane is a beautiful woman, there's no denying that...but could you have got with Faizon?"

"Nah, I never saw Faizon that night. I only saw Lane, but she told me she was at the game with her two friends."

"Now that you know Faizon, do you ever regret choosing Lane?"

"Never. Why in the hell would I regret it? You said it yourself—you've seen Lane. Your problem is you're only concerned with the outer appearance—that's why all your relationships only last a minute. You'll get it together one day though and learn all that glitters ain't gold."

"True, but I ain't gon' lie, Faizon is mad sexy. There are some women who have to work hard to look that damn good, but she's just sexy." I watched as Shon made an orgasmic face while he described

111

Faizon's curvaceous body and thought she may have been correct when she said she felt Shon jerked off when they spoke on the phone. Shon had been my confidant for years, and I knew whatever I shared with him he'd take it to his grave—and I had to get this Faizon situation off my chest before I lost it.

"I feel you, man. She almost got caught out there the other night."

"What night? The night you rushed to leave the Vodka after-party?"

"Yeah, Boy, she damn near got the filler, but just as I was about to let her get it in, Lane's face popped in my head, and I got the hell outta there.

"You buggin.' You tellin' me Faizon was about to give you some head and you bounced? You do know that getting head isn't considered cheating?"

"Bruh, didn't we have this same argument the night Ebony left you, when she caught one of the models giving you a 'bonus'? She considered it cheating, and so do I." Shon and I debated a bit longer on what we constituted as cheating, but the real shade came when I told him the play by play details of that night. He listened intently, and at some parts of the story, he looked as if he was envious of me. After I told him everything, Shon and I watched in horror as the Lakers spanked the Hawks by twenty-two points. After the game, Shon asked if I wanted to take a ride with him down to Strokers. I still had the Faizon fiasco on my brain, so I passed. I reached home a few minutes after one o'clock, and I just wanted to shower and hit the sheets, but my phone vibrated.

"Hello Clay, this is Faizon returning your call," her tone was direct, and business-like. "I apologize for calling you at this hour, but I'm just getting in."

"Hello Faizon, don't worry about it. I'm glad you called me back."

"Well, in your voice mail you said something to the effect of it being urgent, is there a problem with my launch?"

"No, no. . . everything's good. I wanted to talk to you about what happened between us the other night."

"I think that's a good idea. I wanted to call you too, but I didn't know how to broach the subject. So, now that you've brought it up, I would like to apologize for my conduct. I know you're involved with Lane, my friend, and I should have never put you in that situation. I just got caught up in the heat of the moment."

"I appreciate that Faizon, and I hope there's no hard feelings."

"Well, maybe for you there was," she laughed. "You should have seen the way you ran out of my house, pulling your pants up." When I flashed back to that night, I laughed at myself.

"Good one, Faizon. You know, I hate that I let it get that far, but when you came downstairs and modeled for me I tried my best to restrain myself, but you're a beautiful woman, and it would've been hard for any man to resist."

"Thank you, Clay. I'll say this, and I'll leave it alone; Lane is one very lucky women. I just hope she knows how lucky she is."

"I believe she does, which brings me to the other reason I called— Lane will be home in the two weeks, and I was hoping she'll never hear about what took place at your place." I thought Faizon would have been relieved, especially since we both wanted to put it behind us for everyone's sake. But instead she became strangely splenetic as if she was a jilted ex-girlfriend of mine who'd been replaced. Her temperament went from apologetic to mean-spirited. I told her she was being unreasonable, and there wasn't any need for me and Lane to lose our relationship over something that should've never happened in the first place. But before we hung up she insisted she would one day have the last laugh.

"You're right, Clay. There's no need for me to break Lane's heart as soon as she gets back to Atlanta 'cause that'll happen soon enough. And no matter how much you try to forget that night, you and I will always remember the night you wanted me badly enough to throw it all away. When I think about it, you and Lane deserve one another." I didn't know what she meant by that, but I was afraid that one day I would find out. When I finally went to bed, it felt as though I had sparred with Mike Tyson just to get her to promise she wouldn't say a word to Lane, but it was worth it. Lane was coming back to Atlanta and I couldn't have that shit looming over our relationship.

Lane called me early the next morning concerned about where she'd live. She mentioned moving back to her old Brookhaven neighborhood. I suggested we should live together, but she was dead set against it. She claimed she needed her independence and living together wouldn't have allowed it. Since she refused to move in with

113

me, I wanted her as close to me as possible. I told her to let me handle everything, and I would have my Realtor get right on it.

Since I'd been back from Brooklyn, I had signed three new artists and booked two major events, one of which was Faizon's launch. With the success of my record label and entertainment company, I spent an excess of twenty hours per day away from home. There was even a time with all I had going on, Lane consumed my thoughts. I hoped when she returned, my late night fantasizing about Faizon would stop. I didn't want to think about her sexy mouth about to go down on me or her partially naked symmetry standing in front of me. Those were now the images that swarmed in my head.

After my conversation with Faizon, I had barely gotten any sleep, and I dragged myself to the work. I had just finished with a branding meeting with my team when Tom, my Realtor, called. He said he found a two-bedroom condominium that was in foreclosure and thought it'd be worth Lane taking a look at it. Tom said it was also in the heart of midtown which was also in proximity to me, so I hoped Lane liked it. It all started to feel real to me that Lane was coming back. I went to my office and called Lane to tell her the news. "Hi, Clay."

"Hey Bae, what you doin'?"

"I just had my eyebrows done, I was starting to look like the Unibrow," she chuckled.

"Nah, you could never. Anyway, off that, I called to tell you some news."

"What it is?" she asked.

"Tom found you a place in midtown today, and he said it's a great buy. It has two-bedrooms and nearly four thousand sq. feet. I'll shoot you an email with all the information, and you can do a virtual tour; get a glimpse of it yourself."

"Wow that does sound good. I can't wait to see it, how much did he say it is?"

"Don't worry about that now. You just focus on getting back to me."

"Cla – – ."

"Not now, Lane. I love you, and I'll call you tonight." Immediately after we hung up I sent Lane the details that Tom sent to me. Tom found my house, and I was sure that Lane would love the condo as well. I was not about to allow anything or anyone keep us apart. Not even Faizon's scheming ass.

FORBIDDEN SEDUCTION

Lane

I never thought I'd be as excited as I was to go back to Atlanta, but after Clay had given me an ultimatum, I had to realize what was important to me. And being in Brooklyn, away from Clay, gave me time to think about what he really meant to me. I came to the realization that he deserved much better than what I'd given him, and when I got back to Atlanta, it would be a clean slate for us. No drama. No Dre. No cheating. Clay insisted I look at a condo his Realtor, Tom, had picked out, and I wanted it the moment I looked at it.

Between Dre and Charmine my phone stayed lit up. Char called me everyday to make sure I hadn't changed my mind, and Dre continued to try to persuade me to meet him at his place. Even after I made it clear to him that I didn't want him to call me any more and that I was done cheating on Clay, he seemed even more determined to have me in his bed once more. I wished he were that determined to be faithful to me when we were together; we may have had a chance. I hadn't told Dre of my plans to move back to Atlanta, but I knew I would eventually have to do it soon. Not because I felt I owed him anything, but I wanted him to know I meant what I said when I told him I was in love with Clay.

From the day I learned that 'Ms Prissy' Faizon had shoved her tits in Clay's face and God knows where else, I couldn't wait to see her. I was dying to tell Char about it, but Clay made me promise on my red bottoms that I wouldn't breathe a word. I wanted to catch Charmine before she left for work, so I called her first thing in the morning. I gave her all my details for my flight back to Atlanta, and I also asked her to drive past my new condo to get a sneak-peek for me. "Girl, if your place is as near to Atlanta Station as you say, please believe I'll be stopping by your place for lunch errday, Boo," she shrieked.

"How are you gonna stop by my house for lunch, and I'll be at work?" I asked.

"Because you know your ass will be giving me a key. You not talking about nothing, so let me get off this phone. I have a few things to do this morning before I look at the condo, but I'll call you as soon as I see it."

"Okay, Char, thank you. Talk to you later." I went on about my morning and waited in anticipation for Charmine to call me back with her seal of approval on the condominium. I liked what I had seen on the computer, but I trusted Charmine's up close and personal opinion more. I had just prepared lunch for my dad and me when Charmine called me back all hyped about the condo.

"Lane, I know you asked me to drive by the condominiums, but I wouldn't be able to give you a true assessment, so I went inside. Luckily there was an on-site manager who showed me an empty model of a two bedroom, and it's gorgeous. The building is really nice. There's a gym, and it's a good neighborhood. Girl, either you put something on Clay's ass, or he's feeling mighty guilty about something," she said.

"Why in the hell would Clay have to be feeling guilty about something? And let me clarify something, I'm buying my own condo." Charmine was the one who appeared guilty about something, because after I posed the question to her, she changed the subject and turned the conversation to my dress fitting. What was worse, I noted a change in her attitude as if she was hiding something from me. Was there more to what Clay had told me about Faizon that she knew of? So I asked her to be straight with me.

"Lane," she started plaintively, "the last time we spoke you mentioned that Clay had an issue with Faizon and how he removed himself from her launch. And lately I've noticed that whenever your name is brought up, Faizon's been quite hostile towards you, and I put two-and-two together. So, the other night I confronted her with my suspensions and she basically admitted something happened, she just didn't say to what extent."

"And you believed her nonsense? She's a liar—I know exactly what happened—Clay already told me everything. This is the reason why I wanted to get in that ass, but Clay told me not to because he'd handle it." I went on to tell Charmine, Clay's version of what really happened and that I couldn't wait to get back to Atlanta to settle this once and for all. After Charmine and I hung up I was still fuming, so I splashed cold water on my face to calm myself down. I was beginning to feel like Faizon wanted my man, my best friend, and my life, but I would handle all that soon enough. I wanted to spend some time with my aunt Bernice before I left for Atlanta, so I called her to let her know I'd be there later on in the evening. I asked my dad to come along for the ride, but he said he had some business to take care of, so I should just go by myself.

When I arrived at my aunt's door, I immediately smelled her apple crumble pie as it seeped through the door. Aunt Bernice knew it was my favorite and made one especially for me. I enjoyed the time I spent at my aunt's house. She told me she was proud of me for moving back to Atlanta and not to worry about my dad because he would be in good hands. Aunt Bernice sent me home with some food for dad and some advice before I left. "When you get back down South, you hold on tight to that man of yours. I ain't never seen a man look at a woman the way that he looks at you. Wait...let me take that back. Your daddy was a fool about your mama." She laughed and slapped her knees. "Oh, Chile, I could tell you some stories, and if you treat Clay right, he'll love you just as much as your daddy loved your mama."

"Thank you, Auntie. I will."

"That means you gotta let that worm go—he ain't no good for you, Lane."

"I know, but I haven't done anything with Dre..."

"Shhh. . . don't lie to your old auntie. I was a young woman once, and even if Bev ain't tell me nothin' I know something went on with you and that boy. I'm not saying the boy ugly 'cause he surely ain't. I'm just saying he ain't for you." I stopped before I lied to her any further.

After our conversation I thanked her for everything and gave her an open invitation to come to Atlanta any time she wanted. When I got home, my dad was in his bedroom. I knocked on the door and told him about the food Aunt Bernice sent home for him. He asked me to join him in his room after I put his food in the microwave. I put his food away like he asked and entered his room. He was sitting on his bed with his head hung low enough to be in his lap. I hadn't seen him look that sad in a while, and I thought he may have had a change of heart about me moving back to Atlanta. When I sat on the bed beside him, he reached in his bible and handed me a white envelope.

"What's this?" I asked.

"It's for you, open it," he said. I looked at the envelope suspiciously and turned the envelope over to see if I could recognize the handwriting, but both sides were blank. I pulled out the contents of the envelope and I was astounded. It was a cashier's check made out to me. I sat there speechless with my mouth agape for a few minutes.

"You know I can't accept this, Daddy." I extended my hand to give him back the substantial check, but he got up and walked over to the window.

"You can, and you will. Your mother left that for you, and you'll take it. We always wanted the best for you, and now you can start a good life in Georgia." The back of my throat started to close up on me, and my tears seemed to burn my skin as they rolled down my cheeks.

"What about you, Daddy? I don't need anything close to this much."

"Baby Girl, listen. I'm fine. The house is paid for, and I don't have no expensive habits; Old Betsy might need a few new tires soon, but she's even paid for. What does an old man like me need? Take the money Baby Girl, and do what your mother intended it for... and that is to make your life a little more comfortable," he said, nearly in tears himself. My dad walked back over to me and kissed me on my forehead. He told me to be up by nine the next morning because he wanted to take me to breakfast. He wanted my last few days at home to be a memorable one for the both of us.

The next morning, we had an old fashion breakfast at a diner on Linden Boulevard, and afterward, we stopped by the bank and I deposited the insurance check. I thanked my dad for our morning out

FORBIDDEN SEDUCTION

together, and then I took him home. I dropped my dad off in front of our house and told him I'd be back shortly. He looked at me strangely but didn't question me. He opened the iron gate and headed up the stairs. I had one more thing I had to resolve before I left, and the time had come for me to tell Dre I planned to leave New York.

I called Dre and he answered his phone way too cocky. He told me that he knew that I would call, because I couldn't stay away. I ignored his egotistical comments and asked his location. He said he had just left the barbershop and was headed back home. I asked him to meet me at Dottie's, the spot we used to frequent in Prospect Heights, but he used every excuse to dissuade us from meeting there. I lied and told him I had something else to do in that area and convinced him we wouldn't be there long. When I arrived, Dre was already there and was seated in the very rear of the coffee shop. He stood and greeted me with a friendly peck on the cheek. "What's good, Lane?"

"Hi, Dre. Thanks for coming, but why'd you give me such a hard time about meeting me here? You used to love this place."

"It wasn't a problem. I just don't drink coffee like that no more since we broke up. I can't afford these high ass coffee bean prices."

"Whatever, Dre," I said, tired of his excuses.

"I see you Lane, you looking good in dem jeans."

"Thanks, Dre." I avoided looking directly into his addictive brown eyes and looked up at the big screen TV that showed continuous BET videos. We hadn't even ordered our coffee before Dre started to make sexual innuendos.

"Lets grab a couple of those muffins, some coffee, and shoot back to my crib. I wanna help you out of dem jeans," he said, as he rubbed my thigh suggestively from under the table. I jerked my leg away from his touch, and for the first time since I had sat down, I looked him firmly in his eyes.

"Alright Dre, stop. I need to talk to you seriously." I started by telling him how badly I had missed Clay and my life in Atlanta. The way he laughed at me you would've thought I had practiced a stand-up routine for him. I told him I wasn't playing and that I was dead serious. I felt free when I told him that this would be my last week in New York, and I was going back to be with Clay. Dre asked me had I missed Clay on those nights that we made love, and I was curled up in

121

his bed til morning.

"Lane, you fooling yourself. You think 'cause dude got a little change, he's a boss—but that don't mean shit. That just means he can buy you stuff, but he can't make you feel the way I do. I know your body better than you do. And it's not only because the sex is crazy, I'm in here," he said and thumped his right temple three times lightly. I let Dre have his say, but I told him he was wrong. Dre finally accepted the fact I was going back to Clay, but he continued to make his plea for us to have sex once more before I left for Atlanta.

As Dre pestered me about going home with him, I glanced out of the window to the shop and noticed two loud women as they passed. One of the women caught my glare as she passed and doubled-back. She pressed her face against the window, and she looked somewhat familiar to me. The woman entered the shop and walked towards us, and then I remembered exactly who she was. Dre's back was turned to her and couldn't see the ambush which was headed his way.

"This is why I had to leave you my money for the barbershop today—so you could look fly for some next bitch?"she snapped. Her voice shook Dre, and he turned quickly to face the voice. The last time I saw her, Dre's face was buried happily between her thighs in our bed. Her friend had now joined her inside. She looked as if she had sucked on a whole lemon as she stood next to Renee. The last thing I wanted to do was to have a shouting match in the neighborhood coffee shop. So I ignored her high schoolish behavior and insisted Dre calm the situation before it got too far out of hand.

"Dre, you need to handle this before I do," I said, as I lifted my cup of coffee to my lips.

"C'mon Renee, let me talk to you outside." He stood up to face Renee and attempted to usher her outside, but she snatched her arm from out of his hands.

"No, I'm good! You can talk to me right here," she said, as she drilled a hole in my face. "What's going on Dre?"

"Nothing. I'm having a coffee with an old friend, what's the matter with you?" I knew all about Dre's antics as I recognized his spin. He was about to make her feel like she was crazy for assuming something was going on. "This is Lane," he said.

Renee looked at me and squinted. "Lane? But I thought you said she lived in Atlanta?"

"She does, she was here for her mother's funeral." Renee looked as if she wanted to sympathize with me.

"Oh, I'm so sorry. ...I didn't know. I didn't mean to call you out your name." It was as if she was on mute and only her lips moved, because the words of my aunt Bernice 'he's no good for you' blared repeatedly in my ears. Her friend, who hadn't spoken a word, pulled her cell phone from out of her bag and walked off.

"If you hadna came in here with all that mad rah-rah bullshit, you wouldn't have to be apologizing, coming up through here embarrassing me. Lane is headed back to Atlanta and wanted to see me before she left. We was about to leave anyway, just meet me outside I'll only be another minute." I watched in amazement as he used his verbal gift— Dre knew his fine-ass could get away with anything; this was child's play to him. Renee nodded in shame and proceeded to walk out.

"I'm really sorry to hear about your mother," she said and walked out with her friend as Dre directed. Dre sat back down and rubbed his hand down his face. As he sat across from me, I took a long, good look at him as I knew it would surely be my last time so close to him. As I watched how the episode unfolded between him and Renee, I relived all the times that I waited up all night for him and how I'd be angry as hell with him. But as soon as he'd come home—he'd slither in my bed —and make pillow biting love to me and all was forgiven.

"So, when you told me two weeks ago that you and Renee weren't together, that was a lie?" I asked.

"I didn't want to have to tell you about Renee, I know how you feel about her. I'm sorry, Lane."

"I know you're sorry, but so am I for continuing to allow myself to get carried away with your lies. I should know better by now." I started to put my jacket on to leave. Dre looked at the front of the shop to make sure Renee hadn't snuck back in the shop. He looked relieved when he saw she was still standing outside the shop with her arms folded in front of her while she talked to her friend.

"When are you leaving?"

"Wednesday morning."

"Baby, I wanna get with you so bad right now. Call me later tonight; let me make you happy just once more before you leave."

"Are you serious right now? Bye, Dre." Dre was never going to change and not that I hoped for one, but there was never going to be a future for us. I walked out of the shop and caught the gaze of Renee. Funny enough, this time I sympathized with her. I wasn't out of their sight a good minute before I pulled my phone out and blocked Dre's number. That was the first step towards ending my addiction. I had a couple of days left at home with my dad, and we spent that time together. He hadn't gone to the club or played golf with his buddies as he normally had. And yes, I even forgave my cousin, Beverly.

On my last night in Brooklyn, I picked up my clothes from the cleaners and cooked all of my dad's favorite dishes while he spent most of the day waxing Old Betsy. I tried to tell him that he didn't need to take me to the airport, and I could get a cab. But he wasn't hearing it. It wasn't long after dinner that my dad went to bed for the night, and I packed all the rest of my things for my trip back to Atlanta. I wrapped my hair and moisturized my face before I called Clay. He said he waited on me to call him before he went to bed. He told me he didn't know if I had asked Charmine to pick me up, but he wanted to be the one to pick me up from the airport. I told him that Char had texted me earlier and stated that she expected him to pick me up, but she would be there as well. That night I was so excited to see both of them that I couldn't sleep. What I wasn't so excited about was the inevitable showdown with Faizon.

When morning came, my dad knocked on my door to wake me. It brought me back to the first day of school. It reminded me of the anxious feeling you have in the pit of your stomach to see all your old friends, but not wanting to leave the comfort of your bed for the unknown. My dad and I planned to visit my mother's resting place before I went back, so after we ate a good breakfast, we stopped by the florist shop and picked out my mother's favorite flowers. Aunt Bernice and Uncle Snuck dropped by to see me off. I thanked them for being there for me and my dad. As the time started to wind down, my dad and Uncle Snuck took all my luggage downstairs and put it in the trunk of Old Betsy.

My aunt began to tear up as she started to tell me about what we all meant to her. "Listen, Lane, I knew that I wasn't always your mama's favorite person, and a lot of days she just put up with me for your daddy's sake. I know I can be a handful a lot of the times, but always remember your old aunty Bernie loved her, and I love you too. And I'm gon' take care of your daddy as long as I got breath, so don't you worry 'bout that." We hugged until my dad came back upstairs and said we had to leave. I told my dad I had to do one more thing before I left, and I'd meet them downstairs. I went to my mother's jewelry box —put on a pair of her favorite earrings and sprayed some of her perfume on me. When I got downstairs, my dad looked at me and smiled.

"You look pretty in them. I know your mother smiling on you."

"Thanks, Daddy." Uncle Snuck and my aunt drove off before we did, and they honked at us as they passed us by. My dad joked about having to find a part-time job to keep himself busy to prevent my aunt from driving him crazy. As we approached the Eternal Gardens Cemetery, I began to feel light-headed and overwhelmingly cold. My dad advised me to sit in the car until I felt ready. He sat patiently and waited for me to compose myself. After a few minutes had passed, I felt that I was able to make it out of the car. My dad reached in the backseat and grabbed the bouquet of white orchids. We walked hand-in-hand to my mother's plot. My dad stayed with me for a bit and talked to my mother, but then he got up from the ground and told me to have some time by myself.

When he walked out of my sight, I cried openly. I told my mother that I was leaving to go back to Atlanta to be with Clay, and that I planned to enjoy my life. I also thanked her for leaving me the means to be able to do so. As I talked more about my future plans in Atlanta, I felt so calm and peaceful. I felt it was a sign that I had made the right decision, and I had my mother's blessings. My dad walked back over to me, pulled me up from the ground, and kissed my forehead. He told my mother he loved her and that he'd be back next week. When we got to the car I looked at my dad and said 'I'm ready now.'

FORBIDDEN SEDUCTION

Clay

I had been up since the crack of dawn and busied myself with my work as I waited for Lane's return. Ever since Lane had been gone, I had neglected my house terribly, and as I looked around the house at the dirty dishes, clothes piled on every chair, and papers that missed the trash can on the floor, I knew something needed to be done. I still had more than a few hours before Lane's flight touched down in Atlanta. So, I looked up a few of those house cleaning services on the internet, and I chose the first one that promised they could come out immediately. When the cleaning people arrived, I showed them the problem areas I wanted them to pay the most attention. As they started to tackle the job, I went to Publix for some essentials.

When I returned home from the store, I noticed the house started to take form, and it looked a lot better. But because my house had been in such shambles, the cleaners had taken longer than I expected. After I discarded the moldy leftover food in the fridge, I put the groceries I had just brought away. One of the cleaners entered the kitchen with a cleaning bucket in hand and insisted my cleaning package came with a bathroom cleaning as well. I promised her that I wouldn't report her if she skipped the bathrooms and rushed them along. I waited for this day for two months, and I wasn't about to let a dirty toilet keep me from being at the airport on time. Before I left for the airport, I called Shon, and I told him that he would have to handle things at the office 'cause I wasn't coming through all at. Lane's flight was scheduled to land at five, but I arrived at Hartfield's International an hour earlier. I found a Starbucks, got a cup of coffee, and waited in the arrivals section of the airport.

As I looked around the airport, I saw Charmine as she dashed through the crowd of folks like she was late for one of her court dates. "Charmine, Charmine," I called. When she heard her name being called she followed the direction of my voice. "Over here." I flagged her over towards me. She walked over to me and greeted me coldly—nothing near the warm and cheerful bond we had in Brooklyn.

"Hello Clay," she said. She looked down at her watch like she was bored with my presence. I found her reaction towards me odd but dismissed it as she may have had a lot on her mind.

"Thanks for the invite to your big day. I sent the RSVP back already."

"Yeah, I got it."

"Charmine, are you okay?"

"I'm fine."

"I thought you'd be happier than what you are to see Lane, yet you seem a little distracted."

"Oh, I am happy to see Lane. . . are you?" That shit threw me for a loop. I looked at her and sunk my neck into my chest.

"That's a fucked up question, of course I am. Why wouldn't I be?"

"Look Clay, I don't know how to be anything other than real, so I'm not going to play with you. Faizon is running around here insinuating that there's something going on with you two, and I don't know if it's true or not. I simply don't want Lane to catch wind of it, because if there is some truth to it, it's going to break her heart." I maintained my cool, but my heart was racing 'cause I didn't know what had been reported to Charmine, and I definitely didn't want to show my hand.

"Charmine, I know you don't know me like that, but you know enough about me to know I would never do anything to jeopardize what Lane and I have. Since we 'keeping it real,' yeah, when I first met Faizon there was a slight misunderstanding on my part, but we got it all out in the open. She said I mistook her intentions and we squashed it."

"Well, I hope you got through to her, because if I don't know anything else about Faizon, I know she's a firecracker, and we don't need that in our lives." If I had known all of this would have jumped off with Faizon when Lane asked me to help her, I would have never gotten involved. Charmine's right, I don't need this in my life right now, and in eighteen minutes, Lane's plane would be on the ground. Now, I got to be worried if Faizon's gonna be running around Atlanta saying I ran out of her house with my dick in my hand. I asked Charmine's advice on how I should handle it since she knew Faizon much better than I did. I wanted to keep Lane out of the mix all together, except for the small piece she already knew of.

Charmine said she wasn't implying that anything had gone on, but suggested that if something had happened, I needed to be the one to break it to Lane. I agreed with her and said I would, but it wouldn't be on her first night back. Once Charmine said what she had to say she was back to her pleasant disposition, and we talked about how glad we were to have Lane back. But I knew I couldn't celebrate just yet, I still hadn't gotten through to Faizon to stop talking about the night that never happened. If Faizon was as dangerous as she appeared, I'd be on edge every time she went out with Lane, and I couldn't have that shit on my brain.

Charmine grabbed me by my arm, and squeezed it when the arrivals board posted: Flight 247 from New York had just landed. We watched as all the people from that flight met their loved ones with hugs and kisses. Some had already picked up their luggage and was on their way out of the airport before Lane even made an appearance. It appeared that there weren't any more passengers on that flight, except for the one or two late passengers who casually strolled off.

I started to think that Lane had changed her mind about coming back to Atlanta and never boarded the plane. As I walked over to the information desk to ask if there was anyone else on that flight, I spotted this beautiful woman who had walked out and looked around the airport. I yelled out to her and sped up my pace in her direction. "Lane! Baby, over here!" She looked over and started to run to me—I snatched her up in the air. We kissed and held onto each other tightly.

"You're finally here, I can't believe it," I said and we kissed some more.

"Eww. . . get a room, why don't you," Charmine said. She pulled Lane from my arms and they roared loudly with joy. I asked Lane to give me the description of her bags, so I could retrieve them while they talked. I walked over to the conveyor belt and waited for Lane's luggage to be shot up from out of the mouth of the metal ramp. When my phone buzzed from a private number, I started not to answer because I had distinctly told Shon I did not want to be disturbed under any circumstances. But since I hadn't spoken to my mother or sister in a few days I picked up.

"Hello, this is Clay."

"Hi, Clay. I heard your girlfriend is back today, and I can't wait to see you two lovebirds."

"Faizon? You gotta stop this. Nothing happened, so why you buggin'?"

"I'm not bugging yet, Sweetheart. Tell Lane I'll talk to her later," she said, and before I had the chance say anything else, she hung up. I had to make a decision about what I needed to do, I wasn't gonna allow Lane's homecoming to be disrupted by anyone. Lane and Charmine walked over to the baggage claim just as I hung up the phone. They were both so occupied as they talked to each other that they hadn't even noticed I was on the phone in the first place. Lane walked up behind me, slipped her arms around my waist, and rested her head on my back.

"I missed you so much, Baby. I can't wait until we get home," she said.

"I missed you too. I have a surprise for you, but I'll give it to you later."

"Oohh...I can't wait!" Lane purred.

I laughed at her suggestive tone. "You can get that too, but I was talking about something else."

"Ahh, I have to know what it is now, I don't think I can wait."

"Later," I said

"Aren't those your bags, Lane?" Charmine said and pointed to the two black bags as they were about to go around the ramp again.

"Yeah, both of them are mine, Clay." I yanked up the large bags before they made another trip around. Charmine told Lane that she had to get back to the office and would call her later. Lane told Charmine she would call her instead, and she looked at me and winked. They said their goodbyes, and Charmine left to go back to her office. As we walked to the parking lot, Lane continued to grill me to tell her what her surprise was, or at least give her a tiny hint, but I refused to give her even the 'tiny' hint she begged for.

I opened the passenger's door for Lane to get in the car before I put her bags in the trunk. I looked in at her from the back of the opened trunk. I'd waited two long months to see her and now she was just a foot away—it seemed surreal. Lane appeared just as happy to see me, when I got in the car she gently grabbed my locs, and pulled my face towards hers. She pressed her opened mouth on mine and kissed me affectionately. When she started to kiss me behind my ear, I begged her to wait until we got home otherwise I wouldn't be able to make it. It was a good thing I didn't live too far from the airport, because at every stoplight, Lane touched a different area on my body, and I was tempted to pull over.

I drove recklessly into my driveway and parked. Lane pulled her set of spare keys from her purse and hopped out. "Hurry up, Clay," she yelled. "Meet me upstairs!" I slammed the car door and raced upstairs behind her. Wildly, Lane striped the clothes from her body, and then button by button, she undressed me. I laid her gently on my bed; her luscious body felt like cotton as I kissed my way down to her treasure. Lane's low, soft moans escaped her trembling body which excited me even more. As I entered her, I looked into her beautiful eyes and with each thrust I felt her pussy tighten around my dick as if she were thirstily sipping my juices. In one motion, Lane flipped my body over and got on top of me. Her nipples teased my lips as they brushed against them while she rode me masterfully. "I missed you so badly, Clay," she whispered in my ear just, as I exploded inside her. Lane rested her head on my chest, and as I held her body tightly, I knew I genuinely adored this woman.

Lane started to doze off, so I rolled her off of me onto her side of the bed. I wrapped a towel around my waist and went downstairs to see what I wanted to cook. I had stocked the shelves with fresh foods but hadn't thrown away all the outdated containers of takeaways that I lived on while Lane was away, so I quickly discarded them. I shuffled through the assortment of foods and realized I wasn't in the mood for cooking and would order some Chinese instead when Lane woke up.

With dinner plans decided, I went into my living room and poured myself a glass of Hennessy—I sat on the sofa and thought I couldn't have been more satisfied with my life than at this moment. My woman tucked away upstairs, my businesses are doing well, and I have a nice home and cars. Then in an instant, that thought was overshadowed by Charmine's advice for me to tell Lane about Faizon before she heard it from someone else, and that someone being Faizon. But I wasn't prepared to tell Lane about that night, and that on occasion, I still had sexual thoughts about Faizon.

Lane woke up when I entered the room and asked me why I allowed her to sleep for so long. I told her she looked so peaceful, and I wasn't about to disturb her. Lane climbed out of bed and put on one of my wife-beaters and a pair of her sexy panties. She asked me the time, and I told her it was after eight o'clock. Lane said her father should have been back from her aunt's house and that she wanted to call him. As she dialed his number I asked her if she wanted Chinese for dinner, and she nodded that she did. So I called in our order while she spoke to her father. When she finished her conversation with her dad, she told me that he sent his best, and then she reminded me of her surprise. I told her I'd have to take her to it, but it had to wait until after our food was delivered.

I was so starved by the time our food came that I picked at it with my fingers as Lane tried to dish it out. Lane slapped my hand down and insisted I wait until she put it on plates. We sat in the kitchen and ate our Chinese food, and we talked about all the things that had happened in her absence...well, almost everything. Lane grabbed a bottle of wine and we took our food upstairs. She expressed how pleased she was to have her old job back and wouldn't have to go through the hopeless process of having to look for another one. After we ate, Lane placed my head in her lap and lovingly stroked my face as she looked down on me with her enticing eyes. As she continued to talk about how much she missed me and that she never wanted to leave me again, she stroked my manhood until I got an erection and we made love again.

After we made love, we took a quick shower together. I hopped out before Lane and went downstairs to the car and brought in her bags. When I got back upstairs she had already dressed into some sweats and her own t-shirt this time. Lane put her hair in a ponytail and said she was she ready to see her surprise. I went downstairs to my studio and grabbed a medium sized brown envelope. When she asked me if her surprise was in the envelope, I replied 'sort of.' We hopped in my car and drove into Atlanta, and we passed a tall building on 17th Street, and Lane said it looked as if she had seen it before. I parked across from the building, we got out of the car, and walked inside the building.

I pressed the button for the elevator and gave Lane the brown envelope. I told Lane the building had looked familiar because she had seen it before. When Lane opened the envelope I told her, her new home was on the second floor and she looked at me stunned. "What do you mean my new home?"

"As of this morning the condo belongs to you." The elevators doors opened and we went up to the second floor. When Lane opened the door to the condo she said it looked exactly like it did in the virtual tour. She told me she always wanted a home with a bright, modern design and this was exactly what she wanted.

Lane turned to me in disbelief. "How, Clay?" she asked.

"What do you mean how? I called my agent, Tom, and he took care of the rest."

"Okay maybe not how, but why? I told you I didn't want you to do this. I told you I was going to put a deposit on it myself."

"And now you don't have to." I walked upstairs and looked around further, and a few minutes later, she joined me. She said she had to ask me a question which started to make me get slightly nervous.

"Charmine and I were talking the other day, and after I told her that you wanted to get me this place, she made the statement 'He must have done something and is feeling guilty.' Is that true? Do you have something to feel guilty about?" It was no way I was about to have this conversation with her now, and I wanted to put her mind at ease. So, I asked her to trust me just as I trusted her when she told me nothing happened between her and Dre.

FORBIDDEN SEDUCTION

Lane

As soon as I stepped off the plane and saw Clay's face, I knew I'd done the right thing. My first night back in Atlanta was great. I missed being held by Clay, and he held me all through the night. He made me feel secure, loved, wanted, something I could never say about Dre, and our last encounter proved as much. Clay is a man in every aspect of his life: how he manages his business, family, and me. And a couple of nights of quickie booty-calls with Dre could have cost me everything. I had a long conversation with Clay about why he purchased my condo. He assured me that there weren't any strings attached, and he had done it purely out of love.

The next morning, Clay slept later than usual, and I went downstairs and made him breakfast before he had to leave for the office. I called Char to find out what she had planned for the day as I didn't start work until next week. Charmine told me that she would pick me up from Clay's house after lunch and take me to her new office. I still hadn't heard from Faizon, but I knew it would be soon enough, because I still had to be fitted for my dress. This was my second time as maid of honor for Char's wedding, and I prayed that this time would be the dream wedding she's always wanted, and deserved.

I placed the breakfast I had just prepared for Clay on a tray and took it upstairs to him. He was still sound asleep when I entered the room. I called his name several times before he cracked his eyelids opened. "That looks good," he said when he saw his scrambled eggs, beef sausage, wheat toast, and juice placed on the night table. "Thanks, Bae."

"No, Clay, thank you. I truly appreciate all you've done, and this is the least I can do."

"What are you going to be doing while I'm at the studio today?" he asked and took a forkful of his scrambled eggs.

"My day is booked. Char is picking me up to see her new office, then I'm taking her with me to the condo, and later this evening, I have to see Faizon for my dress fitting."

"Yeah, sounds like you're booked. What time do you think you're gonna see Faizon?"

"All I know is, it'll be sometime this evening. I told you she's been acting weird lately. I haven't heard from her since the last time she called me at my parents' house, and from what Charmine is saying she acts as though there's a real problem between us."

"I wouldn't take it too personally. She sees that we're happy, Charmine's getting married—she probably feels left out. If I were you I wouldn't put too much into anything she says these days. Or, she could be a little jealous of you and Charmine—you know how y'all women are." I would have accepted Clay's theory to be a fact if Faizon wasn't as beautiful and talented as she is. However, she possessed both qualities, and there was no need for her to be jealous of me or Charmine, but something was going on. I had noticed that after I told Clay about seeing Faizon he appeared a little jumpy. He repeatedly asked me did I have any idea of when I'd see her and reminded me at least three times before I left his house not to take everything she said to me at face value. Clay didn't even finish his breakfast. He hopped in the shower and shortly afterward, he left for the office.

After I cleared the breakfast dishes, I got dressed. The weather was beautiful for April, and I didn't have to be as overdressed as I was before leaving New York. I threw on a pair of my favorite jeans, a V-neck black cardigan, and my Christian Louboutin spiked heels. When

Charmine rang the bell I was ready. I invited her in, but she said she was on a tight schedule and had to leave right away. I could see the fear in Charmine's eyes, and I knew that the stress of the wedding had started to get her. We stopped by her new office first. There were still a few areas which needed some attention, but overall their office was very impressive. We stepped over half of the used paint cans and some other builder's junk which was left on the floor as we made our way to one of the four offices.

Charmine tore the plastic off of one of the new chairs and offered me a seat. She sat behind this beautifully designed hand crafted desk with gold brackets. I looked around the office and each corner screamed with her personality. The cabinets and chairs were finished in the same gold brackets as the desk, and she still had furniture in boxes. I asked her if she had someone pick out the furniture for her, and she screwed up her face. "Girl, you know me better than that! I'm not trusting just anyone to put things in a space where I have to spend my days and probably most nights as well. I handpicked all of these items myself."

"Umm, calm down. I was only asking. What about Anthony's office, did he decorate it?"

He wanted to do it himself, but I was like no sir, I'll be in charge of all the office décor. And he's fine with it."

"I guess so, if you came at him like you just did me."

"Oh, shut up." Charmine got up from her chair and walked over to me.

"Listen Chica, I can't tell you how happy I am you're back. This is going to be a great year for us.

"I believe you—I have my old job back and a new home. I have a brand new start here. And I'm going to take advantage of it this time. How much longer are we going to be here? I'm dying to get to the condo."

"Not much longer, I'm just waiting on a delivery and then we can leave. You must be itching to hit the stores today to shop for the condo; it's going to be beautiful once you get it all decorated."

"I know. I already have some things in mind that I want to get for it," I said. I started to list all of the shops I wanted to get my furnishings from when my cell went off. I looked at the screen and

Clay's face popped up. "Hey Sweetie, what you doing?" Clay really didn't have much to say, he was more concerned with if I had seen Faizon yet, and when I told him I hadn't, he seemed relieved. When I got off the phone, Charmine asked me what all that was about, and I told her I honestly didn't know. The way I looked at it, I should have been the one who was so nervous. The fact that Faizon had such flammable ammunition about me and Dre was too much for me to grasp. And it appeared she was waiting on that exact moment to strike her match.

The furniture for the other two offices had arrived, and after they were set up to Charmine's satisfaction, we left her office. Charmine was accurate in her estimation of the distance from my condominium to her office. We could have walked there as she stated. When we stepped into my living room, the panoramic view was the first thing you saw. I couldn't wait until nighttime fell—to be able to see the Atlanta skyline—as it would join me in my living room. As I showed her the entire layout of the condo, we talked about what I needed to make it look like the cover of Home Design magazine.

As I fluttered around the condo and started to designate where I wanted things to go, Charmine cut me off in mid-sentence. "We've talked about everything today except for how in the world you ended up in Dre's bed again?" My face dropped as I was a bit caught off-guard because we were just discussing kitchen appliances.

"That's because there was no need to bring it up. I told you everything there was to know when I was back in Brooklyn, and I'd like to forget all about it."

"No, you didn't. You gave me some quick version of a night you claimed you had partied and drank too much. You're an intelligent woman, and I'm trying to understand how you allowed Dre to coerce you into having sex with him. Unless, he didn't have to coerce you at all," she said. She walked around the empty space, and where we agreed moments earlier a table should go, she stood there with her arms folded and questioned me as if I were one of her hostile witnesses. I was so over this conversation and wished I had never said anything to her about it.

"Char, I don't know why you are so bothered by it. I've already told you more than I wanted to tell you. What's done is done, and I can't change it."

"I'm not bothere---, yes, I am bothered. It wasn't like you two had the best relationship in the beginning. He cheated on you several times, so what would make you go down the path already traveled, I don't know. You better pray Clay never finds out about this."

"And you know what? There wouldn't have been any chance of that if you hadn't opened your fat mouth to Faizon! Now she's around here on some bitches running wild shit, thinking she's gonna blackmail me, and that's not about to happen."

"Listen, Lane. By no means am I defending Faizon, but you knew her moral back story when she lied to our faces about her affair with Darnell. Remember how she swore to us she didn't know he was married; we didn't find out the truth until she was already in the hospital. And you see what it cost her."

"Yeah, and look at what it might cost me. Do you think I want to lose Clay? And thanks to you, that may be what the hell happens."

"No you don't. You don't get to make me responsible for your actions with Dre. I didn't slip his dick inside you. If nothing else, take ownership of your own mistake." She walked over to me and rested her hand on my shoulder. "Lane, you're my best friend, and I love you like my sister. I just want you to be happy, but I'm afraid that if Clay finds out, that will be the end of your relationship."

"Don't worry about it. Nothing is going to come between us." I softened my tone as I knew that Charmine was concerned about the possibility of my relationship with Clay ending over this.

"Why, are you going to tell him?"

"Hell no! Like I said, there's no reason to hurt Clay. And please stop worrying about it so much. You have enough to think about with your wedding day right around the corner."

Charmine closed her eyes and took a deep breath. "I know, which reminds me we need to be leaving soon. We have to meet Faizon." I looked at my watch and realized how late it was, but I wasn't looking forward to seeing Faizon at all. Charmine and I left my condo and started the journey to Faizon's. After Faizon had fully recovered from her injuries inflicted by Darnell, she moved out of her parents' home and bought herself a nice house in the Lithonia area. Her over protective father had a fit when she first suggested she wanted to live on her own, but Faizon can be quite persuasive when she wants something...or someone.

The normal thirty-minute drive from Atlanta to Lithonia took over an hour due to the standstill Atlanta traffic. When we finally arrived at Faizon's, I couldn't help but admire her beautiful brick house from the outside. Before we got out of the car, Charmine told me she wanted to avoid any confrontation, and asked that I adopt the same mentality. I told her I would as long as Faizon stayed in her lane. Charmine popped her trunk, and she pulled out a garment bag with her bridal veil inside. This would have been the last fitting before the actual wedding —the first time I laid eyes on my dress and Faizon since I had been back.

I waited for Charmine by the passenger's side door while she gathered some papers from the backseat of her car. Charmine's nervous actions were perceptible as she fidgeted over the stack of papers in her car. "Did you leave something at the office?" I asked.

Charmine picked up a piece of paper from the floor of her car and scanned it briefly. "Got it," she said, and she waved the paper in the air to show me. "And Lane, please remember what I said."

"Oh please," I said. I walked ahead of her and rang the doorbell. Faizon opened the door. She was dressed impeccably in an off the shoulder grey dress and black designer boots. With all that had been said, I was taken aback when she pulled me into her home and gave me a big hearty hug.

"Hey Girl, welcome back," Faizon said. I couldn't see Charmine's reaction to my welcoming reception from Faizon from where I stood, due to the extended hug she'd given me, but I felt the heat from her eyes as she brushed passed us to enter the house. Faizon gave Charmine a hug once she turned me loose. "Y'all come on in. I was just about to call y'all—I thought you had forgot." Charmine and I followed her in her living room.

"Faizon, you know better. You know I wasn't about to forget I had to be here today. I also brought my veil to see if it'll match with the dress," Charmine said. Faizon told us to take a seat in this lovely room surrounded by eclectic pieces which suited Faizon's artsy and creative personality.

"Lane, you looking good, girl. It looks like you lost some weight since the last time we saw each other," Faizon said.

"Thanks, Faizon, I have lost some weight. I guess from all the stress."

"I hear that. Again, I hate I couldn't be there for you. I had a lot going on here with that whole Darnell thing still."

"Forget about it. I told you I understood when you called." Charmine looked back and forth at us as if she were watching a tennis match as she listened to our cordial exchange. But you could detect the underlined phoniness from the both of us. I guess we were feeling each other out to see who would strike first.

"Y'all want something to drink? I have some wine chilling in the fridge," Faizon said. Charmine and I both wanted some, so Faizon got up to fix our drinks. "I'll be back in a sec."

"Cool," Charmine said, and she unzipped the garment bag with her veil. It was a stunning long- lace white veil. As Charmine handled the delicate lace, she smiled broadly, and I suddenly felt bad that I hadn't been there with her as she shopped for the most important day of her life. While Faizon was still in the kitchen, I touched Charmine's elbow to grab her attention. "Char, I want you to know I feel horrible that you had to do all of this by yourself. I wish I could rewind time, I'd do everything differently."

"Let's not talk about that here. The main thing is you're here now." Charmine lowered her tone when she noticed Faizon had returned with our drinks. "Oh, I need that," Charmine said as she took the glass of wine from Faizon's hands.

I had taken my glass from the tray and put it straight to my lips, but Faizon interrupted me. "Not yet!" She pushed my glass away from my mouth, and raised her glass "We have to make a toast. To Charmine, here's wishing you and Anthony long life, perfect health, and a solid loving marriage. Cheers!"

"Cheers!" Charmine and I both chimed in. Although we talked, drank, and laughed together the atmosphere was strained. After Faizon finished her wine, she asked Charmine to follow her upstairs to her sewing room to try on her dress. Charmine started to giggle with jubilation. She looked at me and smiled, then made her way up the stairs behind Faizon. While they were upstairs, I checked my phone for texts and emails. Although I had blocked Dre's number from my phone before I left Brooklyn, I still checked regularly to see if he tried to contact me. What I couldn't block were the vivid memories of us as I lay collapsed in Dre's perspired arms after he'd brought me to delicious orgasms.

Charmine stood at the top of the stairs and called my name which broke my concentration. I swung my head to answer her call, and I walked over to the stairs to be faced with a stunning Charmine. I threw my hands over my mouth and gasped—the dress couldn't have been any more perfect. The white lace mermaid dress with a sweetheart neckline fit her like skin. Charmine walked down the stairs and modeled her dress up close for me. When she turned around, she revealed the stunning dipped back aligned with pearls. She held onto her veil as she twirled around and around like a little girl. "How do I look?" she asked.

An unexpected tear escaped my eye. "You look radiant."

"Don't cry, Lane," Charmine said. "You're gonna get me started."

"And me too," Faizon said, as came from out of the shadows. "Charmine, I had no idea you'd look this fabulous." Charmine grabbed Faizon down from off the last step and embraced her. When Charmine released her, Faizon told me I was up next. Faizon warned me in advance that since this would be my first fitting, I shouldn't be too upset if my dress didn't fit me as nicely as Charmine's had. Charmine joined us upstairs. She carefully took her dress off and placed it back in the bag. Faizon walked over to her clothes rail and pulled down another garment bag. She unzipped it and pulled out a gorgeous purple strapless gown. I took my clothes off and tried the dress on, and surprisingly, it fit my body nicely for it to have been my first fitting. Faizon hadn't completed the dress as it still had a few pinned areas which needed to be sewn up. She cautioned me not to lose any more weight between now and the wedding because she would have to make alterations to the dress at the last minute.

After I took my dress off, Faizon put the lovely garment back into its bag and hung it next to Charmine's dress. We went back downstairs to the living room and finished off the bottle of wine. Charmine kicked off her shoes and put her feet up on the sofa. "I better call Anthony and tell him not to make dinner for me tonight 'cause it looks like I'll be drinking my dinner," Charmine said. The way we keeled over from laughter at Charmine's corny comment—I could tell we were on our way to being tipsy

While Charmine was on the phone with Anthony, Faizon asked me if I was glad to be back in Atlanta. I told her I definitely was, but her next statement was when I knew it would take a nasty turn from there. "Girl, it seemed like you were never gonna come back to Atlanta. Clay must have told you something, 'cause you hurried your ass back here pretty quick."

"Something like what?" I asked, and placed my glass of wine on the glass coffee table.

"Never mind. But you should've known better than to leave a man like that alone in Atlanta for too long," she said as she emptied her glass of wine in one sip, and poured another.

"Meaning...?"

"Just what I said—a man like Clay shouldn't be left alone." I heard the inflection in her voice, and I knew I wouldn't be able to keep my promise to Clay or to Charmine now.

"I agree. Especially nowadays with these ratchet-ass women who have no regard if the men they sleep with are in relationships or not. But some women are just dirty like that and knowingly sleep with married men, their friend's man...it just doesn't matter to some women. Does it Faizon?" I clenched my teeth and dared her with my eyes to continue. I was ready for her. It was apparent that Faizon wanted me to know something as she continued on.

"A woman can't sleep with their friend's man, or any man, if he isn't a willing participant," she fired back.

"Okay, let me stop talking in riddles and let you in on something. Clay already told me about how you made a fool of yourself by rubbing your fake-ass tits all up in his face. And I can guarantee you, Clay wasn't a willing participant."

"First of all Hun, these are as real as yours," she said and squeezed her breasts together. "And if that's what he's told you, and you believe him...okay. But I can guarantee you there's a lot more to this story." Charmine took the phone away from her ear in disbelief and frowned in our direction.

"Babe, let me call you right back," she said. Charmine rushed over and stood in between us as we were now in each other's face in a heated argument. "What the hell happened? she shouted, "I was only on the phone for two friggin' minutes."

"There isn't anymore to this story, but if it is, it's real fucked up on your end because we were supposed to be friends!" I was so upset my mouth got as dry as sand and my eyes started to twitch. I totally ignored Charmine as she pulled me back from Faizon's face, but I had a lot more to get off my chest, and I finished. "I don't know what you've conjured up in that little brain of yours, but I'm here to tell you —Clay don't want you, Boo."

"Lane, believe it or not, I am your friend. I could have told Clay all about you and Dre. I certainly had the opportunity, but I decided not to." I shot Charmine a resentful look, because if it had not been for her gossiping, Faizon would not have known anything about what happened. Charmine hurried back over to the sofa and put her shoes back on and motioned for me to do the same. I got my things to leave Faizon's house before it went any further. But before we left I had to let Faizon know one last thing.

"Clay doesn't want you, Faizon. And if you think I would trust anything you say, you're mad. Especially after the way you chased Darnell's married ass down. Look how you tried to break up that man's family 'cause you thought he wanted you too. But what did it get you? A week in ICU, AND you can't have any more children."

"LANE! Stop." Charmine screamed. "Now you've gone too far, let's just go." As soon as those words left my mouth I wanted so badly to have been able to retract them. Faizon just stood there seemingly unfazed by my venomous words.

"You can say and believe what you'd like, but you're wrong about one thing. I wouldn't have to chase Clay. And if I were you I'd ask him how I know that." With that, Charmine practically ran out of the house, and I certainly didn't have the energy to keep up this exchange, so I surrendered and followed Charmine out to her car. We got in the car and Charmine drove off in huff. Other than the occasional grunts and deep sighs which Charmine expelled, we rode home in complete silence. Several different emotions stirred within me: anger, sadness, hurt, and I felt sorry for some of the things I said to Faizon. I remembered when I first met her. One of the first things she said to me was 'women don't like me, and I don't like women.' At the time, I laughed about it, but now I completely understood why that was.

Charmine finally broke her silence and asked me if I was going back to my condo or to Clay's. I told her to take me to Clay's as I had to get things sorted out. I wanted to put this issue between him and Faizon to rest. Charmine looked at me with one raised eyebrow and creased her forehead. "Normally, I wouldn't advise this because I'm a firm believer that honesty is the best policy, but do us both a favor and leave that shit alone," she said and rolled her eyes at me. "Don't start a fight you can't finish; your hands aren't clean Lane, or have you forgotten?"

"So you think it's okay for Faizon to imply that she may have been intimate with Clay?"

"I think implied is better than fact in this instance. It is a *fact* that you slept with Dre. She's only made up some silly story to wind you up. Plus, didn't you tell her that you would never believe her word over Clay's?"

"I do believe Clay. But even you have to admit, he's been acting kinda scary ever since I told him I was going to see her today."

"Do what you want to do, Lane, but be prepared for any repercussion that you'll bring on yourself. And this may sound selfish on my part, but I'm getting married in two weeks—do you think I want or need this craziness from you and Faizon right now? Please Lane...as your best friend, I'm asking you to please leave it for now. If anything did happen between them you'll find out soon enough." Charmine dropped me off in the driveway of Clay's house and sped off without a goodbye or anything. I put my key in the lock, but before I could turn the handle, Clay pulled the door opened and let me in.

"How was it? Did everything go good?"

"Yeah Clay, everything went fine," I lied. And I decided that I would keep up the lie until after Charmine's wedding. Her happiness had now become my priority.

FORBIDDEN SEDUCTION

Charmine

Unbelievable. Everything that could have gone wrong had gone terribly wrong. Planning permission for the extension to our new office had been denied. I allowed Emily to take Jayla's junior bridesmaid dress home against Faizon's wishes, and while Jayla played dress-up, she spilled grape Kool-Aid on the dress. Oh yeah...and my two best friends are at war. Lately, the only peace I had gotten was in the courtroom with the murderers, rapists, and the career criminals. I tried my best to remain neutral in this Lane and Faizon fiasco, but it's gotten harder each day. I've had to be the sounding board to both ladies as they've bitched about each other, and I was tired of it.

Anthony had been a real sweetheart. He'd seen the stress the girls had been putting me under, and he had done his best to alleviate most of it. So he set up a mini office for me so that I could work from home. But that wasn't all: he did all of the shopping, cooking, and fought with the building inspectors to get Martin & Martin opened. It was bad enough that the official date had to be pushed back because of the issues that surrounded the planning permission. First on my agenda was to make sure that Emily found another dress for Jayla before the wedding.

FORBIDDEN SEDUCTION

When I had no choice but to tell Faizon about the dress catastrophe, she ranted for the better part of an hour on how she begged me not to take it from her home. She voiced her concern that any dress we bought for Jayla wouldn't be up to standard, walking alongside her original creations. I tried my best to assure her that we would look for a dress very similar to Jayla's original dress. We had one more rehearsal before the wedding, and when I received calls from two of my bridesmaids saying they couldn't attend, I was done.

Lane had gone back to work at the bank, but she managed to get an afternoon off so we could shop for the bridal party gifts. I picked her up from Clay's house after I left my office. On the surface it appeared that Lane and I were fine, but I still detected some underlined displeasure, which I assumed was because I had broken her trust. I wanted us to get it out in the open, but Lane refused. Lane and I drove to Tiffany & Co. in Phipps Plaza for the gifts. I knew I wanted all the ladies to have a piece of jewelry, but hadn't determined if I wanted them to have a bracelet, earrings, or a pendant. The saleswoman who assisted me saw I had a hard time deciding on what to buy and innocently hinted that Lane should be more helpful. Lane exploded on the poor woman. "This isn't my damn wedding," she howled, and then she turned to me. "Maybe you should have brought your friend Faizon. You two seem to share everything nowadays."

I turned to the saleswoman apologetically and said, "Excuse us for a minute." The puzzled woman gave Lane the evil eye as she walked over to another counter. "Where did that come from?"

"I'm really not feeling this."

"Not feeling what? Shopping...what?" I was confused as to why Lane decided to spazz out now.

"Since you want to talk about it so badly, lets," she said.

"Here? Right now? Why don't we wait until we can sit down and discuss it properly." Lane backed away from the counter while I walked over to the saleswoman for help. The saleswoman returned and I asked her for advice on the silver pendants in the display case, and we both agreed that the pendants would make a lifelong gift. I gave her my credit card and the initials of all the bridesmaids to have them all engraved. She returned with my receipt and told me the pendants would be ready in two days for collection or I could have them

148

delivered; I told her I would pick them up myself. Since neither Lane nor I had anything to eat, we chose this Italian steakhouse inside Phipps Plaza.

We were seated and handed menus. I told the waiter I knew what I wanted and ordered a grilled chicken salad—Lane chose the same. Lane looked across the restaurant with her elbows on the table, fingers interlocked, and soundless. "Now, back to what you were saying in Tiffany's," I said.

"Charmine, I tried very hard not to say anything on the subject because I thought it was all resolved, but I can't seem to let it go."

"I thought it was over too, and I apologized to you. So what else is bothering you? I want us to be able to move on."

"It's easy for you, because you weren't the one who was betrayed. I still don't see why you had to tell Faizon about me and Dre."

"Lane, as I told you before, there were a lot of factors which led me to tell her. It wasn't like I called her up one day and said 'Girl, let me tell you what I heard' it was nothing like that. I had a little too much to drink, and I was stressed the hell out. We've been friends for years, and you should know that it wasn't done out of malice. Faizon sensed that I was worried about you, and it just slipped out and I've regretted it since."

"I do know that, Char. My feelings are hurt, and now that Faizon has something like this on me, it's made me sick to my stomach. We both know she's planning her attack—like a jungle animal."

"I know she is, but I believe it's more to it than that."

"Like what?"

"If I tell you, can you handle it?" Lane thought a minute and nodded she could. "I believe you're questioning if you're truly in love with Clay, because if you are than how could you have slept with Dre." Lane unclasped her fingers and hid her face in her palms. After the waiter brought our salads to the table and left, Lane told me that she loved Clay and hoped one day to marry him, but she felt Dre was her addiction. For the first time, Lane openly confessed that she had known for some time that Dre had cheated on her numerous times, and even when she caught him in the act with Renee, she still wanted to be with him.

"Is there something wrong with me to still have feelings for him?"

she asked.

"That's hard for me to answer. On my wedding day, Kamel left me at the altar. As soon as I left the church, my feelings for him died. The hate allowed me to cover up my humiliation, but that was how I chose to deal with it, all women are different."

"But you're so happy now. No one would ever suspect you were going through anything. How do I get where you are?"

"You have to know you're important and love yourself wholly. What you've done is made Dre more important than you—which is why you've always accepted his behavior." Lane said that's exactly what happened during their relationship and beyond. Lane said she felt better now that she had completely opened up. I told her to make sure she had gotten it all out of her system as I didn't want us to have this same discussion two months from now. We finished our meal and I took Lane back to Clay's house. She said her first day back at work had her pooped out. I asked her when she'd be moving into her condo, and she said over the weekend when her furniture would be delivered.

I drove up Clay's driveway and parked. Lane turned to face me. "Thanks for being a good friend. I know I haven't been such a good friend to you lately, but I'm back now. I'm even going to make amends with Faizon. You really don't need the added pressure from our childish rants."

"That means the world to me. I'll call you when I get in, love you."

"I love you too, Girl. Talk to you later." I watched her walk in the door before I pulled off this time. Whew, that was one burden lifted off me. Now, if we could find a replacement dress for Jayla I'd truly be stress free. When I got home Anthony was in the shower, and he didn't hear me come in. I got undressed and joined him the shower.

"Aaahh. . . you scared me," Anthony shouted with his eyes full of soap. "Where have you been? I've been calling you all day." I hugged him and laid my head on his hairy, lathered body.

"I didn't get any calls from you, but I told you this morning I was going to buy my bridesmaids gifts today. Then, Lane and I had dinner at this nice restaurant in Phipps Plaza. We should go there sometimes."

"I know you're just coming in, and I don't want to dump anything else on you, but I've got some good news and some bad news. Which do you prefer to hear first?" he asked and continued to vigorously wash his hair.

"Oh, God...goods news first, I guess." I moved Anthony's body to the side so I could let the water beat down on my body.

"OK, Emily called and said she found Jayla another dress at this vintage shop, and she picks it up tomorrow.

"Oohh, that's great news, Baby! I was worried about that all afternoon. I almost don't want to hear the bad news 'cause it'll take away from the good news."

"Well, it's up to you," he said and switched our positions again so he could stand under the water to rinse the soap off his body. "You don't have to know."

"No. Go ahead, shoot."

"I'm too tired to have sex with you tonight," he said and started to laugh hysterically."

I slapped his wet butt, and I joined in with his hearty laughter. "I must say I'm a bit disappointed that you won't be performing tonight, but I'll just have to get over it. And tonight at dinner, Lane said she'll work things out with Faizon. Everything is finally coming together." Anthony stepped out of the shower before me and continued to tell me about what happened at the law firm. He explained that the building inspector said we'd be able to extend out and not up as we hoped. I asked Anthony if there was anything I needed to do, but he said he'd already called our architect to draw up some more plans. And worse case scenario the work will be finished a few weeks behind schedule.

Anthony stopped talking to me, so I thought he was waiting for me to finish with my shower to discuss the situation further. But when I walked into our bedroom, Anthony was stretched out on our bed in a deep sleep. I covered him up with a duvet, kissed him, and went into my office to finish some work. I checked my emails and opened one from Emily. She had sent me a picture of Jayla's replacement dress to have a look at it. I was pleasantly surprised to see how well she'd done in choosing Jayla's dress. The lace was very similar to my dress, and it was a pale purple which would contrast nicely with the other bridesmaids dresses. I replied back to her email and thanked her for helping me find one so quickly.

We had one more hurdle that we needed to contend with and that was the sell of our house. One man had showed extreme interest in the house and even agreed to our asking price. Anthony and I were confident that his paperwork would be fine and that our old house would be sold in a matter of weeks.

Before I went to bed, I called Lane. We talked awhile before she said Clay had just come home, and she wanted to make his dinner. I snuggled next to Anthony and mulled over how well everything turned out for us today. I hadn't realized how enervated I was until I felt the pressure as it left my body. I woke the next morning to Anthony's rendition of How Deep Is Your Love, and thought I would have to introduce him to my collection of Barry White's greatest hits real soon.

I stumbled into the kitchen where Anthony had prepared breakfast and placed it on the table. He was dressed and about to leave for the office. "What's on your agenda today?" he asked.

"I have a consultation this morning, but I'm free pretty much the rest of the day. Why, what's up?" I asked.

"Nothing really, but it would be nice to have supper with you tonight. Ever since Lane's been back, she's been commanding a lot of your time."

"Oh, sweetheart, I'm sorry about that. Of course we can have dinner together tonight, and you know what…I'll even cook."

"Sounds great," he said and gave me a peck on my cheek. "See you tonight." I finished my breakfast before I left for my consult. I called Faizon while en route to my appointment and told her the good news about Jayla's dress. I told her I would send her a picture of it when I reached my destination. Faizon continued her tirade about the dress having been bought online, but I disregarded her annoyed sighs and told her the dress looked fine.

"If I don't like it she won't be wearing it, and I mean it Charmine."

"Please, stop trying to create a problem. And she will wear the dress because this is my wedding, and I make those decisions. I just happen to know you'll love it."

"The only person I know who creates problems for herself is Lane."

"Faizon, I'm not going there with you. The only reason I called was to tell you about the dress. …But since you brought her up, you're actually wrong about Lane. We were together last night and she said she wants to put all of this behind her, so maybe you'll meet her halfway.

"I want nothing more," she said sarcastically.

"I bet. Anyway, I'll send you the picture in a few."

"Okay, I'll look out for it. I'll call later to tell you what I think." I told her that would be fine. I was a bit perturbed by Faizon's statement about Jayla's dress. I don't think I could have appreciated her any more for making all of my dresses for the wedding, but Faizon was a bit presumptuous to think she'd dictate who'd wear what at my wedding.

I agreed to meet with the couple at their home since our office wasn't ready yet. As I approached the neighborhood of the million-dollar plus homes in Sandy Springs, I thought how nice it would be for Anthony and I to live in one of them. I found the address to my potential new clients and pulled into the driveway of their home. It was suited for a top grossing movie star, and it intrigued me to know why they needed a lawyer. I was greeted warmly by the polite husband and wife, and after a short briefing, the young couple revealed they were suspected of being drug dealers. I was suspect myself. During our consult, I learned they weren't gainfully employed and avoided any inquiries to explain their wealth. At the end of the consultation, I advised them it would be wise to seek legal counsel, and they immediately retained me before I left their premises.

I promised Anthony a home cooked meal, so I stopped by the market. I bought the ingredients for Chicken Alfredo and a bottle of wine. I called Anthony to tell him I was on my way home. He said he'd be home later than expected as he had to go over a few things with the architect. In the meantime, I received a call from Tiffany & Co to say that the pendants for my bridesmaids would be ready for pick up tomorrow afternoon. As I looked over my to-do list, I felt the brunt of not having hired a wedding planner. I had been swamped with work and didn't have time to get everything done on my own. So I called Lane and read her an excerpt from an article titled: Duties of A Maid of Honor, I found in one of those bridal magazines.

Lane agreed she hadn't been the best help to me and asked me to email my list of things which still needed to be done. I told her she would have it first thing in the morning, and I started to cook dinner. At first glance everything seemed to have fallen apart. I made things out to be bigger than they actually were. Now that Lane has assumed more responsibility to help me, what could possibly go wrong?

Clay

Ever since that day Lane had her dress fitting at Faizon's house, she'd been a little standoffish. Every time I asked her if anything wrong, she swore to me that nothing was the matter. If Faizon's launch date wasn't as close as it was—I would have directed her to hire another company. But I was mindful that it wouldn't have looked good on my company or on me as a businessman. And more importantly, it would have definitely raised a red flag with Lane.

I had removed myself totally from Faizon's event this time, and she hadn't created the fuss like she did the first time I'd done it. And when I told Shon, he couldn't have been happier. He called her everyday for any kind of bullshit just to hear her voice. Regrettably, there were times I wanted to hear her voice myself, but I avoided her like the plague and with good reason. We had a lot of upcoming scheduled events with my company, so I held a meeting with my market and development team. And twenty minutes into it, Shon left in an unexplained hurry.

After the meeting finished, I called to ask him why he rushed out of the meeting the way he did. He told me that Faizon had called him and wanted to meet with him. He said she wanted to discuss the models that would be used to model her clothes. I didn't believe that pretext and asked him what she really wanted.

155

And he made it clear something other than the models roster was discussed. When he finished bragging on his morning's performance, I became heated. "Shon, tell me you didn't sleep with her?"

"Nah. There was no sleeping involved."

"You know what the fuck I'm asking! Did you fuck her?" I barked.

"Why you trippin'? Why are you worried about what happened between us, sounds like you jealous or sumthin."

"Jealously has nothing to do with it. I'm trippin' cause you're mixing my business for your pleasure, and I can't have that."

"You can't have that...or her? I thought you was madly in love already, or did you forget about Lane?"

"Now who's tripping? Hell nah, I haven't forgotten about Lane. I was mainly thinking about you and Pamela. Y'all just got back together."

"Man, you could give a fuck about me and Pam's relationship. You just tried to hook me up with a broad at the Hawks game a couple of weeks ago. Let me put you out your misery, I didn't tap that but she did shine me up though. And yo, the bitch is bad." As Shon proceeded to tell me how skilled she was with her tongue, I sat down at my desk and envisioned her full, luscious lips going down on him. Before I spoke another word to Shon, I turned down the volume on my aggression before he completely exposed the fact that I was crazy with jealousy.

Shon and I came to an agreement that he wouldn't see her any more unless it was business related. But when I got off the phone with Shon, I realized I'd made a fool's agreement with a fool. Faizon was a temptress, and Shon was no match for her seductive nature. I had to be a hundred percent sure that Shon wouldn't be tempted to put my business at risk any more, and I knew how. I called Nikole, my entertainment manager, to my office. "Yes, Clay?" she asked.

"It's about Faizon Hill."

"Oh, how ironic. I just met with Amani; she'll be performing three tracks off her new album on that night. I also spoke to the owner of Danielle Danielle Models, and she'll be providing the models for the event."

"Sounds great, but I wanted to talk to you about taking lead on this one. I feel Ms. Hill needs a woman's touch. So, I need you to email her and let her know that you'll be taking the helms as of today." Nikole seemed happy to hear the new development. She wanted this event from the beginning. She once said to me, an event like this would have allowed her to showcase her talents and stamp her signature in the Atlanta entertainment arena.

"Oh Clay, thanks! I won't let you or Ms. Hill down. But what about Shon? He just told me this was his best gig ever."

"Don't worry about Shon, I'll deal with him." I passed Shon's notes on to Nikole, and she left my office a very happy woman. Later that evening I told Shon he was removed from the project, and he hit the roof. Shon didn't want to admit that Faizon had played him to get at me or that she plotted and used him, knowing he would tell me what happened at her place. Shon questioned my motives once again. He said I needed to make sure that Lane is who I really wanted, because my actions proved differently. Throughout the day I tried to tune out Shon's words that played in stereo sound over and over in my head. He was dead wrong when he stated I had forgotten about Lane. That would never happen, but I had to admit that my fantasies about Faizon grew.

I arrived home before Lane that evening and poured myself a double Hennessy. I turned on the TV to watch the game, but I wasn't interested. I laid back on the couch and reminisced about me and Lane's first date. I recalled how proudly I stated to her that I'm a man, and I handled my business like a man. And it was important to me that Lane respected me as a man, so I knew what had to be done. Of course, I would have rather been able to ignore my feelings instead of what I had to do. But, when Lane got home I would have to come clean about my fantasies and worse...that night at Faizon's house.

I called Lane and asked her how far she was from the house, she said she had just dropped off some kitchen stuff she purchased for her condo and was on her way to the house. The distance from her condo to my house was less than an hour. That would had given me time to get relaxed and go over what I wanted to say—soften the inevitable blow. Lane arrived with a full Chinese meal from Hsu's. She said I had gotten her hooked on their barbecue ribs and had the taste for them. I waited for her upstairs in my bedroom while she plated up the food.

Lane came upstairs with our food. She placed some napkins in between us and hopped on the bed. Lane grabbed for the remote and turned to the HBO channel. "Let's find a good movie," she said and tossed some soy sauce in my lap. "But nothing too violent, I want a good night's sleep."

"Yeah, go 'head, Bae," I said. I didn't have much of an appetite, so I just stared down into my plate. Lane noticed that I hadn't ripped into my Chinese ribs as I've been known to do, and she stopped flipping through the channels and looked over at me.

"Are you okay?"

"Yeah Bae, I'm good." I said, and she went back to the TV. I put a rib in my mouth, and it just didn't taste as good. I really just wanted to get this over with. I reached over and took the remote from Lane's hand.

"Hey, what you doing? I just found something for us to watch." I placed my plate of food on my night able and turned to her.

"Lane. I need to talk to you."

"Uh-oh, I guess this is about your mother's picture frame. The other day I was looking at how much you resemble her, and it slipped right of out my hands. I'm sorry I didn't tell you this right away, but I was hoping that you didn't notice it. I've already ordered another one just like it and it'll be here in two days.

"No, it's not that." When I told Lane that wasn't what I wanted to talk to her about, she looked confused. She also put her food on the night table on her side of the bed and sat with her back pressed against the headboard.

"Then what is it?" she asked. I started from when Faizon and I first met, but since I have already told Lane about that, she seemed to have handled that well. But as I disclosed the full accounts of that night I went over to Faizon's house is when I could see she started to get really upset. I watched in agony as her eyes filled with tears. I knew she had suffered enough, but I wanted her to know everything so I continued. When I confessed I had been fantasizing about Faizon, Lane cried openly. I reached over to touch her, and she pulled away from me violently. "Don't touch me, Clay! You lied to me! I kept asking you had anything happened, and you kept telling me nothing happened. And Faizon...that bitch! She kept throwing hints that something happened between you two. Argh. . . no wonder she was laughing at me." She edged off the bed in a huff and attempted to run out of the room. I pulled her back into me and held her with my arms wrapped firmly around her waist.

"Lane, do you think this was easy for me to tell you this? It wasn't, but I want our relationship to be an honest one. So, I'm telling you this because I don't want any secrets between us. I love you, Lane." She squirmed to be released, but I held her tighter.

"I don't want to hear any more. I'm leaving," she said.

"Please, Lane. Please don't go—let me explain."

"Explain what? How you allowed a woman I called my friend to almost have your dick in her mouth, and how you've still been having lustful thoughts about her?" she screamed. All at once she mustered up enough strength and broke free from my embrace. "Get off of me, Clay!" She ran down the stairs, grabbed her bag, and left my house. I sat back down on my bed and pounded the top of my night table. It went just as I thought it would go. I never expected Lane to accept my transgression—I only wanted her to know the truth, my truth.

FORBIDDEN SEDUCTION

Lane

I'd left Clay's house in a dizzied fury and drove at top speed to my condo. The entire way home Clay repeatedly called my cell, and each time, I pressed the ignore button. It was a mystery how I made it home without having killed myself as I don't remember if I even stopped at any traffic lights. I parked my car and rushed upstairs to my condo. I fumbled to get the door opened and tripped over the shopping bags I had put there in a hurry. I closed the door with my back, crouched over my knees, and cried wildly. I slumped to the floor as the images of Faizon's mouth on Clay and him enjoying it flooded my head.

I resisted calling Charmine as long as I could, but I needed to talk to her. I crawled to my bag a few inches from me and pulled out my cell phone. "What's up, Chica?" Charmine answered all cheery.

"Char...Char," I cried.

"Lane? What's happened?"

"Clay...Faizon, they were at her house, he's been. . ."

"Lane! Calm down. You're not making any sense, and I don't understand what you're trying to tell me. What about Clay?" I sat against the kitchen island with my knees in the air and composed myself.

"Tonight, Clay admitted to me that he's been having sexual

fantasies about Faizon, and it almost got physical."

"What!? In his thoughts or for real?"

"For real."

"When?"

"The week before I came back to Atlanta, Faizon got him to come over and she...and he." I couldn't force myself to verbalize any further.

"Where are you now?"

"I'm at the condo. I left his house as soon as he told me."

"Well, you can't stay there. You don't have any furniture yet."

"I can, I'll sleep on the floor."

"Now you're talking crazy, and you have to be at work tomorrow. I'm on my way to get you."

"No, Char. I'll be alright, right here."

"Shut up, I'm on my way. I'll call you when I'm downstairs and you come on down."

"Thank you, Char."

"I'm on my way." I was glad Charmine suggested she'd come get me. I wasn't in the right frame of a mind to stay in an unfurnished condominium. I found two Tylenol's in my bag, opened the box of glasses I bought earlier, and poured some water for my splitting headache. I followed Charmine's advice and calmed down. After I drank several tall glasses of water I started to think somewhat more clearly. I focused my attention to Faizon, and how she had been the main culprit in this sham. I went to my call log and dialed her number. I wasn't surprised when she didn't answer, but that didn't stop me.

"Hello Faizon, this is Lane. I want you to know that Clay told me everything tonight, and I know what you've been up to, you sneaky bitch." I pressed the end button and put my phone back in my bag. As I waited for Charmine to call me, I picked up the bags I had tripped over earlier, and I was placing them on the counter when my phone rang. I thought it may have been Charmine, but it was Clay again and I sent him straight to my voice mail. About a minute later, my phone beeped indicating he'd left a message. I was tempted to listen to it, but just as I lifted the phone to my ear Charmine called and told me she was downstairs. I turned my lights off, locked my door, and met her downstairs.

It was evident I had interrupted Charmine's night. She was dressed in a baggy t-shirt, flannel pajama bottoms, and her hair was pushed up under one of Anthony golf hats. I slid in her front seat, and we just looked at each other and shook our heads. It was such a familiar scene from our old college days. One of us would have had a traumatic breakup, and we always ended up consoling each other by the end of the night with a large pepperoni pizza and some tissues. Charmine told me to tell her everything that Clay had told me and not to leave anything out. By the time we arrived at her front door, it was nothing more to tell. When we approached Charmine's house, she pressed the remote and opened the garage door. She passed me her keys and told me to go inside while she rolled her trash cans to the curb. When she got in the house, she told me to get comfortable while she got the guest bedroom ready for me. I told her I would do it, but she insisted.

While Charmine was in the guestroom, I went to the kitchen and poured a glass of apple juice. Anthony joined me in the kitchen. He told me he had no idea what was going on because Charmine hadn't told him anything. However, he said if my reason for needing a place to sleep concerned Clay, he wanted me to give him a pass. Anthony felt Clay was one of the 'good guys' and deserved a second chance. We talked a bit more about his upcoming wedding before Charmine returned, and when she did, she shoved Anthony off to their bedroom. Charmine also poured herself a glass of juice and sat down next to me on the couch. "So, what are you going to do?" she asked.

"For number one, I'm going to get in Faizon's ass! That's why that bitch was so smug the other day. She knew she had a dirty little secret at my expense. I tried calling her before you picked me up, but she didn't answer. And it's a good thing she didn't."

"You're damn right it's a good thing she didn't answer. You can't afford to make Faizon your frenemie. Have you forgotten she knows all about you and Dre? And if you go at it with her, Clay will know everything too. So keep your cool, try to get a good night's sleep, and think about it before you make any foolish decisions."

"And let that trick continue to laugh at me? I expect that kind of shit from her, but Clay? I feel so betrayed; I certainly didn't come back to Atlanta for this."

"Betrayed? Lane, I hope you don't take this the wrong way, but I have to keep it real. You really can't be too mad at Clay for telling you the truth when you've lied and cheated on him. I know you have some cause for being hurt...but you actually had sex with Dre." I hated to admit it, but Charmine was right, how could I be such a hypocrite. Clay is the first man in my life who even had the decency to tell me the truth. Dre would have fucked her for sure, and then he would have come home and ate his dinner with me like nothing ever happened.

"What should I do, Char?" I asked.

"I can't answer that for you. But if you plan on continuing your relationship with Clay, respect him enough to tell him the truth like he did you, because Faizon is going to be waiting in the cut for you to leave Clay. I bet this is what she was hoping for."

"You're right, I won't make any decisions tonight. I'll get some rest, and my mind will be fresh in the morning."

"Sounds like a good idea. I know you didn't bring anything to wear, so you can go through my closet tomorrow morning and see what fits you."

"You know I can't fit none of your tight-ass attorney suits. I had planned to go back to Clay's in the morning. He usually leaves out by seven, and I don't have to be at work until ten tomorrow."

"That's up to you, but Anthony will have to drop you by your house to get your car. I have to be in Sandy Springs at eight." Charmine got off the couch and gave me a hug. "Sleep well, Chica. See you in the morning."

"Good night, Char, and thanks for letting me stay here tonight." She fanned her hand at me as she walked away. I watched some old black and white film on TV until I remembered I had a voice mail from Clay I hadn't listened to. I walked over to the kitchen counter, grabbed my bag, and returned to the sofa. I entered the password to my cell and pressed play. In the three minute message, Clay had poured his heart out to me. He acknowledged he wasn't blameless, and he knew that what he admitted to would be devastating, but he wouldn't make it worse by lying to me. The last thing he said was that he loves me and would give me my space.

I replayed his message a few more times before I put my phone away and went to bed. I was exhausted, and I had a major decision to make which would determine my fate with Clay. The next morning, I awoke with the most nauseated feeling, but I needed to get to Clay's to get dressed for work. So I hopped straight out of bed and staggered into the kitchen where Anthony and Charmine were having their breakfast. "Good morning, you two. Why didn't you wake me?" I asked.

"You still have plenty of time. It's only five-thirty, but I have to leave soon. Anthony said he's fine with dropping you off," Charmine said and got up from the table.

"Yeah, I don't have a problem with that. Do you want some coffee?" Anthony asked.

"No thanks, Anthony, I'm good. I'll be ready to leave in a few." I went back to the bedroom, made my bed, and cleaned up before Anthony and I left. When we got in the car, I checked my phone to see if Clay called again, but he stayed true to his word and hadn't called me since his last message. As I gave Anthony directions to my condo, he talked to me about the dynamics of a man. He explained how some men could take one look at a woman and know she'd be his wife. And then he schooled me on the class of women who men would never take to their house unless they wanted to get freaky. I didn't know where he was going with all this, but I listened just the same.

Anthony dropped me off in front of my condo before seven o'clock, and if Clay followed his schedule, he had left the house already. And I would have avoided seeing him. I thanked Anthony for dropping me off, and I got in my car and proceeded to Clay's. As I drove down the hill on Clay's street I noticed that one of Clay's cars wasn't in his driveway, so I felt confident he had gone to the studio. I pulled into the driveway and crept into the house as if I was about to burglarize it.

I unlocked the front door and went upstairs to Clay's bedroom. I laid out my Ann Taylor black suit and white blouse for me to wear to work. I stepped in the shower and exhaled as the forceful water shot from the massive shower heads and massaged my frazzled body. I contemplated taking the day off, but I hadn't been back a full week yet. I turned off the water and stepped out of the shower. I'd left my towel on the bed as I thought I'd be alone. Naked and still drenched from my shower I walked into the bedroom, and I realized I wasn't alone. Clay had come back undetected and sat noiseless on his bed. "Oh God, Clay! You scared me!" I said and touched my heart from fright.

"I'm sorry Bae, I didn't mean to."

"I didn't expect to see you. I thought you'd be gone to work."

"I did. I left something and had to come back for it." I became aware of my nakedness and reached for the towel to cover my body. But Clay grabbed my arm and pulled my body close to him as he remained seated on the bed. He wrapped his arms around my waist and nuzzled his head on my damp stomach. "Lane, I'm sorry. I would never deliberately hurt you, you know that. I love you." I wanted so badly to resist this: 6'1, fine, chocolate masterpiece who held onto me so tightly that I felt his electricity surge throughout my body. I couldn't pull away from him, so I stayed in his arms and melted from his touch.

"Oh, Clay. I love you too." Clay kissed around my navel and started to go higher, but I stopped him because I wanted to establish what his feelings were towards Faizon. "But how are we gonna work through this? Do you have feelings for Faizon or what? Because if you do, I'm not going to compete with her."

"C'mon, Lane. You know I don't have feelings for her like that."

"Then what kind of feelings do you have for her?" He released his hold from around my waist. I picked up the towel, wrapped it around me, and sat down next to him.

"My feelings for Faizon are superficial. Of course I can't deny she's a sexy, beautiful woman, and I've thought about her more than I should have. But I never want you to feel like you're competing with her 'cause there's no competition. I love and want only you." I believed him. I believed that Faizon had flaunted her ass around him and came onto him so strongly. What man wouldn't think about it? And plus, I was in no position to throw stones.

"Clay, I really want to get over this. Faizon thinks she's got one up on me, and I gotta address it with her."

"Do your thing. I've told you everything now, and I did it so there wouldn't be any secrets between us. Come back here tonight after work, we'll get through this together, Bae, I promise." I told Clay I would and rushed to get dressed as I needed to get to work. Clay grabbed something from his chest of drawers and left the house again. I walked in the bank with five minutes to spare. I wanted to fix a cup of coffee, but Mr. Wyatt, my boss, called me in his office.

"Good morning, Lane. We haven't had the chance to have a chat since you've been back. I'm glad to have you back."

"Thanks, Mr. Wyatt. It's good to be back."

"I know it's only been your third day back, but I hope you're finding things all right."

"Yes, I'm fine."

"I was so sorry to hear about your mother."

"Thanks, Mr. Wyatt. And I really appreciate you holding my position open for me."

"Don't mention it, Lane. Well, if there's nothing more we'll catch up during the week." I went into the staff's break room and fixed a cup of coffee and attempted to call Faizon again. I still didn't get an answer, and I knew for sure she had purposely evaded my calls. I didn't get too bent out of shape because I knew we had to see each other sooner than later. I had just left Mr. Wyatt's office and told him everything was fine when I realized I didn't have a clue about this new system.

I called Jade, the Customer Relationships Adviser, into my office to help me. I was told she was the know-it-all of the branch, and she'd be the one most able to give me a brief synopsis of the system until I had more time to learn it for myself. Jade was so meticulous with the details that she had me bored to tears and yawns as she took me step-by-step through the new complicated procedure. I was so happy when Charmine called, and I had an excuse to send Jade on her way. "You made it to work?"

"Yeah, barely. Girl, how 'bout I took a shower at Clay's this morning, stepped out the shower, walked into the room butt-ass naked, and guess who's sitting on the bed?"

"Stop playing!" Charmine started to laugh. "I thought you said he wouldn't be there?"

"He wasn't when I first got there, but he forgot something and came back for it. Char, for as long I've been staying with Clay he's left the house at seven o'clock and has never had to come back for anything."

"I don't know, maybe it was just meant for y'all to bump into each other. So, what did he say?"

"He told me what I wanted to know, and some I didn't want to know. The main thing is he isn't tryna get with the tramp"

"I guess. I will say he's a better person than you are for telling you the truth about it all."

"I don't know what you're trying to hint at, but if you think I'm about to tell him about Dre, who I'll probably never see again and dig a deeper hole in our relationship...girl bye."

"And what about Faizon, have you spoken to her?"

"No. Not yet, but we'll see each other real soon."

"Wait a minute. If the 'real soon' you're referring to is at my rehearsal dinner on Saturday, you can stop that right now. I don't want no bullshit between you bitches that night. I mean it, Lane."

"Ooh. . . I wonder does Anthony know his future wife has such a potty mouth?"

"If he doesn't, he'll soon find out if y'all bring that nonsense to my rehearsal dinner. I told you his mother already thinks us 'coloreds' are too aggressive. And that's all I'll need is for her to witness an episode of Jerry Springer right there at my rehearsal dinner."

"So when am I suppose to see her? I told you she's been avoiding all my calls."

"I don't know what to tell you. Just don't do it on my time." Before we hung up, I told Charmine I promised Clay I would go back to his house after work. A few minutes after my call with Charmine, Jade came back to my office and informed me she had emailed me the new procedures on the FATCA compliance. I quickly realized I made a mistake by getting her involved. By lunchtime, I determined that Faizon and I should meet to talk about her trying to get with Clay before Charmine's rehearsal dinner. I called Faizon for the fourth time before my lunch ended, but this time I left her a cordial message and asked her to please get in contact with me. I figured the theory "you catch more flies..." would work in this instance.

The afternoon went at a much faster pace, and when I looked up, it was after six o'clock. Clay called and said he made reservations for us at Bone's. He said he heard me talk a lot about their Sautéed Wild Salmon dish. I told him I was nearly finished with my work and would meet him at his house directly. I cleared as much as I could from my desk, including reading up on the new procedures which Jade kindly emailed me. I stopped by Mr. Wyatt's office, and thanked him for our afternoon catch-up and said goodnight.

As I drove home, I received a call from the Midtown Furniture store where I ordered my furniture. They wanted me to confirm my details for my Saturday delivery and told me I'd be their first stop. Traffic wasn't as bad as it normally was, so I made it to Clay's house in good time. When I turned into the driveway and parked, Clay pulled in right behind me. I exited my car and waited for him to exit his. He walked up to me, kissed me on my cheek, and took my workload from my hands. Once we were inside the house, Clay told me our reservations were at eight o'clock, and he went upstairs to get changed. Clay was stripped down to only his boxer briefs which revealed his six pack, and I understood why Faizon wanted to get with him. As he rubbed body cream all over his smooth chocolate body—he caught me as I watched him lovingly. "I look aight?" he asked.

"You look more than all right, and we better go before we end up having something from the fridge tonight."

"You're right, we better leave soon 'cause you're looking real good yourself." Clay set the house alarm and we left, headed for Bone's restaurant. I had just secured my seat belt when my phone alerted me that I had received a text; the text was from Faizon, and in it she agreed to meet me the next day at her new shop on Amsterdam Ave. I texted her back and told her I'd be there after work. Clay noticed I had been occupied and asked me if everything was okay—I didn't want to say anything to Clay just yet about the meeting, because this was something I wanted to get resolved by myself.

We entered the restaurant and were seated by an olive skinned waiter. He placed two menus on the table, and asked us if we needed time to look them over. But we knew exactly what we wanted, and he took our orders right away. After the day I experienced, I needed a cocktail, but since I had work in the morning, I ordered a glass of red wine instead, and Clay had his Hennessy. "This is a nice place," I said as I looked around. "One of my colleagues, Syreeta, told me that their Maine Lobster dish is the bomb as well."

"Yeah? Well, hopefully what I ordered will taste good too. I'm glad you agreed to come over tonight. I never meant for what I told you to be the shit that pulled us apart. I just wanted to be honest and let you know where my head was at."

"And I respect that, but you gotta admit that you knew it was gonna be hard for me to hear. Who wants to think that their man is having those kinds of thoughts about their 'friend'?"

"I did know it was going to be hard for you to hear, because it was just as hard for me to tell you. I should have just followed my gut when I told you that I didn't want to get involved with her in the first place."

"So now it's my fault because I asked you to help her with her launch?"

"No, Lane, that's not what I'm not saying. What I'm saying is: I wasn't feeling it when you asked me, and I should've have stuck to it. Look, Bae, I didn't bring you here to talk about Faizon. You said you wanted to work pass this, and that's what I'd like to do too. Looking back I should have done some shit differently, but it never changed the fact that I'm still in love with you."

"I love you too." Clay was right. I wasn't about to spend my evening talking about Faizon, so I switched gears, and we talked about our day. Clay asked me if I had spoken to my dad and how was he doing. I told Clay that I had talked to him earlier, and he was fine—I also mentioned that my dad would be here in a couple of weeks to look at my new condo. Clay appeared genuinely excited to hear it and said he would make sure he'd take my dad to the East Lake Golf course while he's here. The subject turned to Charmine's wedding, and Clay asked me what I thought he should wear. I told him that when we got back to his house he could model some of his suits for me as I loved to see him get undressed.

Our food arrived, and just the look of my dish made my neck roll and after my first bite. I had gone to fine dining heaven. "Let me ask you this, because ever since this whole mess started it's been on my mind," he paused. Should I even attend the wedding?" I had a mouthful of salmon, so I couldn't answer immediately.

"Of course you're going to the wedding. Why would you even ask me that?"

"Look, I'm not trying to make things more difficult than they already are. It's already a fucked up situation, and I hate I got you tangled up in it," he said and bit into his crab cakes.

"Honestly, me too, but Faizon isn't innocent in this. She knew exactly what she was doing. Furthermore, she and I were friends, and she crossed the friendship boundaries when she tried to stake her claim on forbidden territory."

"I feel you. And now that I've come clean I hope that's the end of it. Now we'll be able to fully trust each other."

"Yes we can," I said. I sipped my wine hoping it hid the shakiness in my voice. "There are no more secrets." Clay and I finished our dinner, and he asked me if I wanted some desert, but I was too stuffed to put anything else in my stomach. When we got home, Clay played a few tracks from off his new artist, Amani's, self titled album for me to hear. The girl was hot. Clay compared her sound to Elle Varner, and I understood why; I told Clay that he definitely chose a winner when he signed her. He said he felt the same way, and that she would be introduced for the first time at Faizon's launch. I asked him if he would have to personally deal with Faizon any longer—he told me that he handed her over to Nikole.

It had been a long but good evening, and we were both very tired. The next morning I wanted to sleep late so badly, but I had to get to work. Clay had the independence to sleep all day if he chose to, but he was an extremely hard worker, and since being with him, I had never known him to take a day off. I slowly dragged myself out of bed and dressed for work. Clay had been up. He'd already made calls to set up a meeting for the huge birthday party for one of the Atlanta housewives cast members. People in Atlanta had created a buzz about Clay's entertainment company for being a major player in the city, best known for its music and parties.

I called Charmine and told her about my plans to meet Faizon after work. Charmine asked me if she needed to have a referee or an ambulance sent over to the shop just in case. I laughed, but I assured Char it wouldn't be that serious. Charmine mentioned she had picked up the bridal gifts and wanted to know if I would help her get all the gift bags ready. I told Charmine that as soon as I left Faizon's shop, I'd be on my way over to her house. I heard the anxiety in her voice, so I told her I could meet Faizon another time and come straight over, but she favored the idea of having the issue between us resolved before her rehearsal dinner which was two days away.

Although I was tired, as soon as I walked into work the day had gone by smoothly. Things had started to come back to me like second nature, and I managed to use the new FATCA procedure without any help from Jade. Before the bank closed its doors for the day, I went to the ladies room and checked my make-up before I left for my meeting with Faizon. I entered the parking lot of Faizon's shop and spotted her as she transported clothing rails from a van into her shop.

I parked my car next to hers and got out. She acknowledged my arrival, but continued to take things from the van and rolled them inside. I walked inside the packed shop with rails all along the walls. "Hey, Lane. How do you like my shop?" Faizon asked.

"It's nice. When did you get it?"

"A few days ago. I'd been looking for something eccentric, yet stylish, and I found it in this shop. Which is why I haven't gotten back with you, this was occupying all my time." Yeah, whatever Faizon—let's just get this shit over with.

"Well, you know why I'm here—there are some things we need to discuss."

"I know we do," she said, but she continued to arrange the clothes on the rails. "Do you want something to drink?"

"No, I think we should have this conversation sober."

"I was actually speaking of juice this time."

"No, I'm fine. Well...Clay told me everything that happened that night. He told me how you lured him to your house under the pretense of, whatever lie you told him."

"Lure isn't the term I'd use. I asked, and he came. Did I have too much to drink and cross the line a bit? Yes. Did anything happen as a result of that? No. So why are we really here, Lane?" she asked. She then came over and sat on a used leather sofa that had mounds of clothes on it.

"Is something the matter with you?! You tried to suck his dick! And the only reason why you didn't succeed is because he didn't allow you to. Now, to be honest, I thought it was bad enough when you started messing with Darnell, knowing he was married with children. But for you to stoop as low as to try to get with Clay...I see you just dirty like that."

"Oh, I see. So you thought it was okay for you to get some from Dre whenever you wanted, but Clay is off limits?" It was crazy how Faizon felt some sense of entitlement when she spoke of Clay.

"Dre is one of the biggest mistakes in my life, but he has nothing to do with this, and I not gonna lose Clay because of it either. But you Faizon, you were supposed to be a friend, and I trusted you. I have a chance to be happy with Clay, and I'm not about to let you ruin that for me." We went back and forth verbally, and at times we were so loud people peered inside her shop to be nosy. We shouted at each other until I became hoarse, and I finally concluded that this ridiculous drama wasn't going anywhere. "Well, Faizon, I only want to know how we are gonna move pass this? We have to be in close quarters for Charmine's wedding, and for her sake, I hoped that we could at least try to get along."

Faizon took a long time to respond to my proposition. She crossed her long legs and looked at her nails as if she was bored with me. "Of course we will, and for what it's worth Lane, I apologize. I'm so use to women hating on me for whatever reason, that I don't know how to treat the women in my life who have treated me decently." I looked at this heffa like she was out of her mind; I wasn't as gullible as she thought I was. And I certainly wasn't about to fall for her lies, but I wanted to end on a relatively good note, and we decided we would.

I got up to leave her shop and was only a few steps away from having stepped outside the door when Faizon called my name. I turned to face her. She walked over to me and said she wanted me to know that Clay was a good man. She added that was happy for me and that she would never tell Clay what she knew about me and Dre. Honestly, after her statement, I was more nervous than ever. I left her shop not feeling totally assured that she was telling me the truth, but for now that would have to do. As soon as I got in my car, I called Charmine and gave her the full details of our little chit-chat, but Charmine insisted I wait until I got to her house.

When I got to Charmine's, she was in her garage with a lit cigarette in her hand. "What the hell? I haven't seen you smoke in years," I said.

"Girl, I get married Sunday, my parents will be here tomorrow, and my friends are at each other's throats. You should be glad you didn't find me out here sniffing something," she said and took a long drag from her Benson Hedges cigarette.

"It can't be that bad. You're marrying the man of your dreams, your parents refused to stay at your house, and your friends are on the mend."

"For now y'all are." Charmine took two more quick pulls, and clipped her cigarette in an ashtray. "Come in, and tell me what the hell happened between you two loonies." After I told her what had taken place, the only thing Charmine said was 'um em.' We went inside of Charmine's office and sat at a table full of ribbons, trinkets, and the pendants for the bridesmaids in their classic blue and white boxes from Tiffany's. I called Clay and discovered he was still at work. I told him not to expect me until much later because I was at Charmine's helping her with her wedding stuff. Anthony entered the room and stated he was going to his parents' house to see his sister, Emily. Emily recently filed for a divorce and had to move back home. She needed a lawyer to settle her divorce, and who better than her own brother and future sister-in-law to advise you.

When Anthony left the house, Charmine pulled the good stuff from the fridge and poured us two glasses. She made me promise we wouldn't get too toasted until the gift bags were at least done. I promised, and we drank as we wrapped the gifts. As we wrapped the gifts, the Sauvignon Blanc started to take its effect on Charmine. She started to talk about how she thought she'd never find anyone to love again after Kamel, especially someone like Anthony. She said it wasn't that she was ever opposed to interracial dating, but just that she had never thought about it until Anthony. And said she would go as far to say that this was the happiest she'd ever been.

Charmine and I had wrapped all the gifts, and then I placed them inside a large decorated box. During the night, we had scratched a lot of things off Charmine's list, and she said she could breathe a lot easier. Since we were done with the gifts, I went into Charmine's hidden stash and poured us a glass of Patron. "Raise your glass, Boo," I demanded. "Here's to my best friend and sister. I love you and hope that you two have plenty of babies."

"Hear, hear! I'll drink to that, and thank you for always being there for me, I love you too," she said. "You and Clay will be next."

"We'll see, hopefully one day. I love Clay very much and I'd love to be Mrs. Clay Roberts, but could you imagine me fighting these thirsty bitches off him everyday. You see the shenanigans I just went through with a 'friend.'" We laughed until tears rolled from our eyes. "Don't laugh Charmine, you're gonna have the same problem with Anthony's fine, David Beckham lookin' ass." We cut up a little more before Charmine made me drink plenty of coffee, and water before I considered leaving her house. And by the time I was ready to leave I was absolutely fine.

On the way home, I thought about what Charmine said. Clay is the best thing in my life, and I wanted him so badly. Just the idea of marrying Clay made me smile. When I arrived at Clay's house, he was asleep, stretched out across the bed in only his underwear as one hand cradled his head. I got totally undressed and laid on top of him. Clay mumbled he loved me in his sleep, wrapped his one free arm around me, and we slept peacefully

FORBIDDEN SEDUCTION

Charmine

Anthony and I had picked my parents up from the airport and took them straight to their hotel. We made sure they were settled in before we left for work. I told them that I would be back to take them to dinner after work. I selected a hotel location that wouldn't have prevented them from taking in the sights on foot if they decided to get out before I returned. My mother was very fond of Anthony, but my father still wasn't a fan. Anthony and I went straight to our new office, as we were about a week behind schedule, and I hadn't seen it in a couple of days. But once on-site I was pleased it had made such vast improvements.

Anthony moved some of the boxes to their respective offices and asked me to be in charge of the coffee runs, which I was more than happy to oversee. I had called to check on my parents and was speaking to my mother when another call beeped in. I told my mother I would see them around five o'clock, and I took the other call. It was Faizon. "Hi Charmine, what you doing? she asked.

"Hey, Girl? I just got off the phone with my mother."

"That's right, they are in town. Look, I'm not going to hold you. I know you've probably already talked to Lane, and you

177

know what happened with me and Clay. I just wanna know are we good?"

"We're okay, but to be honest I think what you tried to do to Clay is messed up. I'm quite sure Lane could have done without that in her life. And, I could have done without the unnecessary drama right before my wedding as well. However, if Lane said she's okay with it now, then I'm cool too. I'm glad that you two came to some mutual understanding that you would try to get along."

"I hear you, but we have discussed it. And I have apologized to her for it. Another reason for my call is I wanted you to know Tracey was the last of your bridesmaids to pick up her dress from my shop yesterday, and that ass got kinda fat. I had to let her dress out two full inches."

"What? Girl, I think she might be pregnant. She doesn't want anyone to know yet, but I can tell by her tits. How do you go from iron board flat to Dolly Parton in a matter of a couple of months, unless you paid for them? And I know Tracey well enough to know, she does not have that kind of money." We had a few laughs before Anthony called me for his first coffee run. "Listen I gotta go, but I do appreciate the call."

"I know you do, Hun. See you at the rehearsal dinner. Bye." We hung up, and I drove down to the nearest Star Bucks for Anthony's coffee. When I returned to our office, I hung pictures, certificates, and our degrees on the walls as Anthony moved all the heavy stuff. By lunchtime, the office looked great. The contractors had a few minor things to do, but it wouldn't be long before the doors of: Martin & Martin would be opened to its community. Anthony and I left the office to go home to change before we picked up my parents for dinner.

"Will you be coming with us to dinner tonight?" I asked.

"I'd love to join you, but I don't know how your father will feel about that," he said.

"I think you should come. My father will come around, I promise you. It's just going to take him some time, just like your mother eventually will."

"My mother? Why do you say that, she loves you."

"Love? I'll settle for she likes me. She still has a lot to learn about

178

African Americans, and I'm gonna be the one to school her."

"Like what?"

"For God's sake, Anthony! She still calls us 'coloreds.'"

"That's fair," he chuckled. "Both of our parents will come around soon enough. You know, I think I will go tonight. I'll show your father I'm not all bad." We picked up my parents from the hotel and took them to the Sun Dial restaurant. I thought it would have been a nice treat for them to enjoy their meal as the restaurant slowly rotated around the dazzling Atlanta skyline. I knew my mother would have enjoyed it as she was excited with just the elevator ride up to the restaurant. Once we reached the top of the restaurant, we were seated at our table. My dad never bothered to pick his menu up. "Do you know what you want already, dad?" I asked.

"I sure do. I'll have some collards, fried chicken, some sweet potatoes, and corn."

"I'm sorry dad, but this restaurant doesn't serve that. Their steak is delicious. Look at your menu."

"I'll pass. I never been to no food establishment that doesn't serve soul food. You haven't even walked down the aisle with him yet, and he already got you eating peach salad and tomato surprise," he said with a big frown on his face. When he finally picked up the menu, it was only to criticize the selection of food on it.

"Paul. Now you just carrying on," my mother interrupted. "You like steak, so why are making such a big deal out of it? Charmine and Anthony brought us somewhere nice to try something different for a change." My father raised his eyes over the menu and looked at me. He decided to skim through the menu again for something to eat.

"Mr. Grant, if I may make a suggestion, I know of a good soul food place. Actually it was my first choice, but Charmine felt this would be a nicer treat for the both of you," Anthony said.

"Do they have sweet potatoes, and collards?" he asked. My mother looked like she wanted to wring my dad's neck and scanned the restaurant as if she thought someone had heard my him. I knew my mother well, and I could tell she was so ashamed of my father's behavior.

"They'll have everything you want, and it isn't too far from here," Anthony said, and he looked at me for approval. I saw how important this was for him to be able to connect with my father, so I said nothing. My mother and I were fine with it, so Anthony concocted a story to tell the waiter as we left out table. We may have been a block away from Busy Bee's Café, and my father said he could smell the butter dripping off the biscuits. It was there my father found all of his soul food favorites, and he ate until he loosened his belt. As he put the last bite of collard greens in his mouth, he said he enjoyed their cooking almost as much as he did my mother's. My father thanked Anthony as he ordered some more peach cobbler for my father to take back to the hotel for a late night snack.

We walked around the downtown area a little while before we took my parents to our new law office. I emphasized to them how Anthony and I had done most of the work ourselves, except for the extension to the building. My parents said they were very proud of all my accomplishments. My father walked over to Anthony and patted him on his back. "Good job. I see you'll make a good husband for my daughter, and that's all I could ask for." We left our office and took my parents back to their hotel. I reminded my mother that I would pick her up early so we could get an early start before the rehearsal dinner.

On the way home, Anthony and I talked about the evening with my parents. "So, I see the saying 'the way to a black man's heart is through his stomach' is true."

"Oh shut up!" I laughed. "You and my father seemed to get all chummy-chummy tonight. Now, it's one down and one to go." I wondered if a double serving of some peach cobbler would have worked on Mrs. Martin as miraculously as it had with my father. Lane called to tell me that she was taking the afternoon off and could help me with any last minute preparations. I was thrilled to hear that, because I needed all hands on deck before the rehearsal dinner.

When Anthony and I got home, we checked our messages, and there was one from our Realtor. He stated that Mr. Kanavagh, the gentleman, who wanted to buy our house had been approved, and our house was now officially sold. Anthony called our Realtor back and talked about some of the formalities while I looked up moving companies.

The next morning, I picked up my mother from the hotel and brought her back to my house. My father said he didn't want to interfere with 'woman's work,' so he chose to stay at the hotel until time for the rehearsal dinner. I put on the coffee machine for my mother and left her in the kitchen while I went to my office and gathered all the wedding items. I brought all the items back into the kitchen and put them on the table for my mother and I to get started on the decorations.

My mother picked up one of my personalized matchbooks, and she reminisced about her wedding day. She relished in the fact her mother was able to give her a real string of pearls which was a big deal back in her day. My mother told me the story of how her mother had worn fake pearls to her own wedding and promised herself that if she ever had a daughter, she would own a real string of pearls. And as a child I remembered how much my mother cherished those pearls; she would wear her pearls proudly when she went out with my dad or to church.

By the time my mother finished with her story, the only thing that was left for us to do were the name placements for the seating order. Lane and I had already wrapped all the other gifts beforehand which allowed my mother and I to just enjoy each other's company. "I'm so happy for you, Precious. You've done so well for yourself, and you deserve it all. I've never told you this because as hard as it may be, sometimes you must let your children go through stuff to help them become the person who they are meant to be. Kamel wasn't meant to be. He would have drained you, your spirit, and your bank account. And you've grown so much after that situation"

"Thanks, Mother. I didn't see me ever getting over that. I thought my ability to love or be loved left me at the altar along with Kamel that day. I couldn't have imagined me at this point in my life. It made it so much easier for me when you accepted Anthony—and hopefully Daddy will too."

"He will precious...he will," she said and kissed my cheek. Lane called and said that she was on her way over. When Lane arrived, my mother greeted her warmly. She hadn't seen Lane since her mother's funeral and was very glad to see her back in Atlanta. Lane hugged my mother sweetly and became a bit teary. They've always had such a good relationship, and I could tell that Lane missed her mother. We three ladies sat around my cluttered kitchen table and mapped out our day. Lane said she wanted to treat us to the spa and get our nails done for the rehearsal dinner. On our way to the spa, my mother asked Lane how she liked being back in Atlanta. Lane expressed she was happy to be back, but wished she wasn't met with the absurdity she had faced since she'd been back. My mother didn't have any of the inside story, but she consoled Lane as if she knew what Lane was talking about.

We arrived at the spa and entered the tranquil establishment to the calming sounds of ocean waves. Lane and I had been regular faces at the spa, but since Lane's time away in Brooklyn and with me planning my wedding, we hadn't been there in a while. Sharin, the owner, mentioned how she missed not seeing us and was glad to have us back. She asked if we wanted anything to drink, and we all settled on mimosas. When Sharin returned with our drinks, she mentioned she added something new to her massage package list and recommended we treat ourselves to it. We all agreed we would have the Luxurious Body polish and massage like Sharin suggested and after we finished our mimosas, we were called back to our rooms. As I laid there stretched out on the table, I allowed my masseuse to freely grope my nude body. I thought about my mother and laughed. I remembered when she said that the first time she had gotten a massage, she kept all her clothes on. When I asked her why—she told me that she cringed at the thought of a man, other than my dad, seeing her naked, so I didn't doubt she was in the next room fully clothed.

Lane and I had finished with our treatments and had gone back up front to the reception area to wait on my mother as she still hadn't come out from her session yet. Minutes later, Lane elbowed me as my mother exited the room all smiles and giggly, with her arm interlocked with her masseuse as he escorted her back up to the reception area. I figured the mimosa had helped her relax a little which made this time a much different experience from her first. Lane asked if we could stop at the mall so she could buy a dress to wear to the rehearsal dinner, so we made a stop at Lenox Square Mall. Once we got inside of BCBG, Lane quickly found a cute black dress with a sheer back. As Lane paid for the dress, she told my mother that Clay would be at the rehearsal dinner, and she joked that she wanted to look as good as her. My mother always enjoyed Lane's sense of humor, and Lane's banter cracked her up. Lane left her car in the parking lot of the spa, so I dropped her off to pick it up. Lane said that she had to meet Clay before the dinner and left. My mother and I made our way back to my house to get ourselves prepared for the evening.

As I approached my driveway, it was packed with the cars of Anthony's family. I was relieved that my dad opted to remain at the hotel until closer to the time of the rehearsal; just the thought of Mrs. Martin and my dad in the same room made me tremble. As we walked up the driveway, I warned my mother about the ignorance Mrs. Martin still harbored towards African Americans—I didn't want her to be shocked by Mrs. Martin's lack of race sensitivity.

We walked into a house filled with family: Anthony's parents, his two brothers, their wives, his sister Emily, and her three children. Anthony's oldest brother, Andrew, and his family weren't there. When Anthony asked his mother if Andrew was coming, she made up some pathetic excuse for him. Andrew always pretended to be interested in me, but I had gotten the impression he never liked me very much. Jayla ran up to me and showed me her store bought bridesmaid dress. I took it from her hands immediately and hung it safely in my office along with my dress.

Anthony had already introduced my mother to his folks by the time I rejoined them in the living room. Emily followed me in the kitchen, and she apologized again for her negligence with Jayla's dress. We talked about her divorce being nearly final. She said she couldn't wait to be single again and was thrilled about the prospects of meeting new men. However, she was concerned about the negative behaviors one of her twin boys, Jordan, started to exhibit since their father didn't live with them anymore. I watched Mrs. Martin as she inched her way over to the fireplace where my mother and Anthony stood talking. My mother has a very loving spirit...that is until someone does or says something outrageously stupid. And I could see that was about to happen.

I waited a few minutes before I excused myself from the kitchen, and left Emily talking to her younger brother, Jeremy. I walked over to where my mother, Anthony, and his mother stood. I pretended I wanted to know what time we had to leave in order to pick up my dad from the hotel without being late for the rehearsal. But what I really wanted was to monitor the conversation between my mother and Mrs.

Martin. As I walked up on them, they seemed to have been engaged in a polite conversation. "Is Charmine your only child?" Mrs. Martin asked.

"Yes, she is." my mother replied, and I thought the conversation would have remained harmless. That was until, just as I had expected, Mrs. Martin pressed the, 'stupid button.'

"Your hair is lovely, Marjorie. Is it all yours? Or is it one of those weave jobs you women would rather have than pay your mortgage? You know, I will never understand how you people can justify buying hair that costs just about as much as a small used car."

"No, Dixie, it's all mine," my mother said, as she ran her fingers through her long ebony curls that fell neatly back into place. After my mother proved her locks were her own and not from Su Ling's Beauty Mart, she motioned to Mrs. Martin lip area. "Dixie, you have something right above your lip." Mrs. Martin wiped and scratched at the spot my mother directed her to for over a minute. And that is when I knew my mother had a little thing called: payback on her mind. "Oh, never mind, Dixie. It's just a few lip hairs. Nothing a little wax won't fix." My mother winked at me and moved to the other side of the room while Mrs. Martin's face turned bright red. To prevent his mother from being flustered any further, Anthony suggested we all leave for the church. I reminded Anthony that I had to pick up my dad, but he said he wanted to pick him up instead. I called my dad to inform him that Anthony would be the one who picked him up, but he said he was just about to call me because Lane and Clay had just walked in and would bring him to the church with them. I asked him to let me speak to Lane. "Thanks, Girl. You saved us a trip.

"You're welcome, Char. How is it over there? I just heard all your new in-laws are there."

"Lane, it's a mad house. We're about to leave now, see you at the church."

"Bye." We all piled in our cars and headed for the church. When we arrived, it was a pleasant surprise to see that everyone in the wedding party, except for one of Anthony's groomsmen were already there seated in the church pews. This was the first time that Faizon met my mother, and she rushed over to hug her and told her how much we looked alike. I admired Faizon's outfit and told her that after her launch I wanted her to make me the same design, but in black. Faizon's traits were horribly flawed, but her style was impeccable. She looked better than most models because she knew exactly what suited her curvy well proportioned body. I left them to talk while I thanked everyone for being a part of my wedding day. I asked that we waited a few minutes more for Lane to arrive with my dad.

I couldn't have timed it more perfectly. As soon as I finished my mini speech, my dad walked in the church followed by Lane and Clay. My dad and Lane walked down to the front where we all were, but Clay sat in the rear of the church as far away from Faizon as possible. I called my dad over to meet the rest of the Martin family, and Lane walked over to where my mother and Faizon were. The body language from Lane and Faizon was a bit contrived, but I don't think anyone else paid much attention to them.

After everyone met, Anthony asked all his groomsmen to get lined up in the back of the church. He positioned his groomsmen, and I asked the same of my bridesmaids. I asked Lane to play wedding planner and direct the wedding party to where they needed to stand as they walked down the aisle. Anthony paired the couples together in the back and made a discovery. "We need someone to walk with Faizon because Luke isn't here yet," he said. He looked around for one of his groomsmen to double for Luke during rehearsal. Anthony realized that his idea would be a hassle and spotted Clay who sat quietly in the back. "Wait, Clay's here. Hey man, would you mind helping us with this? You can be Faizon's partner, just until Luke gets here."

"Nah, man, I'm good on that. Let one of ya boys handle that for you." Clay said from his seat. Lane's head snapped in my direction and then turned to Clay, but Anthony pressed him for his assistance.

"C'mon man, you are one of my boys," he said. Anthony rushed down the aisle and grabbed Clay's arm. "You're holding us up. Lane won't mind, it's not like you and Faizon are the ones getting married." I stood fretfully cemented in my spot. I wanted to yell for my father to walk with her, but I didn't want to raise any suspicions, so I said nothing. I glanced over in Lane's direction once more. Her face was screwed up, and she had pursed her lips tightly. If her glum face was a presage of how she felt, I feared that at any minute she would have erupted in the church. But she too said nothing. Lane watched painfully as Faizon and Clay linked arms and stood in line.

The couples marched down the aisle to my favorite Charlie Wilson song "You Are." Clay and Faizon were the next couple cued to walk down the aisle. Midway to the altar Faizon leaned in and whispered something in Clay's ear and he responded with a quick nod. From where my father and I stood in the vestibule of the historic church, I noticed Lane's mouth move as she mumbled something inaudible. Lane stared Faizon down until she reached the front of the altar. She almost forgot to direct them where to stand. Lane finally pointed for Clay to go to her left and Faizon her right. Lane remained chilled throughout the remainder of the rehearsal, and I knew she'd done so because she had promised me.

After my father and I rehearsed our grand entrance, the priest explained in great detail what he'd say during our ceremony. I asked the wedding party to practice the entire routine once more, and they obliged. When everyone appeared to be confident with their roles in my wedding on Sunday, we called it a wrap for the night. Faizon walked over to Lane and attempted to say something to her, but she looked through Faizon. Lane walked over to Clay as he waited for her by the doors of the church, and I knew from the back of Lane's head movements she had discharged some choice words for Clay. I wanted to catch up to them to find out what had been said, but instead I attended to the rest of my guests and family. I told everyone we'd meet them at the Quiones Room for our dinner.

Anthony gathered from the strange behaviors Clay, Lane and Faizon had displayed something was off. "Is everything okay, or was my request for Clay to stand-in not such a good idea?" he asked.

"No...not really, but you didn't have any idea on what's been going on. I'll tell you all about it later. Tonight is our night." My parents, Anthony, and I walked out of the church, we thought everyone had left for the restaurant already until Faizon got out of her car and ran up to me. Anthony walked ahead with my parents so that Faizon could speak to me in private, and she waited until they were out of earshot.

"I know how important tonight is for you and Anthony, but I had to let you know this before we got to the restaurant. I don't know why your girl freaked out. All I said to Clay was that I was sorry for everything." Faizon said.

"Really, Faizon? You know it's a delicate time for Lane, and now it looks like you're just provoking her."

"I hate that you feel that way, but that wasn't my intention." she said. She told me she'd see us at the restaurant and got back in her car. Anthony waited outside our car while we talked, and once I reached the car, he let me in and we left the church grounds.

"What was that all about?" My mother asked.

"Oh nothing, Mother. Just girl stuff."

FORBIDDEN SEDUCTION

Faizon

This whole "Lane is a victim" thing has played out. I apologized to her and Clay for my part in the blotched evening. Really, if anyone should be upset is me, so why is Lane still with the 'Faizon is evil' looks. I know Lane drilled him when she whisked him off after the rehearsal only to find out that I apologized to him like I said. Clay had made it clear that he chose Lane, and he further confirmed it when he decided to tell her what took place at my house. Who expected Clay with his fine ass would be a one woman's man—we could have had so much fun together. In the past when I fooled around with men who had wives or girlfriends, mum was always the word.

The real reason I decided I wouldn't tell him about Lane and Dre is I would have looked like a fool; he wouldn't have believed me anyway. It would have just been the case of me trying to break them up because I wanted him all for myself. I was aware that my actions haven't always supported that I do care about Charmine and Lane. They've both been there for me at times when I've questioned myself why they haven't kicked me to the curb yet, but they can't hold me responsible for being who I am. I was very honest with them. I told the both of them how I was, and they

189

should have believed me. And furthermore, Lane has thrown the fact that I only care about myself in my face so many times during one of our many arguments that she definitely should know who I am.

Clay may have had Lane convinced that he hadn't been aroused when he saw me at rehearsal and pretended as if he felt nothing for me, but I'm not fooled one bit. He was the one who held onto my arm a little longer than necessary. I knew when he saw me the first thing he thought about were my lips on Shon, and he wished it were him. It was through Shon, I allowed Clay to have his fantasy about us. Shon had been an easy target and now I can't seem to shake the leech. Even after Clay had replaced Shon and had Nikole manage my launch, he called me regularly in hopes my mouth would bless him again. But there would be no way in hell I'd make that mistake twice.

Charmine's wedding dress would be the introduction to Faizon Hill, the designer. It would be the visual business card that would be seen across Atlanta. Their wedding had already been printed in the Atlanta society columns as one of the most elite weddings of the year, so by the time of the launch, my name would have appeared in most of the Atlanta newspapers as well. Nikole had been extremely professional and guided me through strategies I hadn't even thought of to build my brand.

I needed to contact Lane because the last time we met at my shop, we only briefly discussed Charmine's bachelorette party at the Whiskey Blue. Lane had been so uptight over this Clay issue, I didn't know how I'd be received by her, but I had no choice as she hadn't called to finalize the details of the party. I got out my phone and called her anyway. "Hello," Lane said.

"Hey, Lane, it's me."

"I know. What's up? Lane talked to me so dryly, I started to just hang up and plan the rest myself

"You could show some signs of life. I am calling about *your* girl's bachelorette party," I said.

"I'm at work, Faizon. Did you expect to hear a marching band playing in the background 'cause you called?

"Whatever, Lane. I just need to get some details for tomorrow night."

"I'll ask Char to help me Saturday because my furniture is coming in the morning, and I'll keep her with me most of the day. Then later, I'll tell her I want to take her out to show my gratitude for helping me."

"So... you think the day before she gets married, she'll want to spend the whole day with you arranging your furniture, and her mama is here?"

"You just can't help yourself. You always want to be in someone else's stuff. But I got this...all of it."

"Cool. I absolutely want us to have a good time tomorrow night, Lane. I don't want this tension between us. I've said sorry—I don't know how many more times you want me to say it. It's like you don't believe me or something."

"No, believe me. I know you're sorry. Talk to you later." If she truly wanted to know what I was sorry about—it was that I didn't get Clay in bed as I wanted. When Lane and I finished our phone call, I received a call from Nikole and she asked me to check my emails for the written details to my launch. I immediately checked my emails and read hers. In it she had the guest list, sponsors, and the artists who'd be performing. She also attached some photos of the beautiful models from the Models agency who'd be dressed in my fashions. It all read like a fantastically organized celebrity event with me as the star.

I called my mama because I wanted her to share in my good news, and as expected, she and my daddy yelled so loudly through the phone they almost pierced my eardrum. After I finished my conversation with my parents, I looked around my beautiful house, with all my beautiful things, and there I was... lonely as hell. I poured myself a glass of Pinot Grigio and reflected on all that I had accomplished and sadly, all the years I wasted with someone else's man. I had all of these wonderful things taking shape in my life and no one to share them with while Lane and Charmine started new chapters in their lives.

FORBIDDEN SEDUCTION

Lane

As soon as I woke up, I called Charmine so she'd be ready by the time I picked her up. My furniture was being delivered to my condominium by eleven, therefore, I had to be back in enough time to let them in. Charmine suggested she drive her own car as there may have been things she needed to do during the course of the day. But I assured her she wouldn't need her car, because if there was something she needed, she could use mine. She agreed, but she said she wanted to see Anthony off because he was going with his brothers. They had planned something special for him on his last night of being a free man.

Clay had an early morning at the studio, but he told me he'd meet me at the condo later. He said he hoped to be there before the furniture was delivered so he could help us move the heavy things in its place. I was surprised that he even wanted to help me after the way I went in on him after the wedding rehearsal. I demanded he tell me what was said as he and Faizon walked down the aisle, looking like a happy couple. He confirmed what Faizon tried to tell me before I walked off which was she was sorry, and he also told me that he wasn't going to put up with paranoid behavior. He reminded me that he hadn't been caught with his hands in the cookie jar, but that he told me everything that happened. And I needed to trust him. He kissed me and said he'd see me later at the condo, and I left for Charmine's house.

When I reached Charmine's house, Anthony let me in. We joked around a bit before his brothers came and took him off to a camping trip. When Anthony left, Charmine said she was a little worried about him. She thought he may have been stressed out from all the wedding hoopla. I could tell that Char was a bit loopy herself when she got in my car. "I'M GETTING MARRIED TOMORROW!" she yelled exuberantly with her fists in the air. "Girl, this has been one crazy year."

"I know, right. What time is Anthony coming back home tonight? 'Cause I don't need him blowing up your phone looking for you, I have a nice day planned for us."

"He isn't. His brothers are having some kind of Martin men tradition for him, so the next time I see Anthony will be at the altar."

"Ahh, that's good, and what about your parents?"

"They're fine too. I spoke to them right after we hung up. Do you remember my uncle Henry who lives in Macon?"

"I think so."

"Well, he and his wife are driving up for the wedding, and they are spending the day with them."

"Alrighty then, it sounds like it's just us today."

"Where's Clay at today?"

"He had to take care of something at the studio, but he's gonna meet us at the condo later."

"Okay. What did he tell you about that scene at rehearsal?" she asked.

"He told me that Faizon said sorry and that's it, but it was the way she did it that pissed me off."

"I don't know, Lane. That girl is a trip. You have to admit you can see why she tried something with Clay, the brotha is sexy."

"No, I don't have to admit to that. As good looking as Anthony is, I would never try to sleep with him under any circumstances."

"I hear you. But some women just wasn't born with that moral component, something's missing."

"It's gonna be her teeth if she don't stop fucking with other women's men," I snarled. Charmine and I arrived at my condo right on time to meet the delivery truck with my furniture. They unloaded a packed truck filled with my stuff and hauled it upstairs. As the furniture was placed in the rooms, I instantly started to feel at home and was glad that I had returned to Atlanta. Charmine and I hadn't done a bad job when we shopped for my home's accents last week. Everything we bought matched so nicely with my new furniture. We arranged some of the lighter furniture that we could move easily in the rooms downstairs.

Charmine playfully complained about how I had her engaged in manual labor the day before her wedding. She had been saved by the bell when Clay called from the building's intercom and said he was on his way upstairs. When Charmine heard Clay was on his way upstairs, she dropped the cushions that were in her hands on the sofa and stretched out on them. I cracked the door opened for Clay so he could come in, and I continued to pack away some more kitchen items. "What's up ladies?" he said.

"I'm in the kitchen," I said. Clay entered the kitchen, kissed me on my forehead, and placed two large pizzas on the counter for our lunch.

"Ahh...thanks, Baby."

"Hiya, Clay. You see how your woman got me moving these heavy-ass boxes and furniture around? I'm sweating my hair out," she laughed.

"Anyway, Charmine. You've done more complaining than anything," I said. Clay chuckled as he walked out the kitchen and joined Charmine in the living room. She sat up from her reclined position and hugged Clay.

"So tomorrow's the big day, huh? You ready?" Clay asked.

"Yeah, I'm ready. I can't wait to see Anthony's face when he sees me walk down that aisle in my dress. You know, two of Emily's friends are having Faizon make their wedding dresses after they saw what stunning dresses she made for Emily and Jayla."

"She's a talented designer," Clay agreed.

"And if you hadn't of left when you did that night, you would have found out just how talented she is. Skank!"

"Oohh, Lane! Stop." Charmine laughed.

"Lane, I thought we've been through this," he said.

"We have, I just get heated every time I think about it." I looked at my watch and realized that we still had a lot of work to do at my condo before I took Charmine back to hers to get dressed for her party. "Okay, Char, station break is up. We still have the upstairs to do." Clay asked me how much more I needed done, and I told him I only needed to put the beds together. Clay knew what I had planned for Charmine, so he offered to stay back and put up the beds for me. I took my key off my key ring and handed it to him, but Clay told me that he had Tom, his Realtor, make him a copy and gave mine back.

I informed Charmine that I wanted to do something special for her and had planned an evening out for us on her last night of being single. Charmine accepted right away, but she asked if we could stop by the hotel to check on her parents before we went out. I told her we would. Charmine asked me what I had planned to wear. I told her I still had the black dress I bought for her rehearsal dinner, but had changed my mind about wearing it. I grabbed a pair of heels from the box of shoes I had brought in earlier from Clay's house. I told Charmine that I would get dressed at her house after we left the hotel.

By the time we left my condo, Clay had fixed one of the beds for the guest room. He told us to have a nice evening and for me to 'behave' myself. I told him I would be spending the night at his, so not to put the alarm on. Charmine told Clay she'd see him at the wedding and walked out of the door. Before I left, I asked Clay what his plans were for the night. He told me that he planned to kick it with Shon, but he would text me later on. When I got downstairs, Charmine had a cigarette in her mouth, the second one I'd seen her smoke within the last few days. "You might as well say you started smoking again."

"I haven't, this is only to calm my nerves," she said. We entered my car and headed in the direction of the hotel. When we arrived at the hotel, Charmine's parents, her uncle Henry, and his wife, Thelma, had just come back from dinner. Mr. Grant said he enjoyed the food at Busy Bee's so much he had his brother take them back. Charmine's uncle was so pleased to see her. He told her how badly he felt about them living so close, and he never invited her to his house down in Macon. Charmine told him he shouldn't have felt that way because she could have invited him to hers as well. Henry's wife appeared to be much younger than he was. She was dressed very nicely, and her

Brazilian weave was on point, but she was quite reserved and didn't speak much.

Mrs. Grant asked Charmine what time we needed to be at the hotel in the morning to take the photos, and Charmine told her she'd pick them up by nine. After Charmine was satisfied that her family was fine, we left for her house to get dressed ourselves. Faizon texted me and said she had just arrived at Whiskey Blue, along with a few of Charmine's colleagues. I replied back that we needed more time as we had just made it back to Charmine's house, but I would text her when we were close. When we got to Charmine's house, I hopped in the downstairs shower, while Charmine showered and dressed upstairs.

When Charmine emerged from her room, she looked amazing in a black shimmer, one shoulder dress by Anne Klein. I told her that I didn't want to get all sentimental, but I had to let her know how glad I was that I hadn't missed all of this by being in Brooklyn. She said she didn't want to bawl and ruin her make-up, but said she was glad I hadn't missed it either. "Okay Lane, where are we going?" she asked.

"I don't think you've ever been there."

"There are very few places in Atlanta I don't know about, try me."

"Char, I don't think you've ever been there. It's a new place in West Buckhead," I said. I purposely tried to sound annoyed so that she'd stop asking me questions. On the way to the bachelorette party Anthony called Charmine. She didn't have too much to say, but whatever he said moved her as her eyes shined with liquid that soon streamed down her face. I dug in my bag, pulled out some tissues and handed them to her. They were on the phone a bit longer. She then said she 'loved him more' and hung up. At the next light, I texted Faizon and told her we'd be there in ten minutes.

I parked in the parking lot of the club, and Charmine stated she had heard of this place. However, she still hadn't caught on that we had planned a party—she thought we were there just for a quick drink. I sent one last text to Faizon to let her know we were in the elevator. When we reached the rooftop and the doors opened her guests yelled "Surprise!" She stumbled backwards and I took her arm and escorted her back out of the elevator. "Oh my God!! I can't believe this is happening," she cried.

"Yes, it's happening," Faizon said and wrapped a Bride banner across her body. "Now we can party!" Charmine looked at me and shook her finger in my face.

"I can't believe we've been together all day and you didn't say a word about this."

"If I did, then it wouldn't have been a surprise." I said. Charmine gave me a tight squeeze.

"Don't I get one of those? Lane and I planned this together," Faizon said, as she slithered from out of nowhere.

"Of course you do." Charmine walked over to her and gave her a hug. A host of Charmine's friends were there: her friends from her old law firm, some of our old college friends who now lived in Atlanta, and all of her bridesmaids. We drank, and danced the night away to the thumping sounds of the DJ as we overlooked the romantic Atlanta skyline. I looked to my left and spotted Charmine as she danced wildly on top of a table to the energetic sounds of Rihanna.

I was feeling particularly sexy, and I wanted to hear Clay's voice so I called him. Clay answered his phone, but I barely heard him from all the noise in the background. However, I was able to establish that he was still at the Gentlemen's Club with Shon. I was a bit inebriated and promised him that I would perform sexual favors for him when I arrived at his house. Clay told me to just promise him that I'd make it home safely, and if I felt I wasn't in any condition to drive, to call him. After I finished my call, I sat down on one of the V-shaped couches and finished my drink. Faizon and one of Charmine's colleagues pulled her down safely from the table and guided her over to the couch next to me. "So. . . you enjoying yourself?" I slurred.

"Hell yeah! I'm having the best time with my girls. Y'all hooked-me-up!" Charmine said and snapped her fingers offbeat.

"That's what's up. It's good to know that Lane and I could let bygones be bygones and do this for you," Faizon said.

"And me too, 'cause y'all bitches were getting on my nerves," Charmine said. Faizon wrapped her arm around my neck, leaned in, and whispered in my ear that she wished that she had never betrayed me. It could have been the three mojitos in her system, but she appeared to be genuine, and for tonight I chose to rid myself of all the hostile feelings I had towards her. The night climaxed when Charmine's colleague had the bar hostess bring up the cake, lit with colorful sparkles. We all tried to sing a verse of "Congratulations" by Vesta which didn't go to well, so we gave up. And Charmine cut her cake.

As Charmine's guests started to leave the party, they wished her well and told her they would see her at the wedding. Charmine thanked them all for coming out to celebrate with her as they left the rooftop. Faizon looked at her watch and reported it was three in the morning, and we should be headed home as well. "Faizon is right. I have to get some sleep, or in the morning my face is going to look like it took some hits from Laila Ali," Charmine said.

"I would love to take you straight home, but we've all had way too much alcohol to drive. There's a Waffle House not too far from here. We should get us some coffee and something to eat from there, and then go home," I advised.

"I'm with it. I can't even remember how many drinks I had tonight," Faizon chimed in.

"What about you and Faizon's cars?" Charmine asked.

"We'll catch a cab. I'll explain to the owner why we're leaving our cars so he won't have them towed. Then after we eat, we'll have the cab bring us back to get our cars"

"Sounds good, because now I have the taste for a pecan waffle," Faizon said. We waited on the elevator to take us downstairs. I asked Faizon to call the cab while I spoke to the owner and explained the situation. Ross, the owner of the club, told me our cars would be fine in the parking lot, and as I walked out of the building, the cab was just pulling up. Faizon and Charmine tripped over each other as they staggered into the cab. They were both super drunk, and I wasn't much less. I asked the cab driver to take us to the nearest Waffle House, and he drove at top speed because Faizon kept threatening to puke in his cab. After the cab driver took the money for his fare, he hurried us out in fear that Faizon would hurl in his backseat. Once we were inside the noisy Waffle House we all ordered pecan waffles with scrambled eggs, and I told the waiter to keep the coffee coming. It appeared we weren't the only ones coming there to sober up by the looks of the other drunk customers.

As we recapped the events of the party, Faizon confessed her highlight of the night was when Charmine danced on the table. I held my stomach and laughed until I cried with the vision of Charmine as she swung her bridal banner in the air. Charmine made us swear that we wouldn't post any of the photos of her out of character on Facebook. She said it wouldn't look good for her or her new law firm. I realized the Waffle House may not have been the best idea as it had gotten even more crowded with what seemed like all of Atlanta's club-goers who wanted a bite to eat before they hung up their six inch heels. I noticed the far away look in Charmine's eyes. Her thoughts were a million miles away from the small booth we shared. She looked down at her watch and rocked her body to the jukebox music being played. "Well, this is it. Tomorrow night at this time I'll be Mrs. Charmine Grant Martin," she said. I sipped some of my coffee and placed the cup back on the table.

"Everything just seemed to happen so fast with you two. It went from you not wanting to date him because he was a colleague, to this."

"I know. I still can't believe it sometimes," Charmine said.

"You better believe it.'Cause after tomorrow it's no turning back," Faizon said.

"I don't want to turn back."

When our food was brought to our table, we ceased talking to one another and devoured it. We had asked for so many refills on our coffee that our waitress got tired of going back and forth and left the pot in front of us. After multiple cups of coffee my eyes had regained their focus, and I was able to string together a complete sentence without bursting into laughter about air. After Faizon ate her second pecan waffle drenched in maple syrup, she appeared to have sobered up as well. She pulled her phone out to call the cab back to pick us up.

We remained seated in our booth until we saw the cab drive up. I paid our check and told our waitress to keep the change. The same cab driver who dropped us off had returned to pick up us. When he dropped us off at the Whiskey Bar, he told us get home safe, then he pulled off. We walked Faizon to her car and as we talked, my phone vibrated, it was Clay. He was concerned and wanted to know where we were. I told him I'd be home in about an hour, because I still hadn't dropped Charmine off at home. "You two don't understand how lucky you are," Faizon said as she opened her car door, and got in. "To be loved the way Clay and Anthony loves y'all...some women will never get to experience that. See y'all in the morning...I mean in a few hours," she laughed.

"Get home safely, and thank you for such a wonderful night," Charmine said.

"Yeah, tonight was the bomb. Text me when you get in the house," I said. Faizon nodded, put on her seat belt and drove off. Charmine and I got in my car, and I proceeded to take her home.

Charmine expressed how badly she felt about Faizon's admission of not feeling like she was loved. Faizon's statement had brought Charmine to tears. "Are you kiddin' me, Char? She's got you fooled. I know we said we put all that shit under the bridge, but I'm not falling for that."

"Easy for you to say when you have a man like Clay at home waiting on you, but she has no one."

"Now I know you're joking. You saw firsthand all of the losers I had to deal with before Clay, but I've never slept with anyone's man, and that's exactly what she looks for. Look at her. She is a gorgeous talented independent woman. Why in the hell would she need to sleep with my man?"

"I don't know, Lane. I feel sorry for her that's all."

"And I don't know either. If you want to feel sorry for someone, you better start feeling sorry for yourself. 'Cause you're gonna need some teabags and Preparation H to reduce that luggage under your eyes. And you have less than four hours to sleep before we need to pick up your parents and get over to the hotel for your photos. Charmine dropped the subject of Faizon and closed her eyes the rest of the way to her house. When we got there, I nudged her gently and told her we had arrived. She got out of my car and walked into the house. I waited until she waved me off and closed her door before I pulled off.

On the way home, I thought about what Faizon said about being lucky, and contrary to what Faizon may have thought, I did know how lucky I was to have Clay in my life. I never knew what genuine unconditional love was until him. I thought about Dre, but not because he genuinely loved me, but because when I was with him, I felt like Faizon...unworthy and lonely. I thought how those two would be perfect for each other and grinned.

I got to Clay's house just as the sun peeked from out of the darkness. I grabbed my shoes from my backseat and walked up the driveway barefooted. When I got in the house, Clay was in the living room wide awake, but he looked exhausted. "You finally made it in, huh? Come to bed," he said. He led the way to the bedroom—I pulled my dress over my head and tossed it on the leather chair next to the chest of drawers. I climbed into bed and curled up next to his partially naked, warm body and slid my hand in his briefs.

"I am so lucky," I whispered as Faizon's words rang in my head.

"What'd you say?" he asked.

"Nothing, Baby."

"Glad you're home, Bae. Goodnight."

"Me too. Goodnight, Clay."

Anthony

With all of our new projects scheduled so closely together, Charmine had been greatly stressed out lately, but her Superwoman mentality wouldn't allow her to ask for anyone's help. I knew she was a tigress from the first time I had ever laid eyes on her in the courtroom. She had demonstrated an aggressive and ruthless "in your face" courtroom style which was a real treat to watch, and I enjoyed watching. And for those very same reasons, I was too intimidated to approach her on a personal level.

It was ridiculous how tongue-tied I used to get around her, and I tried to build up enough confidence to at least say hi. Over the course of a few weeks, I looked forward to watching her as she dissected witnesses' alibis and testimonies and D.A theories in order to save her clients. Then one day she wasn't there. One day turned into two, and finally I realized she wasn't coming back. I had missed my chance to get to know her. As time passed, my reputation for being a formidable, dynamic attorney had caught the eye of several of the major law firms. One in particular was: Holland Thompson & Harrington. Mr. Thompson invited me to come in to meet with him and his other partners to see if we'd be a good fit.

Holland Thompson & Harrington was a very reputable law firm, and I was honored that they'd shown an interest in me. The morning of my meeting, I was so stoked I arrived for my meeting an hour early. I sat in a conference room and waited until they were ready to see me. I had my eyes closed to meditate when I recognized a female's voice as she talked to the receptionist outside of the conference room. Mr. Thompson and Mr. Holland entered the room, and while the door was left slightly ajar, I noticed it was the voice of Charmine 'Tigress' Grant that I heard. Mr. Holland caught my eye as I stared at her.

"I see you spotted one of our brightest stars, Charmine Grant. She joined our team nearly two months ago, and if everything works out, hopefully we'll be able to say the same about you," he said.

"Thank you, Sir. I hope so too." They apologized for Mr. Harrington's absence. They explained he was out of the country for his son's wedding. The meeting lasted for almost three hours, but I knew in the first hour I was going to accept any offer on the table just to be near Charmine Grant. I had already messed up one time, and there wouldn't be a second.

"Well, that is it for us. Do you have anything you'd like to ask, or add?" Mr. Holland asked.

"No, Sir. I believe you've covered it all, and I appreciate you both meeting with me today," I said.

"In that case, we'd like for you to join us here at: Holland Thompson & Harrington. You can take a week to mull it over and get back to us."

"Thanks, Mr. Holland, but I don't need a week sir. I'd like to accept your offer now if I may."

He chuckled at my avidity. "Of course you may. We'll get our administrative department right on it." We all shook hands and walked out of the conference room. Mr. Thompson stopped us as we approached an office a few doors down from the conference room, and knocked on it.

"Come in." We walked in, and there she was again. She stood up from behind her desk and walked over to us.

"Charmine, I'd like you to meet Anthony Martin. He's decided to be a part of the team," Mr. Holland said. She extended her hand and grasped mine.

"I thought that was you," she said, then turned to Mr. Holland. "We've worked together at the Cobb County Courthouse."

"Okay, yes. I thought you looked vaguely familiar," I said, as I looked around her office for a family photo with her husband and kids. But I didn't see any such photos.

"I hope you'll have a lot more to say in the courtroom," Mr. Holland teased, as he sensed my timidity. "We'll leave you to it then, Charmine."

"Nice to see you again, and welcome," she said. And from that introduction in her office I promised myself I would never let her out of my sight again, and I haven't.

At work I did fine around her, because it was all business and very professional. But when she invited me to social events outside of work, it took me awhile to feel totally at ease around her. It wasn't that she made me feel uncomfortable, it was just that growing up I didn't have too many social interactions with people of color in my everyday life. I was born in Cumming, Georgia, in Forsyth County and it's known for two things: for being the wealthiest county in the state of Georgia and the most racist. So I hadn't been exposed to other races or cultures as much as I would have liked. Hell, I went through my entire elementary to high school years without having a single Latino or African American in my school. It wasn't until I attended Georgia State University in Atlanta that I shared classes with African American people.

I'm aware that people liked to dispel the concept of love at first sight, but that's exactly what it was for me when I met Charmine. The day we had breakfast together while we waited on our clients for a meeting, I gathered up enough nerve to finally give her a kiss—and I knew then I wanted her to be my wife—and in a matter of a few hours she would. I talked to Charmine several times throughout the night. I wanted to make sure she still wanted to get married and hadn't pulled a 'runaway bride' on me, but she seemed to be just as ready as I was.

Ever since my oldest brother, Andrew, had gotten married, my brothers and I had started a Martin family tradition, which is we all go camping on the eve of the brother who's getting married. And although I was the second oldest, I was the last to get married. My brother, Andrew, called me the day before we were due to go on our camping trip, and said he was undecided if he could go with us. He claimed that something unexpected had come up, but he never revealed what would have caused him to break our family tradition. When I asked him if everything was alright, because he had also missed the rehearsal and dinner, he said he was fine and would get back to us if he decided if he could go.

As the night progressed, he never called back to confirm if he could go, so I was unsure if the trip was even still on. I called Shade, my youngest brother to see if he had heard anything that may have been troubling Andrew. "Hey there, Shade."

"Hey Dude, what's going on?"

"I'm trying to figure out what's going on with Andrew and this camping trip. Has he said anything to you?"

Shade drew a long breath and paused. "... I don't know what's going through his head. You know Andrew can be a real dickhead sometimes. But if he doesn't pull his act together soon, we'll just go without him."

"OK, if you say so, but I still would like to know what's troubling him?" Shade and I had to make an alternative plan just in case Andrew hadn't changed his mind about going camping with us. He had all of the camping equipment in his van. I really wanted him to go, but if not, I wasn't going to be boggled down with why.

The next day, I called my mother. I wanted to wear my dad's diamond cufflinks on my wedding day, and anything you had to ask my dad had to be approved by her first. We talked for a bit, and then she told me I could wear the cufflinks and that she'd send them to the hotel with one of my brothers. She asked me about the camping trip, and I told her I wasn't sure if Andrew was going because we still hadn't heard from him, but we still planned to go. My mother told me that Andrew was at the house and that he was out back with my dad. Shocked, I asked her to call Andrew to the phone, and while I waited, I composed the question I really wanted him to answer without losing my cool. "Yeah," Andrew said.

"Yeah? What in the hell is going on with you, Bro? I've been calling you all morning about us going camping tomorrow night, and I haven't heard anything back from you," I said.

"It slipped my mind. I've been busy helping dad with the roof half the afternoon."

"That's fine, but I want to know what is your deal, and plus you have all the camping gear in your van."

"Can't you use Jeremy's? I just don't want to be a hypocrite."

"What? Now you've lost me. What does going camping have to do with you being a hypocrite?"

"Nothing. Forget I ever said anything."

"No. I don't want to forget about it, say what's on your mind," I pressed.

"Alright, just remember you forced it out of me. Don't get me wrong I like Charmine, but. . ."

"But what?"

"She's. . . well. . .you know."

"What? Beautiful? Intelligent? About to be my wife? What? Just say it." I asked through clenched teeth.

"She's black, Anthony!"

"You don't think I know that, you idiot! You've known Charmine for over a year now, so you knew she was black too. Why is that an issue now?"

"I thought she was just a fling. I never thought you'd be serious about marrying her." I love my brother dearly, but never have I wanted to rip his throat out as I did at that moment. His statement hurt me deeply because out of all my siblings we have always been the closest. As kids we did everything together, and to know that he felt that way about my future wife made me sick. For years, I have dealt with my parents' ignorance and their foolish beliefs. Not that I felt it was acceptable, but because I honestly believed they didn't know any better...but Andrew? In that conversation I made sure he understood that if he didn't approve of my choice for a wife and couldn't be supportive, then clearly he couldn't be my best man at my wedding. The conversation with my oldest brother had unsettled me, but I knew I'd done the right thing, especially after I resigned that I hadn't excluded him, but he excluded himself.

I downed a beer before I called Shade to tell him it'd be just us three, and the lack of surprise demonstrated by Shade, implicated he knew why Andrew had refused to take my calls and pulled out of the camping trip. I needed to know if Shade felt the same way, so I grabbed another beer and went out on my deck "Shade, I gotta ask you this, and I don't want you to beat around the bush. Do you feel the same as Andrew?"

"Aw, c'mon Dude! Why would you ask me something like that? You know I think Charmine is awesome."

"I thought I knew Andrew, but what a shocker he turned out to be."

"I'm not defending him, but give him a break he's a bit screwed up. This is all unfamiliar territory for him. You know how we were raised." I would have loved for all my brothers to have thought Charmine was 'awesome' but I'm glad to have two brothers on my side. Before Shade and I hung up, I asked him to be responsible for getting the camping gear from Andrew as I couldn't bear to look at him, and he agreed he'd handle all of that. Shade told me that he would pick me up from my house at nine o'clock, and not to let what our brother said put a damper on my trip.

That night, I tried to get a good night's sleep, but instead I tossed and turned. I became so unhinged that I got out of bed, and I sat in the chair and watched Charmine while she slept so peacefully. I wished that my parents and Andrew could have seen her as I do. Charmine stirred from her sleep and looked up at me. "What's the matter, Baby?" Charmine asked still hazed.

"Nothing, Sweetie. I'm only sitting here looking at how beautiful you are."

"Oh, Baby, come back to bed it's late."

"I will. You go back to sleep." Charmine rolled over and went back to sleep, but before I joined her I had resolved within myself that I may have loss a brother, but gained a wife. I eventually fell asleep, and Charmine woke me. She said she knew I wanted to be up by eight o'clock for my camping trip. I lagged as I got out of bed, and Charmine said she noticed I didn't seem as enthused about the camping trip as I had been previously.

"Anthony, you're worrying me. Last night I caught you staring at me while I was sleeping, and this morning you look like you've loss your best friend. Are you sure you still want to go through with the wedding?"

"That's the one thing I'm a hundred percent sure of. I can't wait until I hear you say, I do.

"Then tell me what's bothering you?"

FORBIDDEN SEDUCTION

"Nothing. Nothing at all. You go and have a great day with Lane." How could I have possibly found a way to tell her that my brother doesn't want to be my best man because of the color of her skin? I hopped in the shower, got dressed, and waited for my brothers to pick me up. When my doorbell rang, I thought it was my brothers, but it Lane. She had arrived at the house early to take Charmine away for the day. "Good morning, Lane."

"Good morning, Mr. Grant, or will you not be taking your wife's last name?" Lane laughed.

"Funny, Lane. Where are you taking my wife-to-be?"

"Uh um, Hun, she has one more day as a free woman. After tomorrow you can ask those type questions."

"You're a regular comedienne this morning, I see."

"I'm just joking. My furniture is coming this morning and she's gonna help me arrange it, and later on I have something nice planned. Where are you headed?"

"My brothers and I are going down to the Chattahoochee Oconee forest for some camping."

"You're going camping the day before you get married? OK. Lions, tigers, and bears, oh my. Be sure you come back in one piece, and don't be out there trying to play nice-nice with them damn bears either." Lane and Charmine thought that was hilarious and crumbled with laughter.

Charmine attempted to defend me as she wiped tears from her eyes as she laughed hysterically. "Leave him alone, Lane," she said and walked over to me and apologized for laughing so hard. I asked Lane to excuse Charmine for a minute. I wanted to talk to her alone because I wouldn't see her again until we were at the church to exchange our vows. Charmine followed me into our office, and I closed the door. I grabbed onto her and hugged her close to me.

"I want you to know you've made me the happiest man on Earth, and I can't wait to see you walking down that aisle tomorrow."

"I feel the same way, Baby. I love you so much," she kissed me softly and pulled away. "I better not give you too much now, or you won't have anything to look forward to tomorrow night." I tried to get her to change her mind but she wouldn't budge. She opened the door when she heard car horn beeps from outside our house. "That should

209

be your brothers," she said and sent me off with a quick peck on my cheek. I grabbed my rucksack from inside my room, told the girls to have a good day, and left my house.

`When I got outside, Jeremy and Shade were in the front seat of Shade's SUV. I walked around to the back to put my things in the back of the SUV and there stood Andrew. I hadn't expected to see him there, and he startled me, but it was a good startle and it meant everything to me that he was there. "I could never let you down," Andrew said, and he pulled me in for a bear hug. I held back tears as I was too choked up to respond. He threw his arm around me and we hopped in the SUV.

We stopped at Wal-Mart and Q.T. for some last minute camping trip needs. Andrew filled our coolers with ice and bottled beers while Shade filled the SUV with gas. The journey was a little over an hour and once we got there we set up our site; Jeremy and I started a rousing fire. It was such a good feeling to be surrounded by all my brothers. When Jeremy and Andrew bickered over who pitched the better tent, it took me back to when we were kids arguing over the Saturday morning cartoons.

As night fell and the beer cooler emptied, we sat around the fire and talked about life, wives, and kids. I was the last brother to do this marriage thing, and as we sat hunched around the fire, all the advice that was given was directed at me. "A few things you gotta look for, Anthony. Once you say 'I do,' headaches will become a perpetual condition. Your time has now become her time, and you can forget about Sunday night football in peace," Jeremy said.

"No, I have one for you," Jeremy said. "Every time you see her in a brand new outfit, tags could still be swinging from the armpit, but this is what you'll hear: 'This old thing, I've had it forever.' that's Madison's favorite line." We all laughed at him as he turned beet red, it was like it had just happened to him. Shade noticed we had drunk our last beer and he asked Jeremy to go with him back to his vehicle to grab some more beers and some other stuff. As they walked back to the SUV Andrew and I remained seated in our camping chairs. I rubbed my hands over the blazing fire for warmth as the night chill had set in.

"Uh, I wanna thank you for putting your differences aside and coming out here with us, it means a lot to me," I said.

"Don't mention it baby bro. As your older brother, I should've never put you in that predicament. I was worried that you were gonna tell me to scram once you saw me, but I had to take that chance."

"Absolutely not. Although I was prepared to let you go, I'm glad I didn't have to."

"You love her that much?" Andrew asked.

"Yeah, I do. Charmine is an amazing woman, and given the chance you'll think so too."

"You know, on our camping trips there are no restrictions—we can ask, or do anything, right?"

"Right?"

"Well, I have a question to ask that I've been dying to know the answer to, and I hope you won't think my question is distasteful, but I'm just curious."

"Alright, ask away."

"How does it feel to kiss a black woman?" At first I didn't know how to take the question. I didn't know if I should have been offended or angry, but his question meant he wanted to learn about something he apparently felt uncomfortable about.

"When you kiss Brittany, how do you feel?"

"That's irrelevant, I know she's white."

"In this particular instance I'm not asking you what you know, I'm asking you what you feel.

He thought on it for a minute as if I had asked him a trick question or something, and he thoughtfully responded. "I feel love."

"Exactly. And that's precisely what I feel when I kiss Charmine...love." When I said that, he looked at me as if a light bulb blinked on above his head. He left his chair and gave me a second bear hug tighter than the first. "So does this mean you're back on for being my best man?"

"Of course it does, you couldn't stop me." When Jeremy and Shade returned with the beer, Andrew and I were still locked in a hug.

"Cut that sissy crap out. It's time to get wasted," Shade said. We looked at Shade who stood near his chair with two beer bottles in his hands. Andrew picked up a rock and threw it at him. Jeremy defended his baby brother, and he picked up a rock and threw it back at Andrew.

FORBIDDEN SEDUCTION

I cracked opened my brew and watched the intoxicated trio as they engaged in a rock toss—happy that the Martin boys were all together.

Charmine

The steam from the tea kettle had seared my knuckles as I gripped onto its handle, still half asleep from the bachelorette party held in my honor. I had just poured myself an oversized mug of green tea and sat at the table when Anthony called to wish me a happy wedding day. I told Anthony I appreciated his call, but I had to get ready because Lane would be at the house at any minute to pick me up to take me to the hotel. He asked me to allow him another minute, and at that moment, someone rang my doorbell; I thought it may have been Lane so I dragged myself to the door.

I opened the door without checking the peephole, and there stood a man in a black tuxedo with a bouquet of flowers in one hand and a small box in the other. I asked Anthony did he know anything about the unexpected visitor. He said he did. It was his way of thanking me for being his wife. The man who was dressed as if he was getting married himself handed me the flowers and the box—I thanked him, and he left. Anthony remained on the phone while I opened the red velvet box from the Solomon Brothers jewelry store. "Oh, Anthony," I cried, as I pulled out a pair of platinum diamond drop earrings. "Oh my God, Anthony. There are absolutely beautiful."

"Not nearly as beautiful as you. I wanted to be the one to give you the something new to wear today. Just as you have given me a new beginning; a new life. I love you sweetheart."

"Oh Honey, I love you too. See you in a few hours." After we hung up, I stood at the table and doted on my precious new gift. When my doorbell rang again, this time I knew it had to be Lane. I opened the door for her, and she looked about as rough as I did. "Girl, you look crazy. Do you want some tea or some coffee?"

"Are you serious? Have you looked at yourself this morning? And I'm not the one who's getting married."

"Aw, shut up! I asked you do you want something to drink?"

"No, we're already behind schedule. And please tell me why you are still in your robe?" I held up my diamond earrings and showed her. "Who gave you those? Anthony?"

"Yes ma'am, he did."

"Anthony don't be playing! These are gorgeous—you've got to wear these today."

"I am. Anthony bought them for me to wear today." I left my earrings in Lane's hands as I grabbed my wedding dress and shoes from my office. Lane reminded me that the glam team would meet us at the hotel at ten o'clock to do all of the bridal party's hair and make-up. I called my parents to tell them that Lane and I were on our way to pick them up, but my mother told me that my uncle had just called and agreed to bring them to the hotel. Before we left my house, we rechecked all the rooms to make sure I hadn't left anything behind.

I had gotten a blinding headache since my phone had buzzed from the moment I opened my eyes. Emily called in an alarmed state which only made my headache worse; she said that her ex-husband had the children for the weekend, but he hadn't brought them back at the agreed time. I panicked because they were my: ring bearer, junior groom, and junior bridesmaid. She told me that Jeremy and Shade had left for her ex-husband's house to get the children, but she hadn't heard anything back from them as of yet. Faizon called, she said that after she had seen the state that Lane was in last night, she wanted to be sure that Lane hadn't overslept, and picked me up on time. After Faizon's call my phone rang again, and this call had to be by far the most shocking. "Hello," I said

"Good morning, Charmine. This is Andrew."

"Andrew?" I hadn't recognized the voice straight away although the name was familiar, but then it clicked. "Oh, Andrew."

"I know you're busy getting ready to marry my brother, today, so I won't take up too much of your time, but I wanted to take this time to welcome you into our family. I've never seen 'Squirt' so happy."

"Squirt?" I chuckled.

"Yeah, that's the nickname I gave him when we were younger. I'm not surprised he never told you, because as he's gotten older, he's always been embarrassed about that. He earned that name because he used to squirt milk from his eyes when we were kids." Boy. How we both laughed about it. Before he hung up, he apologized for not having taken the time to get to know me—I accepted his apology and told him that I'd see him at the church. We pulled up to the front of the hotel as I ended my call with Andrew. The hotel staff greeted us and helped us up to our room with our bags. We had a large suite and another adjoining room for my mother to get dressed all to herself; she never liked the idea of women getting dressed in front of one another.

Emily called me back as soon as I entered the room. She sounded much more cheerful and her news put me at ease. She reported that Shade and Jeremy had picked up the children from her ex, and that she would see me at the hotel soon with Jayla. My bridesmaids had arrived. And as they came in the room, the hair stylist grabbed them first for their hair, and when they were finished, they were sent straight to the make-up artist. By the time Faizon had arrived, I was a wreck. And it didn't help that she came with her personal team which consisted of a manicurist, make-up artist, and hair stylist.

The large suite was already overly crowded with my bridesmaids who trampled over each other as they tried to get dressed, and now Faizon's mini entourage only made it worse. Lane detected I was about to blow my cool. She brought me a glass of wine and told me to find a seat. Lane wanted a reason to cut Faizon to shreds and seized the opportunity. "Faizon, you do understand that this isn't your wedding, and you're being real extra right now, don't you?"

Faizon looked at Lane from her one opened eye as her make-up artist continued to put on her lashes. "What are you talking about? I just got here."

"I told you last night I had my people coming to the hotel to take care of all that. Why are you acting like this is the Faizon show. I. . . I don't get it."

"And I don't expect you to get it. I am my own brand, and I represent my brand from the minute I wake up until I go to bed and every minute in-between. So, excuse me if I didn't want to use *your* people who you probably found in the Yellow Pages." Lane stepped closer to Faizon, and I shouted out to Lane immediately. Faizon's lashes were still being applied, and she hadn't realized just how close she came to having them ripped from her eyes.

"Forget it Lane," I pleaded. "They're here already, just let them finish." I returned to my seat, and my hair stylist continued her work. I grabbed my wine from the tray and gulped the last bit of it and demanded someone pour me another. I looked around the room and realized my mother, Emily, nor had Jayla arrived at the hotel yet. I asked one of my bridesmaids to take my phone and call to find out the location of my mother at least. I seriously needed her to be at the hotel with me seeing that I knew Lane would have never behaved badly in front of her. Simone dialed my mother's number and handed me the phone. "Hello," my mother answered.

"Mother, where are you?"

"We're in the elevator now, Precious. We'll be up in a minute."

"Hurry, Mother." Here I sat, a prestigious attorney, with credentials that could have lined the walls of three offices, yet I cried for my mother. When I told Lane my mother was on her way up, she opened the door and poked her head out. Lane called out to my mother and directed her to the room. When my mother and father entered the room, everyone greeted them, and they also straightened up their language just as I suspected they would. My parents walked over to where I sat and kissed my cheek.

"Good morning, we're here now," she said. I wasn't even fully dressed and my father took his handkerchief from his jacket and wiped his eyes.

"Please don't get me started, Daddy," I said.

"He's alright, Precious. He's been like this all morning," my mother said.

"I'm okay, Angel. It's a big day for you," he said.

"I'll be fine. I'm worried about you, now."

216

"We'll both be fine Angel, as long as we don't trip up the aisle."

I asked my mother where my uncle and his wife were, she told me that after they had dropped them off at the hotel, they went to get some breakfast. After my parents spoke with Lane and the rest of the bridal party, they excused themselves to their room to get dressed. Faizon and Lane hadn't spoken three words to each other since the argument over Glamgate, and they stayed out of each other's way. By the time most of the bridesmaids were dressed, Emily and Jayla had finally shown up and jumped right into the flow of things. I yelled for Tracey to give me the time. She said it was nearly noon and time for the photographer to arrive for our photos.

I started to get nervous, and my make-up artist positioned her mini fan directly on my face as beads of sweat trickled down my temples. As the last few of my bridesmaids were finished with their hair and make-up, they got dressed in their Faizon Hill designs. At first glance, I was proud to say all of them looked as if they had stepped straight out of a magazine. Faizon had designed a different dress for each of the ladies which complemented their bodies so perfectly. Even the ladies were amazed at how beautiful the dresses looked on them.

Lane hated to admit it, but her face radiated once she slipped on her dress, and everyone told her how amazing she looked. "Girl, I look too damn bootylicious in this dress. Clay may not let me make it all the way down the aisle once he sees me in this," Lane said, as she eyed her rear-end in the full length mirror.

"Pardon me, Lane," Emily shouted, as she shielded Jayla's ears. "You do have a minor in the room."

"My bad, Jayla. Don't pay any attention to your auntie Lane." The hair, and make-up team that Lane's hired had finished with me, and I wanted my mother to be in the room before I stepped into my wedding dress. I called their room and told my mother I was ready. The photographer showed up just as I ended the call with my mother. He entered the room and immediately started to take photos. My mother opened the door that adjoined our rooms, and when she saw the all the bridesmaids her mouth dropped opened.

"Oh, my goodness, you all look so pretty. I know my baby already thanked all y'all, but I want to personally thank you too for taking part in Charmine's day. And thank you, Faizon for making all these lovely dresses." The photographer asked the ladies to follow him as he wanted to take shots of them together. As they all focused their attention on the photographer, my mother and Lane unhooked my dress from the rail. Lane unzipped the garment bag and pulled out my masterpiece—I held onto my mother as I stepped into my dress—Lane zipped up the side and stood back to look at me.

"Oh my God, Charmine. You are stunning." When all the bridesmaids heard Lane's exclamation, they left the photographer and rushed to see me in my dress, and they all echoed the same. From the moment I put on my dress, I felt like a princess, and all the 'Ooh's' and 'Aahs' confirmed it. Faizon walked over and fluffed the lace at the bottom of my dress for more pouf and adjusted the back of the dress a bit more. Faizon smoothed, tucked, and fluffed the dress a few times before she was satisfied with how it looked.

"I'm one bad bitch! Atlanta ain't gonna know what hit 'em once my fashion line is out." The photographer snapped us as we cried during this monumental moment. My dad knocked on the door before he entered the room filled with women.

"Look at my baby. Charmine, you look so elegant," he said and stepped back to stand alongside my mother. "I'm speechless."

"Thank you, Daddy. You look very handsome yourself." The photographer snapped photos of me and my parents. When he finished, he said he'd shot enough frames of all of us at the hotel, and he'd meet us over at the church. The make-up artist stayed at the hotel just in case she had to retouch any of the ladies faces. My father had been in the military for most of his life. He was a stickler for time constraints, and he rounded up all the bridesmaids to prepare to leave the hotel. All the ladies obeyed my father's direct orders, gathered their bags, and headed for the door. Once the room was cleared out, my mother patted a spot on the bed for me to join her. I sat down next to my mother. She pulled a long leather case from her purse and handed it to me. I opened the case and in it was the long stringed pearls my grandmother had given her, and now she had given them to me.

My mother unpinned the secured pearls from the case and draped them around my neck. I placed my hands over the cherished pearls. "Are you sure you want me to have these, Mother?" I choked up again. "These belonged to Grandmother."

"I'm positive I want you to have them, Baby. Nothing would make me happier."

"I don't know why I can't help but to feel so nervous, like something is going to go wrong like it did the first time."

"You get those silly thoughts right out of your head, 'cause God got His hands in and on this union. Today has nothing to do with yesterday." She hugged me and assisted me off the bed. She also fixed the bottom of my dress as she had seen Faizon do earlier. "I don't want to have to kill that chile."

"Her name is Faizon, Mother."

"I know what that chile's name is. I still don't wanna have to kill her."

"Well, that makes you and Lane both." My mother looked at me very puzzled. "Long story, I'll tell you another time." I held my mother's hand as we walked out of the hotel room and into the elevator. Once we got downstairs, my dad, my eight bridesmaids, one junior bridesmaid, Lane and Faizon were seated in the Range Rover limousine. The chauffeur assisted my mother and me up in the limo, and off to the church we went. As I sat in the limo packed with friends and family, I marveled at how differently things had changed for me. A year ago I would have never believed that I would have fallen in love, opened my own law firm, purchased a new home, and get married to the love of my life. But it's really happening for me this time, and I feel so good.

FORBIDDEN SEDUCTION

Lane

Faizon sat next to me in the limo, and she continued with her over-the-top dramatics. It took everything in me not to have reached out and touched her. She had irked my nerves from the moment she came to the hotel, but I promised Char and her mother that I wouldn't create a scene. The street long, limousine was well-stocked with every drink imaginable, and Tracey had guzzled down two flutes of champagne before Charmine and Mrs. Grant even came downstairs. Jayla hopped from spot to spot, fascinated by the TV and other amenities while the other ladies were just as excited about the wedding itself. The noise level in the limo was that of a basketball cheer-leading squad, and I had missed several of Clay's calls because of it. So, he texted me, and he told me he loved me and would see me at the church.

Charmine and Mrs. Grant emerged from the hotel. The chauffeur assisted them up into the limo and closed the door. Charmine sat in-between her parents, and she looked extraordinarily beautiful and happy. She had on the diamond earrings that Anthony had given her earlier, and a lovely string of pearls hugged her neck. She beamed with joy as she talked about her readiness to see Anthony and finally be his wife. Tracey asked

Charmine if she wanted a glass of champagne, and she accepted. "Whoa, Charmine, you better slow down. You've already had some wine upstairs. You want to at least be sober when you say your vows," Faizon said.

"Give it to her Tracey," I interjected. "She doesn't need Faizon to be her drink monitor."

"Okay, Boo. I was only looking out for her. It's not gonna be a good look if she's up there at the altar, slurring her vows."

"Some people can have a drink and not lose a sense of self."

"I see where this is heading. Tracey, please pour Charmine a glass of champagne too if she wants."

"You two chill out! Tracey I will have a glass, but just a little bit," Charmine said. Tracey poured Charmine the drink and passed it to her. When we arrived at the church, the chauffeur hopped out and escorted all of us out of the limo. Mrs. Grant and Charmine took a hold of Mr. Grant's arms, and they entered the church through a side entrance to avoid being seen by the guests, but more importantly Anthony. As promised the photographer and make-up artist were there and had set up in a designated room in the church. The photographer informed Charmine that he'd already captured shots of Anthony, his family, and the groomsmen.

I wanted to see if Clay had arrived, so I walked through a side entrance and peeked inside the church. The church was filled with guests, but no sign of Clay. However, I did see Anthony. He looked so good as he stood at the alter in his tailored ivory suit and a purple tie that matched the bridesmaid dresses. I glanced once more for Clay before I went back in the room and joined the others. Mr. Grant exposed his watch from the cuff of his suit and informed us of the time. The bridesmaids lined up at the door and waited for the cue.

Mrs. Martin came to the room for the first time since we'd been there. She walked over to Emily, wiped a smudge of lipstick from the corner of her mouth, and told Jayla she looked beautiful. When she approached Char, Char's shoulders immediately tensed up. Charmine told me that Mrs. Martin was known for saying the most uncouth things, but I hoped she'd exercise some decorum today. Mrs. Martin took Charmine's hands in hers, and smiled. "You are beautiful, Dear," she said, and she initiated a hug from Charmine and left the room.

With everyone lined up at the door, I asked Mrs. Grant if I could have a minute with Char by myself. She walked off and stood by her husband. "What's the matter, Lane?" Charmine asked.

"Nothing's wrong. I know this will be my last chance to get you by yourself before the wedding starts. I just want to tell you how happy I am for you that you've found someone who loves you as much as Anthony does. You two are going to be so happy together. I love you, Girl."

"Ah, thank you, and I love you too, Chica," she said. I then pulled an envelope from my clutch bag and placed it in Charmine's hand. "What's this?"

"My wedding gift to you and Anthony."

Charmine opened the envelope and read the contents. "Oh my God! Are you freaking serious? Greece for seven days?" she said, and grabbed me tightly.

"Yeah, I wanted to pick a place I knew you haven't been yet, plus I heard the weather is wonderful this time of year."

"What the hell? Did you rob your bank, or something?"

"Err... how 'bout it's rude to look a gift horse in the mouth."

"I'm not. I just don't want you to have over extended yourself on a trip this extravagant, and when I come back, I find out that you've been eating Ramen," she said.

"Not at all. Let's just say it's a gift from me and my mother. She made sure that I wouldn't have to worry about money as much." I kissed Charmine on her cheek and told her I'd hold on to the tickets until after the wedding. She gave them back to me, and I placed them back into my bag. The music had started which was our cue the wedding had officially commenced. I joined the wedding party line, and we walked out of the room into the vestibule of the church. Mrs. Grant and Mrs. Martin were the first to be escorted down the aisle. I watched with butterflies as the bridesmaids sashayed down the aisle with Anthony's groomsmen on their arms.

After Faizon and Jayla walked down the aisle, Anthony's brother, Andrew, and I were next in line. As we glided down the aisle, I searched for Clay through the sea of faces in the pews. I finally locked eyes with him—and the way he looked at me I knew it was on when we got home. Anthony's twin nephews, Jayden and Jordan were the ring-bearers; one carried Anthony's ring, and the other twin carried Charmine's. The organ music stopped, and Charlie Wilson's "You Are" started to play and the entire church rose to their feet. The ushers reopened the doors and presented Charmine to everyone.

The church gushed at the sight of the beautiful bride as she held onto her father's arm. Anthony, boyishly wiped tears from his eyes as Charmine walked towards him, and the closer she got to him, the more tears he shed. Andrew gripped his brother's shoulder firmly and handed him a handkerchief. Mr. Grant and Charmine now stood side by side with Anthony. The priest started the wedding procedure, and once Mr. Grant said he handed his daughter's hand in marriage to Anthony, he kissed her sweetly on her cheek and sat down next to his wife.

After the priest performed his part of the ceremony, Charmine and Anthony recited the vows which they prepared for each other. As they exchanged their vows, I looked in their faces. They genuinely looked so happy together. It was such a lovely, touching part of the ceremony, and all you heard were sniffles from the guests as they witnessed the tender moment. I drifted off to a time in my life when I thought I desperately wanted to be married to Dre, and thought someday we would, but I had to learn the hard way with him.

After Charmine and Anthony exchanged their vows, the priest pronounced them 'man and wife' and they bolted down the aisle as the guests applauded. Once we all piled outside the church, the photographer took more pictures of the entire wedding party and families. The guests disbursed from the church steps, but Clay stood there and watched as we posed for more pictures. After the last snapshots were taken, Charmine and Anthony fled to the reception venue in a classic '64 Rolls-Royce. Clay walked down the steps of the church, strolled over to me, and he kissed me delicately on my lips. "Damn, Baby, you look so good. I wish we could go home now," he said. "We could go and come back, no one will miss you." Clay tried to persuade me as rubbed his hands up and down my waist. "Clay, you know I'm not leaving Char's wedding, I wouldn't do that to her."

"I know. You just look so good in that dress. I wanna take it off."

"You're looking fine too," I said. I tried to convince him to ride in the limo with me to the reception venue, but he said he wanted to take his own car. He kissed me again before I had gotten in the limo with the rest of the wedding party. Jayla decided she wanted to ride in the other limo with her uncles and brothers to the reception, and Charmine's parents rode with her uncle, so us ladies acted a plain fool in the limo. Faizon was seated next to Tracey, but when she looked over and saw me and Emily, she left her seat and wedged her body to sit between us. Emily had dominated my attention about how stressed she'd been from her pending divorce, so I almost welcomed Faizon's intrusion, but I should have known she was up to something.

Faizon asked Emily the name of the groomsmen who walked her down the aisle, and Emily told her that he was her cousin, Luke.

"Ooh, Girl, you got some fine men in your family. That Luke is hot!"

"Thanks, I guess," Emily said.

"Lane, did you see the way Luke was checking me out? I'm gonna have to try me some of that white meat," Faizon said. Emily looked a bit offended by Faizon's ill-mannered remark.

"Don't pay her any attention, Emily, she's extremely crass. And plus, Faizon thinks every man wants her," I said. Faizon didn't say anything after I made my comment. She only rolled her eyes and started to apply another coat of lipstick on her lips

"I'm quite sure he'll be flattered, but Luke's in a relationship," Emily informed her.

"You got to come better than that, Emily. Luke having a girlfriend or a wife doesn't stop Faizon. Does it Faizon?"

"Oh, don't start that shit, Lane. We settled that, and you said that you forgave me." Emily looked shocked and confused by our conversation, and she decided she didn't want to sit with us anymore. She took Faizon's old spot next to Tracey and poured herself some more champagne

"I'm a lot of things, but stupid isn't one of them. I did forgive you, Faizon, but that doesn't mean I'll ever forget what you did. I hope that eventually I'll be able to chop it up with like the old days, but it's gonna take some time."

"Me too, and I understand and respect that."

"And I'm not gonna hate on you, you really did the damn thing with the dresses."

"Thanks, Lane. That means a lot, and with my launch around the corner, I need all the encouragement I can get."

"You don't have anything to worry about. You'll be very successful." Surprisingly, Faizon and I continued a pleasant conversation, and when we looked up, we were at the hotel. None of us waited to be assisted out of the limo this time. We were so ready to party that we hopped out in single file and danced our way inside the ballroom. Clay was seated at a table of single women who apparently thought he was single too. These ladies had their flirtation game turned all the way up. They flipped their weaves and batted their eyelashes so much that when I approached the table, I felt a cool breeze. When Clay excused himself from the table and pulled me aside, the ladies turned to each other and started to whisper as if I had taken their male prospect away from them. Clay couldn't keep his hands off of me. He caressed, kissed, and touched me in places that should have been left for our bedroom. "I want you so bad right now," he said.

"I want you too, Baby."

"Then let's leave."

"Clay, we already discussed that. And Char and Anthony haven't even been presented to their guests for the first time yet."

"Aight, I'm gon' chill for now, but when we get home imma need for you to come up out that dress real quick." I was flattered that Clay desired me so much, and I giggled like a teenager each time he flirted with me. Clay and I sat at the bar and had a few drinks, and again, I was interrupted by Faizon who watched us from afar. I'd noticed her staring at us earlier and had a feeling she would eventually make her way through the crowded dance floor to come over.

"Hey, you two."

"Hello." Clay said.

"The wedding was beautiful," she said, and she looked around the ballroom. "Now, this is what I call luxury."

"Yeah, it's tight," Clay said.

"I agree, everything is beautiful." I said.

"Clay, how are things looking for my launch?" Faizon asked.

"That's something you'll need to address with Nikole."

"I will, but since you're right here I thought I would ask."

"No, talk to Nikole, like I said."

"Faizon, he doesn't want to discuss it, so just leave it," I said. Faizon accepted she wasn't getting anywhere with Clay and walked away. Andrew, Anthony's brother, clinked a fork against his glass of champagne to get the guests attention. He took the microphone from the DJ and asked us all to stand as Charmine and Anthony made their entrance.

"Ladies and gentleman, family and friends, I'd like to present to you for the very first time, Mr. and Mrs. Anthony Martin." The ballroom of guests applauded thunderously as the newly married couple entered the ballroom and danced their first dance together. After their dance, Charmine and her dad danced to the Nat King Cole classic "When I Fall in Love," and they moved the guests to tears as he twirled his little girl around the floor. After their dance ended, I joined the wedding table for dinner, and Clay went back to his table of drooling women.

Before we started our dinner, Andrew wanted to make his toast to the couple. He cleared his throat and turned to face them. "When Squirt was born, I didn't think I'd like having a baby brother in the house, but as time went on I grew to love him very much. I felt it was my job to teach him how do things, like how to be a man. But this past week the roles were reversed, and he taught me something—he taught me that love is colorblind. I've never seen him as happy as he is right now with his beautiful new bride. And I want to wish them both a long and very happy life together. So join me, in raising your glasses to them both. Salute!"

Andrew walked over to Charmine and they embraced. He said something to her that couldn't be defined by the guests, but she smiled and nodded. Andrew hugged Anthony, and they both sat down to eat. Just as I thought, Charmine was whisked from table to table with guests who wanted to congratulate her and Anthony, so we didn't have much time to spend together. The DJ opened the floor to everyone, and guests young and old met on the dance floor. I left my table to relieve Clay of the starry eyed chicks, who had sucked in their bellies, and poked their breasts out to attract his attention. I walked back over to the table and asked him to dance.

As we danced, Clay held me close to his delicious body, he kissed the back of my neck, and whispered how badly he wanted to make love to me. The intense sexual chemistry between us caused me to leave the dance floor and locate a restroom. I entered the restroom and dabbed my skin with one of the moist linen towels provided in the guest toiletry basket. As I was about to leave and go back to the reception, Charmine entered the restroom. She was well over the legal limit, and she threw her arms around me. "Lane, this day has been amazing! Everything was perfect. Even Anthony's mother came over to me again and kissed me without wiping it off this time. I couldn't have dreamed better than this."

"I know, Sweetheart. Everything is perfect. And I can't think of two more deserving people, but I'm gonna have to leave you soon or give Clay some ill na-na in one of these stalls. I'm in her now tryna cool myself off."

"Eww, you nasty," she laughed. "But the good news is you won't have to do it in the bathroom. Anthony and I are leaving as soon as I toss the bouquet, and we make our goodbye rounds. We have a room upstairs, and we'll leave from here to the airport in the morning."

"What time is your flight?"

"7:10 in the morning."

"Okay, call me before you leave. I'll take your parents back to their hotel tonight before Clay and I go home."

"Thanks, but don't worry about it. My uncle is taking them to his house tonight since they leave for home tomorrow; he's taking them to airport as well."

Charmine was so drunk that as she talked to me she left out every other word. But from what I could decipher, she wanted to thank me for everything, and told me to hold onto the tickets for Greece until they got back from France in a few weeks. We kissed each other, and she rushed out of the door so she could throw her bouquet. I followed her to back into the ballroom. I asked Clay to give me a few minutes so I could tell Charmine's parents and Anthony goodbye. Clay told me that he had just talked to Anthony and wished him a good honeymoon, and said that he would get the car from the valet. I told Clay that my car was still parked at the hotel, but he said not to worry about that now, he'd bring me back later to pick it up. I located Charmine's parents—I told them that I would be leaving soon and wished them a safe trip back home.

Andrew made the announcement that the newlyweds were about to leave the reception area, and that Charmine wanted all the single ladies on the floor so she could throw her bouquet. The way the single women stampeded the floor, you would have thought Andrew said come collect the winning lottery ticket. I casually strolled on the floor and waited for Char to throw it. Faizon looked over and discovered I was on the floor and she immediately went into competition mode. Faizon took off her shoes, pulled her tight dress above her knees, and crouched down like she was on the scrimmage line. Charmine faked her first bouquet toss, but the second toss went in the air and landed easily in my hands. Faizon tried to stir up some bullshit and told the single ladies in her area that it was fixed, because I was Charmine's best friend.

As Charmine and Anthony made their exit from the ballroom, the guests waved and shouted for them to have a good honeymoon. I walked past Faizon and Luke who were engaged in a conversation by the bar. I shook my head as I witnessed him put his card in her hands. When I got outside, Clay already had the car and beeped for me as soon as he saw that I exited the hotel. I gathered the bottom of my long gown and held it in my hands as I ran to his car. I hopped in and Clay peeled off.

As Clay dashed through the traffic, I groped his visible hardness through his suit pants, and at the first traffic light, he moved my hair from my neck and kissed me behind my ear. As the sexual tension grew between us, I anticipated a night of romantic but rough lovemaking. By the time we reached the neighborhood, my desire for Clay to be inside me had greatly intensified. The tires on Clay's CLS550 screeched as he swerved into his driveway. He parked the car, and we simultaneously got out and rushed up the stairs which led to his house.

Clay opened the front door, and I hurried to the stairs where I removed my Louboutin Peeps. He straddled me and gently laid me back onto the plush carpeted stairs. Clay unhooked my bra and swirled his warm tongue over my nipples. My body shivered as it responded to his erotic touches. My body was inflamed with crazed passion. I gripped onto Clay's collar and slid up one step. The friction of the carpet had pulled my dress down and exposed my half covered body even further.

Ungracefully, I unbuckled his belt and released his throbbing manhood—Clay's hands clenched both sides of the staircase banisters and groaned as I took him fully in my mouth. I teased Clay's thick rigidness with my tongue. "Ooh...Clay, you taste so good. I want to feel you inside me." Clay lifted me from the stairs, yanked my dress off that had fallen around my ankles, and threw it to the bottom of the stairs.

Once inside Clay's room he laid me across his bed and rolled my purple lace panties off my ass. Clay's manhood throbbed against my thighs as he kissed my breasts and slid his fingers slowly in and out of my wetness. I purred as his hands explored my body, and he kissed his way down to my yearning sweetness. Clay penetrated me and breathed heavily in my ear. "I love you, Lane."

"I love you too, Dre," I said. As Dre's name left my mouth I realized my grave error for which there was no pause or rewind button. I prayed that I had said Dre's name in my mind, and Clay hadn't heard me. But when Clay pulled out of me instantly and sat up I knew he had.

"What did you say? Who did you just call me?" He yelled.

"Clay...Clay." I called out to him, horrified. I reached out to him, but he pulled back. He picked his pants up from the floor, and put them back on.

"Clay, hell! That's not what you said—you just said 'I love you too, DRE.'"

"Clay, I'm sorry, let me explain."

"Explain what? Explain how I'm making love to you, and you call me by another muthfucka's name?!" I got out of bed and wrapped myself with the sheet. Even I tried to come up with a logical explanation to why I would have called Dre's name in the most intimate moment between us. But I struggled with the answer myself to why that happened. And Clay wanted nothing to do with my lame excuse or me. Every time I tried to get near him, he moved away as if I had some contagious illness. Clay left me in the room and went downstairs. I followed him to the living room where he had poured himself a drink.

"Clay, please. Just give me a chance to explain. The only reason I can think of, is that he did cross my mind at Charmine's wedding. I...I don't know how else to explain it."

"So, that's supposed to make me feel better? The fact that you thought about him at the wedding, and I'm sitting less than ten feet away from you? And then while I'm making love to you, he just so happened to cross your mind again? Fuck outta here...who the hell you think you talking to, Lane?" My tears blinded me as he angrily fired questions at me, but I knew that if he allowed me to hold him everything would be fine.

"Clay, I'm telling you the truth. I don't know why it happened, but please, let's just sit down and talk about it."

"Now I see maybe there was some truth in what Faizon was telling me, she knew something happened between you two in Brooklyn, and she tried to warn me."

"No, no, that's not true. Nothing happened between us. Faizon only wanted to stir up some shit so she could be with you." Clay refused to take his eyes off me, and I started to sweat profusely. I felt he somehow knew I had been lying to him.

"Nah, that night at that party. The night you claimed he just showed up; the night I couldn't get a hold of you till five in the morning. You fucked him that night didn't you?" Clay asked as if he'd been given a revelation. He downed his glass of Hennessy, and sat on the edge of the sofa. "Don't lie to me Lane, or I'll call your girl right now, and I know she'll be more than happy to tell me everything." I was so confused. I didn't know what to do. My stomach had balled up into knots, and I felt sick. I thought about what Char had advised me to do; tell him the truth, but I was so scared of losing him that I dismissed her advice altogether. But if I allowed him to ask Faizon she would surely tell him everything she knew and throw in some bits of her own, then we'd be done forever.

Clay badgered me with his unending questions—I felt pressured to tell him something happened that night, but just how much to tell him was my dilemma. I stalled for time as I hadn't expected my night to take such a dreadful turn. I had a lot at stake, and none of my odds were good. Clay walked over to the bar and poured himself another drink. He gulped it down in one shot. He indignantly informed me that he wasn't going to wait another minute while I contrived a story. He

231

walked over to the coffee table and picked up his cell phone. "Am I gon' have to hear this from Faizon, or are you gonna tell me what's up?"

I had never expected Clay to find out about me and Dre, so I never prepared myself on how to answer Clay's barrage of questions. I asked Clay to pour me a drink first, and he obliged. I took a long sip of the rum drink Clay had poured for me and prayed for a miracle by the time I had gotten to the bottom of my glass. I sat down on the couch opposite him. I still had the sheet clutched so tightly above my chest that I started to lose circulation. "You don't need to call Faizon. I'll tell you what you want to know." I paused yet again by taking another sip, and this time I emptied the glass trying to get every drop. He sat in his leather chair with the look of fury on his face. "Lane...I'm not waiting much longer."

"Okay, err...that night at the party. I swear I didn't expect to see Dre there. I didn't know he knew Beverly's boyfriend, and by the time he got there, Beverly and her boyfriend were so high they were zonked out, and I just wanted to get home." I started to cry, but Clay was unfazed by my tears. "I had a little too much to drink myself that night, and Dre suggested we ride home together in a cab..." I said, but I slowed down the pace.

"Keep going," Clay said and shifted his body in the chair as if he had prepared himself to hear the worse.

"We, I went back to his apartment. . . and. . . and," I cried, and covered my face with the sheet. I was distraught. Devastated, that I had hurt Clay so badly that it broke me down, but Clay wanted to hear me say it.

"Lane, did you sleep with him?" I nodded slowly through the tear dampened sheet, but still that didn't satisfy him. "LANE! Did you sleep with him?!"

I took the sheet down and looked him face on. "I'm so sorry, Clay. I never wanted to hur---."

"Get out of my house," he stated firmly and remained seated.

"Clay, please!" I moved towards him to make him understand, to make him forgive me.

"Lane, don't make me ask you twice." I got up from the couch and stood there a few minutes more, covered only in a bed sheet, and tears.

I walked to the bottom of the stairs where Clay had thrown my dress and picked it up. I grabbed my bag and walked upstairs to Clay's bathroom where I put my dress on and called for a cab on my cell. I asked the dispatcher to have the cab driver call me on my cell when he arrived as I had no intentions of leaving the bathroom until I received his call. I wanted to call Charmine so badly, but I would have never done that to her on her wedding night, and unfortunately for me, she wouldn't be back for a few weeks.

It seemed like an eternity, but finally the dispatcher called me and said my cab was out front. When I emerged from the bathroom, my eyes were swollen from crying, and I looked disheveled. I walked down the stairs, picked up my shoes, and headed for the door. As I walked to the door, I peered into the living room where had Clay remained, and although his back was turned to me, I noticed he had an unopened bottle of Hennessy in his hands about to pour another glass. I wanted to run to him, throw my arms around him and tell him everything would be fine, but I walked out of his house, a despondent woman.

I slid my body sorrowfully in the backseat of the cab. I composed myself enough to give the cab driver the address to the hotel where I had left my car and leaned my head against the window. The cab driver took note of my disorganized attire and hair through his rearview mirror. He seemed concerned for me, and he asked if I needed any medical attention. I told him I didn't. I just wanted him to drive. The cab driver dropped me in front of the hotel, and I gave the attendant my ticket to pick up my car. I entered my car and started to head home. I was nearly there when my cell phone rang. I had hoped it was Clay telling me to come back, that he hadn't meant what he said. I almost broke a nail as I pried opened my bag in a hurry. "Hello, Baby Girl, how are you?"

"I'm fine Dad. How are you?"

"I'm good, but you don't sound so good. What's the matter, are you sick?"

"No Daddy, I'm fine. It's late, are you sure you're okay?"

"Yeah, I called late because I thought you'd still be at the reception. I wanted to know how the wedding went?"

"The wedding, Charmine, everything was just beautiful, Daddy.

They leave for France in the morning"

"You sure don't sound like you're happy that your best friend got married. You sound almost pitiful, are you thinking she won't have time for you no more?"

"No, that's not it. We celebrated late last night, and it's been a very long day. I'm just tired, that's all."

"Well, take you some of those vitamin tablets. They've been working for me. And how's Clay doing?"

I fought hard to hold back my tears. "He's fine too, I'll be sure to tell him you asked about him."

"Alright then, Baby Girl, I'm gon' let you go. I look forward to seeing you in a few weeks. Well, I love ya, and tell Clay I said hello."

"I will Daddy, and I love you too." I was happy to hear from my dad, but I wanted so badly for it to have been Clay. I was tempted to call him, but I couldn't bear any more rejection from him in one night. I slinked into my building, and my downstairs neighbor stopped me as I was about to get on the elevator. He asked me if I was okay, and I motioned that I was fine without having looked at him. I pressed the button for my floor, and my neighbor watched me until the doors of the elevator closed.

I went directly upstairs to my room and fell hard onto the brand new bed still covered in the plastic. I didn't have the strength to disrobe, and so I laid in my maid of honor's dress. I hated myself for having told Clay the absolute truth, and I cried until I was empty. Just as life had started to look up for us, this happens and it was all my fault. I knew what I had done was unforgivable, and sadly it didn't mean anything, but it was too late now. As I recanted what had just happened, the look on Clay's face made me physically sick, but I couldn't move. I placed a mini waste basket by my bed and hung my head over the basket just in case my insides came up. I took my phone from my bag and placed it in my eye's view on my pillow, and every time a text came in, I prayed it was from Clay.

At some point I had dozed off, and when I woke up in the middle of the night, I had an excruciating headache. And I was drenched in my own sweat from the plastic on the mattress. I went downstairs to get the bag that contained my new bedding and returned to my room to put the sheets on the bed. I stopped in my bathroom, opened the medicine cabinet, and popped two Tylenol's in my mouth. I climbed back into my bed and prayed I would fall back to sleep. I had such an incredible view of Atlanta's skyline from my bedroom window, but as the sun beamed through my window and awoke me the morning after my world had come to an end, it looked dull. I peeked at my cell phone through my one opened eye and blew heavily as there weren't any missed calls or texts from Clay. I flipped my phone over on its screen and pulled the covers back over my head.

I struggled to make a decision about whether I should go to work or stay at home. I had leaned more towards going to work, but when I raised my head from my pillow the pain overtook me, and I laid back down. It was still too early, and no one would have been at the bank to take my call. I set the alarm on my phone to ensure I called Mr. Wyatt to let him know I couldn't make it in. I tried very hard not to think about last night, but it replayed itself as if to taunt me. I had nearly dozed back off when my phone buzzed, and rattled me out of my sleep. I just knew it was Clay, as it was too early for it to be anyone else, and he'd be up at this hour getting ready for his day at the studio. "Hello, Clay?"

"No, Girl, it's me. I know it's early, but you told me to call you before we left, and we're about to leave for the airport."

"Okay...I thought you said your flight was at seven o'clock, why are you leaving for the airport so early?"

"You know, with international flights the airline asks that you be there two hours earlier. Wait. It's not even five yet, Clay left for the studio already?" Charmine asked.

"No."

"Then why did you answer the phone and think it was Clay? I thought y'all spent the night together?" I tried to dodge her questions, but Char continued to dig—I crumbled and burst into tears. "Lane what's the matter? What's happened?" I tried to articulate to Charmine through my tears what had happened at Clay's, but what she had gotten were a string of incoherent sentences. She tried to calm me down so I could tell her what happened.

"I said, Clay found out what happened with me and Dre," I started to bawl again.

"Lane, stop. Breath...how did he find out, Faizon?"

235

"No, I told him, and he made me leave."

"Oh no, Lane. Anthony and I are coming right over."

"NO! No, you're not," I pulled it together at once. "You are going to go to the airport and get on that plane, I'm fine. I promise."

"Lane, how in the hell do you expect me to be in France having a great time when I know you'll be here hurting like this?"

"And if you miss your plane to come over here, I'd feel even worse. And plus you said it yourself, no one forced me to sleep with Dre, and now I'm suffering the consequence." I begged Charmine not to come over and go to the airport, and after much effort, I coaxed her to do just that. I promised her that if I needed someone to talk to, she'd be the very first person I'd call. I overheard Anthony in the background as he told Charmine they needed to get moving. I told them to have a safe, enjoyable trip and to take plenty of pictures.

After Charmine and I ended our conversation, I was able to get some sleep. My alarm went off, and I woke up to call Mr. Wyatt. I informed him I wouldn't be at work; I explained to him that I was ill, and although he sounded a bit agitated, he told me to get well soon. Now that I had the whole day to myself and no one to spend it with, I had a lot of time to think of Clay, and how royally I had messed it all up. It was afternoon when I finally climbed out of bed, and I tried to unpack the rest of my boxes I still hadn't completely finished arranging.

Midway through my task I gave up and pushed the rest of the unpacked boxes back in a storage closet. I had cried so much during the night that I felt weak, and it didn't help that I hadn't eaten a morsel of food all day. I called information for the number to Clay's favorite Chinese restaurant and ordered some of their chicken noodle soup to replenish my strength. When my food arrived, I went back upstairs to my bedroom and turned on the TV. I sat on my bed with my legs crisscrossed while I enjoyed my chicken soup and an episode of Everyone Loves Raymond. I wanted to go back to bed, but I knew I'd be up in the middle of the night again. After I ate my soup, I went to my closet and selected an outfit for work the next day. I realized I hadn't brought all my belongings from Clay's house, and I now had an excuse to call him, but I shuddered at the thought.

I picked up my phone and dialed Clay's number, but it went

directly to his voice mail. And I was too afraid to leave a message. I had been cramped up in my condo all day and decided to take a drive to get some much needed fresh air. I hadn't been out long when my cell phone buzzed, and my heart dipped. "What's up girl, you still are work?" Faizon asked.

"Nothing much, just taking a ride downtown. I didn't make it in to work today, I called out." I didn't want to divulge too much information to her. I'd been burned by her once, and hopefully that was my last time.

"Girrl...you still hung over from Charmine's reception? That's why I'm glad I don't have anybody to answer to. You better get like me," she gloated.

"No, I'm good. What do you want?" I wanted her to know that we wasn't about to 'kick it' like we were besties.

"I'm calling to find out if you heard from Charmine yet?"

"Yeah, she called me this morning before they left for the airport. I told her I'd call her tomorrow, give them a chance to get their groove on."

"I hear you. So what you got going on later? Girl, my bad. You and Clay may already have plans, so call me when you get a chance. I'm getting super excited about my launch and want to run a few new designs by you."

"Okay, I'll holla at you tomorrow after work—maybe I can drop by then."

"Alright, sounds good. Talk to you tomorrow." It seemed odd that Faizon still thought our relationship was intact as if nothing ever happened and even odder that I continued a relationship with her. I certainly didn't know of too many women who would've forgiven her for what she'd done. With Charmine in the air to France, I wished that Faizon and I could have talked the way we did in the past, but those days were long gone. Of course it would have been nice to be able to share with her what happened, but if I had given her an inkling that Clay wanted nothing to do with me, she would have been at his house offering him her shoulder to lean on and a whole lot more.

The drive hadn't done what I had expected it to do, so I turned my car around and headed home. I realized I couldn't drive my problems away, because even as I drove around the serene locations in Atlanta, I still spent the entire time thinking of Clay. When I got home, I made a second attempt to put some things away from the many boxes I had hid in my storage closet. While I moved and emptied boxes, I wondered if Clay had thought about me or if he wanted to call but was too angry to make the first move. I held my phone in my hands and willed him to call. I needed to hear his voice, and I had convinced myself that he needed to hear mine too. So, after nothing transpired from my willing him to call, I called him for the second time.

This time there was no mistaking that he intentionally ignored my call as his phone had rang twice, and then I was sent to his voice mail. I threw my phone on my nightstand and got ready to go to bed. I concluded it'd be wise if I gave him a cooling off period before I tried to contact him again. The next day at work I was so irritable. My colleagues steered clear of me. I stayed in a funk until after Charmine called and said that they landed safely in France. She wanted to know if I had spoken to Clay. I told her that I had called him, but we still hadn't talked since the night of her wedding. She told me not to give up and said she would call me tomorrow.

Six o'clock felt like an eternity as I watched the clock. Faizon called like she said she would, but I was in no mood to go over any designs with her. I told her I had to stay at work to make up for the day I had missed. She sounded a bit disappointed and told me she had depended on me to help her, but if she only knew I could have cared less at this point. Faizon told me she'd be at her shop well into the night and hoped I'd reconsider. I told her I doubted if I would change my mind and hung up.

At the sight of six o'clock, I shut down my computer and lunged for the front door. I had thought about what Charmine said about not giving up and I didn't plan to. I left work and hit the highway in the direction of Clay's studio. I wasn't going to let him off the hook that easily. I had accepted I was the one who messed things up, but I hadn't accepted we were through. I exited the interstate, and as I stopped for a red light at the top of the ramp, I asked myself was I prepared for Clay's reaction when I showed up unannounced at his office.

I almost lost the courage to proceed with my plan when I pulled into the parking lot and saw Clay's car parked in his reserved space, but I knew I couldn't spend another day without him. I sat in my car and rehearsed what I wanted to say to him that would make him take me in his arms and forget about everything. I finally built up enough nerve to walk in the studio and demanded that Clay speak to me. I checked my hair and make-up in my rearview mirror before I stepped out of my car.

I walked in the reception area and told the pretty, young receptionist that I was there to see Clay Roberts—she picked up the phone and dialed his extension. When he answered, she told him that he had a visitor at the front desk. She listened for a minute then covered the mouthpiece on the phone and looked at me. "Can I have your name please?" she asked.

"Sure, it's Lane." On her end there was a long silence, and then she placed the receiver back on its base slowly.

She seemed very reluctant as she relayed Clay's instructions to me. "Umm. . . Ms. King. . . Clay wants me to tell you, you need to go home." I was so humiliated that I stood at the desk too embarrassed to move from that spot. When I felt my legs were stable enough for me to walk out of there without falling, I started to head for the exit. I had gotten as far as the front door when I heard my name being called.

"Lane? Is that you?" I turned around, and Shon had started to walk up to greet me. "I thought that was you, it's good to see you. I was sorry to hear about your mother, but I know Clay told you all that already."

"Oh, hi Shon. Yeah he did, and thanks for the flowers you and Pam sent." The receptionist looked like she wanted to tell Shon I had been asked to leave the building at Clay's insistence, but she never did.

"Does Clay know you're here?"

"Yes, but he must be busy so I was just going to leave."

"You know he's never too busy for you. You might be just what he needs, he's been acting like he's had something stuck up his ass all day. C'mon, I'll walk you back there," he said.

"I better not, Shon. I'll talk to him later."

"Why later, you're already here." I just shrugged my shoulders and followed Shon to Clay's office. I felt this could be bad on so many levels, but I was in too deep now. We stopped at Clay's office door. Shon knocked once, but before Clay could ask who it was, Shon had pushed his office door opened. "Do you know this pretty lady? I stopped her before she was about to leave." Clay remained seated behind his desk. Shon kissed my cheek, he told me it was nice to see me again, and left the office. Clay waited until he thought Shon was clear away from his office.

"I thought I told you to go home," he said.

"I know what you said, but I really needed to see you. Clay, please, can't we talk about this?"

"Lane, we don't have anything to talk about any more. You forfeited all that when you slept with Dre."

"And I'm sorry about that, I never mea---,"

"What?! Never meant for me to find out? Here it is I'm here in Atlanta feeling bad that I had to leave you in Brooklyn grieving over your mother and you being comforted by that muthafucka? Nah, I'm good, Lane." Clay hopped out of his seat and rushed towards me. "It's time for you to go, and don't come back here." He walked over to his office door and opened it slightly, but I closed it shut and propped my back against it so that he couldn't open it.

"Not until you listen to me. I don't have any excuse for why I slept with Dre. If I could take it all back I would, I hate myself for doing this to us. But it happened and I can't change it. I know we can get over this. . .I love you Clay." When I told him that I loved him, he moved in so close that I felt his breath on me. It looked like he wanted to kiss me, but when I stepped in to kiss him he pulled away.

"You might be able to get over this, but I can't. I loved you so much, and now it's all fucked up."

"Clay, you can try. I forgave you when you told me about that night at Faizon's, and how you were having fantasies about her after that. That wasn't easy for me but I overlooked it."

"But I didn't fuck her—the moment I realized it had gotten out of hand I got the hell outta there. But you, you went to Dre's knowing what was gonna happen."

"No, I didn't go there for that purpose, it just happened."

"Don't lie to me, Lane. I've told you too many times, I don't have room in my life for this kinda shit, and I thought you understood that. I thought you knew I loved you, and I wanted to be all that you wanted. But I guess was wrong, so it's best you do you." I started to cry uncontrollably, and I begged him for another chance, but he wouldn't discuss it any further. He said he'd be back in ten minutes, and I should be gone by the time he returned.

I knew Clay was serious about not wanting to see me in his office when he got back, so I wiped my tears on the sleeve of my dress and left his office. I hoped his receptionist had left her station as I was too ashamed to even look in her direction. She spotted me coming out of Clay's office and asked me to sign out in the book. I ignored her request as I tired to escape without her noticing my teary eyes and hurt pride. I opened my car door, hopped in quickly, and dashed out of the studio's parking lot.

When I got home to the quiet emptiness, it gradually sunk in that Clay and I were done. I should have listened to my instinct and never went to his studio; the wound was still too fresh. I should have waited a few more days before I forced him to talk to me. Sadly, my old habits had resurfaced, this time at the expense of a relationship and a future with a great man. Clay genuinely loved me, and I tossed it all away for nothing. It wouldn't have been so bad if my aunt Bernice hadn't sat me down in her kitchen before I left Brooklyn. She had warned me that Dre would be the demise of me and Clay's relationship, and in a matter of just a few weeks, I had done just that.

FORBIDDEN SEDUCTION

Faizon

M_y shop had increased its traffic since Charmine's wedding, and I was approached by several women who were amazed with my designs and wanted high-end fashions. I needed an assistant to help me at the shop, so I could be focused on my launch7, and build my brand. I had placed an advert in the newspaper, but everyone that responded either didn't have the experience or the look to represent me. Lane promised me she'd come by the shop after work later on, but she flaked out on me two days in the row, so if she didn't show up tonight I wouldn't be surprised.

Nikole and I had one last meeting before my launch in five days, and she asked that we meet at Platinum Plus Entertainment office. I asked my mother to help me down at the shop so I could keep the shop opened while I met with Nikole. When my mother arrived, I showed her what needed to be done and asked her to hand out the new catalogs I designed myself. I watched her as she charmed the clients, helping them as they looked through the catalogs. She raved that since I was her daughter she'd make sure

I got right on their garments. My mother was a natural, and so I left her as she was engaged with a client who stopped in wanting a special dress made for her son's bar mitzvah.

I had arrived at the PPE office early and waited in the reception area for Nikole to see me. Ten minutes past our appointment time, Nikole finally greeted me in the reception area. She walked over to me and apologized for being late. Nikole asked me to follow her into her office. When we got in her office, she apologized again for having kept me waiting, but she explained that she was on the phone and had secured another sponsor for my launch. Before we got started into the business of the launch, Nikole offered me a cup of coffee, but I declined. As we discussed the full run-through of the evening, I was impressed with how well her vision coincided with mine. She had the evening set up to be a musical event as opposed to just a typical blasé runway show.

Before my meeting with Nikole concluded, she asked me if I feel good about what had been done so far, and I told her that my expectations had been exceeded. Now we only had to wait until the night of my launch to see what happened. After I left Nikole's office, I stopped by Clay's to say a quick hello and thanks for all of his help. I knocked on his door twice before he opened it and when he did, he opened it so abruptly that it spooked me. "Oh, I'm sorry Clay, I didn't want to disturb you. I just finished a meeting with Nikole, and I just wanted to drop in and say I really appreciate all you've done to help me with my launch."

"No need for thanks, that's what we do," he said, as he kept me at bay. I asked him if I could come in, he paused for a second, and then reluctantly he opened the door.

"I have something I want you to look at," I said and walked over to his desk. I pulled a new sketch from out of my bag. "What do you think about this?" He hadn't moved or let go of the doorknob as I waited at his desk for him to come over and offer his opinion. "You can't see it from over there, Clay."

"Faizon, look...I was in the middle of something when you knocked."

"I won't be long. I just want a man's opinion on it." He pushed the door closed and walked over to his desk. He looked uninterested at the sketch I had laid down.

"It's not too bad," he said and sat down behind his desk.

"That doesn't sound very promising. So, I take it you don't like it as much as you did the piece I tried on for you at my house."

Clay became very agitated. He picked up my sketch and handed it to me. "Look Faizon. Like I said, I was busy. I appreciate you coming through, but I got a lot going on at the moment."

"Okay, Okay. I didn't mean to stir up anything. And I particularly don't want to get on Lane's bad side again. She's just started to chill with me again. As a matter of fact I'll see her later on tonight, I'll tell her you said hello."

"I didn't ask you to do that, so don't tell her nothing," he said.

"Ohh. . . that doesn't sound good. What's going on with y'all?"

"You just said you're gonna see her tonight, ask her." And with that he got up from his chair, walked me out of his office, and slammed the door behind me. He didn't have to tell me anything, and I surely didn't have to ask her anything. His reaction to Lane's name was evidence enough. No wonder she's avoided me, something was definitely wrong in paradise. I looked forward to this evening with Lane if she didn't back out again. I hoped to get her to open up about what had caused the rift between them.

I wanted to call Lane, but I knew if she found out I was at the PPE office she would have canceled on me tonight as well. By the time I had gotten back to the shop, my mother had changed a few things around which looked rather good and I told her it was clear where I got my eye for fashion from. My dad pulled up in front of my shop with his new Cadillac. He had plans to take my mother out to dinner and asked me if I wanted to join them. I told him I would have if Lane wasn't on her way, but I told him I'd take a rain check on dinner. Because my mother had done such a marvelous job at the shop, before they left, I asked her if she wanted to help me run the shop part-time, and she gladly accepted.

Lane called and said she'd be at the shop about six thirty if traffic wasn't too heavy—she still sounded unlike herself, but at least today I knew why. Lane offered to bring some food for us. She said she was starved and needed something to eat. I told her whatever she decided would be fine with me. Lane estimated her arrival time accurately and arrived at the shop at six-thirty precisely. I left my chair and helped her in the shop as both her hands were full. Lane put the food down on the table and plunked her body in my swivel chair. "Girl, you look tired," I said.

"I am, and I'm starving," she replied, and ripped opened the bag with the barbecue platters in it. "Wait, are you closing the shop? I'd hate to look ghetto eating out of the bag like this in the front of your shop."

I snickered as I walked over to the door and locked it. "Yeah, I meant to do that after my mama and daddy left."

"Ah, they were here? I hate I missed them."

"Yeah, my mama helped me tremendously today while I met with Nikole down at the PPE office." Lane practically choked on her spoonful of coleslaw when she heard 'studio'. I played it cool and waited for her to take the bait.

"How did it go?"

"It went very well. After I met with Nikole, I had to stop by your man's office to tell him that he is a genius at what he does. He told me I can pretty much guarantee I'm the next big thing in the Atlanta."

"Okay... So you saw Clay?"

"Only for a minute. I told him you'd be here tonight."

"What'd he say?"

"He didn't say anything. Was he supposed to?" For Lane to have claimed to be so starved, she seemed to have lost her appetite when I mentioned Clay's name. She placed her fork back in the food container and closed the bag. I don't even think she had realized it when the tears filled her eyes and streamed down her face. I felt ashamed that I had taken so much pleasure in seeing Lane so deeply upset, and I reached out to console her.

"Lane, why are you cryin'?

"It's all over. Clay and I are over."

"What? No, you just had a bad argument, y'all will get over that."

"No. We won't get over this. He found out about me and Dre."

"Oh my God! How?"

"From me, I told him." Lane explained the circumstances of that night, and why she had no choice but to tell Clay about the night she shared with Dre. I felt horrible for her as she relived her pain, and the pain she said she saw in Clay's eyes. When she told me how sick she had felt when Clay threw her out of his house in the middle of the night, I knew exactly how she felt. About four years ago I had dated this guy named Trevor, and I was madly in love with him. The only problem was he had a girlfriend. But he promised me that he would end it with her, and this went on for months. Well, one night while I was at his house, I gave him an ultimatum. I told him that he to needed to choose who he wanted to be with. When it seemed like he was having trouble deciding for himself, I figured I'd help him make the decision and threatened to tell his girlfriend. Trevor went bananas. He physically pulled me from his bed, dragged me down his stairs, and pushed me out of his apartment—that was the last of saw of him. So, I knew first hand of the trauma Lane felt.

It wasn't a secret that Lane and Charmine had always considered me to be the most heartless of the three of us, and most times I would agree with them. But, I couldn't help but feel badly for Lane now, and even though I had made a foolish move on Clay, it was clear that they loved each other. Lane went to the bathroom in the back of my shop. She returned several minutes later composed and with a fresh application of make-up. "You and Clay will be fine. You gotta know that he still loves you. I knew Clay was madly in love from that night I tried that craziness. I've never had a man turn me down before, ever. Married, single, it's never happened—not until Clay.

"That's why it's hurts so much. I've never experienced a man love me like that before, and now it's too late."

"It's not too late. You gotta make him see that y'all have something too good to just throw away, it's salvageable."

"Thank you, Faizon. You know, I was terrified to tell you that Clay and I had broken up. That's why I've been avoiding seeing you," she said.

"Why?"

"I was afraid you'd jump at the chance to move in, to use our breakup to your advantage."

"Girl, I ain't gon' lie. . . if I thought he'd give me a chance, I'd be pushing up on him right now, but he doesn't want me. And anyway, I met someone at Charmine's wedding"

"Who? Please don't say that Luke dude, 'cause I could've sworn I heard Emily tell you he was in a relationship."

"That's what she said, but that isn't what he said. Love it or hate it, I'm gonna always go after what I want. That's why I'm the most hated woman in Atlanta. And, you better take a page from my book—go fight for your man and stop playing."

"That's exactly what Char said, but after the other day, I better leave it for a while."

"Don't wait too long. Men like Clay are a rare commodity, especially here in Atlanta." I knew it would be a long time before Lane considered this to be water under the bridge, but I was thrilled that she had considered restoring our broken bond. Lane looked over the designs that I wanted to see returned to a woman's wardrobe. I also showed her the pieces that would be featured on the evening of my launch, the jumpsuits, skirts, lingerie pieces, and a wedding dress. I had never thought about bridal wear, but Charmine's dress inspired me to do it.

Lane expressed how much she liked my creations and how she looked forward to my 'coming out' night. Lane's appetite came back, and we both grubbed on the barbecue meal she bought for us. I asked her when Charmine and Anthony were due to come back from France, because I wanted them both at my launch, and she told me they'd be back in three days. As Lane cleaned up her mess from my table, she said had to call it a night because she had a busy morning and needed her rest. I thanked her for coming to the shop and reminded her that Clay's rejection towards her now wouldn't last.

After Lane left, I closed my shop properly and headed home myself. When I got home, I opened the door and called out into the air 'Honey I'm home' it was a sad, running joke I played on myself for years. I just wished that there would come a day someone would be there to answer me back. As I looked around my beautiful house and my lavished lifestyle, it was inconceivable that I didn't have someone in my life to share it all with. I thought Darnell would have been the man I would have settled down with. All the years I invested in him emotionally and financially—I was sure he would have left his wife for me. But, instead he showed me how important I was in his life, with a trip to the emergency room where I nearly died, and unsure if our unborn baby would survive.

FORBIDDEN SEDUCTION

I flicked through the hundreds of TV channels to see what I could watch, and I stopped on an episode of "Grey's Anatomy." A few minutes into the show I realized it was a repeat, so I turned the TV off and went upstairs. Since my mother agreed to help me at the shop, I didn't have to be there so early in the morning, and I'd use that time to scout out some new fabrics.

I wanted to unwind with a hot bath, so I went to my bathroom and turned the water on. I added my favorite bath salts, and stepped my tired body into the lavender and vanilla scented water. I closed my eyes and Clay's sexy body flashed across my mind as I lathered my body with the bewitching scents. I thought of Clay as my soapy hands washed my breasts, causing my nipples to harden. I presumed Clay must have been lonely since his break up with Lane, and wished I could have eased his loneliness in my unforgettable, Faizon style.

As I relaxed my head on my bath pillow, I explored my curvaceous body and fondled my throbbing nipples. My clitoris twitched and yearned for attention, so I slid my fingers up and down slowly as I pretended it was Clay's smooth chocolate dick inside of me. My pussy tightened around my fingers and I moaned with delight as I pleasured myself. I orgasmed loudly as Clay's attractive face was burned in my memory.

I rinsed off and stepped out of my bath, convinced that Clay had mad swagger—as he had been the only man I knew that could make me cum without physically being in the same room. After I finished with my bath-time sexual release, I dried off and prepared myself for bed. I almost regretted that I promised Lane I wouldn't push up on Clay, but I never promised her I wouldn't fantasize about him.

FORBIDDEN SEDUCTION

Clay

Shon knocked violently on the door to my office, and jarred me from an unintended late afternoon snooze. "Bruh, don't say you up in here sleeping? That's why shit ain't getting done!" Shon shouted.

"What are you rambling about? I wasn't sleep." I jumped up from behind my computer like I had been awake the whole time.
"Yo, whatever you and Lane going through you need to get that shit sorted, 'cause you fuckin' up." I'm not prepared to say Shon was a 'yes man,' but he had never spoken to me like that before. "Ms. Diva from the Real Housewives is talking about pulling her birthday bash from us 'cause she hasn't heard back from anyone yet."

"That can't be right, I spoke to her myself and I was suppo---."

"Exactly! YOU were supposed to get back with her. You didn't just drop the ball on this one, you dropped the Mack truck. If you don't handle this one ASAP it could mess up our reputation around Atlanta. You've heard those chicks during their interviews, they're ruthless." I told Shon that I would handle the damage control from here as it was my fault it had gotten to this level.

251

However, before he left, I tried to dissuade his allegation that my situation with Lane had caused this screw-up. After he left my office, I called Nikole in and asked her to get the super dramatic Housewife on the phone for me. When I got on the phone with the Atlanta Housewife diva, I asked her to forgive me for my lack of professionalism. I further vowed that Platinum Plus Entertainment was committed one hundred percent to giving her the best celebrity birthday celebration that Atlanta has yet to see. That appeared to be all she needed to hear and said she was happy to let us continue with her party. Women had their outlets when they needed to talk about their personal issues: their girlfriends, co-workers, and Oprah. But who could I have talked to about the hurt I suffered since I found out about Lane. Shon had accused me correctly when he said that Lane had me fucked up, but it wasn't like I could talk to him about it over ice cream and cake. So I got up every morning handled my business and suffered in silence. I had started to miss her so badly that one morning I drove by her job and watched her as she walked inside the bank. I was tempted to go inside to talk to her, but every time I thought of Dre's hands and mouth on her it disgusted me.

I had never allowed myself to love a woman like I did Lane, she was very special to me, and I hoped that we'd be in it for the long haul. So when she hit me with the whole Dre bullshit, I honestly wanted to lay hands on both of them. After I broke it off with Lane, she called me at least once a day, but I wasn't ready to talk so I always ignored her calls. Now that she hasn't called me in a few days, I missed seeing her face when it popped up on my cell phone screen. I knew that I would eventually have to see her, because she still had some of her shit at my crib.

I tried to keep myself occupied with my work but even that wasn't enough distraction for me. Faizon's launch was scheduled in a couple of days, and I needed to be around her about as much as I needed a hole in my head right now. Faizon reminded me of that old BBD song "Poison." She's definitely dangerous; she knows she's beautiful and that her body will hypnotize a muthfucka. She had my boy Shon fucked up—had him thinking she was seriously interested in him, and he got hooked real quick. When I told him that he was a mere pawn in Faizon's game to get at me, he got all bent out of shape and claimed I was just 'hating' on him.

The entertainment division of Platinum Plus Records was still young, but we had done a few things around Atlanta. And they were all successful. The clients spread the word about us. And because of it, our clients are more upscale and aren't concerned about their budget. They're looking for the most lavish and talked about event in Atlanta. I could have made some real money from Faizon's launch if I hadn't eaten most of the cost as a favor to Lane, but I still wanted it to be the talk around Atlanta. This was the first fashion industry event for PPE, and I didn't want it to be our last. From the moment I put Nikole in charge of Faizon's event, she worked her ass off. She managed the budget meticulously, hired the models and even worked on building the set for our first signed R&B artist, Amani. Nikole had also secured several key sponsors from and around Atlanta. So when Coca-Cola confirmed, I was more than impressed, and I predicted Faizon's launch would be successful. It was also to my benefit that Atlanta is a city hungry for entertainment and looked for a reason to party.

I spent more of my days at the studio, because I hated being home alone with my thoughts. I knew Lane wasn't completely out of my system, and I was too afraid I would have picked up the phone and asked her to come over. The night before Faizon's launch, my team and I were swamped with last minute preparations. The models of the DDM agency had flown in a day early for their final fittings for the show, and Amani had rehearsed so much she had laryngitis. Faizon contacted Nikole earlier that day and said she wanted the models to be brought to her shop just in case she had any alterations to make. She also requested that I call her. I prolonged that last request for as long as I could, but I knew as the CEO I would have to make myself available at some point to all my clients. I went into my office, picked up the phone, and called Faizon. "Hello," she said.

"Hello Faizon, this is Clay. I'm returning your call."

"Well, that's nice considering I left a message for you this morning."

"You're right, but I was busy getting everything ready for you to blow ATL out of the water."

"Oohh...I like the sound of that."

"Good. Now what can I do for you?"

"Don't ask me that if you don't want the answer," she giggled. I hadn't been on the phone with her for a minute before she started to flirt with me.

"Pertaining to business, Faizon—you know that's what I meant," I said sternly. Faizon had proved you had to be blunt with her as to not get any wires crossed. And I most definitely wasn't gonna engage in anything other than the business at hand with her. "I'm quite busy, Faizon, I still have things to do before tomorrow night gets here."

"Okay. You may not consider this business, but I think it is. I know all about you and Lane, and of course she'll at my launch tomorrow night. I want to know if that's going to be a problem for you?"

"Why would it be? There will be over two hundred people at the venue. Lane and I probably won't even see each other."

"I just want to make sure you'll be alright."

"Don't let what happens between Lane and me concern you. You just focus on doing what you need to do, and I'll handle me." I indulged her a while longer about issues she had created in her mind before I ended our conversation. I hung up the phone, pulled out my cell, and looked at the picture of Lane I had stored in it. When Faizon said the word 'breakup' it finally seemed real. Yet, I hadn't told anyone on my end that we had split—not even my mother.

It was after two a.m. when I finally left the studio, and on the way home, I stopped at one of those fast food joints. I ordered a couple of burgers and some chili cheese fries. When I got home, I hadn't realized how starved I'd been until I wolfed down the tasty burgers, and wished I had bought a few more. After I finished my food, I hopped in the shower, and when I got out, I surfed through the channels as I stretched out on the bed. I had dozed off with the remote in my hand when my phone rang. I woke in a discombobulated state when I answered. I picked up my phone and Lane's face appeared on my screen. I cleared the frog from my throat before I answered as I wanted to be fully alert for this call. "Hello," I said.

"Hi, Clay. Were you sleeping?" Lane asked.

"Nah, I was just getting in. Why are you calling me, Lane? I thought I ---."

"Clay, please. I couldn't sleep for thinking about you, and I need for you to hear me out... I love you, and I don't believe you stopped loving me just like that. I've been miserable without you and I want you to give us another chance. I know we can work it out."

"You're right. I never stopped lovin' you, but I don't know if we can work this out."

Lane's voice quivered as she spoke, and she started to cry. "If you still love me than why won't you forgive me? We can start over."

"We can't... I can't. Lane, as badly I want you lying next to me right now, we gotta move on." Lane cried even harder as I attempted to close the chapter on our relationship.

"Why, Clay? Whyyy?"

"Because you gave him what was meant for me, and I, I can't get over that." We continued to compare the hurt we both felt since our separation, but I explained to her my hurt was far too great. In the past, I had to let a few women go, but it was easy. And once they were gone, they were gone; I had no feeling about it. But to tell Lane to move on wasn't that simple, but I didn't know what else to do. Just as Faizon had done, Lane told me that she'd be at the launch and asked if we could have a private moment to talk and, I told her I preferred we didn't.

After I got off the phone with Lane, I couldn't get back to sleep so I put in a DVD. I watched "American Gangster" with Denzel Washington for the hundredth time until it watched me. It seemed no sooner than I got to sleep, morning had arrived, and I was still dead tired from my late night drama with Lane and Denzel. I checked my phone for the time, it was five a.m. and although I could have slept another two hours, I threw my legs over the bed and got my morning started. I had so much that needed to get done today, and it required all my skills to make it happen. Nikole had set up some press for Faizon's launch, so I knew Nikole was hyped this morning as her talents would be unveiled tonight through the success of this event.

Of course I had to be well-groomed tonight as we had media coming to the event. I thought about what Lane said about us having a private moment to ourselves to talk, and I contemplated her appeal for us to at least be friends. I never really understood why after a relationship had ended, women always wanted to remain friends, 'cause in my past relationships that whole 'friend' shit was a joke. As the morning quickly turned into afternoon, Shon, Nikole, and Faizon contacted me with a few issues which concerned them about the venue.

I asked Shon to meet me at the downtown venue as I was on my way there with one of my boys from the Atlanta Journal Constitution. He was there to write an article about the event for the paper. My team had arrived and started with the set up for the night. Shon and Amani arrived together because he needed to do her sound check for her performance. Amani showed some signs of strain as she had never performed on this scale before. I managed to calm her down before she started with her rehearsals. The company with the red carpet and backdrop turned up and their staff got busy with their work.

Faizon pulled up in a van with her parents. Her father jumped out and asked some men who he saw outside the venue if they would mind helping them. The men agreed to help and pulled the racks of clothes and other accessories from the back of the van. "Hi Clay, are you really just going to stand there doing nothing, while I do all this manual labor?" She joked.

"I'm never doing 'nothing' even if it may appear that way. I'm talking to the man who is getting ready to put your name and face in the AJC." Faizon handed her mother some of the garments bags, and walked over to us and shook Malik's hand. "Faizon, this is Malik Watson from the AJC."

"Hi Malik, I'm Faizon Hill. Atlanta's newest and hottest designer," she charmed.

"You're confident. I like that. I've been waiting on you, and if you don't mind, I'll be following you around to catch you during this process so the article will capture your true essence," Malik said.

"I don't mind at all. But definitely not before my make-up artist gets here."

"I think you're beautiful the way you look right now. You don't need any make-up and plus that defeats the purpose of your true essence." I listened to them as they talked about how Faizon wanted the story to introduce her to the city. When they both agreed on what angle Malik would take, Faizon and her mother walked inside the venue. "She's bad. I look forward to writing this article about her. Then I can find out if she got a man in her life." I shook my head, and turned

256

to see how far Faizon had gotten. "What's up? Why you looking like that?" Malik asked.

"Nothing's up, just be careful," I said.

"Why? You must have tried to get at that."

"Nah, nothing like that. Only a friendly word of advice." Nikole came out to the front and asked me if I could listen in on Amani's rehearsal. I asked her where Shon was as I thought he would have been in the rehearsal with them. Nikole said she hadn't seen Shon for nearly an hour, so I told her I would be right there. "C'mon man, let me get you set up before I get missing," I said.

"Sure. But don't get too lost, I wanna do a small piece on you too after everything settles down tonight."

"Aight, cool." I showed Malik to an area that he could set up, and left him to locate Nikole. I found Nikole and Amani in the main room where the actual show would take place. I listened in on Amani's set and knew instantly I had hit melodic gold, and tonight she would give Atlanta a small preview of what's to come when her album dropped in a few months. Mr. Hill and his wife walked past the main room and stopped when they heard the sultry songstress. They listened as if they'd been fans of hers for years, and when Amani finished her song, their applause filled the room. Mr. Hill spotted me in the back and walked over to me, he asked me if I was Clay Roberts. When I told him I was, he shook my hand and thanked me for helping bring his daughter's vision to fruition.

When the rehearsal for the models was done, my team poured in the room and put the finishing touches in the main room as it wouldn't be much longer before the guests started to arrive. This was the second rehearsal that Shon had missed, and no one had seen him for at least an hour. I called his cell, but he didn't answer it. I walked back into the main room one last time and still he was M.I.A. However, Nikole was still in the room with the work crew.

"Hey, Nik, have you seen Shon yet?"

"Yeah, he was just here with me and Amani, but when he saw Faizon and that guy from the AJC, he followed them down the hall," she said.

"What the fu---. Aight thanks, Nik." I walked back to the area that I showed Malik he could use to interview Faizon, puzzled as to why

Shon needed to be present for that. I turned the corner of the hall and saw Shon as he stood at the door where Malik and Faizon were. "Shon, what's good? Why you playin' security guard when we got mad shit to do?

"What you talkin' 'bout? I was getting something from the back and just so happened to see Faizon. I wanted to see if she needed anything," Shon said.

"Nah, she's good. But I need you to assist the lighting engineer up front." Shon glanced into the room once more as Malik interviewed Faizon and walked off in a huff. I stood at the door a minute longer myself and then joined the team back up front. I had just signed for a delivery when a van pulled up and out walked seven gorgeous models from the DDM agency. Nikole greeted them and took them all to the back where a dressing room was prepared for them. Shortly after the models arrived, Faizon's hair and make-up team came. I was about to take them to the back to join the others when Malik and Faizon walked around the corner. Malik told me he had just finished his very candid interview with Faizon and reminded me that he wanted one with me after the show.

Faizon beamed as she talked to the models, and she led them all to the dressing room. Shon and I conducted our walk-through and ensured that everything was finished completely and correctly. I had ordered an ice sculpture from a company in Marietta with Faizon's initials and logo, and the men from the company had it set up by the bar. Everything had been executed well, and I was pleased with how things looked. I went home to get changed so that I could make it back in time before we opened the doors to the guests.

Nikole had been busy with the models and Faizon's team. I called her on her cell and told her I would be back shortly. She said she'd be fine, but would call Shon if she needed any help. I left the venue and headed home. On my way there, I thought of Lane and on the low I was excited that I'd get to see her. I pulled in the driveway to my home and dashed inside the house. I checked my mail briefly before I went upstairs to get dressed. I didn't want to wear too much flash and decided I'd keep it to a minimum. I opened my drawer and pulled out my platinum diamond chain. In the crevice of my drawer, I noticed a pair of diamond studded earrings and picked them up. I remembered back to the night that Lane had taken them off and placed them in my drawer. She must have forgotten she'd left them there. I placed them inside of my jacket pocket so I could give them back to her later on at the launch.

After I got dressed, I hopped back in my car and headed back down to the venue. When I walked in, I was blown away by the end result PPE had produced. It definitely looked like a winning night was about to go down, and as the CEO this would definitely go down as one of my proudest moments. I briefed my team one last time before the guests started to walk the red carpet. When our meeting concluded, I peeked in on Amani. She had made herself comfortable in one of the rooms next to the models until it was time for her to perform. She looked sizzlin' hot in her red dress which highlighted all of her assets in a very classy way.

Shon called my cell and said the photographers had started taking photos of Atlanta's elite as they hit the red carpet. I left Amani's room and walked around to Faizon's area. I wanted to let her know that things were about to get started and that she should be out front as we had agreed earlier. I knocked on the door of the room filled with glamorous models, and I tried hard to divert my eyes away from the few who were scarcely dressed. One of the stylists who continued to curl one of the models hair told me that Faizon had gone next door. I walked over to the next room and knocked on the door. "Come in," Faizon said. I entered the room and couldn't turn away as Faizon turned to face me. She was dressed in only a pair of hot pink panties and some thigh high black stockings.

"Err...I'll come back when you're dressed," I offered. But, I absolutely couldn't move; my eyes were glued to her body. "Just have one of the ladies come look for me when you're done."

"No need for all that, you're already here," she said. She turned back around to look in the mirror and revealed her sexy round ass. "Is it almost that time?" I played it off like I wasn't turned on at all. I folded my arms and leaned against a dressing table affixed to a mirror.

"Yeah, just about. You have a few minutes to play with before you come out front to greet your guests."

"I've changed my mind about that, Clay. I don't want to be seen until the end of the show. I'll mingle with the guests during the after-party."

"That's up to you. I just wanted to give you that option." As we continued to talk, I crossed one leg over the other as I tried to conceal my hardness. Faizon walked over to a wheeled Louis Vuitton bag, pulled out her bra, and walked back over to me.

"Will you help me with this, Clay?" she asked and held the bra in the air on her pointer finger.

"Ahem...yeah." Faizon slipped her arms through the loops of the bra, backed her apple-bottom shaped ass into my crotch, and asked me to fasten it. My hands trembled as I touched her silky smooth skin and inhaled her alluring fragrance, but I managed to get it done. After her bra was fastened she turned to me and unexpectedly threw her arms around my neck.

"Now, that wasn't so hard was it?" Faizon asked, as she slid her hand down to my groin and grabbed my swollen dick. "Oohh...but this sure is." Faizon pecked lightly on the nape of my neck, and gave me a pleasurable bite on my earlobe. In my mind I had pushed all the contents off of the table onto the floor, lifted Faizon onto the table, and buried my dick deep inside her hungry pussy until we both came. But in reality, I removed her hands from around my neck and placed them gently at her sides.

"It's time to get ready, Faizon." Faizon tried to grab at me again, but I stepped back this time.

"Why you acting like this? You aren't with Lane any more. I thought we could..."

"You thought wrong. Just because Lane and I aren't together doesn't mean I would get with you. Finish getting dressed. You have a show to do." I walked out of the room, dipped into the bathroom, and waited until the bulge in my pants disappeared. Yep, just like I said: that girl is poison.

Lane

Charmine and Anthony had returned from their honeymoon, and I couldn't have been happier she was back. I needed her support so badly during my breakup with Clay. I've been in a zombie-like state since that day. I barely managed to perform all my duties at work, and yet somehow, I avoided being terminated. Although tonight was Faizon's launch, I'd bet in all likelihood it'd be safe for me to say I was far more nervous than she was. This would be my first time in weeks that I'd be in the same room with Clay.

I was glad Charmine would be there with me as I don't believe I would have been able to go without her. Anthony and Charmine returned to Atlanta with a heap of unfinished projects. Their office needed completing, they still hadn't hired all the attorneys needed for their office, and they had the laborious task of moving house to look forward to. Charmine called and asked me to meet her at the Starbucks on Peachtree Street, and I got there in less than twenty minutes. We met in the parking lot of the Starbucks and when we saw each other, our faces lit up. This was the first time we'd seen each other since her wedding day, and we jumped out of our cars and ran towards each other like little girls. Once we were inside of Starbucks, Charmine handed me a bag filled with souvenirs from France for me and my dad.

Charmine looked so refreshed coming back from her honeymoon on the French Riviera. As she told me everything about her honeymoon, I flipped through her phone and looked at all their pictures. Charmine had skirted around the issue with Clay and after I looked through all her pictures, I recounted the entire horrible night. Charmine even choked up as I told her the story. "Aw, Lane, I'm so sorry to hear that. I really thought Clay was the one."

"He is. And once he calms down and forgives me, he'll know it too."

"What do you plan to do?"

"Nothing. I tried to force his hand before he was ready and it backfired, so I'm gonna wait him out."

"Before you wait him out, are you sure you have Dre totally out of your system?"

"I had Dre out of my system before I left Brooklyn. Don't forget, Char. I had a lot of factors which led me to that; I was very vulnerable. I realized Dre was only a moment of weakness for me when I was home—Dre and I would never make it as a couple."

"Well, I hate that you had this epiphany so late," she said and drank some more of her latte. "Are you going to be alright with Clay in the same space tonight?"

"I'll have to. He already knows I'm coming, so we'll see..." Charmine and I caught up a while longer at Starbucks, and then she came with me to Saks Fifth Ave where she helped me find a bangin' dress for Faizon's launch. I tried on this beaded cowl dress with the back out. I had Clay in mind as I checked myself out in the fitting room mirror. He always told me he loved it when I exposed my back because it reminded him of the night we met, so I bought it. Charmine treated herself to a very stylish blue pant-suit, and a pale blue Donna Karan sequined top. I told Charmine I was prepared to be the chauffeur and would pick her up at six o'clock sharp. I didn't want to arrive at the function by myself—said she'd be fine with that because Anthony had come down with something in France and needed to stay home to recuperate.

After Char and I discussed our evening plans, we left Saks and went our separate ways. When I got home, I called Delta airlines and made reservations for my dad's trip to Atlanta. He'd never been to Atlanta before, and I was elated to have my dad visit me in the next two weeks. I needed to be surrounded by positive energy, and I knew my dad would provide me with that. After I placed my call and steamed my dress, I relaxed in a hot bubble bath. Charmine called just as I stepped out of the tub. She said she had medicated Anthony and was ready any time I was. I told Char that as soon as I got dressed and did my make-up, I'd be on my way.

Tonight appeared to be one of those nights that the heavens blessed me enormously. My hair and my make-up looked great. And the way my curves filled my new dress, I felt and looked amazing. I slipped on my heels, admired myself in the mirror for a few more seconds, and left my condo. I arrived at Charmine's a little earlier than planned because I wanted to talk to Anthony before we left. Charmine answered the door with a face mask on. "What are you wearing?" I asked.

"What does it look like? I told you Anthony is sick," she said.

"Girl, you know you are too theatrical for me. Where is Mr. Dead Man Walking at?"

"Now who's being theatrical? He's in the bedroom." I walked through the hall stacked with wedding gifts and stepped over boxes that were packed for the big moving day. I knocked on the half opened door, and Anthony told me to come in. He was in the bed with the covers pulled over his face. The room smelled like he was sick, and there were used tissues thrown all over the bed. I walked closer to him to see exactly what had happened to him during his honeymoon. His skin was a slimy greenish color and his ears were swollen

"Shit! Char wasn't kidding. What the heck happened to you?" I asked.

"I don't know. It could have been that alligator meat I ate at this French restaurant on the last night we were there. That's the only thing I can think of since Charmine didn't have any, and she isn't sick."

"Are you sure the alligator isn't trying to eat his way back out of your stomach, 'cause you look atrocious. Don't you think your wife may need to stay with you?"

"No, no, I'll be fine. There isn't anything she can do for me if she stays here. I've already been to the doctor. He gave me some medicine, told me to get plenty of rest, and to give it a couple of days." Charmine entered the room with a cup of hot tea and a container of orange juice.

"Well, I sure hope you get better soon," I said.

"Thanks, Lane," he said.

"Are you sure you don't want to me to stay with you? I'm sure Lane will understand."

"Absolutely," I said.

"No, Sweetheart, I'll be okay. Go have a nice time, and if I get worse, I'll call my mother."

"Sure, call your mother and let her know I've left you on your sick bed while I went to a party. Just give her a reason to hate me more."

"Oh, stop. You know my mother doesn't hate you. She called you everyday while we were on our honeymoon."

"Yeah, and I believe that was to prevent us from trying to make a baby." Charmine giggled, and Anthony told her to stop being silly. Charmine arranged the bedside table for his convenience with his medicine, juices, a thermometer, and his cell phone before we left. When we got outside, Charmine discarded her face mask in her trash can and rubbed some hand sanitizer on her hands. I asked her to squeeze some in my hands too because I certainly didn't want to catch what Anthony had.

As I drove to the venue in downtown Atlanta, Charmine claimed I was speeding, and if I were pulled over I could be arrested for my excessive speed on the interstate. I told her to stop being a backseat driver and relax. Charmine knew I was getting nervous and tried to calm me down before we arrived at the venue. She promised she'd be stuck to me like crazy glue. As we reached the exit close to the venue, you could sense something major was taking place in Atlanta: traffic was bumper-to-bumper with limousines and hundred thousand dollar cars.

When we eventually made it off the exit, we were guided by street security into an area where valets waited to park the guests' cars. Once I handed over my car keys, we were directed in the direction of the red carpet where we posed for some pictures. After our pictures were taken, we followed the red carpet until it led us directly into the venue. All the guests congregated in a reception area where we were served champagne and were handed a program which included the bio on the designer, Faizon Hill.

Charmine and I noticed Faizon's parents as they stood by a huge portrait of Faizon, and we went over and joined them. Mrs. Hill thanked Charmine for sending them a postcard from her honeymoon. She said she would invite Charmine over to the house soon, because she wanted to hear about Charmine's honeymoon in France. While Charmine talked to Mrs. Hill about Anthony's absence, Mr. Hill talked to me about Faizon's tenacity and strength. I wanted to include a few more of her attributes myself, but I didn't think he'd be too pleased to hear them.

Mr. Hill admitted if it had not been their daughter's special night, they'd be at home with a hot cup of tea and the TV guide for their enjoyment. Thus far, the night felt truly electric, and as the guests arrived they were treated like Hollywood A-listers. The lights blinked off and on in the reception area which indicated the show was about to begin. Faizon's parents left us to find their seats, and as the last guests took their seats, our ears were graced with the melodic, sultry sounds of Amani. While Amani sang her heart out, I flashed-back to the freezing cold night when Clay went to Kroger for some coffee and came back home all hyped. He said he heard this female as she sang a cappella in the cereal aisle and knew then he had to sign her.

I was so entranced by the magnificence of Amani's voice that I hadn't noticed the extremely handsome Clay had entered the room. He stood tall behind one of the white columns in the room; I elbowed Charmine and pointed in his direction. "Oh. . . girl you better work that out real soon. That man looks so good, and if I wasn't already spoken for, he'd be Mr. Grant." I slapped her hand from my arm where she grabbed me.

"Now you sound like ya girl, Faizon," I said.

"Girl bye. I was only joking about that. I could never do that—spoken for or not," she said.

"Okay, calm down. You were the one who brought it up." I looked back over in his direction to make sure he hadn't left. "I want to talk to him so badly, but I don't want to get up in the middle of Amani's set."

"Just wait, you have all night. You don't want to appear desperate." she said. Charmine turned her attention back to Amani as she continued to soothe the audience. Meanwhile, I checked Clay out from head to toe. He was dressed so swaggerific in his black suit, white shirt, and his diamond pendant as it glistened around his neck. I watched him stretch his neck above the crowd as if he were looking for someone, and I hoped it was me. After Amani finished her performance, a nice looking gentleman came out and escorted her off of the circular podium. After her enraptured performance, the audience whistled and cheered as she walked through the crowd. Amani humbly thanked the guests and disappeared into the back.

It was time for the main event. The lights dimmed over the guests, and the spotlight shined brightly on the runway. Across from me sat one of Atlanta's most popular radio personalities and his wife. A few of the Atlanta Falcons players were there and of course some of Hip Hop's royalty were in attendance. With everything in place and the music cued, the first beautiful model strutted down the runway in an elegant, white, high-necked jumpsuit with exaggerated hair and accessories. Each model walked down the runway in an outfit as breathtaking as the one before. Their strut, sassiness, and the Faizon Hill designs had the audience's attention.

Throughout the show, Faizon's designs ranged from an evening out with your girls to dining at the White House with the President. And last on the runway was the show-stopper which was a wedding dress similar to Charmine's with just a few minor differences. The audience gasped from the sheer beauty of the dress, and the seven strikingly gorgeous, statuesque models walked down the runway for their final time. The runway stayed clear for close to a minute and then, Faizon appeared from the behind the white curtain.

Faizon looked impeccable. She was dressed in one of her incredible creations which was a deep V-neck black lace dress. She strolled down the runway as if she were a model herself. Her head held high, shoulders back, and eyes forward. She ran back up the runway and back behind the curtain she went. She reappeared again with the seven beauties and with what looked like an entire florist shop in her arms. The room was illuminated once again and the show was over. Faizon's parents locked arms and smiled from ear to ear as they watched their daughter take her final bow. It was evident by the look on their faces how proud they were of their daughter's achievements. They excused themselves and walked backstage to congratulate her.

Charmine had to find a ladies room and left me in the reception area. I watched as the women flocked to the Atlanta Falcon's players for their autographs and whatever else they could get from them. A hostess walked up to me with a tray of cocktails, and I gladly took the Georgia Peach martini from the tray and put it to my lips. I swayed to the music, and all of a sudden, I felt a strong presence next to me. "Hello Lane."

"Clay. Hi. " I said and swallowed hard. "What a great show you hosted. You should be very happy."

"Thanks, I am happy. My team did their thing."

"And Amani, she's amazing. I can't wait to get her CD."

"Well, you'll be able to in a few months." Clay and I stood in the reception area and continued our chat as if we had met for the first time. "By the way, I have something for you." Clay reached inside his suit jacket and pulled something out and placed it in my hand. I looked in the palm of my hand and realized that it was my diamond stud earrings that I thought I lost.

"Oh my goodness, where did you find these? I thought they were gone forever."

"They were in the corner of my dresser. You must have taken them off the night we...you...well, the main thing is you have them back."

"Oh yeah, now I remember what happened." I thought this would be an ideal time to get him to open up to me, and I went for it. "Clay, when do you plan to forgi---"

"Not here, Lane. Not tonight."

"Then when, Clay? We need to talk about this." I wanted an answer. It didn't matter to me who was around us or that he felt it wasn't the appropriate time. Clay took a deep breathe and he looked as if he was about to speak when Charmine walked up.

"Hey Clay," she said. He turned to face her and they embraced each other. "It's good to see you."

"Same here, Mrs. Martin. How was your honeymoon?" He looked around the room. "And where's Mr. Martin?"

"The honeymoon was fantastic! We had breakfast on the veranda every morning until Anthony got sick. That's also why he isn't here. He's home now with some unheard of illness."

"Damn. Well, tell my man I hope he gets better."

"I will. And I gotta tell you, you've done an amazing job tonight. Faizon's line is about to sky rocket. And that Amani...Wow!"

"Thanks, Charmine. I appreciate that, and you're right about Faizon. So many people have come up to me and talked about her already. And like I was just telling Lane, Amani's album is about to drop in a few months, so look out for it."

"I will, I will." I wished I hadn't made the agreement with Char when she told me she would be stuck to me like glue, because I could have killed her. Clay was prepared to tell me something until she walked up and monopolized the conversation. I looked at her and rolled my eyes after she asked him the nineteenth question. "Oh, I'm so sorry, I just came right over and started talking. Did I interrupt something?" she asked.

"No," he said.

"Yes, Clay was just about to say something," I said.

"No, Lane, leave it for another time. I have an interview to do, so I better go. Goodnight, ladies." Clay touched Char on her shoulder and walked off. He stopped briefly and shook hands with a few of the guests before he vanished to the back. Charmine knew I was angry about the way she had just barged in on my conversation with Clay, and she tried to apologize for it. But I needed a minute. Some of the models had gotten dressed in their own clothes and joined the after-party. They grabbed a few of the cocktails off the trays and mingled with the crowd.

"Those are some of the models coming out, so I bet Faizon will be out here soon," she said. I shrugged my shoulders like I wasn't interested. "Oh, Lane, get over yourself! You heard him say y'all will discuss it another time. So really you should be thanking me, 'cause the next time you won't have a bunch of folks around y'all." I hated to admit it, but she was right and if there was another chance, I'd pick a much quieter location. When the hostess circled back in our area, I put my martini glass on the tray and grabbed another. Mr. Hill came over to us and said Faizon needed some privacy as she changed her clothes, but she would be out soon.

At last, Faizon came out dressed in an entirely different outfit, and I could tell that she'd had a few of those Martini's that floated around

FORBIDDEN SEDUCTION

freely. "How ya like me now?" Faizon danced over to us as she waved her arms in the air like she was at a rap concert. "You can't touch this!" she sang.

"It was fantastic. The show gave me goosebumps, everything was just spectacular," Charmine said and gave her a hug.

"I agree, Faizon. Tonight was remarkable. Your fashions were amazing, the models were beautiful, and you were breathtaking," I said.

"Thank you, thank you! Tonight was all of that. I've talked to a ton of people from the press, and said that they're going to do a full piece on me. And did you see Mychael Knight up in here? I haven't seen him personally yet, but I heard he was here."

"No, we haven't either," I said. Faizon's parents talked to us a while longer before they announced it was past their bedtime, and they were worn out from all the excitement. Mrs. Hill reminded Faizon that she would open the shop in the morning. Faizon told me and Charmine that she'd be right back and walked her parents to their car.

"Your homegirl is a little tipsy," Charmine said.

"You don't say, but it has to be from all the hoopla she's experienced tonight. You know after tonight, her life will never be the same."

"I know. And you thought she was giving us her ass to kiss before? Bae-bae. . . you gonna need a new type of lip gloss for that ass now." We cracked up from laughter. "Listen, I'm going to that empty room in the back so I can call to check on Anthony. While I'm here having the time of my life, my hubby is at home miserable."

"You know he's probably already called his mommy."

"Oh, shut up. I'll be right back." Faizon returned from outside just as Charmine had walked off to call Anthony. Faizon shared with me what she had planned next for her brand and how she felt that after tonight she'd soon be on everyone minds. Charmine returned minutes later and joined us.

"Faizon, I really hate to do this but, Anthony sounds worse and I gotta go home."

"Aww...I'm sorry to hear that. I was hoping we could bring the morning in together like we used to do. I'm still too amped to sleep," Faizon said.

269

"Another time. I know what, when we get moved into our new house I'll invite you over for dinner," Charmine said.

"Well, you did promise in sickness and in health. Tonight has been amazing and congratulations again on everything. Enjoy the rest of your night," I said.

"No, you're not leaving—I got you a ride home," Charmine said.

"Wait, how do you have a ride home for me when you came in my car?"

"Just give me your valet ticket. I'll bring your car back to you tomorrow."

"No, first tell me who's taking me home?"

"Clay. I saw him after I spoke to Anthony and told him the situation. He said he wouldn't mind taking you home. Now, will you give me the ticket? I reached down into my bag and graciously handed Char the valet ticket. Charmine asked me to call her when I got in and told Faizon she had a great time. Charmine paid no mind to the crowd as she briskly walked past some people who had encircled one of Atlanta's hottest producers to get home to Anthony. Faizon's mood dampened a bit after she heard Clay would be the one to take me home. She offered to take me in his stead, but of course I declined. As Faizon's event drew near to its close, Maria, the young woman Faizon hired to help her, started to gather all of the clothing. Maria packed the rest of Faizon's accessories and placed them neatly in boxes.

Faizon stood amongst her guests and gave them the history of her new brand. Maria walked over to Faizon and told her she'd be back with the van Faizon's father had provided to transport all of Faizon's clothing. The venue was nearly empty of all the guests, except for the handful of attractive businessmen, and the wide receiver for the Atlanta Falcons who refused to leave Faizon's side. I looked around the venue for Clay who seemed to have evaporated. I went and sat down in the reception area and waited patiently for him to take me home. I watched Maria as she came back inside the venue and whispered something in Faizon's ear. Faizon waved her off and continued to bask in the company of the men.

Faizon hugged the men before she left the circle and headed towards me in the reception area. She flopped down in the empty chair next to me and kicked her shoes off. "Phew...girl, I'm beat! It feels like

I've been on my feet forever."

"I bet, but I know you feel it's all been worth it."

"Oh, of course it has. I can see it now, Faizon Hill in New York, London, and Paris."

"I can see it too. Especially after tonight, you really did a great job, and Clay did an excellent job with the event."

"Girl, I couldn't have done it without that sexy-ass man. No offense."

"You're too much, but since we're no longer a couple, you're safe." Maria popped her head back inside the door of the reception area and looked in our direction. She ducked back out once she saw Faizon was talking to me.

"Lane, let me go before I have to fire Maria's ass before she even gets started. She keeps crying how tired she is and how she still has to help me unload the van."

"Alright, goodnight."

"Goodnight. And thanks for coming out to support me, with how I've acted lately, I know it couldn't have been easy for you" she said and put her shoes back on.

"Don't mention it, I enjoyed myself tonight."

"You may enjoy it even more now that Clay is taking you home," she said. She walked off and yelled out to Maria that she was ready. I was now the last person in the building other than the cleaning people who had started to stack chairs and pull down the decorations from the walls Just as I begun to think Clay had changed his mind about taking me home, he and another guy walked into the room where I was. They walked towards me and stopped.

"Malik, this is Lane. She's my...I mean she's an acquaintance of mine."

"Nice to meet you Lane," Malik said and looked at Clay while he shook my hand. "I see you surround yourself with very beautiful women." I cut my eye at Clay, and he let out an uneasy chuckle.

"Hello Malik, it's nice to meet you."

"It's too bad I didn't see you earlier we could have sat together."

"Nah, y'all couldn't have," Clay stated firmly.

"My bad, Man, I didn't mean to step on your toes," Malik said.

"You didn't. You good."

Malik looked confused by Clay's sudden switch but continued on. "Thanks for the interview. I'll call you and Faizon to let you guys know when the article will be ready.

"Aight sounds good. Thanks, Man." Clay pulled Malik in for one of those brotherly chest-to-chest hugs, and after they said a few more words to each other, Malik exited the building. I couldn't help but to be a little flattered that Clay seemed jealous over Malik's comment. When I told Clay that I appreciated that he agreed to take me home, he made it a point to make me aware he only agreed because Charmine was in a crisis and asked him to. By the time Clay and I left the building, all the staff had gone, and the building looked like nothing had taken place there just hours prior. Clay and I walked across the street to a nearby private parking lot and found his car. Clay opened the door for me and slammed it closed when I got in. When he got in, he remained silent. He put his key in the ignition and drove off.

I wanted to strike up a conversation with him, but I feared he would shut me down like he did when we talked inside the venue earlier. I thought of a topic that we could talk about without him feeling pressed about us being a couple again. "My dad will be here in a couple of weeks and he's looking forward to you taking him to play golf." Clay looked at me for the first time since we got in his car.

"That's what's up. Yeah, I told him I'd take him for some holes if he ever made it down here."

"So, I can tell him that you'll still take him?"

"Sure, why wouldn't you? Listen Lane, something happened between us. Me and your pops is still cool."

"That's good to know." I positioned my body so that I could see Clay from my peripherals, because it was too painful when I looked at him dead-on. "Is Malik a friend of yours?"

"Why? You wanna get with him too? Clay snapped.

"No. I was just asking a question. I had never heard you mention him before that's all."

"That's probably because you don't know everyone I know," he answered quite brutally.

"Clay, how long are you going to stay mad at me? I've told you how sorry I am about everything."

"That's the thing. I don't want to be mad at you. Do you think it's easy for me to be this close to you and can't hold you the way I want to or be in the same room with you and can't claim you as my woman?"

"Then why can't you?"

"I can't. Not right now." Clay looked so hurt. I just wanted to put my arms around him. I gathered from his distressed tone he preferred we didn't talk any further, and I respected that. For the rest of our journey I looked out of my window and hummed the songs Amani performed at the launch. Clay asked me if I wanted him to take me to Charmine's so that I could have picked up my car. I told him that Charmine had planned to bring my car back to me in the morning. So he cut over two lanes and exited off the interstate in the direction of my condo.

We arrived at my place. Clay parked in front of my condo and waited for me to get out. "Thank you, for bringing me home."

"No problem."

"I'll call you in a couple of weeks when my dad gets here, that way you two can set up the golf date. I just hope you don't act brand new and hang up on me."

"I wouldn't do that, and if you hadn't fucked up, I'd be taking you to play golf with us."

"Why do you have to keep rubbing it in? Hopefully one day you'll forgive me and take me too." I unbuckled my seat belt, opened my door, and stepped out.

"We'll see. Bye Lane."

"Goodnight Clay," I said and walked inside. I looked back and Clay had already driven off. When I got upstairs I called Char, she said that Anthony had a fever of 103.1 but refused to go to the hospital, and after she brought my car back to me in the morning, she'd be at home with him. I told her not to worry about my car, that I'd take a cab to her house and get it myself. I asked her if she wanted me to get anything for him from the 24 hours CVS before I got to her house. Charmine told me to get anything that treated the flu since he appeared to have flu-like symptoms.

After Charmine and I spoke on the phone, I drank a glass of water and went upstairs to go straight to bed. I tried not be too affected by my night with Clay—I just wanted to forget the entire mess that I had created and hoped that one day Clay would forgive me. I got undressed and prepared myself for bed. After I washed my face, I set my alarm, and climbed into my lonely bed. My alarm went off as soon as I started to dream of Clay. I pressed the snooze button so that I could get a few more minutes to dream of him. But I laid in my bed in vain as the dream had gone for good, so I got up and started to get ready for work.

While I drank my morning coffee, I called for a cab, grabbed my bag for work, and went downstairs to the lobby. When the cab showed up, I asked him to make a stop at the local CVS. When I got to the CVS, I threw different types of flu and cold remedies in my basket for Anthony—I paid for the items and stepped back into the cab. I gave the cab driver Charmine address and we started the trip over there. I called Charmine when I was a block away from her house and told her I'd be there in less than five minutes. She told me that she would leave the garage door unlocked and to come on in.

The cab driver pulled up in front of Charmine's house. I paid the driver and got out. I walked inside of the house and Char was in the kitchen. She had prepared a nice breakfast for us. I asked her about Anthony and she said surprisingly his fever had gone down in the middle of the night. I gave her the bag of medicines, and she immediately fixed him a cup of Thera-Flu and took it in the bedroom where he was still laid up.

When Charmine came back out of the room, I told her that I would have loved to have been able to stay and have breakfast with them, but my performance at work left a lot to be desired lately. And I definitely needed to be on time. Charmine took my car key from off a hook in the kitchen and gave it to me. I told her that I'd come back after work, and she told me to make sure I did because she wanted to hear about what happened when Clay drove me home.

Time ticked slowly as I watched the bank's wall clock from my computer. I'd been bored to death at work lately, especially since I didn't have as much interaction with people any more because of my new position. I had dozed off in open view a few times while at my computer and was afraid of being called out, so I decided to go the ladies room to steal a few minutes for a catnap. As I got up to leave my office, I received a call on my cell. I walked back over to my desk and picked up my phone. The call was from a private number, but before I answered it the caller hung up.

The first person that came to mind was Clay, but I couldn't be for sure. I wanted to call him to find out if he had placed the anonymous call, but I had promised myself that the next time that Clay and I were together, it would be because he wanted to, and not because I chased him. I had sensed that Clay wanted to take me back, but his fear of being hurt again prevented him from making that move. I put my cell phone back in my desk drawer and went for a quick snooze in the ladies room. The ladies room had turned out to be the confessional box for the cleaning staff that were having trouble with their supervisor, and it had gotten quite loud. After about the tenth time of me hearing 'I ain't going fo' dat shit!" I'd given up on any hope of having a ten minute power nap. When I emerged from the stall, I broke up the bitchfest being conducted by the disgruntled staff that stood in front of the mirrors in a huddle. I washed my hands and exited. Before I returned to my desk, I stopped by the break room and fixed a cup of coffee as I struggled hard to stay awake. Ever since my unsuccessful attempt to take a nap in the ladies room, I noticed that Mr. Wyatt passed by my office several times. And when he came back around for the third time, I pretended to shuffle a few papers on my desk around like I had a ton of work to do.

It felt like I'd been at work all day, but when I looked at the clock again only an hour had passed. I called Charmine and asked her to do something that we used do when we were in college to get us out of class, and she agreed. I quickly made up an excuse to go to Mr. Wyatt's office. As I approached his door, I could see he was on his computer from his window, and I knocked lightly on his door. "Come in," he said.

"Hello Mr. Wyatt. I hate to disturb you, but I have a question for you."

"Sure, Lane. You're not disturbing me."

"When I first returned to work, I had such a difficult time with the new FATCA procedures that I had to get Jade to help me with them. She's very knowledgeable on it, and she really helped me a lot. So, I was wondering maybe we should let her be in charge of training the new employees."

"Have you discussed it with her?

"No, not yet."

"When would she be able to do it, because I can't afford to pull her from her station during bank hours. But if she agrees and you can get all the logistics figured out, it sounds like a great idea."

"Maybe she'll consider doing a few hours on the Saturday." I hated I had to throw Jade under the bus, but I needed an excuse to be in Mr. Wyatt's office.

"Well, you talk to her and see what she says about it, and get back to me." It sounded as if Mr. Wyatt was about to excuse me from his office, and I needed to be in there a bit longer.

"I will. Oh yeah, there's something else I needed to run past you," But just as I was about to come up with another fictitious issue, Rita called my name over the intercom, and asked me to pick up line one. "May I take it in here?" I asked Mr. Wyatt.

"Sure," he said, he picked up his receiver and hit the line for me. From the moment he handed me the phone my amateur acting skills kicked in.

"What? You've got to be kidding! No, I can't leave now. I'm at work. Is there someone in the building that can handle it for me?" I hoped my performance on the phone had convinced Mr. Wyatt that I needed to leave immediately, but so far he hadn't seemed remotely interested. "Well, there's absolutely no way I can leave now so---"

"Wait. What's going on, Lane?" Mr. Wyatt finally asked.

"It's Mike, he's the maintenance man for the condominiums I live in. He's saying that the pipes in my new condo have burst, and it's leaking profusely into my downstairs neighbor's condo."

"Oh no, you must go and take care of that. That's an emergency." BINGO! 'Emergency.' The magic word I waited for. I told Char who brilliantly played the role of 'Mike the maintenance man' I'd be there as soon as I could. I hung up, and Mr. Wyatt told me I could have the rest of the afternoon off. I thanked him and told him I would discuss the training with Jade tomorrow when I returned. I hopped in my car and headed straight to Char's house. It was such a lovely spring day and I didn't want to be cooped up in some old bank.

When I arrived, Anthony was curled up on the couch in the living room. He looked a lot better. Some of the color returned to his face, and his fever had gone completely. Anthony said he appreciated the medicine I'd brought him earlier, and I told him that I was so glad that he looked a lot better. I sat out in the living room and talked with Anthony until Charmine called me in the back to her office. When I entered her office, she asked me to shut her door. "I'm dying to know what happened last night." she said.

"First of all, thank you, 'Mike' for getting me out of work. I was suffering with a bad case of work allergies today."

"You stupid," Char laughed. "Now tell me what happened?

"It's nothing really to tell. He barely said anything to me on the ride home. But check this out, did you happen to notice this nice looking man who was standing next to Mr. Hill? He had on a grey suit?"

"No, there were so many people there I don't remember him."

"Anyway, he's Clay's friend and a journalist for the AJC. Clay introduced us last night and when he hit on me, Clay got upset."

"Of course he would, why wouldn't he?"

"Well, if he doesn't want me, why is he mad that someone else might?"

"Do you think it's easy for him, Lane? Clay still wants you, but he's still hurting. Imagine if the shoe was on the other foot. Look how you reacted to the Faizon situation and he hadn't done anything."

"You're right, but I just want him back so bad."

"I'm not saying give up on him—just give him some time to recover." After Charmine offered me some more advice on my love life, she said that since Anthony seemed to be getting better, they planned to move over the weekend. Charmine made her famous pasta dish for dinner, and after I ate, I went home because I needed to do some work there. I had taken a break from working on my laptop and stretched out on my bed when Faizon called. She asked if I wanted to drop by the shop, but I told her that I had been out most of the day and planned to stay in. She sounded like she needed someone to talk to, so I told her that she was welcome to come by my condo, and she said she'd come after she closed the shop.

When Faizon arrived, I made us some mango daiquiris and nachos. We went out on my patio to enjoy the beautiful spring weather. As we sipped on our cocktails, Faizon talked a lot about her event— she told me about how the wide receiver from the Atlanta Falcons had sent her a bouquet of pink roses—and asked her out on a date. I asked her if she planned to go out with him, and she said she hadn't made up her mind yet. She asked me how the ride home with Clay went, and unlike Charmine, I wasn't sure of her motives, but I still dished all about the humdrum ride from the venue to my house. "That man loves you. I can say that for sure."

"I'm sure he does too, he just needs some time to remember that." Faizon asked if she could have another daiquiri, so I went into the kitchen and blended another one for her. Faizon didn't give an explanation to why she wanted to visit me, but after she finished her nachos, she asked if she could talk to me about something. I was a little leery of what she wanted to talk to me about, especially if it had something to do with her and Clay. But my curiosity wanted to be satisfied, and so I told her she could talk to me. Faizon confessed that she hadn't always been a loyal friend to me, and she regretted how she crossed the line with Clay. She said she missed the times when the three of us got together, and she realized she would never have friends like Charmine and I again. Faizon looked sad after she said that. I was bewildered by her sudden need to cleanse her soul and asked her what was the reason for all of this.

"Lane, when people see me, they think I have it all. But what they don't see is that I'm lonely; a sad woman who needs a man's attention to make me feel good about myself. Do you think it's by accident that the men that I get involved with are already in a relationship? ...Attached men have always made me feel more desirable because they're willing to risk it all for me...except for Clay. That's how I know he truly loves you." I would have never suspected that Faizon thought so little of herself, and I saw her in a whole different light.

I asked Faizon if she wanted the last of the daiquiri that was left in the blender, but she put her hand on top of her glass and shook her head no. I couldn't believe that Faizon was so sullen after the phenomenal success she had just a couple of nights ago, and I prayed I would never be like that. However, Faizon did seem excited when she talked about her upcoming trip to New York. She said she had scheduled some meetings there with some of the major stores about her line. Faizon looked at her watch and said she needed to leave. She had an evening appointment with a new client who wanted her to design her wedding dress. I asked Faizon if she planned to help Charmine and Anthony move on Saturday, and she said bluntly 'I don't do moves.' But she did tell me to let Charmine know she could call her if she wanted help decorating.

Faizon asked me before she left if I had forgiven her from my heart or my mouth. I had to be honest, so I told her that I needed some time to genuinely mean it because I was so shocked that she would have done that to me. "I know you're gonna think this sounds crazy, but I don't want you to take what I did personally—it wouldn't have made a difference who you were to me. I saw something I wanted, and I went after it." I wasn't sure how to respond to that, so I left it alone.

After Faizon left I thought about what she said about her being lonely, and I went back to when we first met. And she was right. As long as I've known Faizon she'd never been in a relationship with a single man. The men have always been either married or committed to someone other than her. Even when Charmine and I suspected that Darnell was married and confronted her about it, she continued to lie and insisted he was single. And by the time we had found out the truth and urged her to leave him, it was too late.

The weekend had arrived and spring was in full effect. Georgia has always been a beautiful state with lots of big green trees and picturesque lawns. I would have loved to have been able to spend my weekend in the park, but I promised to help Charmine move. and she had already called me three times before I made it to her house. When I pulled up in front of the two- story brick house, a humongous Father& Son moving truck was parked outside. When I entered the house, I was thrilled to see all of Anthony's brothers were there with their sleeves rolled up and ready to work. I thought with all of these able bodied men I may just be able to catch some sun after all.

Charmine heard me as I came in and greeted the men. She yelled down to me to come upstairs with her. When I got upstairs to her bedroom, she had hardly touched anything. All of her shoes and clothes were thrown all around the room. I wanted to go off on her, but instead I sealed my lips, took her clothes off the hangers, and placed her clothes inside boxes. "Wait a minute! Was that my Dior suit you just threw in that box like that? she asked.

"What suit?" Charmine walked over to me, snatched a black suit from out of the box and shoved it under my nose.

"This suit!"

"I'm sorry."

"Look, Lane. I have a system, that's why I left my clothes and shoes for last. Help me by clearing out the bathrooms."

"Um uh...this is my weekend off. I coulda been lying under a tree in Piedmont Park, but instead I'm spending my weekend taking orders from you."

"Oh be quiet, and take this," she said, and shoved an empty box in my hand. I did as she asked and started to clear the bathroom of her cosmetics, magazine, and towels and placed them in the box she'd given me. As I packed the items in the bathroom, I heard a familiar man's voice downstairs as they dismantled the furniture downstairs. I thought the male voice that I heard sounded a lot like Clay, but I dismissed it until I heard the laugh. I peeked my head out of Charmine's bathroom and met Clay head on.

"What's good ladies?" Clay said.

"Oh great, you did make it! The more help the better," Charmine said.

"Hi Clay. I didn't know you'd be here today," I said.

"Yeah, I'm here. I'm going downstairs to help the fellas 'cause it looks like y'all got it covered up here." Clay slapped the side of the wall twice with his hand, and went downstairs.

"Why didn't you tell me he was going to be here?" I asked.

"I didn't find out until this morning when he called to see how Anthony was doing. Anthony told him we were moving, and he offered to help."

"Did he know I'd be here?"

"Duh...of course he did. He knows we're joined at the hip." During the course of the day, Charmine and I transferred the boxes she didn't want on the truck from the old house to the new one in her car. On the next to last trip, Anthony suggested that Charmine and I stay at the new house so we could start to unload the boxes as they came in. All of the men left out again with what should have been their last trip. Charmine and I pushed the labeled boxes into their respective rooms and unloaded each one. Charmine said she wanted to listen to some music, and while she searched for CDs, Faizon called. She wanted to welcome Charmine and Anthony into their new home and asked Charmine what she wanted as a house warming gift.

Charmine's new kitchen was much nicer than her old one, and it was twice the size. As we unpacked, the boxes we listened to some old school R&B. I had the box which contained the kitchen items, and Charmine worked on their bedroom boxes. She said she needed to sleep in her own bed tonight because she couldn't take another night sleeping on the air mattress. By the time the truck pulled up in the driveway, we had a lot of the unpacking finished.

Anthony and Clay struggled to get the huge leather sectional in the narrow doorway, but once they got it through the door they pushed it to the living room. Both men huffed and puffed like they suffered with asthma and plopped their sweaty bodies on the sofa. Charmine asked Anthony if his brothers were still in the truck since they hadn't entered the house. Anthony told her that since it wasn't much left at the old house he told them they could go home. As soon as Anthony seemed to have regained his normal breathing pattern back, Charmine said she wanted to show him something she had noticed in the bedroom. Clay and I were alone, and it was so quiet that I heard the house as it creaked. When Anthony and Charmine returned downstairs, she announced that she had ordered some pizzas. "Is everything all right upstairs?" Clay asked Anthony.

"Everything is fine. My wife noticed a hairline crack on the wall and freaked. She thought something was wrong with the subsidence of the house." They both had a laugh and teased women's knowledge on houses and car matters.

"I remember one night Lane was at my house during a thunderstorm, and the boiler light went out. Lane was afraid for me to light it. She said the house would 'blow up' if I didn't light it in three seconds." They roared even louder with laughter. Anthony tossed Clay a bottled beer, and when the doorbell rang, Charmine got all excited.

"Our first guest," she said.

"Really, Char? It's only the pizza man," I said.

"Hater," she said and opened the door. Anthony pulled the money from his wallet and paid the deliveryman while Charmine grabbed the pizzas and placed them on the table. I got out the plates, and the guys tried to hook up the 60 inch screen TV in the living room so they could watch the game. Anthony asked Charmine to bring them another beer, and from habit, I fixed Clay's plate and took it to him.

"Thanks, Bae," Clay said. He hadn't realized he directed a term of endearment towards me, and I soaked it up like a sponge. Charmine and I joined them in the living room and pretended to watch the basketball game on ESPN with them. Charmine suggested we play a game of Scrabble, but Clay said he couldn't because he had some stuff to do at the studio. I asked him if I could have a moment with him before he left, and he agreed. I stepped out into the garage and waited for him to tell Char and Anthony goodnight. I had a lot I wanted to say to him, but the words were all jumbled in my head. The side door which led to the garage opened, and when Clay walked out, I still wasn't clear on what I wanted to say to him "What did you want to talk to me about?"

"I thought it was really nice of you to help them out today."

"I didn't have too much to do today, but that's not what you wanted to talk to me about. So what's up?"

". . . Can I come home with you...not to spend the night, just to chill out a bit? I really miss you."

Because Clay hadn't shown any signs of disquietude throughout the day, I just assumed that he would have at least considered my bid. "I don't think that's a good idea, Lane."

I stepped in closer to him. "Please, Clay. We've had such a good time today."

Warily, Clay stepped back away from me. "Yeah, we did, and I'm just beginning to feel comfortable being in the same room with you again. I don't want to take you home with me just to fuck you. That's what Dre did, but I care more about you than that." After he refused, I didn't pursue the issue any further. He got in his car and drove off—I went back inside and sat down on the sofa next to Char. I listened to Anthony and Charmine bicker over what color they should paint the bathroom for almost an hour, and I thought they sounded very much like an old married couple already.

I left them in the living room and went to the kitchen and got another slice of pizza. Charmine invited me to stay over, but I told her I wouldn't intrude on them on their first night in their new home. So, after I finished my food, I prepared to go home. They both thanked me for my help and Charmine said she'd call me in the morning. On the way home I felt like Clay purposely wanted to torture me, and he succeeded. I got home and settled in for the night, I prayed that night that Clay would eventually forgive me so we could be together again. Within one short week things had shaped up nicely for Charmine and Anthony. The law office opened its doors in the Atlantic Station area, and they seemed to attract a steady flow of new clients. And now that Emily's divorce was final, she took on the role as the office manager for some income. And as Charmine had promised, she invited her family and a few close friends over for a housewarming.

Before I went to the housewarming I had stopped by Macy's in Lenox Square Mall and bought them the premium espresso machine they both hinted at. Anthony and Clay seemed to have built a solid friendship, and Clay was invited to the housewarming as well. I pulled up in front of the house and spotted Clay's car. I walked inside the house, placed my gift on the table with all the others and went straight out to the backyard where all the guests were. The kids cheerfully laughed and played in the pool as the adults sat on the side watched them attentively.

I greeted everyone and walked over to the table where Charmine had fixed a nice spread of: fruits, cheeses, salads, and two lasagnas that Anthony's mother had prepared. Jeremy, Anthony's youngest brother, was a big kid himself. He jumped in and out of the pool and played pool games with the kids. Anthony decided he wanted to show how masterful he was on his colossal gas grill and grilled everything he deemed fit for grilling. When Clay saw me and headed in my direction. I thought we may have reached a breakthrough, but instead he bypassed me, picked up one of the patio chairs, and sat down next to Anthony. I accepted that in the past when Clay and I were in close quarters, I've bombarded him with my desire for us to be together, but I decided I'd play it differently. So, when he finally acknowledged me and waved, I just waved back and smiled at him.

When the burgers and steaks were done, the ladies plated up the food for the kids while the men stood around the grill with beers in their hands and cheered Anthony on for his masterful grilling ability. Charmine asked me to grab some more napkins from out of the kitchen. I walked inside and looked around the kitchen for the napkins that Charmine claimed were in eyesight on the table. I looked in the pantry that was the size of a small bedroom and finally found the napkins. When I turned to go back outside, Clay had walked in the kitchen. "Did you find them?" he asked.

"Yeah, got 'em," I said and proceeded to take them outside.

"Lane, wait." I stopped and looked at him. "I'm not trying to make this hard for us. The other night you don't know how badly I wanted to turn my car around and come back here to take you home with me. But I can't get the vision of you and Dre outta my head."

"And you gotta know that if I could go back and do it all over, I would have never slept with him and lose the man I love forever."

"I wouldn't say you've lost me forever." I restrained myself from having jumped into his arms when he said that, but I also didn't want to get my hopes up either. "And I hope you believe me when I say I want to put it behind me . . . but it's hard."

"I understand. And I want you to understand I'm not going nowhere. I'll be right here waiting for you." This had been the second time that since our breakup I felt that Clay wanted to kiss me. Just as he had leaned in, Charmine entered the kitchen and he jerked back quickly.

"Where the hell are the napkins I asked you for a day ago!?" Charmine asked, and she snatched the unopened pack of napkins out of my hand.

"My bad, Charmine. I stopped her while she was coming out," he said and went back outside with the others. Charmine recognized that there may have been a rekindled fire that was taking place in her kitchen, and she winked at me and took the napkins outside. About an hour later a few more of Charmine and Anthony's colleagues arrived bearing gifts. Andrew played the bartender, and he kept drinks in the guests' hands. Charmine looked at her watch and asked if I had spoken to Faizon, because she was expected to come. I told Char that the last time I spoke to her was when she came to my house last week, but I knew she said she would see us for sure at the housewarming.

As Charmine's guests drank more than they ate, Anthony's mother offered to take the kids inside for the evening and put in a DVD. Her daughters-in-law, Kelli and Madison, welcomed the good deed and hurried the kids out of the pool. While Charmine and Anthony regaled their colleagues by the pool, Clay and I sat by ourselves in a quiet corner lit by the garden lights and enjoyed each other's innocent banter. Just as Anthony shut down the grill, Faizon showed up wearing a very revealing summery halter dress. She found Charmine by the pool in some heated debate with her colleagues over some new state law and hugged her. I watched Faizon as she turned it all the way up and became quite vibrant once she clocked the backyard was plentiful with good looking men. I watched to see if Clay's eyes followed her movements, but he seemed uninterested and continued to talk to me.

Faizon sauntered towards Clay and me with an old fashioned Tequila Sunrise in her hand. "Hey, you two. Why are y'all being anti-social in a house full of people? she asked. Clay and I stopped our conversation and greeted her.

"We aren't being anti-social. We just came over here. You're late, had a busy day?" I asked.

"Kinda. I had a lunch date with my wide receiver, and lunch went into dinner," she smirked. Faizon went on to give a full detailed account of her date. Clay stood up and asked me if I would walk him the door as he was about to leave. "Oh, I'm sorry Clay. I didn't mean to run you off."

"You didn't." Clay walked over to the group of attorneys, and said goodbye to Charmine and Anthony. Clay and I walked to the front of the house where he parked his car, and although I was happy as hell to do it, I was curious to why he wanted me to walk him out.

"You sure decided to leave in a hurry. Did Faizon make you uncomfortable?" I asked.

"Pssh. Not one bit.

"Okay, so why did you want me to walk you to your car."

"To help you walk off some of that damn barbecue you've been eating all night," he laughed.

"Ha-Ha! You're real funny, Clay." I watched him get in his car and pull off before I rejoined the others in the backyard. Anthony's brother, Shade, was furious that he agreed to be the designated driver. He complained that he hadn't enjoyed himself like the others, and he was ready to go. Shade rounded up the family and announced that they needed to get ready to leave if they wanted him to take them home. Anthony told Shade that he would take their parents home because their mother promised to help clean up. Charmine told Anthony that she wouldn't need his mother's help, and he could take her home now, because she had me and Faizon to help her.

The housewarming gathering faded out, and Charmine's colleagues started to leave, and when the last guest left, Anthony drove his parents home. Charmine went inside the garage and returned with some Hefty garbage bags. She gave one to the both of us and told us to get busy. Faizon looked at Char like she wasn't having it, and asked why she had been put to work when she had only just arrived. Charmine told her with a serious face that if she was there long enough to have a drink, then she could clean. Faizon and I tackled the mess of plates and cups around the tables and poolside. Charmine ducked back into the garage and pulled out this large electric contraption that allowed her to vacuum up the mess outside.

After we had the yard all cleaned up, we went inside. Faizon and I looked on as Charmine wrapped up the leftovers and placed them in her fridge. Once she was finished, she sat down at the table with Faizon and me. "That was a nice get together," she said.

"It was. Anthony has such a big family," I said.

"Yeah, he does. And why didn't y'all invite Luke?" Faizon asked.

"Girl, forget about Luke. I thought you said you tackled a wide receiver, anyway?" Charmine asked Faizon. But before she could answer, Charmine turned her attention to me. "And what was up with you and Clay all cuddled up by my rose bush? I saw y'all."

I blushed at her question. "Nothing. We were having just a nice conversation."

"I could see that. What was the conversation about?"

"I know right. They did look all cozy-cozy sitting together," Faizon said.

"I'm serious, it wasn't anything major. We talked a little about us, and how he's not ready to go too fast. I did tell him that I'd be waiting on him whenever he was ready." Faizon and Charmine agreed that we would get back together, and from the reception I'd gotten from Clay tonight, I believed it as well. Charmine looked over at all the decorated boxes and wished Anthony would hurry back home. She was tempted to open the gifts without him, but she refrained from doing so. Faizon asked how my dad was doing. I told her he was doing well and that he'd be in Atlanta next week. Faizon said she hoped she'd get to meet him, but she would be in New York around the same time he was expected to travel.

When Anthony returned from taking his parents home, Faizon and I respected that they both had a long day and decided we'd leave. Charmine asked us to wait until she at least opened the gifts that we had bought them—she sifted through the many boxes until she came across ours. Anthony lifted my box onto the table, stepped back, and watched as Charmine tore the colorful wrapping paper from the box. "Aahh. . . look Anthony! It's the Nespresso machine we both wanted."

"Wow. Thanks, Lane. This is going to make our mornings that much more special," he said.

"You know you're welcome. Now maybe your wife won't be such a grouch in the morning."

"She's never been a grouch in the mornings to me."

"I don't expect you to say nothing crazy 'cause you're still newlyweds, but you're forgetting something, Anthony. I lived with her long before you did, and I know how she is in the mornings."

He laughed and measured with his pointer finger and thumb. "Okay, maybe just a little." Charmine playfully threw a kitchen hand towel at Anthony and reached for Faizon's gift. It was in a small, beautifully wrapped box. Charmine looked confused when she opened the box and pulled out a lovely, delicate hand-stitched baby outfit.

"Do you like it?" Faizon asked.

"It's amazing...but you do know I'm not expecting."

"Not now you aren't, but eventually you will be."

Anthony took it from Charmine's hands and held it up for a closer look. "I love it. Thank you very much." he said and kissed her on her cheek.

"You would love it. That's because you come from a big, John Walton sized family," Charmine said and took the baby outfit from his hands. "Thanks, Faizon, it's beautiful."After the gift opening, we all promised to get together for drinks before Faizon left for New York next week, and then we left.

The next morning, I sprung out of bed. I felt as though something had triggered inside me overnight, and I was prepared to take on the world. I had a lot to be excited about and I believed that it was mainly due to my dad's visit at the end of the week. And Clay's change in demeanor towards me was also a contributing factor. However, I refused to put too much credence into his recent change of heart, because I wanted him to be sure 'we' were what he truly wanted. And it seemed like the more I had eased up on Clay, the more he faintly hinted that there may be a future for us.

Charmine asked Faizon and I to meet her at a restaurant on Peachtree Street for lunch, and just as I was about to leave the bank, she called. She said she had to cancel because she felt very ill. She believed that she had come down with the same illness that Anthony had when they returned from France. I told her that since Faizon was at the restaurant already I'd still have lunch with her, and I would be at her house after work. Charmine said she would see me later and hung up. When I entered the restaurant, Faizon flagged me in her direction. "Hey, Lane. I just got off the phone with Charmine, and she sounds horrible," she said.

"I know, and I might need to stay the hell away from France if it's making folks sick like that."

"I been to France several times, and I've never gotten that sick. They must have eaten at one of those dinky, side streets cafes."

"Well, I don't know about all of that. I just know she sounds really bad, and after work today, I'm going to drop by to check on her."

"That's good. I would, but I have to get some things squared away at my shop before I leave for New York tomorrow."

"Who's minding the shop while you're gone?"

"My mama and Maria. Girl, my mama loves it. She says it gets her out of the house."

"Yeah, I see. She was telling me and Char about that at your launch. Mrs. Hill be all dolled up going to work, huh?"

"Yes, ma'am! I gotta keep my mama fly." Our lunch together was the first time in a while that Faizon and I truly enjoyed each other's company. We talked about what she had planned in New York and what she hoped would happen for her and her brand. I talked freely about Clay and how I wanted a relationship with him again, and she said she knew it would happen for us. We finished our lunch, and I wished her well on her journey to New York. After I returned to work after our lunch, I had been so busy that the afternoon crept up on me. I hadn't realized it was time to leave until Jade stopped by my office. She wanted me to know how much she appreciated me for the recommendation. I had almost forgotten I'd recommended her to do the training for the new employees on the FATCA procedures. I told her she was very welcome and that I had a feeling she'd be honored.

After work, I stopped by the CVS and stocked up on the same medicines I'd bought Anthony when he was sick and had him back on his feet in no time, and I wanted the same results for Charmine. I called Charmine and told her I was on my way over. She informed me that she asked Anthony to put the key under the mat in the garage because she wouldn't feel like getting up to let me in. When I got to Char's house, I followed her instructions and retrieved the key from the hidden location. I opened the door and walked upstairs to her bedroom where Charmine was zonked out. I called her name softly because she had dozed off, and I didn't want to frighten her. "Charmine. . . Char." She flickered her eyes before they opened fully.

"Hey, Chica. I must have dozed back off after I talked to you," she said, and tried to sit up in the bed.

"What you doin'? Lay back down," I eased her back down onto her pillow. "How you feelin'?"

"Not good. I don't know what the hell happened. I was fine yesterday. That's the same thing that happened to Anthony. One minute he was playing tennis, the next minute he was sick."

"Have you been to the doctors yet?"

"No, they're only going to tell me the same thing they told Anthony to 'wait it out.'"

"Okay, well here's some stuff I bought you just in case."

"Thanks. Anthony had just given me some medicine before he left, that's probably why I'm so drowsy." Before I even agreed with her explanation, she had fallen back to sleep. I went downstairs and looked through her pantry to see if she had any soup because that would most likely be the only thing she could keep on her stomach. My phone buzzed from inside my pocket and I answered it.

"Hello Clay."

"What's up, Lane? I have a something to ask you?"

"Sure, what is it?"

"I want your opinion on Amani's CD cover. Shon and I are not seeing eye to eye on this one."

"I'd be happy to do it. Are you going to send it to my email?"

"Nah, I was thinking I'd stop by your crib after I leave the studio?"

"That's fine, but I'll have to call you because I'm at Charmine's. Now she's caught the bug."

"Damn. Aight, hit me up later, and tell Charmine I hope she feels better."

"I will, Clay." I found a can of chicken broth that was pushed in the back of the pantry. I heated it up and brought it to her room. Charmine faded in and out of her sleep, but during the brief times that she was able to stay awake, she managed to eat the broth. Anthony called and said he was on his way home. I told him to take his time because she was still sleeping. When Anthony got home, Charmine was still asleep. I told him I'd call to check on her later tonight, and I left. Once I got in my car, I called Clay and told him I was on my way home. I loved Char, but after I left her house, I felt like I had worked a double shift on a sick ward. So as soon as I got in my house I changed my clothes and put them directly into the washing machine.

I put some pasta on the stove and fixed a small salad for my dinner while I waited for Clay to arrive. As I turned to put the pitcher of tea in my fridge, Clay called me from downstairs to get the new code so he could come up. I cracked the door opened for him and went back to the stove and stirred my pasta. Clay walked in and it felt like old times: me at the stove cooking and Clay coming in from work. He had a large square, black binder under his arms, and he laid it on the coffee table in my living room. He walked in the kitchen and looked over my shoulder. "Whatcha cookin'?"

"Nothing special, do you want some?"

"Not now, maybe later. Come over here for a minute, this is what I wanted to show you." I turned the stove off and placed my pasta on another burner so that it wouldn't burn. Clay opened the black binder, and pulled out three large images of Amani. They were all nice, but the one in the middle with Amani standing behind a microphone, dressed in classic attire instantly stood out for me. In the other two images she looked awkward, like she wasn't comfortable with herself.

"I like this one," I said and pointed to my preference. "Her eyes are saying it's all about the music. The other two she looks miserable."

"That's exactly what I told Shon. And this is the one we're going with. Thanks, Bae. I knew you would help me," he said and put the images back inside the binder. He walked out onto my patio and made a call. He stayed out there for a while before he came back in. "You know what? I changed my mind. I will have something to eat."

"I don't have any Hennessy here, would you like some wine?"

"Nah, I'm good." I fixed him a plate of pasta, some salad and sat it on the table in front of him. As we talked it all seemed so natural— nothing forced, and it reminded me of our dating stage. I convinced Clay to have a glass of wine with me, and we moved our conversation over to the sofa. Clay said he really liked the way I had furnished the condo and asked me how my job was going. We talked and laughed at the silliest things. I really didn't want the night to end, and I would have done anything to keep him there with me. Clay wanted to show me something on his phone and when he looked at it, he realized it was after midnight. He hopped up from the sofa, and as he zipped up his binder, he said he had to leave.

"You know you're welcome to stay here. You can sleep in the guestroom."

"Nah, I better boogey." I walked him to the door, he thanked me for my help with the cover and dinner, and he left. Clay and I had gotten so involved that I forgot to call and check on Char. I dialed Anthony's cell and hoped he'd pick, when he answered I apologized for calling him so late. He said it was fine because he was still awake. He informed me that Charmine still hadn't been able to keep any food down, but at least she didn't have a fever. I told him I would call back tomorrow to see if they needed anything. He told me he wasn't going to the office and would be home with her all day. I cleared the dishes and watched a bit of TV before I went to bed. The next morning, I called Charmine before I went to work. She didn't sound great, but she did sound better. She said that Anthony had placed her on a clear liquid diet, and it seemed to help.

I reminded Char that I worked a half a day tomorrow because my dad would be here, and I hoped she'd be feeling better so we could all go out. Charmine said she was sure she would be and looked forward to seeing my dad. She asked if Faizon left for New York already. I told her that she had and that she sent her love.

My dad has never been a man who liked to be fussed over, but I wanted to do it big for him while he was here with me. He had never been to Atlanta before, and I wanted his first trip to be especially nice. Clay had promised to take him golfing, so I knew he looked forward to that. And then it dawned on me, I had never told my dad that Clay and I weren't together, and if he found out the reason why, he would have been so disappointed in me. I panicked and picked up the phone to call Clay. "Hello, Lane."

"Hi, Clay. I hope you're not too busy, because I have a huge favor to ask of you."

"What's that?"

"I never told my dad that we aren't together, and I hope that you won't mention it either while you're out playing golf with him."

"You should already know I'm not gonna lie to your Pops."

"I didn't say lie, Clay, I just said don't mention it."

"I don't know about that Lane. Is that it?"

"Well. . . yeah."

"Aight, 'cause you caught me in the middle of something."

"Okay, goodbye." Clay sounded offended when I asked him to cover up our breakup from my dad. I lifted my phone to call my dad so that I could tell him myself, but I didn't want his short vacation spoiled with my problems. So, I put the phone back down. After I got home from work, I just wanted to take a hot bath, so I went upstairs and turned the water on to run my bath. My cell phone buzzed before I stepped in the tub, and I hoped it was Clay saying that he had changed his mind and wouldn't mention anything to my dad. I looked at my screen and recognized the New York area code, and my heart dropped. I thought it may have been Dre who convinced my cousin, Beverly, into giving him my number.

"Hello."

"Hey, Lane. Were you sleeping?"

"Oh hi, Faizon. I thought you were someone else."

"Who?"

"My cousin Beverly," I lied.

"Girl, I haven't been to New York in a few years, but when they say this city never sleeps...they mean it. How's Charmine."

"She's still not well, but better than yesterday. Anthony stayed home with her today, so she should be fine. So, how's everything going with you in New York?"

"Great! I had two very promising meetings with two buyers today. One with an exclusive wedding shop and the other one was with Neiman Marcus."

"That is great Faizon, I know you must be trippin'. Just two years ago all of this was only a sketch in your head, now look at you. When will you be back home?"

"I don't know. My wide receiver is flying in on Sunday, so it could be Monday or Tuesday before I return."

"Girl...You are a mess," I laughed. "Now he's 'your' wide receiver, but what about your shop?"

"I am a mess, but so far he's real cool, and best of all he's single. So, we'll see how this friendship develops. And I'm not worried about the shop, my mama is gonna hold it down until I get back. Well, I'm about to take in some sights. Talk to you before I leave, bye Lane."

"Okay, bye." After we talked, I soaked my aching body in the tub until the water turned cold. I wrapped my hair before I prepared the guestroom for my dad. Then after I finished with my dad's room, I went back in my room and watched a documentary on HBO about female serial killers. I had fallen asleep and had the strangest dream. I dreamed that I was surrounded by butterflies in a beautiful field filled with pink lilies, and all throughout my dream, church bells were ringing. But when I woke up I realized that it wasn't the church bells in my dream that was ringing, but my intercom. I looked at my cell phone clock, and it was after two o'clock in the morning. I stumbled blindly down my stairs and pressed the intercom. "This better be good! Who is it?"

"It's Clay, let me up." I woke the hell up quick, ripped the headscarf from my head, and threw it in the closet. I opened the door and waited for him to get off the elevator—he entered my house and closed the door behind him. I was genuinely concerned that something may have happened because he didn't sound too good when I had spoken to him earlier. And now the unexpected visit in the middle of the night made it all the more bizarre.

"What's the matter, Clay? Is everything alright?"

"No."

I got worried by his tone and how serious he looked. "What is it?"

"I want you, but I don't want to want you," he said, never making eye contact with me. He walked over to the sofa and sat with his head down and his hands clasped between his legs. I didn't know how I should have responded to him, so I didn't do or say anything. I sat in the chair across from him, silent. I waited. He finally lifted his head and looked me in my eyes. "I love you, Lane, and I can't fight it any more."

"I love you too." I walked over to him and kneeled down in front of him. I placed my mouth on his—I could feel he wanted to resist me as his body tensed up, so I pulled back. I rubbed his face gingerly with the back of my hand. He looked at me, pulled my face back into his, and kissed me. I had prayed for him to want me like this again. Clay slowly pulled my gown over my head and stood me up in front of him. With his hands in my panties he massaged the flesh of my ass and had taken me to another dimension as he kissed my stomach.

Clay remained seated on my sofa while he unfastened his pants and pulled out his hard thick manhood. I straddled Clay as he cupped my breasts and put them in his mouth. He controlled his manhood as he slid it easily inside my wet sweetness. I felt our flesh meet as I gyrated my ass wildly to oblige Clay's thrusts as he pulled me down on him harder and harder until we both climaxed. Clay held onto me as I felt my juices continue to flow down onto his shrinking manhood, and I lay my head in the crook of his neck I hoped this wasn't just a sexual urge that Clay needed to satisfy, and I wanted to know what was next. "What happens to us now?"

"We take it slow," he said. We went upstairs to my bedroom and slept until he left for the studio the next morning. I woke up next to him so grateful for this second chance that Clay had given me. And I vowed on my life I would never hurt him as badly as I had. Later that morning when I got to work, I called Charmine to check on her. She said she felt a bit better, but still wasn't feeling well so she thought it would be best if she went and got checked out by her doctor. I asked her to call me when she was finished with her appointment so I'd know how it turned out. I had already spoken to my dad and he said he was packed and excited about his first flight to Atlanta.

During my morning break, I received a text from Clay, and it simply read 'I love you.' My dad's plane arrived on schedule at Hartfield's Airport, and I felt like a little girl again as I yelled out to him once I saw his face. We picked up his luggage and left the airport. I asked him what he wanted to do first because I wanted this to be a very special trip for him. My dad told me just to be able to spend time with me was special enough and asked if I minded if we went straight home because he was a little tired. I totally understood, and since he would be here for a little over a week, I knew we would have time to get it in. So, with that we went straight to my new condominium. He said he was impressed with everything in Atlanta so far, except the traffic and asked me how I managed to deal with it everyday.

I gave him the grand tour of my new home, and he loved it. I admitted to my dad that I had mixed feelings about my place, because it was only because of my mother's death that I was even able to have something so wonderful. Clay had called to see if my dad had landed safely, and they talked for a while. After they hung up, my dad told me that Clay planned to take him to play golf tomorrow at eleven o'clock. While my dad unpacked his clothes in the upstairs bedroom, I made my dad his favorite dinner which consisted of: smothered chicken, collard greens, corn bread, and rice with gravy. "Dinner was delicious, Lane. Your mother taught you well," he said

"She sure did. How are Aunt Bernice and the rest of them?"

"Everybody is good. They miss you, though."

"Well, you know that we promised each other when I was home that we'd see each other every other month. So, I'll see them in September."

After dinner, my dad and I had our dessert out on the patio and planned what we wanted to do during his visit. Later that evening, Charmine called and also spoke to my dad, and when he put me back on the phone, she said she had been to her doctor. I asked her had the doctor told her what was wrong with her. Charmine wanted to know if I could drop by her house the next morning—I asked her to tell me over the phone—but she refused. I told her that as soon as Clay picked up my dad I'd come straight over.

My dad had been serious when he said he was tired. After dinner and the evening news, he went to bed. Well into the night, I was still worried about what could have possibly been wrong with Char. I tossed in my sleep most of the night, so when I received an early call from Clay to say that he'd pick my dad up at ten o'clock, I got up and started making breakfast for my dad.

I knocked on my dad's door to wake him, but he said he'd been up reading his bible. I told him that his breakfast was ready for him downstairs. Clay arrived earlier than ten o'clock and had to wait on my dad while he dressed. "What's the matter, you look worried," he said.

"It's Char. She went to the doctor yesterday, and she wouldn't tell me over the phone what the doctor told her."

"She could've just had what Ant had. Don't worry so much, it may not be nothing."

"You're probably right. What time do you plan to be back here, because I may not be here when y'all get back."

"Did you forget I have a key?"

"Honestly, I did." When my dad and Clay left, I dressed quickly and drove over to Charmine's house. When I arrived, Anthony was taking Char her breakfast in bed. Although she looked somewhat better she still remained in bed, and that really scared me. Char had never been one to just lie in bed all day unless something was wrong. I just knew she had some bad news to tell me, and it frightened the hell out of me.

"How you feelin,' Sweetheart?" I asked.

"I'm fine."

"Well, you can't be fine 'cause you're still in bed, and that's unlike you. So, just tell me what the doctor said." Charmine reached over the side of her bed and pulled out a piece of paper from her bag.

"Here, look for yourself." she said and handed the paper to me. "I hope you'll take it okay."

I dreaded taking the paper for her hands as I didn't want to play piece the puzzle together. I just wanted her to tell me what was wrong. "What am I looking at, Char?"

"Well, that's your godchild at eight weeks...I'm having a baby!" We both screamed loudly. I jumped in the bed with her and hugged her so tightly.

"I guess you've told her?" Anthony said as he reentered the room with two glasses of champagne and a glass of apple juice.

"Yes, she did. Congratulations! Ahh...I'm so happy for you two. Well, if you're not sick why are you still in the bed."

"Because, I do have a bug. It's nothing serious, but my husband won't let me get up to do anything." I busted out in laughter. "What's so funny?"

"It looks like y'all will be using Faizon's housewarming gift sooner than you thought."

"Oh my God, I completely forgot about that. We gotta call her." We called Faizon's cell, and Charmine put her on speaker. Charmine told her the news of the baby and that it was due in March. She was also thrilled to bits for them. Faizon also had some fantastic news to share. She had gotten the call that her clothing line would be sold in the Neiman Marcus stores in New York. Not to be left out, I told them about the night Clay and I had and that we were taking things slow but he was willing and wanted to work things out so we could be together.

I hung out with Char and Anthony for a little while longer, but I was so overwhelmed with all of our great news that I couldn't contain myself. I told Char again that I was extremely happy for her and Anthony, and I left their home to take in some fresh air. As I drove around Atlanta, I flashed back to all the times that Charmine, Faizon and I shared: tears, triumphs, fights, joys, and now our successes. Charmine has a new law firm and is about to have a baby. Faizon has her own fashion line, and her wide receiver who's unattached. And I definitely got what I prayed for... Clay.

THE END

ABOUT THE AUTHOR

Andreia was born in Brooklyn, New York and now resides in London, England. She has two daughters and one grandson. Andreia and her husband, Lloyd, have been married for more than twenty-five years. This is the second novel for Andreia, and since writing her novels, she's discovered a passion for writing screenplays and has two to her credit. Andreia is currently working on a project with a UK filmmaker to be released in 2015 and a children's book with her grandson, I'Santi.

Made in the USA
Charleston, SC
02 April 2014